PAUL BUNYAN

*Last
of the
Frontier
Demigods*

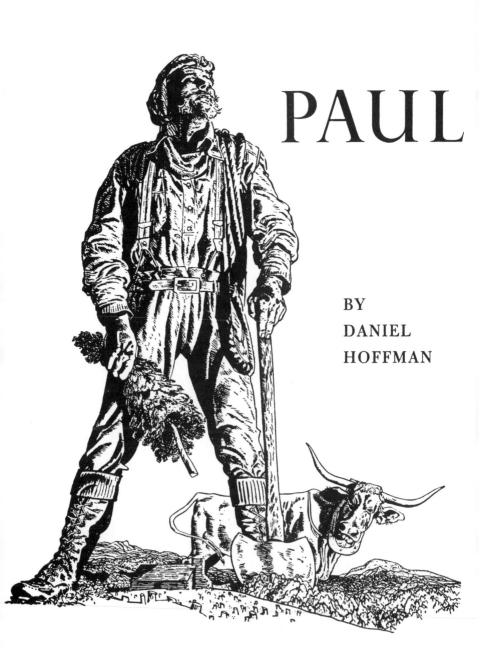

PAUL

BY
DANIEL
HOFFMAN

BUNYAN

Last
of the
Frontier
Demigods

MICHIGAN STATE UNIVERSITY PRESS

East Lansing

♾ The paper used in this publication meets the minimum requirements of
ANSI/NISO Z39.48–1992 (R 1997) (Permanence of Paper).

Michigan State University Press
East Lansing, Michigan 48823-5202

05 04 03 02 01 00 99 1 2 3 4 5 6 7 8 9

Library of Congress Cataloging-in-Publication Data

Hoffman, Daniel, 1923–
    Paul Bunyan, last of the frontier demigods / by Daniel Hoffman.
        p.   cm.
    Includes bibliographical references (p.   ) and index.
    ISBN 0-87013-521-X (alk. paper)
    1. Bunyan, Paul (Legendary character) 2. Folklore—United States.
3. Folklore—Canada. 4. Folklore in literature. 5. American literature—History
and criticism. I. Title.
    GR105.37.P38H63   1999
    398.2'0973'02—dc21   99-27131
                                                                     CIP

HOW WE
LOGGED KATAHDIN STREAM

Come all ye river-drivers, if a tale you wish to hear
The likes for strength and daring all the North Woods has no peer:
'Twas the summer of 1860 when we took a brave ox team
And a grand bully band of braggarts up to log Katahdin Stream.

> *Chorus:* So, it's Hi derry, Ho derry, Hi derry, Down!
> *When our driving is over we'll come into town!*
> *Make ready, ye maidens, for frolic and song!*
> *When the woodsman has whiskey, then naught can go wrong!*

Bold Gattigan was foreman, he's the pride of Bangor's Town,
And there was no other like Chauncey for to mow the great pines down;
Joe Murphraw was the swamper, with Canada Jacques Dupree.
We'd the best camp cook in the wilderness—I know, for it was me.

We left from Millinocket on such a misty day
We dulled our axes chopping the fog to clear ourselves a way,
Till at last we reached the bottom of Mount Katahdin's peaks supreme
And vowed that we within the week would clear Katahdin Stream.

O, Chauncey chopped and Murph he swamped and Canada Jacques did swear,
Bold Gattigan goaded the oxen on and shouted and tore his hair,
Till the wildwood rang with *"Timber!"* as the forest monarchs fell,
And the air was split with echoes of our ax-blows and our yell.

For six whole days and twenty-three hours we threshed the forest clean—
The logs we skidded by hundreds, O, such a drive was never seen!
We worked clear round the mountain, and rejoiced to a jovial strain,
When what did we see but that forest of trees was a-growing in again!

Then all of a sudden the mountain heaved, and thunder spoke out of the earth!
"Who's walking around in my beard?" it cried, and it rumbled as though in
  mirth.
The next we knew, a hand appeared—no larger than Moosehead Lake—
And it plucked us daintily one by one, while we with fear did quake!

Paul Bunyan held us in one hand! With the other he rubbed his chin.
"Well I'll be swamped! You fellers have logged my beard right down to the
  skin!"
"We thought you was Mount Katahdin," Gattigan shouted into his ear,
"We're sorry, but 'twouldn't have happened if the weather had been clear."

Well, good old Paul didn't mind it at all. He paid us for the shave—
A hundred dollars apiece to the men, to the oxen fodder he gave.
And now, ye young river-drivers, fill your glasses—fill mine too—
And we'll drink to the health of Bold Gattigan, and his gallant lumbering crew!

Preface to the 1999 Edition

This book had its unforeseen beginning when, as a college freshman, I attended a performance—one of five, by the Columbia University Theatre Associates—in May, 1941, of the premiere of an operetta, *Paul Bunyan,* by Benjamin Britten with a libretto by W. H. Auden. Returning to Columbia after wartime service, by 1948 I needed a subject for my master's thesis. By then I had become interested in folklore, so an investigation of the sources of Auden's opera seemed a likely topic. Auden, replying to my inquiry, wrote that his sources were in the New York Public Library; these proved to be two books written in the 1920s, so I pressed on to ascertain *their* sources. The consequence of my search was chosen for the 1949 Chicago Folklore Prize, awarded the work as the year's best contribution to the study of that discipline. This led to its initial publication, by the University of Pennsylvania Press for Temple University, in 1952. The present, fourth, printing thus follows completion of my study by fifty years.

So it is now over half a century since I collected the interviews with lumberjacks that comprised the original Paul Bunyan tradition in oral circulation; surveyed the pamphlets, books, and advertisements through which the hero was popularized; and analyzed the uses of some of this Bunyan material in works by Frost, Sandburg, Auden, and Untermeyer. Fifty years before that, woodsmen had told their slender repertoire of Bunyan jokes, exaggerations, and truth-stretchers in smoky bunkhouses in lumbering states from Maine to the Northwest. Much had already changed, and more changes were to come. It's now fifteen years since I last

reviewed these traditions for the preface to the 1983 edition. How
has Paul Bunyan fared since then?

Truth to tell, the great woodsman's fame seems undiminished,
though in other walks of life than lumbering. A year's possession
of The Governor of Michigan Trophy, a statue depicting Paul
Bunyan, goes to the winner of the football game between
Michigan State and the University at Ann Arbor. A century after
his exploits in the woods, the great lumberjack has an affinity with
sports: on the Maine coast for the past thirty-four years there's
been a Paul Bunyan Amateur Golf Tournament. In Bangor, in July
the Paul Bunyan marathon is run and, in August, the Paul Bunyan
Summer Classic Horse Show.

There is a forty-foot tall statue in a little park downtown, where,
in September are held the Paul Bunyan Festival Days. An article
by Dawn Gagnon in the *Bangor Daily News* (Saturday-Sunday,
7–8 September 1996), well describes this celebration:

> Most of Friday night's events dovetailed nicely with the Paul Bunyan
> days theme. Concession stands offered such fare as saucer-sized
> chocolate chip cookies and "Bunyanesque" whoopie pies, each weigh-
> ing in at 2 ounces shy of a pound. Visitors could buy Paul Bunyan cof-
> fee cups, T-shirts, patches and other memorabilia.

Other festivities included a Golf Classic, horse-drawn wagon rides,
a car and truck show, museum tours, music and jugglers, fireworks,
"a silent auction to benefit Habitat for Humanity," and, on Sunday,
"a non-denominational service at Paul Bunyan Park," a five-kilo-
meter run, a champagne brunch, and a band concert. Very like a
State Fair. A little more in keeping with the Paul Bunyan theme was
"The Great Maine Lumberjack Show," with exhibition performances of "such skills as ax throwing, log chopping and buck-saw-
ing with precision." The performers, however, were not actual
lumberjacks but a "team of mostly college students."

Paul Bunyan of course is promoted elsewhere—his roadside
statues stand in Bemidji and Brainerd, Minnesota (where, in the

film *Fargo*, he loomed as two murderers drove through a blizzard), but Peter Daigle, president of Bangor's Chamber of Commerce, "has proof that Bunyan was a Mainer. When the U.S. Postal Service released a Paul Bunyan stamp . . . it did so in Bangor." Among many other attractions of the Bunyan Festival were a craft fair, country music, Babe the Blue Ox at Toys R Us, pony rides, and a reading from his three Bunyan books by author Alan Watts.

These works do not show up in the current listing of 23 publications with Paul Bunyan in their titles in *Books in Print* (1997–98). Justin G. Schiller's article, "The Making of an American Myth: An Early History of Paul Bunyan in Print" (*Biblio*, March 1998, pp. 32–39) attests to the collectibility of early Bunyaniana, and reproduces 16 pictorial renderings of Paul from book illustrations and jackets. But from neither of these sources would one guess that the Library of Congress catalogue lists over 700 Paul Bunyan items, some 200 since 1983, the date of my last survey. Among these are a translation of a juvenile Bunyan book into Spanish, and another one rendered in Braille. Some unprecedented Bunyan adventures appear: Irwin Shapiro's *Paul Bunyan Fights a Dragon* (1975), and Glen Rounds' *The Morning the Sun Refused to Rise: An Original Paul Bunyan Tale* (1984), which, sight unseen, would appear to commandeer for Paul the Davy Crockett tale of stopping the sun from rising (see p. 41–42), in presenting which I had noted that "There is a grandeur here which is nowhere to be found in the lore of Paul Bunyan," a statement that may still be true. There are Bunyan books for children set in just about every state where there ever was a logging industry, all of them claiming Bunyan as their own. Paul crosses the border into Canada in Tom Henry's *Paul Bunyan on the West Coast*, published in British Columbia in 1994. Indeed Paul Bunyan's fame has spread across the seas, as attested by Pavel Strut's *Obr jménem Drobeck; amarické pohédky a povídacky o Paulu Bunyanori*. This volume appeared from Albatros in Prague (1997). A work by Jan Gleiter (1947) was reissued in 1991, entitled *Pao-lo Pan-yang: Shen Ch'i ti fa mu chü jen*. And, no doubt for use in bilingual classes, Steven Kellogg's book *Paul Bunyan, a Tall Tale* (1984) has been republished as *Paul Bunyan, un cuento fantástico* (1994).

*   *   *

Perhaps the most unexpected development of the Bunyan canon in English has been the revival of W.H. Auden and Benjamin Britten's opera, *Paul Bunyan*. But for my having uncovered an acting script of the libretto filed under "Britten" in the Columbia University Music Library in 1948, the work would have been quite forgotten for over two decades; with Auden's permission I published passages in the present book, and for twenty-four years the exerpts in these pages were the only available text of the operetta.

Indeed the work languished in limbo until 1973, the year of Auden's death and Britten's stroke. The composer's companion, Peter Pears, suggested that his reconsidering *Paul Bunyan* might lead Britten to compose again. Pears spoke and illustrated parts of the work to the royal Society of Arts in London in May, 1974, and excerpts were performed by professional singers at the Aldeburgh Festival, where a school choir also performed the three interlude ballads. Britten was not eager for another staging of the work, since its initial production had been ill-received in 1941. But Pears suggested an intermediate version, a radio production, and the result was the entire operetta's being broadcast on the B.B.C. in 1976. Favorably reviewed by the poet Peter Porter in the *T.L.S.*, the work was quickly published at last in pamphlet form by the music edition of Faber and Faber. A hardbound edition, with an essay on Britten's score by Donald Mitchell, followed in 1988.

Paul Bunyan was the inaugural production of the English Music Theatre Company in 1976, after the death of Benjamin Britten. Its next performance was in 1987, staged oratorio-style in St. Paul Minnesota; this was recorded and issued on tapes and CDs (Plymouth Music Series, Vega Classics, 2MCs/VCD 7 90710–4);

packaged with the music was an unpaged little book of over 100 pages. This reprinted the libretto text (in German as well as in English) and included, among program notes, analysis of the music and the essay on the text and the initial production by Donald Mitchell. It also contains Auden's interpretation of the Bunyan legend, originally published in *The New York Times* on 4 May 1941, the day before its premiere. The cover title reads "BRITTEN / PAUL BUNYAN . . ."; there's no mention of Auden's name until the ninth page, where his brief article is reprinted and translated into French and German; I was unaware of Auden's comments until finding them there.

As noted in the present book, *Paul Bunyan* was undertaken at the insistance of the music publisher Boosey & Hawkes, and, as Auden wrote me, was intended to be "something suitable for high schools" (p. 144); there was also a prospect, not mentioned in his letter, of a Broadway production, but this came to naught when the Columbia premiere received at best a luke-warm reception from reviewers puzzled by the contradictions in the script I've discussed on pp 149–50. These contradictions reflect the inconsistencies in Auden's sources, the books by James Stevens and Esther Shepard, both titled *Paul Bunyan,* which I have analyzed in some detail (pp. 87–109).

Auden's conception of the hero of course transcended the banality of those popularizations, which he seems to have accepted as actual folk traditions. His little essay in the *Times* is typically dialogic and philosophical:

America is unique in being the only country to create myths after the industrial revolution . . . The principal interest of the Bunyan legend today is as a reflection of cultural problems that occur during the first stage of every civilization, the stage of colonization of the land and the conquest of nature. The operetta, therefore, begins with a prologue in which America is still a virgin forest and Paul Bunyan has not yet been born, and ends with a Christmas party at which he bids farewell to his men because he is no longer needed. External physical nature has been mastered and . . . can no longer dictate to men what they should do. Now their task is one of their human relations with each other and, for this, a collective mythical figure is no use, because the requirements of each relation are unique. Faith is essentially invisible.

Auden mentions the difficulties his subject presents for an operetta: Bunyan's huge size, the scale of his exploits, and the absence of women. He solved these challenges by making Paul's an unseen voice; having his exploits described in interludes by a ballad-singer; and introducing "a camp dog and two camp cats, sung by a coloratura and two mezzo-sopranos respectively." Auden also introduced Paul's daughter, Tiny, by his wife from whom he is sadly estranged; it's not clear whether Auden was aware of Frost's poem "Paul's Wife," or, more likely, supplied the daughter and explanation for the absent wife himself. Mitchell tells us that when Britten discovered, during the rehearsals by the student cast for the initial Columbia production, that the girl playing Tiny could actually sing, he wrote a song for her not hitherto in the score.

Britten's score is another part of the story. Intended for school production, it could not be too challenging vocally; hence, no sustained arias, no extreme ranges of voice. Mitchell's analysis of the music identifies borrowings, parodic or otherwise, and analogues from a range of sources—Donizetti, Kurt Weill, the blues, Purcell, and Anglican hymns, as well as noting its anticipations of the scores of Britten's later operas.

The next stage in the recovery of this work was its performance in the 1995 Glimmerglass Opera Festival in Cooperstown, N.Y. In December, 1997, the Royal Opera Company gave eight performances at King's Lynn; when the Laurence Olivier awards were given, on 16 February 1998 by the Society of London Theatre, *Paul Bunyan* was cited as the best new opera production. Next came its presentation by the New York Opera Company in April 1998, repeating the Glimmerglass staging of three years earlier, and was telecast on April 22nd over the National Public Broadcasting System.

This production had greater panache than the Columbia premiere, with the telecamera sometimes looking down on the stage as though through Paul Bunyan's eyes; the stage was filled with a chorus of lumberjacks, the cats and Fido crisscrossing stage on roller skates, and the Western Union messenger arriving on his bicycle. Auden wrote that his central character had to be Johnny Inkslinger, a personage originated in the popularization of Bunyan by W. B. Laughead as Paul's bookkeeper (p. 80, supra), and retained by James Stevens, from whose book, propagandizing for free enterprise and the rough lumberjack life, Auden lifted his cast of players. For Auden, Inkslinger is "the man of speculative and critical intelligence, whose temptation is to despise those who do the manual work that makes the life of thought possible." His opposite number is Hel Helson, the man of muscle; both rebel against Paul but are reconciled to him. Inkslinger is a far cry from the titular lumberjack hero, but in Auden's philosophical schematization of the legend he is necessary as representing the civilized, literate society that will replace the woodsman when the forests have been cleared.

Bernard Holland, reviewing the 1998 New York production in the *New York Times* (11 April) was much more welcoming than were the notices of the 1941 premiere. Auden's "clever lyrics use simple language to promote a wonderful continuity of thought, meter and rhythm. There are smart references to American politics and bemused observations on American's social life, a lot of which are probably wasted on the young. Britten and Auden do excellent work, but they have created music for children and texts for grown-ups." *Paul Bunyan*, Holland concludes, "might have a modest success in the theater district. It is cheerful, often frivolous, funny and ends on a high-minded note." At last the work— even if by now over half a century old—seems well established in the repertoire of contemporary opera.

*   *   *

This work of course presents Paul Bunyan at the high-culture end of his public reception. The fact of his broad appeal and recognition was well attested by the issuance in 1996, two years before the televised operetta, of a postal stamp bearing the images of Paul Bunyan and his Blue Ox, Babe. I heard on Maine Public Radio that first-day covers could be had by sending self-addressed envelopes bearing the stamp to the Bangor Post Office before the end of July. Bangor seemed the right venue for such cancellation, with its oversized statue of Old Paul standing before the civic auditorium in Paul Bunyan Park, commemorating the town's past glory as a lumbering capital. The Bunyan statue in Bemidji, Minnesota, however, is accompanied by a mammoth representation of Babe. In Brainerd, Minnesota, the other Bunyan statue has no companion, but in the midst of the blizzard in the movie *Fargo* the two murderers found solace with a pair of preternaturally stupid prostitutes in the Blue Ox Motel. In Bangor, however, Paul stands alone, with no motel honoring Babe, but from 1995 to 1997 the Maine city did possess a minor league baseball team called "The Blue Ox." This team, in the independent Northeast League, unaffiliated with the majors, had to play in the University stadium ten miles away at Orono; Bangor's failure to vote a bond issue to finance a ball park in town led to the loss of the Blue Ox team (renamed of course) to New Bedford. But for those two years, including the summer of the postal celebration of Paul Bunyan, Monday night games on Channel 2 featured, as a mascot, a fellow on the sidelines in a baseball uniform, cavorting about in a horned ox helmet.

I asked for half a dozen Bunyan stamps at the local post office. "I have sheets with Paul Bunyan, Pecos Bill, John Henry, and Casey Jones," our postmaster informed me.

"I just want the Paul Bunyan stamp, doesn't it come separately?"

"No, but I'll give them to you," and she laboriously tore out only the Bunyans. These I affixed to blank envelopes and mailed them to the Bangor P. O. for cancellation and return.

Two days later the rural deliverer left in our box my large s.a.e. containing the souvenirs. The stamps show Paul in bearded profile, the blue ox behind him. The cancellation reads "Paul Bunyan

& Babe Station / Bangor ME 04401 / July 12, 1996," and Paul's face is cancelled with a woodsman's axe crossed by a baseball bat, on which is clearly written, "*Babe Ruth*."

Paul Bunyan & Babe Station
Bangor ME 04401
July 12, 1996

As Mr. Daigle, head of Bangor's Chamber of Commerce had said, "If the Post Office doesn't know Paul Bunyan's address, nobody does," but they seemed not to know for what he was famed. This was a confused conglomeration of legends, both which will most likely survive somehow, in a popular culture where celebrity itself is a value, never mind for what.

*   *   *

Another instance of the hero's saturation of popular culture may be inferred from the crossword puzzle in the *New York Times Magazine* for Sunday, 22 June 1998. In this, the clue defining nine down (six letters) is simply "e.g. Paul Bunyan." The answer of course is LEGEND, from which one may infer that more than any other folk or historical figure in American memory, Paul Bunyan is identified with legend, whatever that legend may be.

Reviewing a book on Muhammad Ali, Budd Schulberg wrote that the champ "is our black Paul Bunyan, except that Bunyan's superhuman exploits were fables and Ali's are real" (*New York Times Book Review*, 25 October 1998, p.11). Fables, yes, but with a reality too, for the accounts of Paul's exploits are cultural facts of many varieties, each present in the real world. In the ninety years Paul Bunyan has been in print as well as in oral tradition, he and his exploits, as the following pages attest, have expressed many other meanings than those Auden found in them. Paul Bunyan has leavened the scary risks faced by hand-tool lumberjacks; he has embodied the exaggerations of folk humor, the inventiveness of pre-industrial woodsmen; he has heroized the exploitation of clear-cut lumbering, and been enlisted as a symbol of conservation. Bunyan has represented management in the lumber industry, and also the workers. He had a spell as hero of oil riggers. Paul has helped to sell lumber, paper products, war bonds, and vacation real estate. He is renowned as creator of the American landscape—the Great Lakes, the Grand Canyon, the Mississippi—and therefore as an advertiser for tourism. He has entertained generations of children with increasingly vacuous accounts of his prowess. He has provided themes for fine poems by Robert Frost, Richard Wilbur, and David Wagoner, a novel by Louis Untermeyer, an epic by Carl Sandburg, and Auden's operetta. The content of the Paul Bunyan legend has constantly changed, now most often invoked as simply a metaphor for gigantic size and strength; doubtless these are permanent aspects of American self-consciousness. Yet who can tell in which more interesting guises Paul Bunyan may yet appear in our culture, whether high or low? Whatever these may be, they will not have come from a woodsmen's bunkhouse, and will have left the original oral tradition far behind. They may still reveal to us aspects of our fantasies and our lives.

Acknowledgments

Thanks to Dana Gioia for sending me the article on Bunyaniana from *Biblio* and the Virgin Classic recording of the Britten-Auden *Paul Bunyan:* to Kamil Siddiqi for providing a video of the televised production of the operetta; and to Ed Fuller, Reference Librarian, Swarthmore College, for his bibliographic assistance.

Introduction to the 1984 Edition

In October 1982 the delegates to a Soviet-American conference on Walt Whitman were given a tour of Pushkin House in Leningrad. We learned that the Institute of Russian Literature there held not only literary collections but an archive of folklore. Responding to my queries about the latter, our host, Dr. N. T. Evdokimov, mentioned that he owned a poster, given him years before, of the giant Russian folk hero Ilya Murometz standing beside his American counterpart, Paul Bunyan. When I exclaimed that my book, the only study of the Paul Bunyan legend, was about to be republished, Dr. Evdokimov presented me with the poster. It had been distributed by the United States Information Agency in 1964. All these years later, to this amiable member of the acadamy of sciences of the USSR, Paul Bunyan still represented folklore.

At the time I prepared this study, over thirty years ago, there was a general sense that Bunyan was a significant point of reference in the traditions of American culture. For instance, writing on the comic element in Whitman's work, in 1955, Richard Chase remarked that "indeed this form of wit is not confined to rural hoedowns, minstrel shows, or tall tales of Paul Bunyan" (*Walt Whitman Reconsidered*, 1955, p. 75). That still seems true; a quarter of a century later Whitney Balliett, the jazz critic, wrote that "Jelly-Roll Morton . . . properly belongs in the nineteenth century mythology of Paul Bunyan and Johnny Appleseed and Davy Crockett, of the Yankees peddlers and tall-tale tellers" (Profile: Ferdinand la Menthe," *New Yorker*, 23 June 1980, p.38).

The republication of this study thirty-one years after its first edition invites consideration of what has become of Paul Bunyan—in folk tradition, in popular culture, in literature—during those three decades. Did the lumberjack hero survive the cold war, Korea, the years of Vietnam and the peace movement, the expansion of the economy, the Great Society, the beats and the hippies, Watergate, Reaganomics? To my knowledge, no further authentic texts of Paul Bunyan tales from oral tradition have come to light since 1952. This is not to say that Paul Bunyan has vanished from public consciousness, for his name and his exploits—as will be seen—linger on. But not in the forests. The economic and social conditions required for the perpetuation of folktales by an isolated, itinerant band of lumberjacks have disappeared. In a feature story on the first page of the financial section of the Sunday *New York Times* for 19 June 1960, John Abele recorded these changes: "Logging Industry's Paul Bunyan Era Gives Way to Age of Machines and Methods/New 'Lumberjack'/ A Look at How the Mackinaw-Clad Rowdy Has Given Way to Family Man." The real folktales were imaginative responses to arduous challenge of hand-logging. The original tradition, sparse to begin with, petered out as the work which formerly pitted men with bucksaws and oxen against an impenetrable forest was now done with power saws; "mammoth cranes and trucks have taken over the log-hauling chores" and huge bulldozers give easy access to remote timberland. "Another victim" of technology is "the picturesque but dangerous practice of 'driving' logs down rivers by nimble-footed loggers wielding picks and peaveys." No room for Paul Bunyan's prowess where "log roads are often better than conventional highways," nor for his unrestrained denudation of the forest now that "timberland has become too valuable to permit the predatory cutting practices of the old days." Besides, the present-day workers in the timber industry spend the winter not in a grungy male bunkhouse deep in the woods but in housing developments where they can watch television with their wives and children. If Paul Bunyan survives, it is not in the timberlands.

The chief addition to the study of Bunyaniana was the late premier folklorist Richard M. Dorson's three-part survey "Paul

Bunyan in the News, 1939–1941," published four years after the present work appeared (*Western Folklore* 15 [1956]). Dorson's collectanea were garnered by his subscribing to a clipping bureau. Although it was in those same prewar years that Herbert Halpert and Alan Lomax collected from aging former lumberjacks some of the genuine folktales of Paul Bunyan published and analyzed in the present study, Dorson's clippings reveal no such folk materials. After all, what he got were news items. Reviewing this book in 1952, Dorson observed that "Mr. Hoffman sharply divides the true folk tale from the popularization and that in turn from the work of art" and "for the first time ... clarifies the important concept of popularization" (*Yale Review* 42. pp. 109–99).

When he published his old file of Bunyan clippings four years later, however, Dorson did not revise his presentation in the light of these distinctions; on his way toward attacking what he would memorably term "fakelore," he dismissed the entire Bunyan tradition as spurious. Paul Bunyan, he wrote, "is the pseudo-folk hero of twentieth-century mass culture, a conveniently vague symbol pressed into service to exemplify 'the American spirit.'" This is indeed true of his items culled from sources as varied as chamber of commerce handouts and features in the *Daily Worker.* Dorson's survey confirms the analysis in the present study of the materials which most resemble them—exploitations in mass media of a few motifs of Bunyan legends manipulated to serve the views and needs of lumber companies, ideologues of unregulated industrialism, and writers angling for the children's market with confections of braggadocio, patriotism, fantasy, or romantic nostalgia. As Dorson observed of the journalistic reports of Bunyan, "a few simple exaggerations circulate in the press, but the tales are the least part of the myth." Bunyan's popularity he attributes to the American desire for "a New World Thor, or Hercules, or Gargantua, with no taint of foreign genesis." Certainly the nativist impulse has run strongly in all treatments of Bunyan, whether for mass markets, or in the arts. Only one is by an author from another country, W. H. Auden, whose opera in

1941, *Paul Bunyan* (discussed herein, pp. 143–53), was, among other things, his own attempt to understand the nation to which he had recently emigrated.

The popularization of Paul Bunyan in mass media of all kinds has continued. Oversized roadside statues of buffoonish Bunyans still attract tourists in Bangor, Maine and in Bemidji and Brainerd, Minnesota.[1] In 1970 a tablet was dedicated to commemorate "The Return of Paul Bunyan" to Yamhill County, Oregon. Real estate developments on the Maine coast bear the names Paul Bunyan Shores in Winter Harbor and Paul Bunyan Estates in Corea. The Bangor House, chief hotel in that city until its recent conversion to condominium apartments, featured Bunyanburgers in its Lumberjack Coffee House. Paul Bunyan is still the name of a lumber company in Anderson, California. His exploits were the series of over 75 full-page advertisements by Mead Sales Company, manufacturers of pulp and paper products through the 1950s. These ads in lumber magazines showed full-page illustrations of Paul by various artists, and were offered, matted, without advertising copy, to all who requested them; thousands were distributed.

Two campaigns in 1959–60 attempted a radical revision of the popular perception of the lumber hero. The "Trees for Israel" cam-

---

[1] Just after submitting this introduction I learned of a claim that the first appearance of Paul Bunyan tales in print antedated by four years James MacGillivray's "The Round River Drive" in 1910 (see pp. 3–4). Steve Bell of the *Bay City* (Michigan) *Times*, sent me his feature page for 6 February 1983 and a photocopy of the typescript of the prior publication. This is identical to MacGillivray's text but lacks its first nine paragraphs and last seventy–five words, and is said to have been transcribed from the *Oscoda* (Michigan) *Press* for 20 August 1906. Since that paper was owned by MacGillivray's brother, his authorship may be inferred—if indeed the typed text did appear in 1906. The member of the local historical commission who says so has misplaced her sole surviving copy of the original; files of the *Oscoda Press* were destroyed in a fire.

These dubious circumstances notwithstanding, boosters in the Oscoda-Au Sable Chamber of Commerce, enthusiasm kindled by this report, are trying to raise one million dollars to build Paul's log cabin, repair the Bunyan statue on Route 23, develop an eighteen-acre Paul Bunyan park with shopping center, and establish a permanent site for the annual Paul Bunyan Festival.

paign of the Jewish National Fund used Bunyan to publicize its efforts at reforestation. A ballad by Bill Galemor, a mosaic mural of Paul at the campaign headquarters in Philadelphia, and presentation plaques with a figure of Bunyan mounted on a brass plate were used in this effort to raise money and export American replanting techniques to Israel. At about the same time, the American Forest Products Industries tried to turn Bunyan's renown from clearing the woods to conservation, but their effort to popularize "Paul Bunyan Jr.—Tree Farmer" did not catch on, since they not only tried to make of Bunyan the wanton logger an ecologist but would turn the epitome of male machismo into a family man.

Although Esther Shephard's *Paul Bunyan* (first published in 1924) is still in print, there has been no book about Paul Bunyan for adults since my own. Old Paul has dwindled into a genial giant playmate for kiddies in the lower grades. His recently written adventures have less and less to do with tradition, yet Paul Bunyan, in print, in films, and on recordings and cassettes, is listed in every juvenile library and in many a grade school curriculum. In view of the recent concentration of interest in all quarters upon folklore from the varied ethnic groups, nationalities, and races comprising the unmelted American population, the persistence in educational catalogues of tales about an all-American hero of an outmoded occupation seems surprising. There still seems to be a vein of nostalgia for alleged versions of a simpler American past, although the juvenile Bunyan books are without exception vapid potboilers of no more historical than literary interest. The current *Books in Print* lists a dozen such ventures, including three oldies discussed on pp. 116–23 herein (Ida V. Turney's *Paul Bunyan, the Work Giant* and the books by Glen Rounds and Dell J. McCormick). The only notable author among the rest is the poet Maxine Kumin, whose *Paul Bunyan* (1966) is clearly written for grades 1–3. J. I. *Anderson's I Can Read about Paul Bunyan* (1976) typifies the reduction of a legend once told by grown men to a first primer. Some juveniles involve Bunyan in fantasy plots unrelated to any tradition, for example, Wyatt Blassingame's *John Henry and Paul Bunyan Play Baseball* (1971), grades 2–5. Each of these volumes tells one or two motifs only, with many illustrations the styles of which for the most part continue representing Paul Bunyan in cartoons, following W. B. Laughead's first sketches in 1914. One should mention, however, Rockwell Kent's illustrations of the 1941 reprinting of Shepard's *Paul Bunyan*, which, while humorous, are drawn with strength.

The *Subject Index to Children's Magazines* lists twenty-one references to Bunyan since 1960, including five articles by the indefatigable McCormick. Here again tradition dribbles away into such fatuous inventions as "Paul Bunyan's Cookbook" (by A. Pond, *Wisconsin Trails*, four issues in 1977–78), or McCormick's "Paul Bunyan and the Chinese Rain" and "Paul Bunyan and the Popcorn Blizzard" (*Children's Digest*, April 1966; February 1970). Seven audio tapes currently offered for sale include redactions of passages from James Stevens's book and items from such audio series as "The Name to Remember," "The Treasury of American Legends and Folk Tales," "Folk Tales Retold," "Tales from the Four Winds," and "The World of Myths and Legends." The unwary parent of teacher might confuse these cooked performances with real folklore. Series of 16-mm. films with equally inviting and misleading titles include shorts on Paul Bunyan. In 1970 Walt Disney Enterprises produced a seventeen-minute film "Paul Bunyan," still available, as part of their "Tall Tales from American Folklore Series," Coronet Instructional Films, in "Paul Bunyan—Lumber Camp Tales" (eleven minutes, 1962), "recounts some of the most famous tall tales of the American folk hero. . . such as the bunkhouse beds stacked 137 feet high, the gigantic flapjack griddle, the popcorn blizzard and the straightening of the Big Onion River." Other such films were made between 1966 and 1978 by Television Enterprises, BFA Educational Media, Pyramid Films, Key Productions, and Encyclopedia Britannica.

And what of literary treatments of this figure whose folk origins have been so overwhelmed by mass-media popularization? No large work of serious literary intent and accomplishment can be added to those already surveyed in the last chapter of this book. I can report, however, that W. H. Auden, and Benjamin Britten's *Paul Bunyan* at last had a second production, on BBC 3, reviewed by Peter Porter in T.L.S. for 20 February 1976. Porter, concerned mainly with Britten's music, opines of "Auden's parable of a new country outgrowing its myths" that "the legend of Paul Bunyan is one of the nineteenth century's few benign myths." So it appears in Auden's treatment, in which the exploitative strains of American life are opposed to the imagined pastoral of Bunyan's camp. The libretto was published by the music division of Faber and Faber, London, in 1976.

Paul Bunyan had figured in a fine poem that somehow escaped my notice while preparing the first edition:

When Bunyan swung his whopping axe
The forest strummed as one loud lute,
The timber crashed beside his foot
And sprung up stretching in his tracks.

He had an ox, but his was blue,
The flower in his button hole
Was brighter than a parasol.
He's gone. Tom Swift has vanished too,

Richard Wilbur's "Folk Tune" (*The Beautiful Changes*, 1947, p. 27), is a poem in which the comic figures of popular imagination—Bunyan, Tom Swift, and Tom Sawyer, who epitomize the dream of work without effort—are juxtaposed to the nightmarish tragic labor of John Henry.

Recently, another poet has written a lament for the vanished hero. David Wagoner, who in several poems reflects his concern for the northwest forests, writes, in "The Death of Paul Bunyan," that Bunyan's was "No common death, not some civilized garden variety/After he'd raised sweet hell from the minute he was born." There follows Wagoner's swift retelling of Paul's growth, his blue ox, his camp of "timber beasts," and how Paul and Babe dug the St Lawrence, the Grand Canyon, Pudget Sound, till he "laid himself off … To fish and hunt and laze around and maybe even think/Once in a while when he could think of something to think of." Wagoner's style replicates the deadpan exaggerations of bunkhouse humor even when his motifs derive from popularizations, as some of them do. His lament continues,

> But they came after him , a new breed of skyline loggers
> (Who didn't even know he was there)….
>
> … smaller men who had never stunk out a bunkhouse

—and Paul was done in by those measly modern lumbermen like the bulldozer and the power saw operators described in the *New York Times* account of contemporary lumbering, quoted above. They caught Paul and Babe asleep and "cut them down with the trees," and the fantastic creatures of Bunyan's bestiary, "far out in the forest . . . Being helpless without someone to dream them,/began lamenting":

> The sausagy walapaloosie …
> The snow snake, the rumptifusel, the gumbaroo
> That would burst near campfires …
> > And the morning squonk
> Wept loud and long for Paul Bunyan, then faded forever.
> [*Collected Poems*, 1956–1976, 1976, pp. 268–69]

Yet Wagoner's terminal report may be premature. The record remains of what a few hundred old-time lumberjacks once told each other to transform the hazards of their work into comic exaggerations, and what half a dozen poets, seeking an image for the resilience of American life, have made of the hero fragmentarily sketched in our folklore. The exploitations of that image in countless ads, tourist promotions, and vapid juvenilia at the least illustrate the sociology of popular culture, though perhaps no further analysis will be needed to show how the Paul Bunyan of the bunkhouse shrank into the bumcombe booby of folklore, how the jests of grown men were reduced to kitsch for the kiddies. That, too, is part of the record. This study of the transformation of a folk legend is offered as an example of the ways of the folk, the popular, and the literary imagination treat a given theme, in the hope that its methods may be applicable to contemporary as well as historical traditions.

Preface to the 1952 Edition

Of all the demigods in the comic pantheon of American folklore, Paul Bunyan is the only one whose fame has continued into the twentieth century. Modern technology and communications, the mobility of populations, and widespread literacy have all but extinguished the fame of Cap'n Stormalong, Mike Fink, and Sam Patch; even the martyred patriot Davy Crockett has long since passed from popular oral tradition into the pages of history. Yet Paul Bunyan is now more widely known than he ever was as the hero merely of lumberjacks or oilriggers. The growth of Bunyan's fame while other folk heroes passed away was no mere accident; neither was his transformation from superwoodsman into a national symbol. Several social, economic, and literary forces combined to make these changes inevitable.

Although there have been many books about Paul Bunyan's adventures, this one is the first to give the history of these changes in his character and fame, and to analyze why they occurred. It is the first, also, to trace the growth of the Bunyan traditions in the three genres in which they have influenced American culture: as oral folktale, as popular literature, and in the works of modern poets who sought a symbol to express the spirit of the American people.

It is hardly surprising that Paul Bunyan should be seen in this light by poets as dissimilar as Robert Frost, Carl Sandburg, and W. H. Auden. The exploits of a national hero—particularly of a mythical personage—are always clues to the character of the people who celebrate him. He embodies their ideals of personal conduct, their ethical code, their goals; although superhuman, he is created in the image of human aspirations, and his preternatural strength helps men to ward off human fears.

In the United States the age-long process by which a national mythology is formed was necessarily foreshortened into a few generations. The tribe of comic demigods of whom Paul Bunyan is the last are our equivalents to the heroes of the great epics of the past. But our demigods are the heroes not of epics but of anecdotes; no bard or scop had time to complete an epic based on native myths before the relentless march of history overwhelmed the folk cultures of the American frontier. Among the poets who wrote of Bunyan, Mr. Sandburg comes closest to emulating the ancient bards; yet it was inevitable that his attempt to use Paul Bunyan as a paradigm of the American character would prove an anachronism. For in this hero's history, between the yarn of the folk raconteur and the shaping intellect of the sophisticated poet there is a line of development to which the lore of Beowulf or Roland or the Knights of the Round Table was never subject. When Paul Bunyan became a popular rather than merely an occupational hero, he ceased to be the product of an homogeneous folk society. In the popularization of Paul Bunyan not only were his adventures revised, but his character and the humor with which his exploits were told were altered still more. His changing lineaments reflect the changing values of American popular culture over the last half-century.

While authentic folktales of Paul Bunyan are now very scarce, and only four notable poets have used him in their works, the popularizations are incredibly widespread. As most of them are inaccurate as folklore and worthless as literature, my reason for analyzing them in detail is their significance in making evident the values cherished in popular culture. Such a study could not be all-inclusive; instead, I have tried to clear a trail through a forest of printed sources and have directed the reader to only the most significant documents in Paul Bunyan's short but varied history.

In tracing this one tradition as it appears in American folklore, popular culture, and contemporary poetry, this book is therefore an attempt to deal with three distinct yet related genres of literature. Each is the product of a different level of culture, each possesses its own values, each is written from its own motives. All three use what is, or is commonly thought to be, the same traditional materials, but each shapes these materials to its own ends. The Motif-Index on page 203 traces the development of typical narrative elements as they appear in these genres.

This study would have been much poorer without the encouragement and assistance of many authors and scholars who generously contributed to my research. Mr. W. H. Auden has kindly consented to the publication for the first time in this book of excerpts from the manuscript of his operetta libretto, *Paul Bunyan;* for his kind coöperation I am most grateful. Professor Herbert Halpert of Murray State College, Kentucky, was similarly generous in making available his hitherto unpublished records of eight interviews with Eastern lumberjacks who knew Paul Bunyan tales. Such materials are rare, and Dr. Halpert has done a great service to the present study by allowing their inclusion here. Mr. W. B. Laughead, author of the first booklet about Paul Bunyan, was good enough to furnish copies of the original and several subsequent editions, and to ransack his memory as well as his bookshelf for the benefit of my research. In the Notes I have acknowledged the assistance of many other writers and students of the Bunyan traditions who responded to letters of inquiry and otherwise aided my project.

Any study of the folk traditions of American character and humor must acknowledge indebtedness to the work of two pioneers in this field: Constance Rourke and Professor Walter Blair. The writings of Professor Richard M. Dorson of Michigan State College provided invaluable aid, but I wish to thank him even more for his kind encouragement extending over several years.

I was fortunate to have the understanding guidance of Professor Paul Spencer Wood when an earlier version of this study was written as a Master's thesis in American literature at Columbia University. Professor John G. Kunstmann encouraged the publication of this book by awarding to the thesis the

Chicago Folklore Prize for 1949. Many good suggestions were offered me by Professors MacEdward Leach, Secretary, and Wayland Hand, Editor, of the American Folklore Society; and Professors Hughbert C. Hamilton and David C. Webster of Temple University. My mother helpfully typed much of a difficult manuscript. To my wife, Elizabeth, I am indebted more than I can say for her steadfast encouragement during the years this book was in preparation. I scarcely need add that while my study has profited much from the comments of those who kindly read the manuscript in whole or in part, any faults or errors are wholly my own responsibility.

I owe a special debt of gratitude, which I shall not be able to acknowledge personally, to the late Ruth Benedict. She encouraged me to undertake this study of the cultural significance of a confused body of literature about a confusing tradition. I had the benefit of Mrs. Benedict's kindly and generous counsel as a student and, for a short time, as a research assistant on the Columbia University Research Project in Contemporary Culture. From her I learned the essential interrelationship of the humanities and social sciences: the disciplines of analysis by which materials as diverse as the Paul Bunyan traditions may be most profitably viewed must combine the techniques of folklore scholarship with those of literary criticism. To her many students Mrs. Benedict was an always generous friend and a continuing inspiration. I hope my practice here does no injustice to the guidance she so graciously extended.

ACKNOWLEDGMENTS

Thanks are due to the following authors, publishers, and institutions for permission to use excerpts from their manuscripts or copyrighted works:

Dr. B. A. Botkin for permission to quote from *A Treasury of American Folklore* and *A Treasury of New England Folklore;* Professor John Lee Brooks for permission to quote from "Paul Bunyan: American Folk Hero," his unpublished thesis at Southern Methodist University; the *Detroit News* for permission to quote from "The Round River Drive" by James MacGillivray; Professor Richard M. Dorson for permission to quote from *Davy Crockett: American Comic Legend* and *Jonathan Draws the Long Bow;* Harcourt Brace & Co., Inc., for permission to cite from *American Humor* and *Davy Crockett* by Constance Rourke, from *The People, Yes* by Carl Sandburg, and from *Paul Bunyan* by Esther Shephard; Miss Charlotte W. Hardy for permission to quote from *The Minstrelsy of Maine* by Fannie Hardy Eckstorm and Mary Winslow Smyth; Holiday House for permission to quote from *Ol' Paul: The Mighty Logger* by Glen Rounds; Henry Holt & Co., Inc., for permission to quote from *New Hampshire* by Robert Frost, copyright 1923 by Henry Holt & Co., Inc., and 1951 by Robert Frost; Alfred A. Knopf, Inc., for permission to quote from *Paul Bunyan* and *The Saginaw Paul Bunyan* by James Stevens; The Library of Congress for permission to reprint an excerpt from the recording of "The Little Brown Bulls" from the Archive of American Folk Song, and to publish written transcriptions of Paul Bunyan tales from recordings in the collection of the Folklore Section; Oregon State Library for permission to quote from manuscript materials from the WPA Oregon Federal Writers' Project files; Miss Ida Virginia Turney for permission to quote from *Paul Bunyan Comes West;* University of Maine for permission to quote from *A History of Lumbering in Maine, 1820-1861* by Richard G. Wood; University of Michigan Press for permission to reprint excerpts from *Songs of the Michigan Lumberjacks* by Earl Clifton Beck; and Louis Untermeyer, for permission to quote from *The Wonderful Adventures of Paul Bunyan.*

Grateful acknowledgment is also due to the editors of the following journals in which portions of this book first appeared: *The Antioch Review, Midwest Folklore, Southern Folklore Quarterly,* and *Western Folklore.* My ballad, "How We Logged Katahdin Stream," was first published by the *Saturday Review of Literature.*

Cover of *Introducing Mr. Paul Bunyan of Westwood, Cal.*, by W. B. Laughead, 1914.
First pictorial representation of Paul Bunyan.

JOHNNY INKSLINGER, Paul Bunyan's
bookkeeper saves nine barrels of ink each
year by not crossing his "t"'s or dotting
his "i"'s.

GET A FREE COPY OF
"PAUL BUNYAN and HIS BIG BLUE OX"
Original printed version of the loggers'
legends. 40 pages, illustrated.

■

Address
JOHNNY INKSLINGER
Westwood, Lassen County,
California.

Laughead's drawing of Johnny Inkslinger,
Paul Bunyan's bookkeeper.

The Marvelous Exploits of

PAUL BUNYAN

AS TOLD IN THE CAMPS
OF THE WHITE PINE LUMBERMEN FOR
GENERATIONS

DURING WHICH TIME THE LOGGERS
HAVE PIONEERED THE WAY THROUGH
THE NORTH WOODS
FROM MAINE TO CALIFORNIA

*Collected from Various Sources and
Embellished for Publication*

Text and Illustrations
By
W. B. Laughead

*Published for the Amusement
of our Friends by*

The RED RIVER LUMBER COMPANY

MINNEAPOLIS, WESTWOOD, CAL., CHICAGO,
LOS ANGELES ·:· SAN FRANCISCO
30th Thousand, See Page 40

Title page to the 1929 edition of The Marvelous Exploits of Paul Bunyan, text and illustration by Laughead.

Frontispiece to James Stevens, *Paul Bunyan* (1925), woodcut by Allan Lewis. Used by permission of A. A. Knopf, Inc.

Frontispiece to Esther Shephard, *Paul Bunyan* (1941 edition), by Rockwell Kent. Used by permission of Sally Kent Gorton.

"One Blow Was Generally Enough," by Rockwell Kent, from the 1941 edition of Esther Shephard, *Paul Bunyan*. Used by permission of Sally Kent Gorton.

Paul Bunyan and Babe the Blue Ox, by Edward C. Smith, number 5 in a series of Paul Bunyan illustrations distributed by the Mead Corporation of Dayton, Ohio. Used by permission.

Poster advertising the premiere performances at Columbia University, week of 5 May 1941, of the operetta by W. H. Auden and Benjamin Britten.

Statues of Paul Bunyan and Babe the Blue Ox beside Lake Bemidji, Minnesota. Photo courtesy of the Minnesota Tourism Division, St. Paul, Minnesota.

Paul Bunyan's statue stands thirty-five feet tall in Bangor, Maine. Photo courtesy of Bromley and Co., Inc., Boston, Massachusetts.

Paul Bunyan Wore Velvet

Gentlemen, get ready...women can't seem to resist hugging men wearing these soft, cotton velvet shirts in a woodsman's plaid. Watch out under the mistletoe. Men's: S, M, L, XL. $125
Blue Plaid: #13609 Brown Plaid: #13709

Paul Bunyan's masculinity makes attractive a huggable shirt in lumberjack plaid, in the Fall 1998 catalogue from Whispering Pines, Fairfield, CT. Used by permission.

The Michigan Governor's Trophy is awarded annually to the winner of the Michigan State University–University of Michigan football game.

The Paul Bunyan Stamp. © USPS 1996.

Contents

PAUL BUNYAN

*Last
of the
Frontier
Demigods*

The question what the American imagination
will make of Paul Bunyan is a curious one.
Will it make him another Hercules or
another Munchausen? Or will it extravagantly
think itself rich enough to afford to neglect him?

CARL VAN DOREN, *The Roving Critic*

CHAPTER ONE

Three Paul Bunyans

1. WHO WAS PAUL?

This book is a study in popular mythmaking, the history of one legendary American hero. We know that the legends of Davy Crockett, Sam Patch, and Strap Buckner began as the embellished adventures of actual men.[1] Perhaps, once, long ago in the woods, there was a strong and skilled lumberjack who bore the name of Bunyan. Perhaps. We shall never know, for the origin of this hero is lost to us now that the woodsmen of the nineteenth century have all passed on.[2] Nobody ever asked them about Paul Bunyan, for no one outside of a lumbercamp had even heard of the hero until 1910.[3] And the early woodsmen did not write their stories down. They told them, though, and so Paul Bunyan's fame spread far and wide.

The most significant fact about such characters as Bunyan and Crockett is not who they were in real life, but what they have become in the imaginary life of the people who cherish them. Paul Bunyan, whoever may have actually borne that name, had by the turn of the century become in story the prototype of the powerful logger. Out of the impetuous humor and slippery wit of the woodsmen a mythical image was fashioned,

an image in which each of them could see himself made fearless, clever, and strong. Thus were the lumberjacks repaid by a
total vision of a stupendous hero to which they each had given
but a part of themselves. This Bunyan grew to be a focal character among them. Innumerable short humorous anecdotes were
told about him. Although many of these had previously been
told in other contexts[4] they now were fastened to his name, and
comprised a widespread lumberjack tradition.

At first Paul Bunyan was but one of a large group of localized occupational heroes, most of whom were similar to him
in size and prowess in their respective vocations. These included the cowboy, Pecos Bill; Cap'n A. B. Stormalong, "Iron
Man of the Wooden Ships"; Mike Fink, "King of the Mississippi
Keelboatmen"; John Henry, the indomitable Negro "Steel-
drivin' Man"; Joe Magarac, Slavic hero of the steel mills; and
a host of lesser regional and occupational heroes.[5] In the years
before 1910 when the exploits of few of these titans had broken
into print and their fame was largely known by word of mouth,[6]
Paul Bunyan already had a great advantage over his fellow
demigods. They were each limited to one region: the sea, the
Mississippi, or the South. But the logging industry spread clear
across the continent from Maine to Oregon, and wherever the
lumberjacks went they took with them their beloved jokes
about Paul Bunyan.

In addition to whatever oral currency these tales may have
had, or may still have, for the past forty years other influences
than this oral tradition have been spreading Paul Bunyan's
fame in ever-widening circles. A few Bunyan tales were first
printed in 1910; after a slow start, in which only a handful of
items appeared in the next decade, printed versions of the
Bunyan stories suddenly deluged newspaper columns and national magazines. Finally, full-length books appeared. As Professor Richard M. Dorson has made clear, this literary diffusion
is the second stage of development typical of the American
comic demigod.[7] Mr. Dorson includes in this second stage a
category which I regard as separate: the use of the Bunyan
stories by talented creative writers, in contrast to their mere

popularization. As I shall demonstrate briefly in this chapter, and more fully in the remainder of the study, these three stages of folktale, popularization, and work of art each arose from different motives and reflects different values; each has its own characteristic style, and it is erroneous to attribute the humor or the hero of one genre to the tales of another. But more of these distinctions below; for the present, let us follow Professor Dorson's survey of how the American folk hero arises.

After the literary phase has grown to full bloom, he finds that:

In the third phase it [the legend] bursts all literary bonds and finds expression in pageantry and a variety of art media: sculpture, ballet, musical suite, lyric opera, folk drama, radio play, painting, lithographing, wood carving, and even a glass mosaic mural. . . . "Paul Bunyan's Day," a gala community festival in honor of the timber god, originated in Brainerd and Bemidji, Minnesota, but spread to Concord, New Hampshire, and Tacoma, Washington.[8]

I have taken from this phase the literary manifestations, such as folk drama and opera, and reapportioned them into my scheme as popularizations or works of art, according to their merits. In Mr. Dorson's final stage, the cycle is completed when the hero passes back into common speech as popular symbol of the huge, the comic, the strong. Divorced now from any specific literary or artistic treatment, these references appear in whatever contexts make allusion to Bunyan's attributes appropriate. This is similar to the first stage, the level of fragmentary folktale, except that here the occupational hero has become the property of the nation at large.[9] However, the hero's virtues and the humor with which the hero is portrayed have both been altered in the growth from isolated local legend to national common denominator.[10]

It is time to give a preview of this metamorphosis. Here is a sample from each of the literary levels of the Bunyan stories.

2. THREE PAUL BUNYANS

On the twenty-fourth of July, 1910, Paul Bunyan made his first appearance on a page of print. The page was in the

Detroit News-Tribune; strictly speaking, Paul himself was hardly there, since he is but a minor character in James Mac-Gillivray's story, "The Round River Drive." The twelve short anecdotes, however, are told by a member of the crew that "'swamped' for Paul," and their adventures could befall loggers only in the crew of the great Bunyan. These anecdotes are strung together in a casual manner, rather than fashioned into a unified narrative. This one is typical of the more amusing incidents:

> Dutch Jake and me had picked out the biggest tree we could find on the forty, and we'd put in three days on the fellin' cut with our big saw, what was three cross-cuts brazed together, makin' 30 feet of teeth. We was gettin' along fine on the fourth day when lunch time comes, and we thought we'd best get on the sunny side to eat. So we grabs our grub can and starts around that tree. We hadn't gone far when we heard a noise. Blamed if it wasn't Bill Carter and Sailor Jack sawin' at the same tree.
>
> It looked like a fight at first, but we compromised, meetin' each other at the heart on the seventh day.[11]

This seems fairly close to the way the tales were actually told by the lumberjacks.[12] Note that the narrator is a participant in the action, and he does not scruple to use such terms peculiar to the logging industry as "the fellin' cut" and "cross-cuts brazed together."

This first appearance did not make Paul Bunyan famous overnight. Four years went by before Douglas Malloch contributed the next Bunyan piece, to the *American Lumberman.* This was simply a repetition of the very same stories told by MacGillivray, written this time in doggerel couplets.[13] Paul Bunyan was still unknown to the public-at-large, and to students of folklore, literature, or history. One of his appearances had been in a local newspaper, the other in a trade journal.

By 1916, however, two more important Bunyan items had found their way into print. Both told more tales than had Malloch or MacGillivray, and in them Paul himself was the major character. One of these publications was an advertising booklet for a lumber company, the other a scholarly paper in the *Transactions of the Wisconsin Academy of Sciences, Arts and Letters.* K. Bernice Stewart and Professor Homer A. Watt, in their article, "Legends of Paul Bunyan, Lumberjack,"[14] presented tales taken down from the loggers of Michigan, Wisconsin, northern Minnesota, and from camps in Oregon, Washington, and British Columbia. This paper is one of the few authentic sources from which students today can estimate the spread of the oral tales before widespread printed dissemination. One tale, "Breaking the Jam," was written down by a lumberjack for Professor Watt, and is a classic of its kind. It will be analyzed in detail in the third chapter.

This paper was Paul Bunyan's introduction to the academic world. At that time John A. Lomax had barely begun his pioneer work of collecting native American folklore. Most of the folklore analysis hitherto undertaken had been done on Anglo-American survivals, such as the Child ballads, and on American Indian customs. Hence Professor Watt in his critical remarks approached Paul Bunyan with the idea of comparing him to folk heroes of the Old World. Here begins the speculation which has continued ever since as to the antiquity and origin of the tales, their relationship to European sagas and legends, and the qualities of humor they exemplify. This type of analysis will be examined in the next chapter.

A larger public was appealed to when, in 1914, W. B. Laughead wrote a pamphlet for the Red River Lumber Company of Minneapolis. Himself an ex-lumberjack who had served in northern Minnesota lumbercamps from 1900 to 1908 as "assistant bull cook, timber cruiser, surveyor, and construction engineer," Laughead put together a thirty-two-page pamphlet, postcard-size, with the title *Introducing Mr. Paul Bunyan of Westwood, Cal.*[15] He "attempted to sandwich hunks of advertising copy between stories about Paul Bunyan."[16] Mr. Laughead christened Paul's ox Babe, and wrote the following story:

Paul Bunyan's greatest asset was Babe, the Big Blue Ox. Babe was seven axe handles wide between the eyes and weighed more than the combined weight of all the fish that ever got away.

Paul saved himself the muss and bother of cutting down trees in the woods, sawing out logs, swamping, skidding, and hauling. Brimstone Bill would hitch Babe to a quarter section of land and drag it bodily to the landing where the timber was cut off of it just like shearing a sheep.

Babe used to pull the water tank with which Paul iced his roads from Dakota to Lake Superior. Once this tank burst and that's what started the Mississippi River and has kept it flowing to this day.

Paul will not need Babe in California for The Red River Lumber Company has installed steam and electric appliances there that would make Babe hang his head with shame.[17]

Except for the last paragraph, this is not at all unlike the MacGillivray story or the yarns Laughead himself had heard in the Minnesota woods. Amusing though these tales may be, however, Mr. Laughead's advertising campaign was not a great success. "Largely because so many of these 1914 pamphlets were filed in wastebaskets that edition is today a collector's rarity."[18] Laughead recalls that "the men to whom our advertising was directed [were] sawmill men, wholesalers, and dealers."[19] Yarns about lumberjacks, with whom they had no direct contact, apparently held little charm for them. And what do "swamping," "skidding," and "quarter section" mean? Such country terms and woodsmen's lingo lack the zing of good advertising copy. Two years later Mr. Laughead rewrote his Bunyan pamphlet, bearing more closely in mind the tastes and preoccupations of his intended readers. The 1916 booklet, called *Tales About Paul Bunyan, Vol. II*, also has a page devoted to Babe, the big blue ox. This paragraph shows a certain change in vocabulary:

Every time Babe was shod they had to open up another Minnesota Iron Mine. He could never be fed twice at the same camp as one meal exhausted all the feed one outfit could tote in one year. In spite of overhead cost and maintenance Babe was a valuable piece of equipment because of high efficiency and low operating cost.[20]

And finally, in 1922, Mr. Laughead rewrote the booklet again. This time he put his stories into the form they have kept with only minor changes ever since. Here is an excerpt from the final version of Babe, the big blue ox:

Babe, the big blue ox constituted Paul Bunyan's assets and liabilities. . . . When cost sheets were figured on Babe, Johnny Inkslinger found that upkeep and overhead were expensive but the charges for operation and depreciation were low and the efficiency was very high. How else could Paul have hauled logs to the landing a whole section (640 acres) at a time?[21]

It is hardly probable that such terms as "assets," "liabilities," "cost sheets," "upkeep," "overhead," or "depreciation" were in the native idiom of the lumberjacks. Obviously these stories have been restyled for a non-lumberjack audience, for readers who don't even know how many acres there are in a section. Mr. Laughead addressed his books to businessmen. Paul Bunyan has been partially rewritten in their lingo. This, apparently, was one way to reach a really wide audience; after the failure of the 1914 and 1916 editions, *The Marvelous Exploits of Paul Bunyan* (1922 *et seq.*) caught on beyond the advertiser's fondest hopes. "Within a few months after its publication the entire edition of 10,000 copies was exhausted. . . . To meet the swelling demand a new edition was put out almost every year until 1944, when the final Thirtieth Anniversary Edition presaged the liquidation of Red River Lumber. In all, over 100,000 copies were given away."[22]

Subsequent popularizations were prepared for still larger audiences, even less intimately connected with the lumber industry than customers of the Red River Company. The implications of writing lumberjack stories in a popular style for readers unacquainted with the environment in which the folktales arose form the critical basis of Chapter Four. There Paul Bunyan transfers his logging operations from the sticks to the slicks.

Several other popularizations appeared in the next few years, but before mentioning these let us take note of the first use of Paul Bunyan as a theme by a gifted creative artist. In 1921 Robert Frost retold a few of the traditional anecdotes in his poem, "Paul's Wife,"[23] but they were only background material for a new story of his own. Paul's wife was a naiad born from a pine tree. She is more reminiscent of Longfellow's Nokomis than of any female American folk figure. To see this, one need only compare her to Sally Ann Thunder Ann Whirlwind Crockett, Sal Fungus, or the other ladies of frontier tradition.[24] As for Paul himself, in this poem,

He'd been the hero of the mountain camps
Ever since, just to show them, he had slipped
The bark of a whole tamarack off whole,
As clean as boys do off a willow twig
To make a willow whistle on a Sunday
In April by subsiding meadow brooks.[25]

The tamarack trick had been told for generations, and was one of the earliest stories to be printed. But in comparing Bunyan's feat to what boys do on April Sundays "by subsiding meadow brooks," Frost puts himself completely outside the story. In MacGillivray's yarn, the author spoke of "Dutch Jake and me." He was there. He was one of the crew. While Laughead tells his stories partly in the vocabulary of his audience rather than of his subjects, his booklet remains a popularization, not a work of art, because he does not impose artistic form upon his material. Frost, on the other hand, speaks an individual diction from a point of view outside the folk tradition, and casts an original tale on a folk theme into a sophisticated form.

3. THE TRADITIONS MINGLE

While the student must critically separate these several genres, actually they are all current at once and each mingles with the others. When one partakes of the special character of another, the problem of separating them is made quite complex. For instance, most of the folktales now recovered from the oral tradition show definite signs of being descended from previous popularizations rather than from the old-time folktales. Thus a new crop of oral tales spreads out, for instance, those concerning Paul's macaroni farm.[26] The stories are johnny-come-latelies to the flux of oral tales, yet after a time they are folktales themselves. But oral tales deriving from Dorson's fourth stage are different in character from those of the first. While it is difficult now to find current oral tales with a purely oral lineage, in Chapter Three I have tried to use typical stories whose origins are most likely in the frontier oral tradition, rather than in written adaptations.

The popularizations themselves present a further ambiguity. Almost invariably, each new story, article, or book about Paul Bunyan purports to be set down out of the mouths of the people. "Here," says the author, "are the stories I heard from old lumberjacks as we sat before a bunkhouse stove. I've fixed them up a little so that you, dear reader, will better enjoy them." But if these authors have actually been in the woods, they often manage to hide that fact in their writing. In style, concept, humor, and attitude they are more prone to resemble each other than the oral folktales they say they are rewriting. There is something of a hoax upon the public here at work, as one author after another comes out of the woods to his typewriter to tell us that Babe, the Blue Ox, measured 42½ axehandles between the eyes. This is presented as a widespread folk tradition, but all it really proves is that the popularizers have plagiarized each other. Chapter Four presents the evidence of this, and shows, too, how their Paul Bunyan came less and less to resemble the hero of the real woodsmen.

A third intermixture is that of the popularization and the work of art. At the risk of iconclasm I suggest that creative artists will do best to select their symbols from the folklore of the folk, rather than from the rehash of the hack writer or the vulgarization of the popularizer. The folk originals of Bunyan, however, are hard to find, and so most of the creative writing has been based on popularizations. This problem is discussed in Chapter Five.

CHAPTER TWO

The Folk and Their Tales

What I write is authentic and truthful, as I am the only man living who knew Paul Bunyan.[1]

So ends the letter which, according to lumberjack Fred Chaperon of Michigan, was written by Joe Muffreau, camp cook to the master logger. If anyone should really know about Paul Bunyan, it ought to be the shantyboys who swamped along Round River with him, or the friends to whom they told or wrote their memories of those grand old days.

Although, according to Richard M. Dorson's recent survey of folklore in Upper Michigan, "Paul Bunyan does not figure importantly in living lumberjack tradition,"[2] some tales still are told there. In addition to those which have been transcribed directly from lumberjack raconteurs, there is a more recent series of Bunyan folktales taken from oral tradition among the oil-well drillers and pipe-line layers of the Oklahoma-Texas panhandle region. Many of these oral tales seem upon examination to be merely variants of written stories. Yet from within these occupational groups there are enough transcriptions of tales whose origin is probably oral to give us a reasonably accurate idea of what that tradition was like in its richer days.

Before examining the tales themselves, however, it may be advisable to present the premises upon which their study will be conducted. In folklore analysis such a definition of principles is especially needed, particularly when the study is literary rather than strictly anthropological. The recent revival of interest in the folk arts has had very confusing consequences for the student of folklore. This revival, certainly a curious phenomenon in a culture as urban, literate, and industrial as ours, has given the very term "folk" a commercial appeal to prospective purchasers of books, phonograph recordings, chinaware, bric-a-brac, and jewelry. Meanwhile, "folk" songs, dances, games, handicrafts, and tales have all been industriously marketed to satisfy this new and somewhat patronizing demand. The result is that many critics, as well as customers, are likely to confuse the commercial facsimile of a folk object with the real thing. When the object is a literary product, such as a Paul Bunyan story, the differences are considerable. If we are to make this distinction, then, it will be worthwhile to examine the conditions under which the actual folktales flourished, and to discover their chief characteristics.

1. WHAT IS A FOLK?

"Folklore," writes Martha Warren Beckwith, "is the study of human fantasy as it appears in popular sources."[3] This definition favors the imaginative forms of communal experience, rather than mere "folk knowledge." The latter is traditional lore, presumed to be fact, handed down through the generations untinged by those distinctive creative qualities in a culture which are characteristic of its popular imagination.

To produce a folklore there must first be a folk:

The true folk group is one which has preserved a common culture in isolation long enough to allow emotion to color its forms of social expression. It has not, that is, lost its emotional reaction to its own particular set of ideas.[4]

Such groups are able to "preserve a common culture in isolation" when they have been separated from neighboring peoples by barriers of either language and national heritage, occupation, geographic conditions, or any combination of these factors.[5]

The folktale, primitive forefather of modern fiction, is one of the most important popular sources in which human fantasy appears among a folk. As Stith Thompson defines it, the term includes "all forms of prose narrative, written or oral, which have come to be handed down through the years. In this usage the important fact is the traditional nature of the material."[6] The Bunyan folktales, then, are the anecdotes which circulated freely among the lumberjacks who lived in geographic and occupational isolation long enough to develop a distinctive expression of fantasy. The tales reflect imaginative reactions of the loggers to the material conditions of their lives.

Folktales are much more closely related to the folk public than is popular literature to American middle-class society. All folk literature has a strongly communal flavor; it is a reflection of a whole group, a culturally classless society, rather than the voice of only one element or individual. This is so because "the traditional nature of the material" is the guarantee that it has been widely accepted and enjoyed. If it had not met these tests, it would be neither retold nor remembered.

But how can a group make a literature? For many years it was thought that the folk arts actually were sprung from "a communal origin . . . removed from the conditions of individual authorship."[7] The phrase is Gummere's, from his speculation on Grimm's theory of ballad origin, of which he was the chief American exponent. More recent scholarship, investigating primitive peoples and surviving folk groups in the United States, where the folk arts are yet a living reality, has brought us to a less speculative view. Professor Benedict, surveying the history of folklore studies, concludes:

All cultural traits including folk tales are in the last analysis individual creations determined by social conditioning. They must, however, each be socially accepted by a process with which the individual has comparatively little to do and which is dependent upon the cumulative social traits and preoccupations of his group.[8]

What these "social traits and preoccupations" were among the lumberjacks and drillers we shall soon see, looking for clues both in descriptions of their life and in their oral literature. But

to examine such literature profitably we should first consider
how such literature comes into being, grows, and changes; and
second, in which aspects of content, form, and function it differs
from the written literature of our contemporary society.

2. THE GENESIS OF FOLKTALES

In a folk group, a folktale arises when one man tells a
story which his neighbors like well enough to remember and
pass on. As the tale is usually told rather than written, the pass-
ing-on is generally oral. Among Old World peoples and most
primitive tribes, the effort is primarily to reproduce the original
story as faithfully as possible.[9] The greater portion of folktale
analysis has been concerned with tracing plots and motifs
through the oral tradition in cultures where retention is the aim
of the tellers.[10]

According to the Finnish folklorists A. Aarne and W. Anderson of the Geographical-Historical School, the many variants
of a given type of story evolve from an ancient archetypal version which is altered in transmission through adaptation to
prevailing environment and through imperfections in the attempt to reproduce it.[11] If the improvised substitutions in the
story are accepted by the audience, they too become part of the
oral tradition. Thus two or more versions of the same tale arise
and spread, often simultaneously. The addition may be a motif,
or a complete element of narrative comprising several motifs
in a sequence. Often the changes are appropriated from other
stories.

Sometimes two or more tales are added together to make
a longer one. The details in the original story may be multiplied
or repeated. The characterization is invariably simple. As the
tale travels from one group or region to another, or as the
level of the folk culture advances, the incidents and background
of the story will be altered to reflect local contemporary conditions.[12]

This formal analysis, based upon extensive study of the European fairy tales, merry tales, animal tales, etc., neglects to emphasize an important difference between Old World lore and the type of material we are considering. The age-old tales of Cinderella or Puss-in-Boots are vestigial productions of the popular fancy. Created many centuries ago, this type of folktale is tenaciously retained among the peoples of Europe long after the social systems it reflects have passed out of their country's history. Today, in the Province of Québec, for instance, the French population retains almost intact a large number of folktales and songs brought over from France as long ago as the sixteenth century. These stories are concerned with *dragons de feu, le bête à sept têtes, sifflets magiques,* etc.[13] The songs celebrate Le Prince d'Orange and Le Prince Eugene; in the ballad "Germine," the knight who returns to die on his doorstep is Guilhem de Beauvoir; he left this earth in the year 1277.[14] Among this transplanted Old World people, popular traditions do not celebrate the exploits of their immediate ancestors in Canada. Their lore is ancient, conservative, and quite uncreative; it is doomed, in time, to slow extinction.[15]

On the other hand, in American folktales—especially tall stories—we are faced with a different situation. The American frontier has always been manned by an exuberant, expansive, strongly individualistic people. Like every unliterate population, they erected heroic self-projections based in part upon the innumerable fragments of older lore which were part of their common heritage. They differed, however, from the French-Canadian and European peasants in this important respect: instead of attempting merely to reproduce the stories they heard (thus changing them by default), the frontiersmen continually and deliberately altered their folktales in the process of retelling them. This characteristic lies deep in the nature of their society; competitive and individualistic in the extreme, they vied with one another in this oral art as well as in every test of physical prowess.

There are many apparent similarities between the tales of Paul Bunyan, Davy Crockett, and Mike Fink, and those told in other ages in distant parts of the world. Such questions as whether the Bunyan stories are based upon myths known in India three thousand years ago seem to me to shed little light on their intrinsic nature. The ebullient self-assertion, preternatural cleverness, and fantastic exaggeration which characterize these American stories are all products of the environment in which they arose. The fragments of folklore from all over Europe which went into their making have been refashioned to fit new situations. If parallels occur between Bunyan tales and the folktales of ancient Europe, they cannot be used alone to establish organic relationships between cultures. As A. I. Hallowell suggests, "Such data are to be studied first of all in relation to their cultural settings, instead of being abstracted from it [sic], or analyzed in their formal aspect."[16] Parallels may well arise independently, where the cultural settings are coincidentally similar.

This perspective has not been enjoyed by most of the critics who have dealt with Paul Bunyan. At one time or another Paul Bunyan has been proclaimed a contemporary Zeus, Thor, Loki, Finn MacCoul, Siegfried, Roland, King Arthur, and Guy of Warwick. For those who are prone to make such comparisons, Ruth Benedict has a word of caution:

Folklore incidents combine and recombine with ease, attaching themselves now to one plot and now to another. In the process they are necessarily reconstructed to suit the new association that has been set up. Only by a study of their diffusion can it be determined which aspects of a tale are present because they are traditional and common property of the entire area or even of a large part of the world, and which elements are the peculiar contribution of the people under discussion.[17]

Thus while there are certain similarities between Bunyan and Beowulf, it is indeed erroneous to imply that the oral tradition has brought Grendel's conqueror to Michigan. What we can say is that both were imagined in societies sharing important traits in common, particularly their struggle against Nature. But there is one further objection to equating Bunyan with any of the heroes of Old World myths and sagas. His personality is different from any of theirs, in spite of occasional resemblances in attributes or adventures. Old World heroes have more dignity than Paul; Old World jokers, less. The particular combination in Paul Bunyan of heroic self-projection, comedy, and exaggeration is indigenous to the American frontier. "The flower of art blooms only when the soil is deep . . . it takes a great deal of history to produce a little literature," wrote Henry James.[18] The moral in the present case is that the soil was shallow and the history short, and so rapid was the change from elemental struggle to urban civilization that the popular imagination has never had a chance to clothe our history in the somber dignity of an epic. Instead, the impulse toward glorification was deflected into ridicule. What might, in other times, have slowly evolved into a national saga was rapidly spawned into innumerable unrelated comic episodes.[19]

I shall attempt, however, to define the development of certain characteristics of humor, personality, and narrative structure which are common (if not entirely indigenous) to the folk literature of the American frontier. The most fruitful direction of this inquiry is, I believe, to trace the development of these folk fantasies in terms of their own environment, treating them as the imaginative reactions of their immediate tellers to their own peculiar way of life. Thus we shall become involved in tracing motifs after all, not in prehistorical migrations from the Indian peninsula, but in their discernible reincarnations in frontier tales from Crockett to Bunyan. This study embraces a span of a little more than a century (c. 1820 to the present), and a geographical distribution which follows the retreat of the frontier from Tennessee to the isolated timber patches of the north woods in the twentieth century.

Such was the route that many of the Bunyan folktales actually followed. I have arbitrarily chosen Crockett as the forebear of Bunyan, not because he was the earliest, or only, comic hero upon whose stories the Bunyan anecdotes were modeled, but because his stories are the most interesting. There were many such figures in the early nineteenth century, but it was the legendary Crockett who best exemplifies the tradition of frontier humor at its moment of widest sweep and most grandilo-

quent inspiration. Needless to say, I do not refer to the actual
Senator from Tennessee, but rather to what he became in the
popular imagination. Tales of previous and contemporaneous
heroes became attached to his fame, just as some of his stories
were later to be retold in lumberjack lingo about Paul Bunyan.
As Bunyan is probably the last major figure in the same tradition, the comparison is valuable in seeing what became of this
vein of American humor and heroic self-projection during these
four generations.

As the proper subject of this study is Bunyan, in the succeed-
ing chapters we shall begin with the lumberjacks and their folktales, looking back to the earlier manifestations of the same
creative impulses only whenever such comparisons are helpful
in evaluating the esthetic merits of the stories.

3. THE FOLKTALE AS A SEPARATE GENRE

One cannot accurately say that these anecdotes are to
the folk who tell them what our magazines and books are to us.
There are at least four significant differences which indicate that
folk literature is a genre distinct and separate from either the
fiction of commercialized popular media, or the works of literary art, in modern society.

In the first place, the forms of the folktale are not those of
contemporary written literature. Folktales fall into several well-
defined patterns, ranging from the simple jest to complex fairy
tales like *Cinderella* and *Snow White*, which involve several
characters and an established succession of episodes. But even
at its greatest level of complexity, folk literature is structurally
simple when compared to a modern novel, play, or opera. Paul
Bunyan stories have been used as themes in some of these complex forms; in the process of adapting the folklore to a more
complicated expression, the nature of the lore has been altered.

A second difference has been suggested above, in discussing
the relationship between the tale and its public. Let us expand
this point to consider the position of the author in his society.

We know well enough what it is in our own; in a folk group, however, a man may be a listener today and a taleteller tomorrow. To the extent that he changes the story in any of the ways we have mentioned, he is partly responsible for its authorship. Thus author, editor, public, censor, and critic are all rolled up together in a folk society. Each man, in his ever-changing role, hears what he likes to hear, and tells—with either realism or fantasy or both—about the life he knows and about himself projected in the guise of an imaginary character.

In the third place, the reflection of society in literature is far more intimate and comprehensive in the folktale than in any but the most ambitious and successful of modern novels:

Among any people . . . the picture of their own daily life is incorporated in their tales with accuracy and detail. . . . Peoples' folk tales are in this sense their autobiography and the clearest mirror of their life.[20]

In a folk group the areas of shared interest and common sympathy encompass almost the whole of the peoples' lives. Hence, from their socially accepted stories we can infer a great deal about the ways in which members of a group look at their relationships to each other, to nature, to the supernatural, and to others outside the group. In short, we can generalize from the folktale about the society it represents. True, we can do this to a certain extent from either the novels of a modern author or the stories in a national magazine. However, because of the interchangeability of the creative, censorial, and receptive roles in the folk society, the folktale is much more nearly a total expression of its culture.

In the fourth place, the folktale differs from both its popularization and the more consequential literary use of its character or theme, since oral and written literatures do not fulfill the same functions in their respective cultures. Popularizers of Bunyan have had to present the humorous projections of an isolated, primitive group of men to the average citizens of an industrial and cosmopolitan culture. Naturally, if lumberjack folktales are to be made interesting, or even palatable, to other classes of people sharing little in common with the woodsmen, the tales cannot be transmitted intact. As we have seen, W. B. Laughead found it unfeasible to tell the stories to his company's customers in their original lingo.

To the lumberjack or rigger, the Paul Bunyan stories, while obviously fantastic and comic, were also *true*. They are true in the sense that they actually represent his imaginative responses to his environment. But the urban (or suburban) reader, who has never lived in continual conflict with the forces of nature, comes to his popularized Paul Bunyan with at least two attitudes the logger and rigger would not share. He views Paul Bunyan as an amusing curiosity, and his imaginary participation in the stories takes the form of a mental back-to-Nature movement. He roams around the woods with Ol' Paul, and gets real mind's-eye dirt on his hands. He trades his white collar for that good old red flannel. He gets away from it all.

For the shantyboy and derrick-rigger, however, Paul Bunyan stories were not a means of indulging in wistful nostalgia; they were an imaginative triumph fashioned from their entire way of life. The modern reader does not share that life. To what extent does he share its ideals and its humor, or believe in the virtues which are admired by these workers on our last frontier? Let us look at their environment and then at their literature, to see what were those ideals and what was this humor, in which forms they were expressed, and to what extent they transcend the way of life from which they speak to us in the boisterous laughter of Paul Bunyan.

4. A NOTE ON SOURCES

The use of written sources for oral literature may seem a contradition in terms. There are few more ephemeral forms of culture than the spoken story. Phonographic recording is its only version which allows completely accurate analysis. Next best is the written transcription of the trained folklorist. Third best is the rewording of the untrained collector or the rewriting of the popularizer. Most of the Bunyan tales in Chapter III have been transcribed from phonograph records. But the Crockett stories with which they are compared present another difficulty. Nobody tells them any more, so current oral versions are impossible to obtain. A considerable body of *written oral tales* about Davy Crockett is extant, however, and for the sake of keeping clear the categories of this study I think it wise to explain how this is possible.

These Crockett texts are taken from a series of almanacs which bore his name. Published between 1835 and 1856,[21] they furnished the frontiersman with his favorite jokes, as well as

. . . Correct Astronomical Calculations; For each State in the Union —Territories and Canada. Rows—Sprees and Scrapes in the West; Life and Manners in the Backwoods; and Terrible Adventures on the Ocean.[22]

These jokes, which had the Colonel as their protagonist, were written versions of the best anecdotes going the oral rounds. They used the same techniques of humor, vocabulary, and concept of character as might be employed by an accomplished raconteur. The authors of these written versions (whoever they may have been) wrote in, and for, the same stream of oral humor from which they took their hero and their style. The same is true of other stories common in many ante-bellum newspapers. Those nearest the oral style are to be found in papers which circulated in regions where the oral stories flourished, notably the *Spirit of the Times* and the *Yankee Blade*.

CHAPTER THREE

Tales from the Pine and the Panhandle

1. THE LUMBERMAN'S LIFE

They [the lumbermen] are a young and powerfully built race of men, generally unmarried, and, though rude in their manner, and intemperate, are quite intelligent. They seem to have a passion for their wild and toilsome life, and . . . possess a fine eye for the comic and fantastic.

So were the woodsmen described a century ago.[1] Few of us today can accurately visualize "their wild and toilsome life," now that power saws topple the timber and the old-time teams of horses or oxen have been replaced by bulldozers, tractors, and trucks. It is difficult now to find even a forest like those they invaded. To find such woods in the East today, one must follow Thoreau's trail to Mount Katahdin. There, in Baxter State Park near Millinocket, Maine, stands one of the few remaining islands of primordial timber, such as confronted woodsmen almost everywhere in the 1840's and 1850's. But what desolation they left behind them! Even in 1846 Thoreau was shocked by the wasteful abandon with which they leveled the forests. With a wry smile and a little tall tale, he writes, "No wonder that we hear so often of vessels which are becalmed off our coast being surrounded a week at a time by floating lumber from the Maine woods. The mission of men there seems to be, like so many busy demons, to drive the forest all out of the country from every solitary beaver swamp and mountain-side, as soon as possible."[2]

Their success is grimly recorded in the landscape for seventy miles above Bangor. Where the great pines had stood and man had been dwarfed, all that now remains are endless swamps of dismal underbrush and arid meadows of baked thistles. Eroded roots and stumps are reminders that this was once a forest. But in the reservation, trees fifty feet tall grow an arm's length apart, and their crowns spread out to hide the sky. Underfoot, the ground is springy where the humus has piled up, hard where the knotted roots and rocks protrude, and soft where mosses creep over the rotting logs. The forest itself is of white pine, spruce, hemlock, and birch; between the trunks are jagged rocks and heavy thickets of spined brambles. Felling these trees by hand and hauling them by ox team on corduroy roads over stump, swamp, and stone must have demanded men of tremendous endurance and vitality.

Thoreau describes how valleys such as this one were logged in the old days, when hand methods—like those referred to in the earliest folktales of Paul Bunyan—were in wide use:

All winter long the logger goes on piling up the trees which he has trimmed and hauled in some dry ravine at the head of a stream, and then in the spring he stands on the bank and whistles for Rain and Thaw, ready to wring the perspiration out of his shirt to swell the tide, till suddenly, with a whoop and halloo from him, shutting his eyes, as if to bid farewell to the existing state of things, a fair proportion of his winter's work goes scrambling down the country, followed by his faithful dogs, Thaw and Rain and Freshet and Wind, the whole pack in full cry, toward the Orono Mills. . . . When the logs have run the gauntlet of innumerable rapids and falls, each on its own account, with more or less jamming and bruising, those bearing various owners' marks being mixed up together,—since all must take advantage of the same freshet,—they are collected together at the heads of the lakes, and surrounded by a boom fence of floating logs, to prevent their being dispersed by the wind, and are thus towed all together like a flock of sheep, across the lake, where there is no current, by a windlass, or boom head . . . and, if circumstances permit, with the aid of sails and oars. . . .

The log-driver, or lumberjack, Thoreau remarks,

must be able to navigate a log as if it were a canoe, and be as indifferent to cold and wet as a muskrat. He uses a few efficient tools, —a lever . . . with a stout spike in it . . . and a long spike-pole, with a screw at the end of the spike to make it hold. . . . Sometimes the logs are thrown up on rocks in such positions as to be irrecoverable but by another freshet as high, or they jam together at rapids and falls, and accumulate in vast piles, which the driver must start at the risk of his life. Such is the lumber business, which depends on many accidents. . . .[3]

By 1847 Maine lumbermen were moving south and west, buying lands in New England, New York, Pennsylvania, and Louisiana, but, as their historian R. G. Wood concludes, "While [they] might stop at intermediate points, it was to the Lake States that they thronged in largest numbers."[4] In the words of Daniel Stanchfield, a pioneer who explored Rum River in Minnesota and imported Maine woodsmen for his camps, "Most of our Minnesota lumbermen, and many settlers in our pine regions, came from that State, and are therefore often called 'Maineites.' The methods of lumbering in the Maine woods in 1830-1850 were transferred to Wisconsin and Minnesota."[5] Such testimony suggests that the methods of logging as well as the conditions of life in the woods were pretty similar all across the timber country. But with the end of hand methods in large-scale logging, the isolated rough-and-tumble environment in which the woodsmen's special ways of life developed has almost disappeared. With this life has gone the distinctive folk arts it fostered; these include the lumberjack ballads and the tales of Paul Bunyan as the shantyboys' hero.

Richard M. Dorson, who has known the aged survivors of Michigan's halcyon lumbering days, thus characterizes the old-time lumberjack as "a traditional type":

. . . hard-drinking, hard-fighting, hard-working, respectful to women, loyal to his camp, titanic in endurance, hopelessly spendthrift. Stock descriptions of the "old American lumberjack," with accompanying cases of eye-gouging, thumb-biting fights in which the winner stamps his caulked boots on the face of his prostrate opponent, are given repeatedly and earnestly by all the oldtimers—testimony that the lumbering life involved a code, a cult, something of an unwritten creed.[6]

The lumberjack's crudity and roughness were intrinsic parts of his isolated culture. The same was true of the cowboy, "for the social life of the Western range was pitched to a key of social conflict."[7] It is surely no accident that Paul Bunyan invaded the plains and replaced Pecos Bill as the dominant figure in cowboy folklore.[8]

However primitive the lumberjack fights may have been,[9] when their aggressions were channeled into a formal contest they were, as their old song says, "bound to conduct it according to law." The story of one classic conflict is told in the well-known ballad, "The Little Brown Bulls," which appears in almost every collection of lumberjack songs.[10] It is said to date from a timber-towing contest between two ox teams "in Mart Douglas's camp in northwestern Wisconsin in 1872 or 1873."[11] (This was the very time when John Henry had his heroic contest with a steam drill.)[12] A few of the fourteen stanzas will enlarge our view of life among the lumberjacks. After each solo stanza the chorus was sung by all within hearing:

> The day was appointed, and soon did draw nigh,
> For twenty-five dol-lars, their fortunes to try;
> A judge and a scaler there soon were found,
> And all did draw nigh on the ap-pointed ground.
>
> *Chorus:* Derry down, down, down, derry down.
>
> With a whoop and a yell came McCluskey in view,
> With his big spotted steers, the pets of the crew,
> Saying, "Chew on your cuds, boys, and keep your mouths full,
> For you easil-y can beat them, the Little Brown Bulls!"[13]

Songs such as these, dealing with the real events of the everyday world, add a necessary background to our study of the Bunyan tales. We find that one set of attitudes toward experience appears in the lumberjacks' ballads, while another, apparently contradictory, is presented in their tales. The songs are realistic, but the stories make excursions into the mythical world as well. To understand the myths, we must also heed the realities.

2. A MATTER OF LIFE OR DEATH

The ambivalence of lumberjack literature is evident when we compare the famous ballad, "The Jam at Gerry's Rocks,"[14] to a typical Bunyan story, "Breaking the Jam," collected by Stewart and Watt.[15] As the titles indicate, both relate adventures concerning a log jam. This was the lumberjack's greatest peril, when a floating log became wedged between rocks or protruding stumps, and the churning timber piled up behind it. These jams had to be destroyed. It demanded great strength, skill, and daring to find the "key" logs under the tottering wall, to pry, chop, or blast them loose,[16] and to escape to shore before the swollen river swept the jam away:

> They had not rolled off many logs when the boss to
> them did say,
> "I'd have you be on your guard, brave boys. That jam
> will soon give way."
> But scarce the warning had he spoke when the jam
> did break and go,
> And it carried away these six brave youths and their
> foreman, young Monroe.
>
> When the rest of the shanty-boys these sad tidings
> came to hear,
> To search for their dead comrades to the river they
> did steer.
> One of these a headless body found, to their sad
> grief and woe,
> Lay cut and mangled on the beach the head of
> young Monroe.[17]

The widespread currency of "The Jam at Gerry's Rocks" and other ballads similar to or modeled after it[18] demonstrates the insecurity with which the loggers regarded their own strength when the hostile elements were pitted against them.

How, then, are we to take their apparent disregard of all

these dangers in the following folktale, written down for Professor Watt by a lumberjack:

Breaking the Jam

Paul B Driving a large Bunch of logs Down the Wisconsin River When the logs Suddenly Jamed. in the Dells. The logs were piled Two Hundred feet high at the head, And were backed up for One mile up river. Paul was at the rear of the Jam with the Blue Oxen And while he was coming to the front the Crew was trying to break the Jam but they couldent Budge it. When Paul Arrived at the Head with the ox he told them to Stand Back. He put the Ox in the old Wisc [River] in front of the Jam. And then Standing on the Bank Shot the Ox with a 303 Savage Rifle. The ox thought it was flies And began to Switch his Tail. The tail commenced to go around in a circle And up Stream And do you know That Ox Switching his tail forced that Stream to flow Backward And Eventually the Jam floated back also. He took the ox out of the Stream. And let the Stream And logs go on their way.[19]

Such a jam was never seen on land or sea! We notice that it baffled the ordinary lumberjacks; they "couldent Budge it." Then comes Paul to the rescue with his prodigious Blue Ox. While Paul is heftier and stronger than his crew, we are not told that he is any braver. After all, he didn't wade into the Wisconsin River and rip the jam apart with his bare hands— which he could easily have done if the tales of his prowess are true. No, Paul Bunyan is not merely stronger than his fellows; he is cleverer! Who but a shrewd, sagacious Yankee would have thought of driving the river upstream? Who but a powerful thinker could have conceived of turning an oxtail into a propeller? And who but a natural-born genius would have set this invention in motion by slinging moose-shot at the great Blue Ox?

This inventive cleverness of Paul Bunyan is a deeply rooted and deeply respected trait in American character. "I now contrived a mould, made use of the lead we had as puncheons, struck the matrices in lead, and thus supply'd in a pretty tolerable way all deficiencies," writes Benjamin Franklin in the *Autobiography,*[20] relating one of his many mechanical improvisations. Here we see that the heroic lumberjack, like the Sage of the Revolution, combined wit with grit to beat down obstacles and "supply'd in a pretty tolerable way all deficiencies."

There is, however, more to "Breaking the Jam" than mechanical wisdom only. We profess to believe in the exploit, yet at the same time we marvel at it, and laugh. This tale, like all the Bunyan stories, and like all manifestations of the comic spirit, demands that we believe in its premises for the duration of the story. We accept Paul Bunyan, we accept his Blue Ox, we accept an oxtail propeller which can spin a river backwards. This suspension of disbelief is essential; every teller of Bunyan folktales assumes that his hearers will take his story as true. Sometimes this is made explicit, as in Joe Muffreau's pronouncement, "What I write is authentic and truthful"; usually it is a casual assertion, planted at the beginning of the tale:

"Boys, did I ever tell you about the time I drove the Naubinway over to Paul Bunyan's camp on Big Mantisque Lake?"[21]

If you stay for the rest of the story, it is because you are willing to believe for the moment that Paul Bunyan really lived and had a camp on that lake.

We admire Paul for accomplishing a task which his crew "couldent Budge," the same task at which young Monroe and the six Canadian boys were crushed to death because they lacked his powers. Yet Bunyan's methods could not be applied by anyone but Paul himself. Dependent upon his superhuman size and strength, his clever solutions are not for the common run of men. Paul's fantastic and impossible improvisations represent an imaginative response to experience, not an account in the historical sense of any possible event.

The direction of this imaginative response is, in a way, perverse, ridiculing by its implausibility what we know to have been a real fear. The loggers are mocking themselves with gusto and good humor. Self-ridicule such as this, neither self-pitying nor cynical, requires a fundamental shift in viewpoint, a complete detachment from the situation. How could the lumberjacks achieve such objectivity toward the danger they most feared? We may say of them as of the backwoodsmen, who faced other perils in the same forests, that "comic resilience swept through them in waves . . . transcending terror with the sense of comedy, itself a wild emotion."[22] Here is a transmutation from fear into laughter. The same reality has been seen through contradictory projections, one tragic, the other comic. In the tragic view we are purged of terror by contemplating the terrible; in the comic, by minimizing it, making it appear ridiculous beside other qualities equally accessible to man—in this case, the strength and ingenuity of Paul Bunyan.

Thus both the tragic ballad and the comic tale were important psychologically in helping the lumberjacks face their daily danger. The ballad is sentimental; the singer and his listeners identify themselves with the unfortunate Monroe, and enjoy the exquisite agony of mourning their own deaths as he is cast up mangled and bloody on the shore. Then they are freer of fear than they were before Monroe, the stand-in and scapegoat of their terrors, died.

But the comic tale is a more affirmative purge. Man is made huge, and his brains match his muscles. The solution is as simple as it is fantastic. Terror is dwarfed, danger ridiculed entirely away. The woodsman identifies himself with Paul, and is filled with the sense of his own strength. From a purely functional standpoint, such tales as "Breaking the Jam" are techniques of adaptation to environment. They are the necessary fantasies men create in order to fortify themselves against the dangers they must face and the threats they cannot overcome except by force of mind. The invocation of courage has always been one of the functions of primitive art.

It is worthwhile examining further the structure of this little tale to see the formal elements which contribute to its effectiveness. Note that the first half of the story is taken up by plausible and realistic description. We are told where the incident occurred and who was present, with only the barest hint, in the exaggerated dimensions of the jam, of the fabulous ending to come. The raconteur, revealing this information in a casual, conversational tone, seizes upon our initial acceptance of the story as "true"; he encourages us to swallow the rest by giving us at first these facts which no one could disbelieve. But suddenly he slips the fabulous into the factual: amazing events tumble at us before we can collect our wits enough to scoff or dismiss them. Then, when we are almost reconciled to the fantastic, comes the perfectly matter-of-fact ending: "He took the ox out of the Stream. And let the Stream And logs go on their way." This undoes our composure again by reminding us that in the beginning we had promised to believe the story. The end is a logical necessity, dictated by the events we have heard and already accepted. We are caught, first by the explosion, then by the calm. In its comic structure this tale demonstrates what Constance Rourke has observed of the composite character of wilderness heroes: "Backwoods profuseness was set off against Yankee spareness."[23]

And yet we may find that we do no more than smile at this elaborate jest, which must have set the lumberjacks a-roaring till the shanty rang with their laughter. Even to those of us who can feel an empathy toward and identification with them, the humorous element may still seem chiefly grotesque. As Boas has remarked about the poetry of primitive peoples, "the effect of [such literature] does not depend upon the power of description that releases clear and beautiful images, but upon its ability to arouse strong emotions."[24] In "Breaking the Jam" there is the erection of a belief and of strong emotional tension; this is suddenly destroyed and resolved by substituting for the fear a fantasy of self-mockery and self-inflation. We are deflected from fear by being tricked into laughter. But unless we can share, or at least comprehend, the magnitude of the oppression, we cannot as fully enjoy the exhilaration which comes with sudden release.

3. DOWN EAST AND BACKWOODS FOREBEARS

We have mentioned the resemblance of this Bunyan story to traits of character and humor in two earlier American folk traditions: the drawling Yankee's canniness, and the tall talk of the backwoodsman. Constance Rourke and Walter

Blair[25] have shown that these traditions were the earliest manifestations of native American humor, and that this humor was
in each case dependent upon the concept of a folk personality.
Yankee and Backwoodsman emerged early in the nineteenth
century as the chief types of regional character seen by the
Americans themselves. First to appear was the Yankee, limned
in Royall Tyler's comedy, *The Contrast* (1787), in which Jonathan appeared as a New England Tony Lumpkin.[26] But it was
the New England village, rather than British authors, which
supplied the chief prototype for the characterization. In hundreds of jokes and anecdotes swapped at tavern, courthouse,
and crossroads, the concept of the Yankee took form. Many of
these stories were printed as fillers in newspapers and almanacs;
some are still told today.[27] The several facets of Yankee guile,
stinginess, keenness of observation, and above all, common
sense, were gathered together in Seba Smith's *Jack Downing*
papers, the first of many written portraits.[28] The Major's career
began when he wrote home to Cousin Ephraim back in Downingville, having come to Portland to sell a load of axehandles
and look at the legislature. These two activities broadly define
the spheres of Yankee interest: outwitting his fellow men, and
measuring the democratic process against plain horse sense.
Gullibility and naïveté were assumed with the comic masque,
and the results reported in a laconic drawl. Yankee talk was
tart as good hard cider, spiced with homely metaphor.

Traces of this early personification of the regional character
remained in the reservoir of popular belief long after Major
Downing, Lowell's Hosea Biglow, Haliburton's Sam Slick, and
a host of other literary and subliterary folk figures had been
forgotten. Their prototype, the Yankee peddler, took to the
western roads and was found wherever there were two people
with one piece of silver between them. He left them Hartford
razors, Rhode Island calico, buttons from Boston, and a caricature of himself in return for their money. Whatever the price
he demanded, in the last item the settlers got a bargain. Below
we shall see how they turned the Yankee's traits against him,
but later appropriated the same guile for their own favorite

sons, Mike Fink and Davy Crockett. And we shall see, too, how later frontiersmen on the last frontier continued to combine these two traditions in Paul Bunyan.

Of the two, the backwoods character is stronger in Bunyan. This predominance is only natural, since the lumberjacks live more like trappers and riverboatmen than like the quiet New England folk of Jalaam or Downingville. Their Yankee traits are recast in lumbercamp settings, just as Crockett's shrewdness consisted in outwitting bears and varmints instead of driving bargains on clocks and axehandles. The traditional backwoodsman, when seen in town, was b'ilin' with braggadocio and sp'ilin' for a fight, leaping high in the air to nicker like a horse and challenge all comers. The Yankee had been a solitary figure, writing satirical letters to the folks Down East, or sidling into western clearings with no companion but his peddler's pack. But the Gamecock of the Wilderness, or the Ring-tailed Roarer, as he was likely to call himself, often traveled with a partner, performed before an audience, and was just as convivial as he was uproarious.[29] We shall see him in greater detail, and hear his own descriptions of himself and his prowess, when we examine more closely the traditional roots of the Bunyan stories in the tales of Crockett and others.

But rather than generalize about this dual background to the Bunyan tales, it is better to take up the points of resemblance as we find them in the stories themselves. Within each resemblance we shall also find contrasts, in imaginative power and verbal ingenuity, and in the complexity of form in which similar motifs are expressed. When we have explored the implications of these parallels and differences, we can arrive at some conclusions about the value of Paul Bunyan tales as the flowering of folklore, and as the seed of literary inspiration.

4. FABULOUS NATURAL HISTORY

The conquest of fear of death was but one of the services Paul Bunyan performed for the lumberjacks. As their symbol of preternatural cleverness, he was far better fitted than they to cope with the lesser discomforts which afflicted their way of life. Here, as in "Breaking the Jam," by identifying themselves with the hero of their fantasies they could partake in some measure of his strength and equanimity in the face of discomfort or danger.

Anyone who has been in the woods at all knows that the tiny mosquito is a formidable enemy. In the spring drives the lumberjacks, making their way through swampy lowlands, were attacked by clouds of furious insects. This particular tribulation became the basis of a Bunyan theme which is known, in one or another of its many variations, wherever woodsmen scratched red swellings on their skins:

Boys, did I ever tell you about the time I drove the Naubinway over to Paul Bunyan's camp on Big Mantisque Lake? Boys, I want to tell you there's some dandy mosquitoes over in that swamp even now, but the modern mosquitoes are nothing like their ancestors.

Well, just as I was pulling into Paul Bunyan's camp that day I heard some terrible droning noise like one of these modern airplanes. Even Paul, big as he was, seemed excited and yelled to me to hurry into his office. So I knew something was wrong.

Then Paul told me that some of the big mosquitoes was loose. He had trapped them several years ago, because they was bothering his cattle. Paul told me that two mosquitoes was trying to kill his prize heifer. They had the critter down and was trying to drag it off, he said, when along came a really big mosquito. The big mosquito simply killed off the other two, picked up the cow, and flew away. So Paul decided then and there to put on a campaign against them. He and his men trapped several of them in live traps, he said, and the rest got scared and flew away.

But this day, when I come to visit Paul, some of the mosquitoes had broken loose. We had barred the doors when we heard the mosquitoes droning overhead. They were landing on the roof. I shook like a leaf, but Paul wasn't scared. Overhead I heard a terrible cracking and looked to see swordlike weapons piercing the roof. Paul said they were mosquito stingers. So he grabbed his sledge and clinched those stingers like a carpenter clinches a nail. Next day he put twelve of his star lumberjacks to executing mosquitoes on that roof. He said he was through showing kindness to the mosquitoes. It didn't pay. They'd stab you in the back.[30]

Naturally, after hearing about mosquitoes that could kill a cow, you wouldn't find your own measly bites of much account.

This story differs in one detail from most of the others: Paul has an office. This, and the contemporary reference to "one of these modern airplanes," indicates the way in which the details of the story are continually kept up to date. The joke itself is no youngster, however. It follows the form of all good Bunyan tales (and most good frontier humor) by setting the story in motion with casual reference to immediate facts. Everybody knew about those mosquitoes on Mantisque Lake. Thus fantasy was introduced with realism. Matt Surrell, who told this yarn, rapidly transferred the scene of his story to the mock-heroic past: "But the modern mosquitoes are nothing like their ancestors." Now we are in the fabulous world of Bunyan.

One might think that cow-killing mosquitoes were climax enough for a joke, but Matt outdoes his own whopper: "a *really* big mosquito" picks up the cow and flies away! When the camp is attacked, Paul is fearless and shrewd, the Backwoods-Yankee combination again.[31]

The mosquito story is typical of an American comic genre: the enlargement of natural objects, especially plaguey critturs. This is often pushed to the grotesque. While the genre contributes some good Bunyan stories, it also exists quite independently of them as a response habitual to the American sense of humor.

Among the lumberjacks, this ridicule of the animal world took still another form than mere exaggeration. The ridicule was based upon fear of the unknown, as well as annoyance from the recognizable. Fear of the wilderness as a stimulus to the imagination is much older in America than any story about the logging industry. Prior to the Bunyan tales, a widespread folk humor dealt with mythical creatures which infested the woods. There are Old World analogies aplenty, many of which arrived here as part of the settlers' baggage. One need think only of sea serpents[32] and werewolves.[33] The snipe hunt is an immemorial practical joke, its object being not the shore bird of that name but a ferocious rodent of the woods, often sought but never captured.[34] And so the animal world of Paul Bunyan is peopled with a variety of furry hoaxes. They transmute fear of unknown dangers into a mock natural history. In Minnesota they include the agropelter, hodag, wild teakettle, snow snake, snow wasset, whirling wampus, and bog hop.[35] There were other monsters in other regions. This tradition, too, is still alive without reference to Bunyan. The Army Air Force, in addition to sheltering the ubiquitous gremlin, was also the habitat of the Schnorrophl. The name had been previously applied to a wild vulture which flew in narrowing concentric circles until it disappeared; a mechanical war changed the myth from a fabulous bird to an impossible machine, and the new Schnorrophl became a secret-weapon aircraft with the same performance as its feathered namesake. Stewart and Watt are of the opinion that the strange animal stories are latecomers to the Bunyan lore. "There is little doubt that [they] existed outside the Bunyan cycle, and are simply appended to the central tales."[36]

While these extravagant creatures have a hoary ancestry in American humor, there is a difference between the lumberman's fantastic versions of the forest's unknown terrors and those of his predecessors, the trapper, raftsman, and pioneer. Matt Surrell and the rest of the lumbering crew always described their gigantic mosquitoes, hodags, and side-hill dodgers with a scientific detachment, as though they were reporting the phenomena to the American Museum of Natural History.[37] This is one side of the coin, the hoax. But the earlier backwoodsmen put another interpretation upon unnatural creation. They didn't *see* the crittur; they *lived* it!

I'm that same David Crockett, fresh from the backwoods, half-horse, half-alligator, a little touched with snapping turtle; can wade the Mississippi, leap the Ohio, ride upon a streak of lightning, and slip without a scratch down a honey locust. . . .[38]

Davy Crockett and Mike Fink became the tarnacious critturs themselves.

Why were not the lumberjacks, too, embodied in the hodags

which they said they saw? Constance Rourke has shown that
the crowing cockalorum of the pioneer was an evocation of
fabulous animal strength to meet the threat of unknowable
animal terror.[39] But the lumbermen did not so keenly need
to fear the beasts which threatened the trapper. The lumberjacks destroyed the woods wherever they went, dooming the
cougar and wolf to extinction. They didn't have to invoke the
speed of the horse or the jaws of the alligator to feel reasonably safe away from the clearing. The forest is awesome at
night, but there is a difference in degree between tremulous-
ness and actual fear for one's life. A little scared, the lumberjacks described impossible beasts with scrupulous patience
and detail, but their major adversary was the mosquito. More
accurate analogies to Crockett's animalistic screams are the
tales such as "Breaking the Jam" in which the lumbermen
conquered their most immediate terrors.

5. VICTIMS OF NATURE, NOT ECONOMICS

Fatigue was as much an adversary as were jams and
mosquitoes. Many lumberjacks must have almost feared to die
in their traces, so endless did their exertions appear in the
face of mile on mile of standing timber. In the old days, after
all, a dozen men pitting their little axes against the virgin
forests may well have been dismayed by the defense in depth
with which the timber seemed to defy them. And once the
trees were felled, they had to be trimmed to logs and driven
by thousands down the rivers and lakes. This was a time of
especial impatience, for the lumberjack lived for his short
spree in town. On the river there were a hundred things
which could delay him: jams, slow current, dried-up streams,
heavy rains. So it is little wonder that the ancient legend of
Sisyphus should be born anew in the woods:

. . . We cut our logs and stacked 'em on the river. And in the spring
when the ice and snow was off, we started a spring drive a logs.
Well we drove those logs down stream for a couple of weeks. And

we come to a set of camps that looked just like Old Paul's camps.
So, we drove for a couple of weeks more, and we come to another set
that looked just like Old Paul's, so we started for a third week, and
we begin to think there might be somethin' wrong. So when two
weeks is up and we come to the set of camps again, we went ashore,
and sure enough, it was Old Paul's camp! And there we'd been
draggin' those logs around and round, around and round, around
and round the river all that time and never knowed no difference.
Didn't know that that river didn't have no beginnin' and no end. . . .[40]

Perry Allen recited this version of "The Round River Drive"
at St. Louis, Michigan, in 1938. "The Round River Drive" was
the title of the first printed collection of Bunyan stories, and
the tale seems to be known wherever Bunyan yarns are told.
Perry's is about the best—and briefest—of the versions I have
located.[41]

"The Round River Drive" is unusual in one respect: Paul
Bunyan is the victim of geography. Just as the death of young
Monroe was the imminent reality balancing the fantasy of
"Breaking the Jam," here is the lumberjack's feeling of futility
and fatigue cast right in the matrix of Bunyan braggadocio.
Swamping, cutting, felling, hauling, and driving sixteen hours
a day was no picnic, even for the mighty Paul.

Yet "The Round River Drive" is by no means a class-
conscious protest. The woodsmen's predicament is treated in
the same fashion as their fears, and the result is laughter instead of rebellion. The antagonist is not the bosses who set
the hours and conditions of their strenuous labors. Paul and
his men accept all these, and expect nothing better. But they
do not expect to be outwitted by Nature, against which they
were continually in battle.

In the same camps at which these tales were told, revolt
and rebellion seethed, and anger at injustice burned deeply.
The IWW spread through the lumbercamps as a forest fire
through the woods.[42] Yet the Bunyan tales, with their good-
natured acceptance of everything in the status quo, were never
captured by the radicals and turned into a revolutionary mythology. The Wobblies made myths and had heroes of their
own, notably Joe Hill.[43] Shot dead by "the copper bosses," he

tells them from the grave: "Don't mourn for me—organize!"
Joe Hill is a tragic hero, Paul Bunyan is comic. The imagination which deified the murdered organizer demands a different
symbol from that which pits Paul Bunyan against every ob-
stacle the lumbering life affords. Bunyan always accepts the
given conditions, and works out his solutions in their terms.
But imagine Joe Hill confronted with a log jam. Would he
put his life at the mercy of the churning logs to make a profit
for the bosses, or would he first demand insurance, social se-
curity, an eight-hour day, and remote-control blasting equipment? Failing these, he'd organize a strike right there on the
spot, and hold the bosses over the barrel with their logs backed
up the river until they came around to his demands. Except
by contrast, there's nothing funny about that situation; on the
other hand, the humorous version of the thing admits of no
rebellion. To Joe Hill, the fate of Jack Monroe is a warning
to the working class; to Bunyan, it is a challenge to prove
himself a better man by conquering insuperable odds.

6. CONQUEST OF NATURE

Except for this one misadventure on Round River,
Paul Bunyan generally has geography and the elements pretty
well under his control. So clever and huge is Paul Bunyan that
we are hardly surprised to find most of Nature's striking for-
mations are his doing. The best of these yarns explain the
features of the landscape as by-products of Paul's ingenious
logging enterprises. Perry Allen tells this story of how Paul
and his crew connected the two sections of a river which had
been burnt dry by a fire:

So we was up agin it, we had our logs in the river, and we wanted to
save our logs, so we had to contrive a plan to connect them two ends
together. So we went at it. We used a match box for a connection,
connected the two ends together and got our logs out. But that match
box is still there. Most people think it's Saint Marie's locks![44]

Paul is continually contriving such plans, and the countryside
is studded with monuments to his ingenuity.

A less imaginative, and therefore more frequent, fashion of crediting the landscape to Paul is to represent lakes as his ox's hoofprints,[45] or Moosehead Lake as the imprint of his "broad shape behind."[46] Similarly, Puget Sound exists because Paul dug it.[47] There are endless variations on the theme, each adapting the idea to whatever features the locality affords. This sort of thing can soon get very tiresome, since all the different stories are simply switches on the same gag. But the collectors have been indefatigable, and, like the tides in the Bay of Fundy, they are a-goin' yet.

The natural prodigies connected with Bunyan include the weather as well as the landscape. The Winter of the Blue Snow is traditional to almost all the tales,[48] but there is no attempt to explain this phenomenon. I suspect that a reference to the Blue Snow served to raise the curtain on the fantasy introduced into otherwise realistic settings. One story about ordinary white snow combines fantastic weather with the previous motif of relief from oppressive conditions. It is one of many tall stories traditional on the frontier which have been drawn into the periphery of Bunyan lore:

Bunyan sent me out cruisin' one day, and if I hadn't had snowshoes I wouldn't be here to tell you. Comin' back, I saw a whiplash cracker lyin' there on the snow. "Hello!" says I, "someone's lost their whiplash"; and I see it was Tom Hurley's by the braid of it. I hadn't any more'n picked it up, 'fore it was jerked out of my hand, and Tom yells up, "Leave that whip of mine alone, d——m ye! I've got a five hundred log peaker on the forty-foot bunks and eight horses down here, and I need the lash to get her to the landin'."[49]

There is more than a casual resemblance between this pedestrian anecdote and a story of some seventy years before:

A traveler floundering through the mire of a cypress swamp in Ohio saw a beaver hat lying crown upward in the mud. It moved, and he lifted it with his whip. Underneath was a man's head—a laughing head that cried, "Hello, stranger!" The traveler offered his assistance, but the head declined, saying that he had a good horse under him.[50]

The frontier hero making natural monuments is an old theme, as old, almost, as the hills he is said to have made.

Here, too, as in the case of the animal tales, the stories were
much richer when the elements seemed a more fearful adversary. None of the Bunyan tales approach the ebullient vitality
of "Crockett's Opinion of a Thunder Storm," in which the hero
absorbs the unbounded energy of Nature in order to with-
stand or overcome it:

Folks may talk and crow as much as they can about the roar of
Niagara, the growlin' o' the sea, an' the barkin' o' them big iron
bull dogs called cannons, but give me a hull team of storm-brewed
thunder, an' your other natral music is no more than a penny
trumpet to the hand organ of a hurrycane. By the great bein' above, a
reglar round roarin' savage peal o' thunder is the greatest treat in
all creation! It sets everything but a coward and a darned culprit
shouting in the very heart and soul till both on 'em swell so etarnal
big with nat'ral glorification that one feels as if he could swoller the
entire creation at a gap, hug the hull universe at once, then go to
sleep so full of thunder glory, that he'll wake up with his head an
entire electrical machine, and his arms a teetotal thunderbolt . . .[51]

The Bunyan raconteurs could not imagine any further than
the mountain, lake, or canyon which they saw. A conceit beyond their creative power lifted Crockett to a demigodlike
stature. This is expressed with greater power and poetry than
any of the Bunyan tales can offer. So many of the Bunyan
stories seem merely peripheral; Paul is but a walking shadow
in spite of all the exploits. It is as though the freshness of diction in the Crockett stories has been lost when Bunyan is
reported doing similar deeds. Many of Crockett's legendary
powers, however, must have passed away with the decline of
the myths about him and the extinction of the Crockett almanacs. In the following excerpt from a mid-nineteenth-
century almanac we meet a creature who is the equal of the
God of Genesis, and is at the same time a nat'ral man. There
is a grandeur here which is nowhere to be found in the lore
of Paul Bunyan:

One January morning it was so all screwen cold that the forest trees
were stiff and they couldn't shake, and the very daybreak froze fast
as it was trying to dawn. The tinder box in my cabin would no more
ketch fire than a sunk raft at the bottom of the sea. Well, seein' day-

light war so far behind time I thought creation war in a fair way for freezen fast; so, thinks I, I must strike a little fire from my fingers, light my pipe, an' travel out a few leagues, and see about it. Then I brought my knuckles together like two thunderclouds, but the sparks froze up afore I could begin to collect 'em, so out I walked, whistlin' "Fire in the mountains!" . . . I soon discovered what war the matter. The airth had actually friz fast on her axes, and couldn't turn round; the sun had got jammed between two cakes o' ice under the wheels, an' thar he had been shinin' an' workin' to get loose till he friz fast in his cold sweat. C-r-e-a-t-i-o-n! thought I, this ar the toughest sort of suspension, an' it mustn't be endured. Somethin' must be done, or human creation is done for. It war then so anteluvian an' premature cold that my upper and lower teeth an' tongue war all collapsed together as tight as a friz oyster; but I took a fresh twenty-pound bear off my back that I'd picked up on my road, and beat the animal agin the ice till the hot ile began to walk out on him at all sides. I then took an' held him over the airth's axes an' squeezed him·till I'd thawed 'em loose, poured about a ton on't over the sun's face, give the airth's cogwheel one kick backward till I got the sun loose —whistled "Push along, keep movin'!" an' in about fifteen seconds the airth gave a grunt, an' began movin'. The sun walked up beautiful, salutin' me with sich a wind o' gratitude that it made me sneeze. I lit my pipe by the blaze o' his top-knot, shouldered my bear, an' walked home, introducin' people to the fresh daylight with a piece of sunrise in my pocket.[52]

Realism and fantasy are deftly intertwined in the very first sentence of this remarkable story. The "nat'ral glorification" of these two passages marks a level of imaginative concept and literary achievement which the Bunyan tales never even approached. These Crockett pieces show considerable subtlety and extraordinary power; note the expert evocation of sounds in the beginning of "The Thunder Storm," and the organization, compression, and structural balance of "Sunrise in His Pocket." Whoever wrote these little sketches was thoroughly familiar with the traditional tone, rhetoric, subjects, and comic techniques of the oral raconteurs. To these he remained faithful, while submitting them to the discipline of even greater craftsmanship, and so brought them to perfection.

All the comic devices in the Bunyan stroies—and more—are found full blast in the earlier doings of Crockett. Bunyan is his heir; the lumberjacks' hero and their humor are both descended from the Ring-Tailed Roarer's. The line is a descent indeed, for the master-logger represents the decadence of the liveliest traditions in American folk humor. Although some of the Bunyan tales have considerable merit, at every comparable point the older strain is racier, fresher, more imaginative, and more amusing.

7. "PAUL'S CLEVERALITY"

In "Breaking the Jam" we have seen the inventiveness of Paul Bunyan, and in comparing him to Joe Hill we have discovered him to accept the world as he finds it, and to proceed with improvements from there. While Davy Crockett's inventiveness took the more apocalyptic form of saving "human creation" itself, Paul concerned himself with the immediate problems of his logging and oil-drilling industries. He found the world rapidly becoming more mechanized than it had been in Crockett's days of glory. In the Crockett stories, machinery is a curiosity, a source of amazement and also of the most energetic images: "He'll wake up with his head an entire electrical machine . . ."; "the hot ile" thaws the sun loose from "the airth's cogwheels." In "The Colonel Swallows a Thunderbolt," Crockett confides that "axletrissity is a screamer." Having seen "a feller in Washington . . . put the thunder and litening into glass bottles" to cure the "roomatiz," he determines to catch "a pestiferous thunder gust." "I opened my mouth so that the axletrissity might run down and hit my heart, to cure it of love." His reaction to this experience is, characteristically, a combination of pioneer animal imagery with a figure drawn from the latest mechanical marvel: "It war as if seven buffaloes war kicking in my bowels. My heart spun round amongst my insides like a grindstone going by steam. . . ."[53]

The Bunyan tales, however, make a different use of machinery. In them the implements are not sources of unusual imagery, but the products of Paul's ingenuity, which functions sometimes in unusual ways. The best of these inventiveness motifs show Paul cleverly solving a real problem. The problems he faced were of two kinds, those which required mechanical ingenuity and those which demanded shrewdness in human situations. The former are much more frequent in the sources I have been able to consult. A third type of story leads Bunyan into improvisations in order to set up a joke rather than solve a problem; these are the weakest of the inventiveness motifs.

Examples of the first type we have already seen in "Breaking the Jam," in Matt Surrell's story of how Paul trapped the giant mosquitoes, and in Perry Allen's of how he joined the ends of the river with a match box. Another favorite is the tale of the stretching harness: the ox was hitched to a pile of logs too heavy to be moved, but the wet leather harness tugs shrank as they dried, and pulled the load to camp.[54] This one is known all over the logging country, and must be derived from such pre-Bunyan stories as that of the man lifted into the sky by his own bootstraps.[55] Colonel Crockett felt like "a grindstone going by steam," but Paul Bunyan invented the original hand-turned model. In one version, his men laid their axeblades on round stones which were rolled down hills;[56] in another, "Paul rigged up the revolving rock" because stones were hard to find.[57] In still a third, the sparks from the rolling rocks set the forest afire,[58] but that is a different story, related, in its explanation of that greatly feared disaster, to the motif of "Breaking the Jam."

One of the rare examples of Paul's ingenuity in a human situation, rather than one of logging techniques alone, is furnished by the following tale. This yarn was told to Professor Herbert Halpert in 1941 by ex-woodsman Albert Peterson of Fish's Eddy in western New York State:

Well, one time Bunyan was skidding logs and they got over the line on another fellow. Well, they'd had these logs cut on this other fellow and he was watching them so they wouldn't get away from them. It was in bark-peeling time when bark slips like it will in the spring.

He didn't know how in hell he was gonna get away with it for the fellow was sitting on the logs. Well, Bunyan's ox team come up. They hooked on to that log, and they jerked it right out of the bark—and the guy was settin' there yet. That was fast work.[59]

Dr. Halpert writes me that he found this same story told in New Jersey about a piney lumber thief, Joe Munion[60]—further demonstration of the way these motifs become attached first to one figure, then to another, in oral tradition.

Peterson's story is also unusual in that Paul Bunyan is poaching logs on someone else's property. Only one other oral tale from my sources depicts Paul Bunyan as crooked; here he is shrewd, and drives a hard bargain:

Discovering in the spring that he had no money on hand, Bunyan suddenly rushed into camp shouting that they had been cutting government pine and were all to be arrested. Each man thereupon seized what camp property lay nearest at hand and made off, no two men taking the same direction. Thus Bunyan cleared his camp without paying his men a cent for their labor.[61]

This is the only yarn I found in which Paul sold his own men down Round River, so to speak. The use of such a ruse might be characteristic of the Yankee peddler, such as the one who offered a shopkeeper his load of brooms for payment half in cash and half in merchandise from the store; the merchant agreeing, the peddler delivered the brooms, pocketed the cash, and then took the other half-payment in brooms again![62] The crafty peddler had emerged as the earliest comic type after the New England bumpkin,[63] and it is interesting to see how, in the Bunyan lore, old stories of his "cuteness" linger. Down East shrewdness won the respect of the people whose pockets it picked; much as the Yankee was detested and parodied across the frontier, his tricks were bought with his calico. On the frontier it might be a swapping of horses instead of brooms, and at horse deals the Yankee had plenty of tricks.[64] Crockett would sometimes turn the trick on peddlers with his superior knowledge of the woods,[65] while western settlers had their own dodges for establishing fraudulent land claims.[66]

But the tricks of the peddler and his imitators are generally too sharp, too crooked for Paul. The peddler is a comparatively unsympathetic character, with whom nobody identifies himself in the way the loggers and riggers see Paul Bunyan as an image of themselves. If all of Paul's tricks were as mean as making his own crew run off without their pay, he would be a different sort of hero from the one he is. In every contest of wits, of course, there must be a loser; all that was needed to make Paul a clever—but still a likeable—fellow was to have his victims be outsiders. Anybody but the woodsmen or riggers themselves would do for a goat. Professor Brooks recorded this Bunyan deception in the Panhandle oil fields in 1927:

... just "a piece of hard luck" that Paul could not help. He had been drilling for several months on the top of a very high hill. One night just before the "graveyard shift" came on a fearful windstorm struck the location, driving with so much velocity that it blew all the dirt away from the hole. There was nothing for him to do but saw the well up and sell it for post-holes.[67]

The lucky purchasers were doubtless settlers and ranchers —not, we may be sure, anyone working in the oil fields. Another time Paul Bunyan disposed of a bunch of dry holes (which yielded no oil) by selling them to Europe, where they could be used for wells.[68]

In the oil fields, Paul was a master technician as well as a dry-hole salesman. "He was equally at home on a rotary or on a standard rig," Brooks reports; "in fact he devised most of the implements and practices of the trade."[69] It was in the Panhandle, too, that ". . . one day without help he built a rig and 'spudded in' [started] the hole with a Ford motor. He boasted that he could dig faster with a 'sharp shooter' [long narrow spade] than any crew could drill."[70]

Paul was thrifty, too:

If any timbers, or even the crown block, fell off the structure [derrick] in the process of building, Paul, who worked below, caught them in his hands to save the lumber as well as the heads of those who might be underneath.[71]

This is also reminiscent of "Breaking the Jam," since the falling of heavy timbers from the top of a derrick is a danger comparable to log jams. But where Bunyan saved the day for the woodsmen by his ingenuity, here in the oil fields it is simply his prodigious strength that protects the workmen's fantasies from dreams of disaster.

The mechanical implements mentioned in stories from lumberjacks in the East and Middle West are usually the hand tools of the lumberman and the old-time equipment for the oxen. (Most of these motifs, recorded by MacGillivray in 1910, Laughead in 1914, and Stewart and Watt in 1916, were from the memories of men already old.) Out on the West Coast, however, lumbering had been mechanized almost from the start. Many of the men in the western camps had ridden McCormick reapers across the broad fields of the grain belt before they went out into the woods. According to them, Paul fitted his camp with more modern equipment. They even remembered his using machines on their farms:

. . . windmills pump water three hours before breakfast for the crew —three men to oil it—three windmills run hot boxes twice a week. . . . Paul's son and his 48-inch cylinder threshing machine in Dakota and their eighty-five 3-horse teams to carry away the grain, looked like the tail end of the Ringling Brothers Circus.[72]

The lumbercamp kitchen gave play to further ingenuity. This is how seventy-one-year-old Gabriel Simon of Elk County, Pennsylvania, described it to Herbert Halpert in 1949:

Paul Bunyan when he eat breakfast. Them days the breakfast was all buckwheat cakes, ham—and the stove they baked his cakes on top of was twenty-four feet long and five feet wide. And in order to keep that griddle greased—the top of that stove—they had an old nigger wench and they took the skins off two hams and tied 'em to her feet—and all she would do was skate around on top of that stove and keep it greased. And it took five chefs,—no, four chefs—to bake the cakes as fast as he'd eat 'em. . . .[73]

"Shock" Wormuth told the same story, and added, "Other men follered 'em up pourin' the batter. Other men'd take 'em off with a shovel—on roller skates too. Other men served 'em; they had little trucks."[74] In many versions the griddle-greasers are Negroes but in Oregon they are Japanese, local prejudice determining the complexion of the lowly "cookies."[75] Another favorite foodstuff story tells how a load of peas got dumped by mistake into a hot spring near camp, so the boys had pea soup all winter[76]—as no doubt they often did. Most of these kitchen stories are little tall tales from the liars' bench, in which Paul Bunyan's dinner horn is so big it took two men to blow it,[77] and the pantry so large that "one cook got lost between the flour bin and the root cellar and nearly starved to death before he was found."[78] Obviously, this is a formula which can easily be overworked *ad nauseam*. It was. These exaggerations become dull rapidly because they do not depend upon cleverness; since the incongruities of comedy are intellectual, the comic solution of problems yields better humorous stories than do mere formula jokes.

In this entire genre of cleverness motifs, as in the tales of animals and the elements, the tradition is in decay. These Paul Bunyan jokes are pretty simple-minded tricks compared to the devious Yankee comedies of deception from which they are derived.[79] Later Bunyan stories, peripheral to his important adventures, are more debilitated still. As Paul's activities venture further afield, the jokes lose the dramatic elements associated with actual problems encountered on the job—such as what indeed to do with dry holes—and degenerate into burlesque. For instance, among a crew digging water mains, Paul is pictured as a macaroni farmer who made spaghetti on the side by drilling holes in the macaroni and selling the cores.[80] Such simple stuff lacks the guile, as well as much of the humor, of the clockmaker a hundred years ago. It seems that as good a source as any for better crafty Yankee yarns than these is still the *(Old) Farmer's Almanack*.[81] Perhaps the better tales of shrewdness in the West are also still alive, but evidently not among the Bunyan stories.

8. CONTESTS OF WIT

The competitive side of the Bunyan tales, faintly sketched in Paul's occasional shrewdness, is revealed fully in the manner of their telling. We have seen that the lumberjacks were incessantly competing, team against team, man against Nature, and man against man. The Paul Bunyan stories enabled them to extend the contests of their physical life into their intellectual existence as well. About the evening fire and in the shanty, Paul Bunyan took his extravagant shape as relaxing woodsmen matched wits in verbal tests of ingenuity.

These lying contests were a source of delight to the experienced lumberjacks. Constance Rourke remarks on "the zest with which situations are pushed to their furthest and their absurdity explored with a tireless patient logic."[82] Sometimes a challenger would match the defending liar story for story; at others, he would question each detail of his opponent's narrative.[83]

From Professor Dorson's description of lumberjack fights, we might expect competition in the Bunyan tales to go beyond mere lying contests. Backwoods individualism was expressed with fists, but there was often a preamble of hortatory speechifyin'; whoever has read *Life on the Mississippi* must remember the oratorical battle between Sudden Death and The Child of Calamity.[84] Though some of their metaphors are a bit highfalutin, Twain's sketch is certainly based upon close observation of the type in real life. The lumberjack, as we have seen, was likewise renowned as a fighter; yet nowhere in the Bunyan tales pertinent to this chapter have I found Paul Bunyan in a fight. What is to be regretted from the literary standpoint is the total lack of grandiloquent bellicosity such as abounds in the chronicles of earlier frontier heroes. Crockett's "half-horse, half-alligator" speech is but a small taste of this business. Just hear Mike Fink scream this one a century ago:

Hurray for me, you scapegoats! . . . I'm in fur a fight, I'll go my death on a fight, and a fight I must have, one that'll tar up the earth all round and look kankarifferous, or else I'll have to be salted down to save me from spiling, as sure nor Massassip alligators make fly traps o' thar infernal ugly jawrs.[85]

What kept Paul Bunyan from being a screamer, too? It was simply this: it takes two to make a fight, and characterization in the Bunyan tales was confined to Paul himself, or, when other individuals appear, to no more than one of them at a time. Many of the stories, as we have seen, are not really about Paul Bunyan at all; they are tacked on to his shirttails in order to place yarns irrelevant to Bunyan in an imaginary setting already familiar to the listener. One example is the joke about Tom Hurley's whiplash. The backwoodsmen, however, traveled in pairs, and teamed up their heroes with partners: Mike Fink with Crockett, and Crockett with Ben Hardin. The subsidiary figures connected with Bunyan are little more than shadows, animated for one joke each, but without personalities of their own. Mr. Laughead writes that "The oral chroniclers did not, in his hearing, which goes back to 1900, call any of the characters by name except Paul Bunyan himself."[86] The lumberjacks simply failed to create more than one giant, and thus there was nobody with whom Paul Bunyan could fight. This failure does not so much enhance the glory of Bunyan as define the limitations of his creators.

The competitive spirit, however, did make itself felt in another fashion. In addition to outwitting each other with stories of Paul, the woodsmen and riggers also used these yarns to string a stranger or a green hand along. The "sell" is one of the hoariest of comic devices; indeed, it is a universal formula in the folk literature of Europe and Asia.[87] It has been the salt, pepper, and spice of American humor since Ben Franklin sold the English on the jump of American whales over Niagara Falls. On the frontier, the "sell" had its practical uses too. Mody C. Boatright defines it:

Frontiersmen, like doctors and lawyers and college professors and gangsters, prescribed conditions under which an outsider might become a member of the group. Hoaxing and practical joking served them as a sort of initiation ceremony. Mountain men, scouts, cowboys, and Texas Rangers felt that they had the right to know the temper of the men who were to be associated with them in such relationships that each man's survival often depended upon his fellows. They would not admit to their fraternity one who could not "take a joke."[88]

The same was true of lumbermen and riggers, whose *rites de passage* often concerned Paul Bunyan.

The Bunyan stories were turned on the tyro in two fashions: to make him swallow preposterous lies, or to plague him about his ignorance of the trade. Imagine the changing expressions on a green hand's face as he is almost persuaded to swallow this one, told by Michigan lumberjack Perry Allen:

That was the winter, the cold winter, that we had such a big crew that the cooks couldn't keep the salt and pepper shakers full, they was all fagged out runnin back and forth tryin' to keep the shakers full. And, y'know a lumberjack likes salt for his beans. Well, Paul and me got the idee a hittin a team of iron greys on a salt and pepper wagon. So I went over that team on the salt and pepper wagon, up and down the cook shack all the rest of that winter except Sunday. Sundays we'd have *prunes,* for breakfast, and it'd take me all day to haul the prune pits out.[89]

Here again is the recurrent contrast between realistic setting and fantastic detail. "And, y'know a lumberjack likes salt for his beans," is matter-of-fact, unquestionable, disarming. Perry Allen tells a story pretty well.[90] He times these contrasts to follow each other so rapidly that an uninitiated listener is always kept off balance. Again, Constance Rourke has a trenchant comment on this quality of humor: "Professor Lovejoy compares the stories as they are told and counter-told to burling matches, a sport of lumberjacks in which they try with deft turns of their pikes to upset each other's balance when poling rafts of logs along the rivers . . . the image seems to fit the scale of the stories as well as their ingenious detail, slyly inserted to catch the unwary listener."[91]

One such unwary listener who was often caught but remembered the traps and wrote them down was Professor John Lee Brooks of Southern Methodist University. In the 1920's he worked in the Panhandle oil fields on a rigging crew, and he has recorded the treatment he received from the old hands:

When the work was going smoothly, there was a continual flow of profane banter which involved always a good deal of 'fancy lyin'.' . . . These yarns were addressed ostensibly to everyone but me, yet even though I didn't say a word, there were huge laughs and elaborately casual glances at me that were unmistakably significant. They watched every move I made with keenly critical eyes, and offered the most ironical, impossible, and serious suggestions by way of help, mentioning Paul as an authority, or they told me some time later, and with apparently no reference to my work, of what Paul Bunyan did to a 'boll-weevil' [novice] who once spliced a rope in a certain way (exactly my way, of course). . . . The name Paul Bunyan came to be a symbol of torment, but I learned to know him and to long for the time when I could invoke his spirit to help me torture someone whom I might call 'boll-weevil'![92]

9. THE COMEDY OF UGLINESS

There is yet another strain of humor traditional on the frontier which some of the Bunyan stories have followed. We have already seen how old-time joke-lore has been refurbished to fit into the Bunyan landscape in the yarns of the whip on the snow and the shrinking harness. Another comic theme is the depiction of ugliness, a time-honored accomplishment among backwoods humorists. "The more misshapen, cadaverous, leper-like, or generally hideous the individual under discussion, the more accomplished the raconteur," suggests R. M. Dorson.[93] The best example of this in Bunyan lore is MacGillivray's story of Sour-Faced Murphy. Here the ugly man is endowed with unusual powers:

Sour-Faced Murphy was standin' in the kitchen one day lookin' worse than usual, and the first thing the flunky knowed the water and potato parrins in his dish began to sizzle, and he saw right away that it was Murphy's face what was fermentin' them. He strained the stuff off, and sure enough he had some pretty fair booze, which was much like Irish whisky. After that Bunyan takes Murphy off the road and gave him a job as distillery.[94]

As Paul is the only character who is clearly defined in the Bunyan tales, the delineation of repulsive physiognomies in others is therefore limited. Even Sour-Faced Murphy represents a comedown from such extravagant hideosities as graced the Crockett almanacs. Hoosiers, Suckers, Wolverines, and Pukes are satirized unmercifully in raucous caricatures. The Colonel, however, owns that ugliness is something of a virtue, since he has so much of it himself: "Now I boast of being too

ugly to get out of bed arter sunrise myself, for fear I'd scare
him back again, but then I ain't sickly ugly; the Pukes [Mis-
sourians] is etarnally so, that his own shadow always keeps
behind him, for fear that his all-spewy lookin' face would
make it throw itself up."[95] A pretty low type of humor, true;
but even in this genre the Bunyan tales reveal decadence.
Crockett's vitality emanates in all directions at once. This encomium of the hideous derives its vigor from the mock-heroic
scale of Davy's own revolting features; he is that same David
Crockett who lit his pipe from the sun's top-knot and swallered
litening to cure his heart of love. Throughout the Crockett
stories in the almanacs, in both the accredited and spurious
autobiographies, and in apocryphal tales in scores of frontier
newspapers, the character of the Colonel came to be clearly
drawn. It is a much more fully realized portrait than that of
Bunyan, and allows Davy plenty of room to make sport of
his own all-spewy ugliness.

Paul Bunyan, however, is represented as being ugly or monstrous only once in the oral tales I have found. This is one
recorded by Professor Brooks, from his oil riggers: "The pipeliners, the roughest crew to be found in the oil fields, tell of
Paul. . . . He was a giant with only one arm in the middle
of his chest."[96] Here is a different species of monster from Sour-
Faced Murphy, whose features were drawn in derision. The
one-armed Paul is, like Crockett, a grotesque but sympathetic
self-projection. The pipeliners had to turn big wrenches all
day long, so their hero is peculiarly adapted for that work.
The man becomes his occupation.[97] But nothing is made of
ʻthis monstrous Paul beyond the barest description. Just as the
ebullience of Crockett showered sparks in all directions, when
the tradition died out all the sparks faded together.

10. THE ORAL STYLE

Thus conquest of fear, conquest of nature, competitive lying, and teasing the tyro were among the principal

themes of the old oral tradition. Ever since the first scholarly treatment of Paul Bunyan by Professor Watt in 1916, students of Bunyan have postulated the existence of a cycle of these Bunyan tales, a group of key stories related to each other, which formed a unified narrative. This nucleus suggests the promise of a national epic, a folk saga which has never grown to fruition. Analysis of the oral style as we find it practiced by Perry Allen, an exceptionally gifted raconteur, should tell us how close`this Bunyan lore came to being an epic, or even an incipient epic.

An important part of the raconteur's technique is the quality of his rhetoric. In this department Perry Allen takes high honors. Occasionally, in stories like this one, the exuberant sweep of the old Crockett almanac stories comes to life again. Alan Lomax asks Perry, "How cold did it used to get in Paul's camp?"

Well, uh, this most particular winter . . . we was lumberin' here up on the Manassee, sixty-eight degrees below zero and each degree was sixteen inches long, froze all the blazes in Paul's lanterns. We couldn't blow 'em out so we hauled 'em off and towed 'em outdoors. In spring when it thawed up, they set the whole north of Michigan afire and burned the Saint Marie's river in two![98]

There is more spirit in the telling than the words alone would indicate. Perry Allen's stories suffer from being reduced to print, for much of their special quality depends upon his casual yet declamatory tone, his irregular but emphatic timing, and the very sound of his close twang swinging into exuberant phrases like "sixty-eight degrees below zero and each degree was sixteen inches long." Comic incongruity sprouts between narrow accent and broad absurdity.

Perry Allen is an accomplished storyteller within the limits of his genre. He has a remarkable memory, a good dramatic sense, and "he once won a liar's contest at Travers City without knowing he was competing."[99] These yarns were recorded in 1938, and some of them show points of resemblance to Mr. Laughead's motifs,[100] while for others I have found no printed sources; the Laughead motifs Perry Allen chose to work with, however, resemble other oral folktales from the frontier and so were probably among the yarns Laughead himself heard from other lumberjacks years before he wrote his pamphlets. At any rate, in Perry Allen's mouth they are transformed again into oral tales whose structure shows the dramatic accomplishments of a talented raconteur. They also demonstrate his limitations. These flaws are not Perry Allen's alone, but are intrinsic to the anecdotal humor of which he is a master.

His achievement is uneven; the high comic tone is not maintained. In the following series of stories the fragmentary nature of the lore—and of this oral method—is illustrated by the way in which he would stop cold at the end of each little set piece, and say nothing further until stirred up again by a leading question from Alan Lomax. (Perry also refused to talk unless certain the recording machine was taking him down!) Note the fitful progress of his narrative, the leading questions, the pauses, and the transitions between the set pieces in this selection:

Perry Allen: . . .They hauled that tree . . . clear almost to the ground, and the rope broke, and the tree slipped back, and it flipped Paul Bunyan clear up here on the Manassee River.

[Pause]

Alan Lomax: What did he do when he got there?

Perry Allen: Well, ye ready for it? Well, he had to lumber. And finally he got him a big ox. The ox was a monster, the biggest ox there was in the world, he was seven axehandles wide between the eyes. And,—uh,—he didn't stop to build skidways and the like of that, he just hitched on a quarter section of land and hauled it up the river and shift the logs out of it and put 'em into the river, and hitch old Babe, the big blue ox, on the rubbish and haul it back, to where it come from.

Well, he heard tell of a big cow down in Vermont that measured that ox for size bein' six axehandles between the eyes, the cow was recommended to be equally as large. So he got in touch with 'em down there, and he made a deal for the cow . . . [and went to Vermont to get her].

Well, she'd a proved to been a great record milker, but he turned her out on evergreens, chestnuts, and evergreen boughs and balsam boughs, and the milk got so strong they couldn't use it on the table . . . so he started to got to makin' butter,—uh,—he had no storehouse.

They tell about makin' a ton o' butter a day, piled it up, near camp. And the boys wondered what he was goin' to do with so much of that butter piled up outdoors there. You know he was askin' the men a question gettin' no decided answer, they just kept pilin' that butter. Finally,—uh,—finally the ice and snow went off, and he used that butter for to grease his loggin' roads and it enabled him to run his loggin' sleighs all summer.[101]

Many of these motifs appear in Laughead's *Marvelous Exploits*. For instance, the paragraph about the ox is based upon the following two excerpts: "Babe was seven axehandles wide between the eyes according to some authorities"; and "So he hitched Babe to a section of land and snaked in the whole 640 acres at one drag. At the landing the trees were cut off just like shearing a sheep and the denuded section hauled back to its original place."[102] It seems that Perry Allen may have found his "facts" in this booklet, if not in oral tradition which either contributed to the book or was instigated by it—since Mr. Laughead kept no systematic record of where he got his own material, it is too late now to pin down such ambiguities.[103] But the most important thing is what Perry Allen did with these motifs, wherever he may have found them. He altered them in two ways: in language, and in structure.

Perry Allen's language is more vernacular than Mr. Laughead's, and his style is more supple and sensitive to the rhythms of the ideas expressed than are the parallel passages in the pamphlet. He omits superfluities such as "according to some authorities" and "the whole 640 acres" but also prunes away more vivid expressions, like the verb "snaked" and the image of sheep-shearing. What he gains by this is rapidity of movement. Compare, for example, Perry Allen's last sentence with this analogous passage from Laughead: "By using this butter to grease the logging roads when the snow and ice thawed off, Paul was able to run his logging sleds all summer."[104] True, the similarity is close; but notice that the raconteur turned the events around to follow the chronological order of the actions, and replaced the participle "using" by an active tense of the verb.

But more interesting than these verbal changes is the structure of Perry Allen's yarns. Although they appeared in widely separated and unrelated parts of the pamphlet, and he himself chose to combine them in the order recorded, he had not worked them up into one continuous narrative. (Neither had Mr. Laughead, as we shall see in the next chapter.) At best, three, or sometimes four motifs are connected, either because they share a detail in common, or because they are different aspects of the same subject. If we look for each "well," "so," and "—uh,—" in the narrative above, I think we can find the points at which Perry paused to think of the next motif to hang on the story to make it longer.[105] These pauses probably indicate the places where Perry expected to be questioned by his competitor, ally, or victim in the performance. That would give him time to think, and the questions might suggest their own answers. The direction of the narrative is typically wayward, for any promising detail is seized upon to be exploited along the way. (Thus the motif about the ox hauling the quarter section of land could have been omitted if the point of the yarn is what Paul did with the butter.) There is humorous climax and anticlimax, but the development is from one joke to another rather than toward the evocation of a unifying emotion, such as suspense, which could run through the component motifs and invest them with a sense of dramatic necessity. It is too bad that this is all there is, for under other circumstances a truly organic development might have produced a genuine indigenous epic.

Since the time of Stewart and Watt and Constance Rourke, the critics have invariably referred to the Bunyan stories as "a cycle." This is precisely what the Bunyan lore is not. Perry Allen's stories are arranged in series of threes or fours at the most. Generally, it is the collectors or popularizers who do the arranging, putting together all the tales concerning each separate phase of Paul's activities. This synthesizes a cycle, but since the stories are taken from different sources such an arrangement cannot be construed to imply that the Bunyan yarns were "cycles" to the men who made them up and told them in the oral tradition. From Professor Brooks' reminiscence

of how the tales were told on him, as well as from the structure
of the stories themselves, we can see the improvisatory nature
of the lore. There were several well-known but unconnected
stories, the number of which cannot be determined today. The
rest was flux, using the materials closest at hand or adjusting
hoary old saws to a new environment. But there was no continuous unity.

The Bunyan yarns cited above often hint at a larger body
of common knowledge, but this is neither defined nor demanded. In Perry Allen's story about the salt shakers, the
opening phrase, "That was the winter . . ." suggests that many
other things happened that winter, but the incident stands
alone. Such phrases are merely a standard device to tie one
anecdote to another with which it has no intrinsic relationship. (For example, Perry's salt-shaker story follows his Round
River Drive; yet the drive was in spring, while the shaker story
was in winter.)

Since folktales are the mirror of a people, from these a
stranger could deduce that the lumberjacks and riggers prized
inventiveness above dramatic organization. The endless and
often banal improvisations in the stories abundantly show
what sort of mental activity was necessary, and hence rewarded, among them. The competitive character of lumberjack society is evident at every twist of the yarns; it also func-
tioned to limit their development to the fragmentary jokes we
have examined. These were born and reared in lying contests.
If the contest was a burling match, you couldn't very well
play chess. And if your opponent has told a joke, you'd tell
another joke. You would not compose an epic.

In American legend, it is easier for the tales of tragic heroes
to approach epical feeling and continuity than for those about
comic figures. This is so because the tragic tales are constructed
around one central incident, the struggle, triumph, and death
of the hero. Such is the core of the John Henry and Joe Magarac
legends, and of the fame of Joe Hill. But Paul Bunyan never
dies, and so the tales about him never reach a climax. Instead,
the "folk mind"—Perry Allen's, for instance—adapts and trans-

forms old stories and even creates new ones, but each is an entity in itself. No one tale is the center of interest, implying the others as necessary background, or giving them dramatic finality.

11. THE FRONTIER AND ITS HEROES DECLINE TOGETHER

A comparison perhaps more relevant can be made between the Bunyan jokes and the legends of Crockett. The tone of all the latter is exuberantly comic. By the time the Mexicans had cut him down at the Alamo, the portrait of the Cockalorum Senator from Tennessee had been so firmly etched with aqua fortis into the popular imagination that not even death could alter the portrait to a tragic delineation. The mythmakers paused to elegize his passing, but even this one memorial ode[106] does not sustain the solemn note. This observance over, the Crockett stories continued for years, surpassing even those of his lifetime in extravagance. What became of this tradition? Why did "the yaller flower of the forest" scatter sickly seeds, and the Bunyan yarns decline so far below the tales of earlier prodigies?

The brags of Mike Fink, the animal impersonations of the boasting riverboatmen, Davy Crockett's triumphs over man, varmint, and the cogwheels of the universe—all are vibrant with apocalyptic power. These shouts and screams and wild adventures were, as we have seen, the defenses against the wilderness of men who had to conquer dangers which they could not always even name. Theirs was a defense by offense; they seized for themselves the strength of what they feared. As violence was the language of their lives in action, so the raging universe showered supernatural energy into the language of their imaginations. At the same time, too, they were well aware of their part in molding the nation's destiny. The national emblem is a screaming eagle, and they screamed the eagle's screams. Expansiveness was in the air. Not since the sea dogs of the Renaissance had history offered so unlimited a field for the individual to conquer. They invaded a continent, and the eagle screamed so loudly and so often that the echoes were said to have worn a track across the country.

But Mike Fink was dead by 1860, buried in old columns of the *Spirit of the Times,* dead and forgotten for eighty years until exhumed as a curiosity. Davy Crockett lingered a while in the almanacs, but after the Civil War little more was heard of him. The permeation of this humorous strain into written literature, beginning with Longstreet's *Georgia Scenes* (1835), lasted a bit longer. It reached its climax in *Huckleberry Finn,* a span of half a century. But the Civil War and the Industrial Revolution combined to clip the eagle's wings. The end of the frontier marked the passing of the Herculean ebullience of pioneer life. The cities witnessed the degradation of rampant individualism in the corruption of the Gilded Age. In back-woods speech and thought, however, the tradition of Davy Crockett did not so much get corrupted as peter out. The Bunyan jokes are the last distorted echoes of the eagle's screams.

It was inevitable that frontier humor should fare better in the earlier days. Bunyan was the hero, originally, of only a few thousand men in an isolated industry; their very way of life was an anachronism in an industrial age. But Crockett was the hero of the whole national consciousness, expressing not only the immediate release from terror of the backwoods-man but also the strutting nationalism of the seaboard dwellers. These myths swayed the imagination of the entire continent for a generation. It was only natural that in this generation there should arise men of literary talent who would seize this native comic strain and enforce its idiomatic strength with the discipline of their craft. Thus in the almanacs and news-papers, Davy was enhanced by their efforts, since they wrote within the oral tradition from which their material was drawn. The fullest possibilities for literature of this material were re-vealed at last by the genius of Mark Twain; no subsequent book based on the background which went into *Huckleberry Finn* has been its equal. The traditions on which it was based were dying while it was being written.

But at that very time, Paul Bunyan had been known for scarcely a dozen years. For most Americans the comic thunder had already shot its bolt. Paul Bunyan stories emerged with the rapid enlargement of the lumbering industry, even as Crockett's had grown with the sudden expansion of the country. But while Crockett had straddled a nation, Bunyan was confined to the lumbercamps, the last outposts of the wilderness Crockett knew. And as the lumberjacks destroyed the forests, that wilderness diminished. The rugged life of the pioneers appears again in the oil fields, but in the Panhandle, too, highways, radio, movies, and now television, break down the occupational isolation.

All these factors point to the conservative character of Bunyan lore, in contrast to the creativeness of the Crockett tradition. In the 1830's the comic tradition was fresh. The national inclination encouraged men who could write, as well as those who could talk, to create, expand, improve, and outdo themselves. Three score and ten years later the jokes were stale. The characters about whom they were told were all but forgotten except in the woods, and even there the old saws rusted in the process of being remembered. The stories were transferred to Bunyan and other latter-day heroes, but their force and freshness were diminished.

Miss Rourke and Professor Blair have shown that American humor developed around the concept of native character. The comic texture of the Crockett stories is woven from the richness of his characterization. Compared to Crockett's personality, boldly defined in several dimensions, that of Bunyan is but crudely sketched. This is partly due to his origin as a self-projection of a limited class of uneducated laborers, while Crockett was the hero of all manner of men. There was many a "larned skolar" in the frontier clearings, for some of the frontiersmen themselves had left behind them backgrounds of education and refinement. The failings of Bunyan are not those of the oral tradition, but the limitations of the isolated men among whom the tradition still lingers.

And just as the Bunyan animal stories lost the vigor of the

cockalorum alligator, so the device of telling Bunyan tales in the third person debilitates the firmness of the portrait. Crockett and Mike Fink spoke for themselves; Paul must be spoken for by Perry Allen and his friends. The comic monologue survives, but the teller is now reduced to an attendant lord who swells a progress at a remove from his hero.

Thus the bragaddocio and cunning of backwoodsman and Yankee persist, but as the characterization dims the vitality ebbs away. Most of the heroic and homely metaphors pass out of mind as the old-time creativeness is more and more replaced by mere conservation of the jokes; outlines remain, but magniloquence shrinks to pedestrian statement.

Mechanical ingenuity, which requires but little characterization, is the most tenacious of the surviving traits. This is to be expected, since it continues to be a necessary virtue. But the skilled and subtle minds such as those which shaped the Crockett stories have either never heard of Bunyan, or have turned elsewhere for their inspiration. The writers who did discover Bunyan do not share the literary method of those who used "David Crockett" as their pseudonym, for they could not in the same way work within the tradition from which their material derived. Advertising copymen, slick-magazine writers, and nostalgic antiquarians have labored long to make backwoods jokes for city folks, but the talents of Longstreet and Twain are scarce among them. Others—poets and playwrights of serious purpose and ability—have turned to Paul Bunyan for symbols of one or another set of social values. What these writers have done with the fading traditions of native American humor will be examined in the following chapters.

CHAPTER FOUR

From the Sticks to the Slicks

1. POPULARIZATION DEFINED

The concept of popularization in literature, as used in this essay, is relatively recent. The popular arts are those forms which are widely accepted by a public that does not directly contribute to their creation. This lack of creative participation distinguishes popular from folk literature. On the other hand, popularization fails to attain the stature of what we are obliged to call, for want of a better term, creative writing. This is so since the author's intention in writing popular literature is primarily to satisfy the demands of a public; as esthetic considerations are often hindmost, the devil usually takes them.

In folk societies, as we have seen, the talented individual who practiced an art gained communal sanction and prestige, since he exercised a skill appreciated by most individuals about him. Both the content and the form of his achievement were related directly to the needs, and produced by the tensions, of a life communally shared on every level. However, with the stratification of society into occupational, economic, social, and educational segments, the unity of expression that once existed in folk and feudal civilizations has necessarily disappeared. The folk artist, like the folk culture, is now almost extinct. The fine artist has been virtually exiled, since it is no longer possible to speak simultaneously for one's self and for all the fragments of one's culture. It is the popular artist who now enjoys communal approval. This approval is a largely passive acceptance of his productions. The modern public has outgrown its folk traditions, and feels the fine arts alien to its taste and morality. The popular arts are widely accepted because they appeal to the common denominators of groups whose differences are often more significant than are the interests they share.[1]

Since the rise of literacy among the middle class in the eighteenth century, writing has become a large-scale commercial enterprise as well as an art. There have been many authors who wrote for a market without sacrificing their integrity; some, like Defoe, might never have written at all under other circumstances. In general, however, the distinction between popular writing and literature creatively conceived is one of kind as well as intention.

The term "popularization" conveys its meaning in another sense: it connotes that something esoteric or specialized has been refashioned in such a form that now a much larger public will find it interesting and comprehensible. Thus Will Durant popularizes philosophy, Sigmund Spaeth popularizes the opera, and Somerset Maugham trims ten great novels to the taste of the multitude. The term is usually one of derogation; to popularize is often to vulgarize. Need the popularizer condescend to his public? That is partly a question of what his public is used to. It also involves the talent and integrity of the writer by whom the public is served. One trend is self-evident: since the public taste is conditioned by what it is fed, on a poor diet that taste will develop without discrimination. Such has been the case in recent popularizations of much American folk material.

For the purposes of the present study it is advisable to re-

strict our examination to two groups of popularizers. The first
of these wrote for ante-bellum newspapers and published their
sketches in books. They include Augustus B. Longstreet, Johnson J. Hooper, Thomas Bangs Thorpe, George W. Harris, Joseph
G. Baldwin, and Thomas Chandler Haliburton. Except for
Haliburton, all were Southerners who wrote short humorous
sketches, often in dialect, about the picaresque exploits of backwoodsmen, and poor-white, cracker, and squatter scalawags.
Haliburton, a Nova Scotian, wrote several books about one
Sam Slick, a Yankee clock peddler who exhibits all the tricks
for which his tribe won widespread folk renown.

The second group of writers flourished three generations
later, from 1912 to the present. They have retold Paul Bunyan
stories to an ever-widening audience. Chief among them are
W. B. Laughead, Ida Virginia Turney, Esther Shephard, James
Stevens, Glen Rounds, and Harold Felton. The second group
is not directly indebted to the first; on the contrary, the latter
writers profess reliance upon lumbercamp raconteurs as their
chief literary dependence. Since the ante-bellum authors also
drew their sketches from folk life, the comparison may prove
valuable.

2. THE SPIRIT OF THE TIMES

The writers of the Old Southwest frontier were men
of many parts. All had at one time or another been lawyers or
journalists except G. W. Harris, and he had been a hunter,
inventor, and river-boat captain.[2] It was no wonder then, as
it might be now, that a sophisticated man like Augustus Longstreet—eminent at the bar and on the bench—should seem at
home among folk traditions. In the 1830's Georgia was barely
settled, still the frontier. After the sessions were over, lawyers
convened from all over the state, held court of their own in
the local tavern, and swapped hoarded yarns with one another.
These authors rubbed their ears against the real oral tales every
day, and some, like Harris, had considerable reputations as

raconteurs themselves. Their humorous writings were immediately rooted in this frontier tradition of oral yarning, best
exemplified in the Davy Crockett stories examined in the previous chapter. The other chief influences upon them were the
Addisonian essay and the European tradition of picaresque fiction. By the early nineteenth century, essay writing was being
practiced by many mediocre talents, and the firmness of style
which had led Franklin to emulate the original *Spectator* papers
had decayed into overblown rhetoric and fustian. This influence
mars the writings of Longstreet and Baldwin.[3] As for the picaresque element, it is hard to determine how much of it was
transplanted from the Old World, and how much grew up
indigenously out of the concept of native character.

These authors were men of considerable cultivation who
lived on the frontier surrounded by "Streaks of Squatter Life."[4]
They looked at their neighbors and were amused; they wrote
sketches of their observations, which, when printed in the
Spirit of the Times and other periodicals, amused thousands
of others. Reprinted in book form, their writings formed one
of the important veins of popular humorous literature until
the Civil War.

Their particular achievement was to capture the extravagant boisterousness of frontier life, and to subject to literary
discipline the fireworks of the frontier imagination. This they
accomplished by integrating into extended sketches the energetic imagery of tall talk, and the explosive fantasies of tall
stories. On the one hand these writings were authentic regional
studies. Longstreet's very title tells us this: *Georgia Scenes,
Characters, Incidents, &c. in the First Half Century of the
Republic.* Scrupulous attention was given to reproducing the
nuances of local dialect. In his preface, Longstreet announced
his stories "to consist of nothing more than fanciful *combina-
tions* of *real* incidents and characters."[5] This suggests the other
side of the coin: despite their verisimilitude of detail, *Georgia
Scenes* and the rest of these boisterous books are studies of
regional character and regional fantasy rather than attempts
at straightforward realism.

One of the most successful of their stories was "The Big Bear of Arkansas," by Thomas Bangs Thorpe.[6] It combines into a single unified narrative the many-sided conquests of terror by comedy which had been achieved only in fragments by the Crockett Almanac tales. As the masterpiece of its kind, this story may well be studied as a model for the use of folk material in literature.

In "The Big Bear of Arkansas," the folktale motifs of fabulous animals, fantastic landscapes, wonderful tools, and extraordinary skill in dealing with the perils of the wilderness are all utilized as accessory elements in a fictional design which transcends the sum of its parts. As the story opens, the narrator is aboard the steamer "Invincible" on the Mississippi. He finds himself surrounded by "professional men of all creeds and characters"; he might "take the trouble to read the great book of character so favourably opened before him," but, as he tells us in inflated, prosaic sentences, as his trip is to be short, he decides to make no advances toward the motley company.[7] Of a sudden there is a loud commotion. In bursts "The Big Bar." He grabs a chair, puts his feet on the stove, and makes himself "as much at home as if he had been 'at the Forks of Cypress.'" He begins to talk. At once his vigorous cadences extinguish echoes of the narrator's cumbrous introduction. As he passes from one subject to another, he is interrupted by doubts, questions, and expressions of disbelief. These come from a Hoosier, a timid man, and an English dandy. He puts each in his place, all the while delineating his own character more clearly by contrast with theirs. His imagination and vocabulary gain grandeur at each new thrust. He plays himself off against the city sissy; in New Orleans, "Some of the gentlemen thar called me *green*—well, perhaps I am, said I, *but I arn't* so at home."[8] City folks deride him for mentioning poker when they'd inquired of the game in Arkansas. "Game, indeed . . . with them it means chippen-birds and shite-pokes; maybe such trash live in my diggins, but I arn't noticed them yet." Now his ire is up, his long bow drawn, and he's off on a tale of a forty-pound turkey. This leads to an encomium of the

State of Arkansas, "the creation state. . . . It's a state without a fault, it is."

But the Hoosier objects to Arkansas' mosquitoes.

Well, stranger, [he replies] . . . it ar a fact that they ar rather *enourmous* . . . But . . . they never stick twice in the same place; and . . . they can't hurt my feelings, for they lay under the skin; and I never knew but one case of injury resulting from them, and that was to a Yankee; and they take worse to foreigners, anyhow, than they do to natives. . . . But mosquitoes is natur, and I never find fault with her. If they ar large, Arkansaw is large, her varmints ar large, her trees ar large, her rivers ar large, and a small mosquito would be of no more use in Arkansaw than preaching in a cane-brake.[9]

A question about bears starts him off in a new direction. "That gun of mine is a perfect *epidemic among bar*." It shoots by itself, at a warm scent. And as for Bowie-knife, his dog,

Strangers, the dog knows a bar's way as well as a horse-jockey knows a woman's; he always barks at the right time, bites at the exact place, and whips without getting a scratch.[10]

Next we learn of a hot fat bear that spouted a column of steam when it was shot. The bear theme mounts in intensity as he offers the English dandy hospitality: "bar-ham, and bar-sausages, and a mattrass of bar-skins to sleep on."[11] Then he describes his land, where beets were mistaken for cedar stumps, and the corn shot out of the ground so fast the percussion killed his sow. "The sile is too rich, *and planting in Arkansaw is dangerous*. . . . I don't plant any more; natur intended Arkansaw for a hunting ground, and I go according to natur."[12]

These exploits occupy the full first half of the story. Beneath their apparently wandering course a broad direction has been firmly fixed. The Big Bar's character has been established, and so has the fabulous nature of the world he inhabits. The conversation touches on many things, but finally gravitates toward bears. We remember that his dog and gun have fabulous powers; and that in vanquishing the discourse of the Hoosier, the Englishman, and the timid doubter, and by disposing of the city sissy and the mosquito-bitten Yankee, he has proclaimed himself the master of the woods. Here the story pivots, as the narrator again interposes, asking "if he would not give me a description of some particular bear hunt." We are told that the ensuing story is set down in The Big Bar's own words, and italicized where he gave them emphasis.[13]

For several paragraphs the stranger confides the bear-lore he has learned in the woods. We see that he is a tremendous hunter, possessed of every skill and power known to man and nature. If there is any beast which can escape him, we may well suspect that *its* powers derive from some other realm. Soon he is pursuing the biggest bear natural creation ever grew. This huge beast continually evades him, until "I would see that bar in every thing I did; *he hunted me* . . . like a devil, which I began to think he was."[14] Here is a chase to compare with Captain Ahab's! After epic struggles and humiliations, after sealing the issue with an oath to flee in shame to Texas if he failed,

what should I see, getting over my fence, but *the bar!* . . . stranger, he loomed up like a *black mist,* he seemed so large, and he walked right toward me. I raised myself, took deliberate aim, and fired. Instantly the varmint wheeled, gave a yell, and *walked through the fence* like a falling tree would through a cobweb.[15]

But this is no tragedy; by the time the hunter reached the thicket, his "bar" was a corpse.

Strangers, I never liked the way I hunted, and missed him . . . I never was satisfied at his giving in so easily at last. . . . My private opinion is, that that bar was an *unhuntable bar, and died when his time come.*[16]

Here, as in the most successful tales of Crockett and Bunyan, the force of the story derives from the comic resilience which parries terror aside. Such comedy is deeply rooted in the tensions of a believable danger. Thorpe has enhanced with skillful literary development the rough folk fantasies of the frontier, but he has not altered the intrinsic nature of this humor. On the contrary, he has fortified it by gathering together its diverse strands and fashioning them into dramatic unity.

After "The Big Bear of Arkansas" the heroes of this folk-inspired fiction changed in character. Our other authors wrote from the settlement, not from the deck of a steamboat penetrating still further into the wilderness. Their protagonists were the scrounging squatters who lived by their wits, a race of coarse-grained Til Eulenspiegels, no longer demigodlike conquerors of thunderstorms and "bars." As we have seen, the Yankee peddler was the first wilderness figure whose wits were his fortune. Haliburton's clockmaker, Sam Slick, was the most popular portrait of him. "We reckon hours and minutes to be dollars and cents," said Sam, who could unload a cartful of clocks on impecunious farmers "by a knowledge of *soft sawder* and *human natur.*"[17] He inveigles the Deacon's wife to take care of his "last clock" for a while. Triumphantly, Sam turns to his companion:

That, said the Clockmaker, as soon as we were mounted, that I call *'human natur!'* Now that clock is sold for 40 dollars—it cost me just 6 dollars and 50 cents . . . nor will the Deacon learn until I call for the clock, that having once indulged in the use of a superfluity, how difficult it is to give it up. . . . We trust to *'soft sawder'* to get them into the house, and to *'human natur'* that they never come out of it.[18]

Sam cavorted about the States and Nova Scotia, and even went to London, in a series of books which were widely reprinted over a period of thirty years. Sam Slick came to have a greater influence along the frontier than had the more localized *Jack Downing* stories; in fact, Sam sometimes appeared in the buckskin leggings and powder horn of the backwoodsman himself.[19]

The frontier imagination was nourished on trickery in these stories of Sam, and in hundreds of individual anecdotes about "cute" Yankee deals printed and reprinted in the newspapers. The itinerant Yankee peddler was soon matched in the settlements by a local breed of traders every bit as sharp. Longstreet's horse swappers battled to a draw when both their animals proved defective.[20] Joseph G. Baldwin drew a masterful

(though ornately written) portrait of his cozening hero Ovid
Bolus, who turned lying into a fine art:

Bolus was a natural liar, just as some horses are natural pacers, and
some dogs natural setters. What he did in that walk, was from the
irresistible promptings of instinct, and a disinterested love of art.
. . . he did not labor a lie: he lied with relish; he lied with a coming
appetite, growing with what it fed on.

Bolus' lying came from his greatness of soul and his comprehen-
siveness of mind. The truth was too small for him. Fact was too dry
and commonplace for the fervor of his genius. . . .
He adopted a fact occasionally to start with, but, like a Sheffield
razor and the crude ore, the workmanship, polish and value were all
his own.

There was nothing narrow, sectarian, or sectional in Bolus' lying.
It was on the contrary, broad and catholic . . . as wide, illimitable,
as elastic and variable as the air he spent in giving it expression.[21]

The satisfaction of the trader and the liar were purely financial or intellectual. Southern settlement life was not yet so
stable that these emoluments could suffice for all. Physical discomfort, still an ever-present reality, was often added to trickery
and gain. In fact, to trick an adversary into unexpected suf-
fering was a greater joy, for some, than walking away with
the better horse. Thus Sut Lovingood, in a story by Harris,
seeks revenge upon a sharp Yankee lawyer by persuading his
victim to mount horseback with an eight-day clock tied to his
back, and a rope around his dog's neck fastened to his waist.

All wer redy fur the show tu begin. "Yu git up, yu pesky critter,"
sed he, a-makin his heels meet, an' crack onder her belly. Well, she
did 'git up,' rite then an' thar, an' staid up long enuf tu lite twenty
foot further away, in a broad trimblin squat, her tail hid atween her
thighs, an' her years a dancin a-pas' each uther, like scissors a-cuttin.
The jolt ove the litin sot the clock tu strikin. Bang-zee-bang-zee
whang-zee. . . . She waited fur no more, but jis' gin her hole soul
up tu the wun job ove runnin from onder that infunel Yankee, an'
his hive ove bumble bees, ratil snakes, an' other orful hurtin things,
es she tuck hit to be.[22]

Sut almost dies laughing when the whole caboodle runs smack into a cart, spattering "splinters, an' scraps perdominant" all over the road.[23]

Sut is an ebullient earth spirit whose desire to get even did not include malice. If meanness were the object, however, there was no scoundrel whose infamy could match that of Captain Simon Suggs, Johnson J. Hooper's hero. "His whole ethical system lies snugly in his favorite aphorism—'IT IS GOOD TO BE SHIFTY IN A NEW COUNTRY.' "[24] Sut Lovingood was content to even a score with a preacher by spilling a sack of lizards into his pants;[25] but Suggs can do no less than make off with the camp meeting collection.[26]

Along with the physical discomforts, bodily functions, animal nature in human beings, and human nature in animals which Sut Lovingood found so amusing, the celebration of ugliness was yet another theme of frontier comedy these popularizers used. Perhaps the best treatment of this is to be found in "A Night at the Ugly Man's," also by Hooper. Old Bill Wallis is *proud* of his ugliness:

It's no use argyfin' the matter—I *am* the ugliest man now on top of dirt. Thar's narry nuther like me! I'm a crowd by myself. I allers was.[27]

And he tells eight little tall tales to prove it, beginning with how he frightened himself at the age of ten by seeing his own reflection in the water. The jests increase in comic power: flies wouldn't light on him; mirrors bust at his reflection; his wife learned to kiss him by practicing on the cow; and lightning started to strike him, but glanced off! His rustic dialect and earthy imagery gain added force from the contrast afforded by the opening pages, in which the beauties of the landscape and Lucy, the Ugly Man's daughter, are floridly described.

These, then, are some typical ante-bellum popularizations of the folktale themes examined above. Each of the frontier authors retained folk humor almost intact, and used realistic depiction of character and *décor* as background for fantasies actually rooted in the life of the folk. The themes, conflicts, vocabulary, and manner of oral story-telling have been incorporated into more highly organized literary forms. The authors can participate in the folk life about which they write, and so record its imaginative comedies with accurate sympathy. But they also stand outside that life, and can dramatize folk comedy by contrasting it with the standards of cultivated society. Significantly, their writings were enjoyed both in the cities and in the settlements. They wrote without condescending to their subjects or pandering to their public. Perhaps the cultural gap between Boston and the Forks of Cypress was not as great as the distance in miles. At any rate, Longstreet, Hooper, Thorpe, and the rest developed an exuberant strain of folk humor with literary craftsmanship and integrity. Their writings became nationally popular, and so added dashes of gusto and guile to the emerging portrait of the American character. As works of literature they successfully combine all three categories, making genuine folk material widely popular, in forms so successfully developed that they can stand on their merits as creative fiction.

3. PAUL BUNYAN IN 1914: W. B. LAUGHEAD'S GENIAL GIANT

The folk life of the old frontier was swallowed by industrialization; the Civil War and shifting populations wiped out or altered all but a few communities in which the Sut Lovingoods and Simon Suggses had flourished. Frontier tensions relaxed, and turbulent settlement life slipped into quieter grooves. Popular humorists turned from the old themes to ridicule village pretensions to urban culture, and to parody literary fads with outrageous acrobatics of orthography. The Yankee trait of crackerbox political comment survived, but Artemus Ward, Petroleum V. Nasby, and the public that followed them turned away from the triumphs of Lovingood, Suggs, or The Big Bear of Arkansaw.

As we have seen, the northern lumbercamps were among

the few places where the frontier life was still being lived by
folk groups as late as 1910. The oral tradition, in somewhat
attenuated form, continued there. What led modern writers
and the modern public to take a new interest in the old folk
yarns of frontier life that lingered among the shantyboys? It
must have been a backwash, on the popular level, of the romantic impulse to seek the natural man.

The popularization of the Bunyan tales began, however, at
the hands of a man associated with the lumbering industry.
"We were not thinking of the Paul Bunyan material as literature but merely as a vehicle for advertising," writes W. B.
Laughead.[28] We have seen in Chapter I how, after the failure
of his first two booklets in 1914 and 1916 to attract the attention of sawmill operators and wholesale customers of the Red
River Lumber Company, he restyled his stories and in 1922
caught the imagination of his mercantile audience. When *The
Marvelous Exploits of Paul Bunyan* caught on, the Red River
people made a good thing out of the old folk hero. "We never
treated him as a myth out of the past, but carried on the fiction
that he was alive and busy running the Red River operation.
This was carried out even in routine business correspondence
both by the company and a great many customers."[29] Soon the
company called its product "Paul Bunyan's Pine," and used as
its trade-mark that phrase encircling a picture of Paul Bunyan,
who resembles Little Orphan Annie in a woodsman's cap and
whiskers. By 1944 the Red River Company had lumbered off
its California properties, as it had logged out its Minnesota
lands by 1913. The Westwood plant is now operated by a fruit
growers' concern, while some members of the Walker family,
who owned Red River, have organized a new enterprise: The
Paul Bunyan Lumber Company of Susquehanna, California.

Mr. Laughead says he "tried to stick to the old-time stories
and to preserve Paul as a character from the pine logging
camps";[30] despite his intentions, however, Paul Bunyan changed
from a mere superlumberjack or old-style crew foreman to a
modern industrialist with his own name emblazoned upon his
company's letterhead and products. The realities of commerce

outstripped this author's imagination in transforming Bunyan, but later popularizers were to close the gap between the hero of Laughead's booklets and Paul Bunyan, industrialist. Some of the outlines of this transformation are, however, apparent in Mr. Laughead's work. Not only in vocabulary do his tales differ from those of oral tradition; the personality of Paul has undergone certain changes, and so has the emphasis of the comic situations in which he and his men are involved.

Yet, at the same time, there is much in Laughead's Bunyan which closely resembles oral tradition. For example, Bunyan's big blue ox was reported in 1910, before Mr. Laughead had published a word.[31] He remembered such yarns, gave the ox a name,[32] and in 1914 wrote down the yarns in his *Introducing Mr. Paul Bunyan* which we have already seen in Chapter I. Here are all the motifs in the 1914 booklet about Babe, the blue ox:

Babe's size: Babe was 7 axehandles wide between the eyes (p. 9). Babe weighed more than the combined weight of all the fish that ever got away (p. 9).
Babe's feats: He dragged a quarter-section of land to the landing, where timber was cut off it like shearing a sheep (p. 9).
Geography: Mississippi River began when the water tank Babe was pulling burst open (pp. 4, 9, 12). Great Lakes were dug by Paul as Babe's water hole (p. 4).

In Mr. Laughead's second pamphlet, *Tales About Paul Bunyan Vol. II* (1916), all of the foregoing motifs were included except the one about Babe's weight. But several new motifs were added:

Babe's size: Babe is as strong as the breath of a tote-teamster (p. 9).
Shoeing Babe: It took a whole Minnesota iron mine each time (p. 9).
Feeding Babe: He couldn't be fed twice at one camp because he ate a year's provisions at one time (p. 9).
Tall Tales: Babe drank up the Mississippi to bring a load of logs upstream (p. 16). Babe hauled Section 37 to the landing. Explanation: There are only 36 sections in a township (pp. 28-29).
Pranks on lumberjacks: Babe drank all the water in the river, leaving the logs high and dry (p. 9). Babe flooded out low-water drives by destroying dams (p. 9).

Subsequent editions included these motifs and added still more. Two motifs, however, were dropped: the understatement in the description of Babe's strength runs contrary to the exaggerative method of all the others; and the flooding of low-water drives must have been too technical for non-lumberjack readers. Later editions, then, presented not only the motifs from 1914 and 1916, but the following new ones too. I cite from *The Marvelous Exploits* (1927)[33] and *Paul Bunyan and His Big Blue Ox* (1944):

Babe's size: Babe could pull anything with two ends to it *(Marvelous Exploits,* p. 7; *Big Blue Ox,* p. 7).
Babe's feats: He hauled whole sections of land at a time *(Exploits,* pp. 7, 16, 36; *Ox,* pp. 7, 29, 36).
   Babe pulled the kinks out of crooked logging roads *(Exploits,* p. 16; *Ox,* p. 29).
Shoeing Babe: Had to log off Dakota for him to lie down to be shod *(Exploits,* p. 29; *Ox,* p. 34).
Feeding Babe: He ate 50 bales of hay for a snack; six men picked the wire from his teeth *(Exploits,* p. 7; *Ox,* p. 7).
Tall Tales: Babe's stretching harness pulled loads to camp by itself *(Exploits,* p. 9; *Ox,* p. 8).
   A settler, his wife, and child all fell into one of Babe's tracks; the son was 57 years old when he got out *(Exploits,* p. 7; *Ox,* p. 7).

Mr. Laughead's motifs were expanded in several ways. Some of the last to be included are among the best: the stretching harness is a genuine tale from oral tradition, and straightening crooked logging roads solves a real problem as the best oral motifs did. The reiteration of detail about Babe's meals and shoes, however, is a weaker vein. The plotless structure of his pamphlets allowed Laughead to juggle the motifs around in whatever order pleased him. Structurally, his booklets are essentially simple; in all editions he has taken the stories he knew, and some he made up, and simply strung them together according to subject. There is no dramatic connection between one group of anecdotes and the next, although several mention details from preceding stories. The sections describing how Paul came to Westwood and what he is doing for Red River are obviously among Mr. Laughead's original contributions. As for the rest, the tales are almost as fragmentary as those from the oral tradition.

In the following discussion I have regrouped Mr. Laughead's tales according to theme rather than subject; this should simplify tracing their development and their deviations from the antecedent material examined in the chapter on folktales.

Paul's character. Paul is as clever as ever, since "being a pioneer he had to invent all his stuff as he went along. Many a time his plans were upset by the mistakes of some swivel-headed strawboss or incompetent foreman."[34] Paul appears to have definite status as manager of the lumber company, and is concerned with the problems of how to "turn the very forest itself into a commercial commodity delivered at the market."[35] In the folktales he was one of the men, not higher in rank than gang foreman, and his problems were the immediate ones of breaking a jam, felling a particular tree, or ending the discomfort caused by forest pests. Now it is his stupid foreman Shot Gunderson who is trapped in the Round River Drive. "Apparently the logs were a total loss." But Paul saves the day by ordering his cook, Sourdough Sam, to mix a batch of sourdough. This he dumps in the round lake; when it "riz," a stream of sourdough like lava carries the logs to the river.[36] Another time Paul had to retrieve a big drive of somebody else's logs which Chris Crosshaul had mistakenly floated down to New Orleans; that was the time he fed Babe salt and drove him to drink the upper Mississippi. "Babe drank the river dry and sucked all the water upstream. The logs came up river faster than they went down."[37] This superficially resembles "Breaking the Jam" in its use of the ox to perform a marvel, but the danger Paul and Babe avert is financial, not physical. The story lacks the immediacy of actual lumbering in the oral tale. Although we may find it more amusing, for a woodsman its comic impetus is diminished.

In addition to using Babe to straighten crooked logging roads, Paul invented identifying log marks.[38] Two further ideas of Paul's seem to have been hatched in the front office rather than the bunkhouse: ". . . he decided to run three ten-hour shifts a day and installed the Aurora Borealis. After a number of trials the plan was abandoned because the lights were not dependable."[39] And the other one:

When Paul took up efficiency engineering . . . he did not fool around clocking the crew with a stop watch, counting motions and deducting the ones used for borrowing chews, going for drinks, dodging the boss and preparing for quitting time. He decided to cut out the labor altogether.[40]

Despite all this ingenuity, Paul is not consistently brilliant. A feeble vein of stories, which later popularizers continue, crops up in a joke about Paul's stupidity. He sets out for Westwood when snow is on the ground in Minnesota. He wears snowshoes but doesn't know enough to take them off as he crosses the desert. One shoe is warped by the hot sands, making him travel in a semicircle. He arrives at San Francisco and has to go three hundred miles north to reach his destination.[41] Here we see the ingenious comic demigod degenerate into simply a giant, who in turn becomes a gigantic simpleton.

Geography. Paul creates geography by being huge, not smart. Babe's tracks are lakes, the Great Lakes are Babe's watering hole, the Mississippi began when Bunyan's water tank leaked. The Black Hills of North Dakota are where they buried Benny, the Little Blue Ox.[42]

Paul in other industries. In another story Paul makes the San Juan Islands to prove to Billy Puget that he was the champion dirt-thrower among the construction crew that built Puget Sound.[43] This tale, completely removed from lumbering, is symptomatic of the extension of Bunyan stories into newer industries.

Mr. Laughead also includes a couple of old frontier yarns about hunters. Paul's shotgun "required four dishpans of powder and a keg of spikes to load each barrel. With this gun he could shoot geese so high in the air they would spoil before reaching the ground."[44] Encountering the skeleton of a moose, Paul followed his trail "back to the place where the moose was born."[45]

Tall tales. Many other little tall tales are included as Bunyan stories.[46] Ole, the blacksmith, sunk knee-deep in solid rock at every step as he carried a pair of Babe's shoes.[47] Another tale often repeated by later writers tells of the boiling coffeepot which "froze so quick that the ice was hot."[48] A more ingenious one, which they do not repeat, is this:

Paul dug a well so deep that it took all day for the bucket to fall into the water, and a week to haul it up. . . . Travellers who have visited the spot say that the sand has blown away until 178 feet of well is sticking up in the air, forming a striking landmark.[49]

Animals. Only two animal tales seem to stem from the old frontier stories. One tells us that "the chipmunks that ate the prune pits got so big they killed all the wolves and years later the settlers shot them for tigers."[50] The other deals with that traditional menace, mosquitoes:

Paul determined to conquer the mosquitoes. . . . He thought of the big Bumble Bees back home and sent for several yoke of them. These, he hoped would destroy the mosquitoes. . . .
The cure was worse than the original trouble. The mosquitoes and Bees made a hit with each other. They soon intermarried and their off-spring, as often happens, were worse than their parents. They had stingers fore-and-aft and could get you coming or going.[51]

In contrast to this yarn, which is worthy of comparison to Matt Surrell's mosquito tale in Chapter III, there is another about the Trained Ants six feet tall "which can run to the Westwood shops with a damaged locomotive quicker than a Wrecking Crew can come out." So far, so good; but a managerial touch appears in the next sentence: "They do not hang around roadhouses or require time off to fix their cars." At first glance this might seem of a piece with the mosquito-bee tale, but the last sentence gives it away as a manufactured story—which indeed it is, according to Mr. Laughead himself.[52]

The rest of Paul's animals are domestic. Having achieved success with Babe, the Big Blue Ox, Mr. Laughead doubled the number of ox-motifs by introducing Benny, the Little Blue Ox.[53] Benny died of gluttony, swallowing a red-hot stove in his greed for pancakes.[54] There is also Lucy, the cow whose butter greased the logging roads in summer. This is evidently the story Perry Allen told his own way as we have seen in Chapter III.[55]

Paul also has a couple of dogs, perhaps derived from old yarns about hunters. Sport was "part wolf hound and part elephant hound and was raised on bear milk"; he was reversible, that is, he had two legs pointing up and two down and could run on either pair. The watchdog, Fido, terrorized the greenhorns but would eat only tailors' agents, peddlers, and camp inspectors.[56]

Minor characters. Naming the minor characters was one of Mr. Laughead's chief innovations. Many of his names are with us yet, if not back in oral tradition, then among the characters in later popularizations. Mr. Laughead has told how he chose these names:

To my best recollection the name "Babe" was invented as a funny name for such a big animal. . . .

Johnny Inkslinger was a natural. Camp clerks were called Ink Slingers, and to provide a character to save Paul's ink I added the "Johnny."

Names like "Shot Gunderson" and "Chris Crosshaul" were always floating around to make fun of the Scandinavians with, so I picked them up for a couple of foremen.

When lumbering was at its height in the Lake States many of the loggers came from Down East. It was fun to mimic the French-Canadians with story cliches like . . . "The two Joe Murfraws, one named Pete," and "The Habitant that wore out six pairs of shoepacs looking for a man to lick." That is the source of "Big Ole" and the bully who wanted to fight Paul Bunyan. . . .

Sourdough Sam came from a reference to a cook whose sourdough barrel blew up and took off an arm and a leg. . . .

These examples will indicate the process of my writing. The point is that they were derived from memories.[57]

Paul has a family, too. "Mrs. Bunyan, with wifely solicitude for his appearance, parted Paul's hair with a handax and combed it with a cross-cut saw." Paul had a son, Jean, who at the age of three weeks chopped the posts from under Paul's bed. This made the father declare, "The boy is going to be a logger some day."[58]

None of the characters are developed beyond their appearances in one or two jokes.

Further developments. In addition to the Trained Ant story mentioned above, Laughead put into his pamphlets several other motifs having little connection with Paul Bunyan. Mt. Lassen had erupted shortly before the 1914 book was prepared, so the volcano was mentioned as Big Joe's bean hole; the boiling mud spring became Big Joe's pancake batter and the boiling lake his teapot. From 1922 to 1935 Mr. Laughead kept a story to the effect that Paul had toted supplies for the A.E.F., who were showing the Kaiser how we log in the U.S.A. This A.E.F. story, Mr. Laughead writes me, "was faked—it was timely in 1922." Earlier, in the 1916 collection, he had included a yarn called "The Anchor." A dumb *Canadien* named Pete Legoux, who "being a fool, knew no higher duty than obedience," heaved overboard an anchor which had not been made fast simply because Paul told him to do it. Of this numskull motif, Mr. Laughead writes:

The "Anchor" story in Vol. II had no Paul Bunyan origin. It was an actual occurrence. The "Pete Legoux" was a French-Canadian character named Charles Butaw (phonetic spelling)—the foreman Mike Sullivan of the Brainerd Lumber Company. I knew both of them.

Esther Shephard used this story [in her popularization, *Paul Bunyan*] but did not get it from me. She told me she got it from a logger in Washington—I know the story was repeated in many times and places.

This may interest you as an example of the circulation and twists of oral tales.[59]

The oral tales got some strange twists in 1935 or 1936 when Mr. Laughead prepared a little folder for the first Paul Bunyan festival at Brainerd, Minnesota. *Paul Bunyan's Playground*, Laughead writes, "shows how material was faked and adapted in special cases."[60] It includes mention of Paul's buttermilk gusher (said to be told among the oil drillers); digging Puget Sound; Paul's motor-driven snowshoes; the origin of the Mississippi and the Thousand Lakes, as in the regular lumber pamphlets; the iron mines Paul opened to get metal for his griddle; the dinner horn. A poetic touch is introduced: "Still evenings or just at dawn when the lakes lie like sheets of glass reflecting every tree on the shore, you will sometimes see a silvery ripple. . . . That's the breath of the Big Blue Ox, sampling the water before he drinks." As the Brainerd show appealed to sportsmen, Mr. Laughead obliged with a yarn of how Paul stocked Minnesota's lakes with fish, another about the reversible dog, and a third on Paul's three-barrel gun which bags birds in the stratosphere and sounds like thunder. Thus was lumber-company advertising adapted to this new use: Paul becomes a national hero, working in several occupations, forming geography everywhere, a benign spirit of tourism as well as the comical Bull of the Woods.

W. B. Laughead never had any literary pretensions for his Bunyan pamphlets; they comprised an advertising campaign to which he brought unflagging enthusiasm and a firsthand knowledge of lumberjack lore. If he failed to write an epic of the woods, it may be that that was never his intention. What he set out to do was to publicize Red River lumber, confident from the start that the jests about Paul Bunyan would help him do it. The gradual changes in his text make evident the fact that Mr. Laughead learned the hard way that the lumberjack jokes he knew had little appeal in themselves for people who had never been in the woods. His first three editions show the education of a copy writer as well as the changing features of a folk hero. But once Laughead discovered how to make Paul Bunyan appealing, other advertisers appropriated Bunyan, too. Now Paul is used to sell almost anything. A few random citations: in recent years Bunyan has plugged the sharpness of Macy's kitchen knives, the pulling power of Dow-Corning Silicone-insulated motors, the advertising lineage figures of the *Saturday Evening Post,* the incomparable qualities of Wisconsin cheeses, and the 1949 Chicago Railroad Fair. Unfortunately for the Red River Company, its rights to the trademark, "Paul Bunyan's Pine," did not cover the use of Paul's name in the advertising of other industries. But Paul Bunyan, of course, is in the public domain. This fact has made it pos-

sible for a dozen more recent popularizers to use and re-use
Mr. Laughead's material as though it were their own creation,
or as though they had found the tales up in Michigan lumbercamps themselves. And, indeed, some of them have! Everyone
who has written on Bunyan since 1916 is indebted to Mr.
Laughead for many of the motifs and most of the names which
now turn up in the "tradition." Mr. Laughead seems surprised
at the far-flung effects of his advertising campaign in oral tradition, in popular literature, and in folklore scholarship. He
has been unstinting in giving trained folklorists whatever aid
he can.

4. PAUL IN 1916: MISS TURNEY'S FARMER

A small chapbook of Bunyan stories was issued in
1916 by Ida Virginia Turney, who did her collecting in Oregon.
The narrative method is similar to Laughead's, except that
there is no advertising matter and the teller is identified as "a
survivor of the 'airly' days, one 'Yank.' "[61] Miss Turney's story
begins as Paul leaves Minnesota for California; then Yank re-
lates a series of unconnected adventures. The book ends with
the death of Babe and the departure of Paul for points unknown, perhaps the Panama Canal or the World War.

Paul Bunyan Comes West is distinguished by its use of dialect,
and by the penetration of its lumberjack hero into several other
industries. Much of Laughead's material, however, is duplicated too. Paul comes west on warped snowshoes, after his
Minnesota coffeepot "froze so fast the durned ice wuz too hot
to handle."[62] The kitchen and dinner horn are described, and
again we get the grindstone story.[63] The cast includes Paul, his
wife, his son Jean, his daughter Teeny, lumberjacks Swede Ole
and Levi Lugg, and the construction giants Dan Puget, Ol' Man
Elliott, and Dad Hood. Babe and the dog Elmer are here too.

At once the question arises how this book could have so
many parallels to Laughead's if its material was actually taken
from men who heard the stories in the woods. If Laughead

really gave the characters and animals their names, is it not strange that those names would be on lumberjack tongues a thousand miles from Minneapolis only two years after his pamphlet's first edition? I doubt that Miss Turney lifted the duplicated material directly. Before suspecting plagiarism, we must take at least two factors into account: the complex interrelation between printed and oral tradition, and the nature of Miss Turney's informants. As to the first, we have seen in Chapter II that printed tales may easily become the sources of new oral stories. The Laughead pamphlets were widely distributed in the industry, and probably had an immediate impetus upon the oral tradition, from which much of his material had been drawn in the first place. Some of Miss Turney's informants may have seen the Laughead pamphlets and simply retold to her what they themselves had read; or they may have heard the stories from lumberjacks who had first read them there.

Paul in other industries. There are three hunting stories; in one, Paul grabs the Timber Wolf by the ears, hollers, and the wolf dies of fright. In another, Paul confronts a Polar Bear; having no railroad spikes for his gun, he rams it full of icicles and kills the bear with them. In the third, he grabs one mountain lion by the tail, and uses it to club two others to death.[64] These yarns, of course, are vestiges of the frontier talk which had in earlier days made Crockett a name all varmints feared.

But Paul takes different shapes in other, less dangerous occupations. He becomes involved in government contracts with the construction firm of Puget, Elliott and Hood. Using Babe hitched to a glacier, Paul digs the Hood Canal.[65] There are several such exploits; fashioning geography is a natural extension of the work of a construction gang.

Paul is also a farmer. He bought a farm in Kansas on which the soil "wuz so rich nobody ever dast plant anythin on it." The story is similar to those taken from oral tradition by Thorpe seventy years before. One kernel of corn grows so prodigiously fast that when Swede Charlie climbs the stalk he can't slide down to earth again. The government inspector orders Paul to cut it down, as "it's drainin' the Mississippi River an' interferin' with navigation." Paul has Babe tie rails a mile long into a knot around the stalk, "an' the faster it growed the more it cut itself. Jist then 'long come a cyclone an' finished it."[66] But the story has no such relevance to a central theme as had the fertility of the "sile" in Arkansas. It is immediately followed by a rather pointless tale of Paul's bad luck in the hog business, in which he had the lack of acumen to place his ranch so far from a highway that "buildin' o' the road to haul the meat out after it wuz cured et up all the profit—an' then some."[67]

Another yarn has Paul in the hotel business:

Paul he tried his hand at ever'thin' goin'—built a skyscrapin' hotel wunst down here on the Big Trail. That thar *wuz* a hotel—spread over more'n ten acres, an' had the last seven stories put on hinges so's they c'd be swung back fer to let the moon go by. The dinin'-room wuz 700 foot long, an' the bell-hops all wore roller skates.[68]

The last sentence tells us what has happened to the famous Bunyan kitchen in this metamorphosis.

Paul retains some characteristics of his old original self, and picks up a few new ones in a yarn about cowpunching:

Paul he'd heard 'bout cow punchin' an' he cal'lated mebbe he'd go into the cattle business; so he took a walk over to Wyoming. He didn't have money 'nough to buy a decent-sized herd, so he made a killin' er two—leastwise they sez he done it, but I got my doubts—an' a posse got after him. Fin'lly they cornered him in a canyon an' got ready fer to string him up. That same day they'd captured the Big Elk an' 'twuz more'n they could do to brand him. Paul he bet 'em he c'd ride the Elk an' they let him try jist fer fun. Wal, that wuz the last they ever seen o' Paul er the Elk. He sent 'em a letter from Argentiny thankin' 'em fer the lift. An' when Paul got back to Oregon he broke the Elk an' hitched him up with Babe an' used 'em makin' roads.[69]

Despite diffusion to another occupation, in this tale Paul retains some of his most vigorous qualities. Probably these adventures were appropriated from the exploits of Pecos Bill, a cowboy hero similar to Bunyan. Here Paul starts as an ordinary mortal, at least in size, yet in the end he performs marvels. He is captured by a posse—though nobody could have laid a hand on the Paul who broke the jam in Chapter Three!—but

gets away by using his wits. Like the original lumberjack
Bunyan, his cleverness involves performing a physical feat impossible for other men. This tale evidently preserves the distinctive features of frontier oral humor. Those qualities, however, are more the exception than the rule in the book as a
whole.

References to women, as well as to farming and construction
work, indicate that these stories have spread well beyond the
lumbercamps—or, equally, that the lumberjacks in Oregon
worked at other trades during the off-seasons and hence were
no longer a distinctive, isolated folk group as of old. Whatever
the case, when we learn that "the women-folks they used a
leetle mite o' it [the blue snow] in the rinse water fer bluin'
an' some o' 'em melted it down fer ink,"[70] we can be sure that
these farmers' wives would have found no place in an old-time
lumbercamp. A similar hint is found when Babe is frightened
by the pink parasol of the Schoolma'am.[71]

Dialect. The book is written in a dialect based partly upon
pronunciation, and partly on bad spelling. It seems pointless to
use "wuz" instead of *was*, "fer" instead of *for*, and so on, since
the deviation in spelling is greater than that in speech. As for
the rest, Charles Oluf Olsen, an ex-lumberjack who analyzed
some Bunyan material for the Oregon Federal Writers' Project,
says this of the odd language in Miss Turney's book:

I should certainly not say that this collection . . . is told in any
distinctive Paul Bunyan dialect.

Quite the contrary. It strikes me that . . . it is told by a farmer
rather than a woodsman.[72]

Both Mr. Olsen and Professor Watt[73] point out that it is virtually
impossible to present any one dialect as typical of all lumberjacks, since their national origins (and speech peculiarities)
derive from all over Europe and Canada as well as the States.
Mr. Olsen is right in saying that the tone of the farmer pervades
this chapbook. When reissued twelve years later, the border
illustrations on every page showed Babe pulling a plow!

Conclusions. One respect in which Miss Turney stays closer to oral tradition than did Mr. Laughead is that Paul remains a superlumberjack, not a foreman or manager. His labors, however, are so diversified that few of the stories possess the intensity which we have found in oral tales that reflected the homogeneous life of the lumbercamp alone.

5. PAUL IN 1924: MRS. SHEPHARD'S CARELESS DOCUMENT

Miss Turney's chapbook gained but limited circulation; it remained for still another writer to assemble a full-length book of Bunyan tales, and to attract wide attention to them. Esther Shephard's *Paul Bunyan* was prefaced with a statement of literary intentions:

. . . some liberties . . . have been taken in arranging them [the stories] in the form of a continuous narrative told by one logger; but I have tried always to keep as close to the originals as possible and substantially the stories are just as the men in the camps tell them.[74]

Since this is Mrs. Shephard's aim, it is only fair to examine her list of sources and determine which "originals" her text is designed to resemble. We find that she has drawn upon Stewart and Watt's article, Mr. Laughead's pamphlet, Miss Turney's chapbook, and tales contributed to West Coast newspaper columns. She has also consulted a dozen friends, including Carl Sandburg, Carl Van Doren, Charles Oluf Olsen, five college professors, a journalist, and an official of a Canadian timberworkers' union.[75] But nowhere does Mrs. Shephard indicate that she recognizes the differences between the oral tales recorded by Stewart and Watt and the popularized adaptations of Laughead and Turney. Although her foreword gives an apparently accurate account of the conditions under which the oral tales were told, she admits of no such distinctions between them and the work of the popularizers as I have tried to make evident in the last three chapters.

Her book contains hundreds of Bunyan jokes to Miss Turney's dozens and Mr. Laughead's scores. To examine them all minutely would be too laborious and unrewarding a task; instead, I shall analyze a few of the most characteristic stories, and list a fair sampling of others, chosen to demonstrate how the outlines of our hero were retained or altered in the printed spreading of his fame.

In structure the book is jumbled and random, although like Miss Turney's it has a logical opening and finale: Paul's birth, and the death of the blue ox. In considering its style, I am fortunate to be able to make a three-way comparison: between a tale from oral tradition which Mrs. Shephard collected, Perry Allen's recitation of the same story based on her text, and Mrs. Shephard's revision of her original text for publication in her book. From these comparisons I trust that certain characteristics of the book will become clear.

Writing in the *Pacific Review* for December 1921, Mrs. Shephard quotes the following yarn about Paul Bunyan's birth:

"Paul Bunyan was born in Maine. When three weeks old he rolled around so much in his sleep that he destroyed four square miles of standing timber. Then they built a floating cradle for him and anchored it off Eastport. When Paul rocked in his cradle it caused a seventy-five foot tide in the Bay of Fundy, and several villages were washed away. It was soon seen that if this kept up Nova Scotia would become an island, and Paul's parents were ordered to take him away. He couldn't be wakened, however, until the British navy was called out and fired broadsides for seven hours. When Paul stepped out of his cradle he sank seven warships and the British government seized his cradle and used the timber to build seven more. That saved Nova Scotia from becoming an island, but the tides in the Bay of Fundy haven't subsided yet."[76]

Perry Allen naturally would not have seen this tale had it appeared only in a university quarterly. But Mr. Laughead reprinted it in the introduction to *The Marvelous Exploits;* that is the most likely source for Perry's recitation, which uses most of the details of the printed story, but puts the yarn back into the strong vernacular of the skilled oral raconteur:

A lot of people wondered where Paul Bunyan was born. But he was born, in Maine! When he was three weeks old he was such a lummox of a kid that he wallered around so much in his sleep that he rolled down four square miles of standin' timber. Well, the natives wouldn't stand for that so they built him a floatin' cradle and anchored it out at Eastport, Maine. Every time he rocked in that cradle, he caused a seventy-five foot tide in the Bay of Fundy. And it, uh, destroyed several villages and a loss of lots of lives. And when he got asleep, they couldn't wake him however, so they called the British navy out and a-fired broadsides for seven hours. When they did awake him, he was excited over so much, uh, excitement, that he tumbled overboard into the ocean. And he raised the water so it sunk seven war ships. Well the natives wouldn't stand for that, so they captured his cradle, and out of the cradle they made seven more ships. But the tide, in the Bay of Fundy, is a-goin' yet.[77]

See how Perry Allen filled in Mrs. Shephard's ellipsis ("When three weeks old . . ."), eliminated every passive construction ("villages were washed away," "It was soon seen . . .," "parents were ordered," "navy was called out"), and dropped the complicating details about Paul's parents, the government, and Nova Scotia's becoming an island. (Perhaps, in Michigan, Perry did not understand the relevance of this last motif; at any rate his story is stronger for leaving it out.) Note, too, the concreteness of the details he adds: "When he was three weeks old he was such a lummox of a kid"; "destroyed several villages and a loss of lots of lives."

Mrs. Shephard reworked her field notes, too. This is how she fixed up Paul's birth for book publication:

If what they say is true Paul Bunyan was born down in Maine. And he must of been a pretty husky baby, too, just like you'd expect him to be, from knowin' him afterwards.

When he was only three weeks old he rolled around so much in his sleep that he knocked down four square miles of standin' timber and the goverment got after his folks and told 'em they'd have to move him away.

So then they got some timbers together and made a floatin' cradle for Paul and anchored it off Eastport, but every time Paul rocked in his cradle, if he rocked shoreward, it made such a swell it come near drownin' out all the villages on the coast of Maine, and the waves was so high Nova Scotia come pretty near becomin' an island instead of a peninsula.

And so that wouldn't do, of course, and the goverment got after 'em again and told 'em they'd have to do somethin' about it. They'd

have to move him out of there and put him somewheres else, they
was told, and so they figgured they'd better take him home again and
keep him in the house for a spell.

But it happened Paul was asleep in his cradle when they went to
get him, and they had to send for the British navy and it took seven
hours of bombardin' to wake him up. And then when Paul stepped
out of his cradle it made such a swell it caused a seventy-five foot
tide in the Bay of Fundy and several villages was swept away and
seven of the invincible English warships was sunk to the bottom of
the sea.

Well, Paul got out of his cradle then, and that saved Nova Scotia
from becomin' an island, but the tides in the Bay of Fundy is just as
high as they ever was.

And so I guess the old folks must of had their hands full with him
all right. And I ought to say, the king of England sent over and con-
fiscated the timbers in Paul's cradle and built seven new warships to
take the place of the ones he'd lost.[78]

Note how discursive, undramatic, and generally disorganized
Mrs. Shephard's story is now. Compare the dramatic terseness
of Perry Allen's: the directness of his opening rhetorical question, instead of her rambling introduction. Note his repetition
of the refrain-like phrase, "Well, the natives wouldn't stand for
that"; the logical proximity of causes and effects; and the knock-
out punch of his last line, where fantasy is overwhelmed—and
thus intensified—by realism! If Perry Allen got his facts and
"figgers" from reading or hearing Mrs. Shephard's first version,
then this Michigan raconteur has in some measure done for her
what Thorpe and Longstreet did for the likes of him a hundred
years ago. He has taken the crude outlines of a good story,
slashed away the extraneous matter, and whittled the narrative
into artistic unity. But it is Mrs. Shephard who should be doing
this; instead she piles detail on detail, insensitive to the dramatic
basis on which the best oral narratives are always erected.

Mrs. Shephard comes off better in her rendition of the Round
River Drive. Here she works on the raw materials of the story,
filling it out by personifying different members of the crew, and,
in three pages, leads up to the climax in stimulating fashion.[79]
She keeps us going, however, right into an anticlimax which
effectively destroys the force of the Round River Drive. It seems

that Paul really knew the river was round all the time, because he had been fishing on its bank, and drawn up round fish. But before the point of this joke is reached we are detoured into an account of how Paul fished (by boring holes in the river for the fish to fall into), how Ole had to make special round bottoms for the frying pans, and how the men had curved backs from eating the fish.[80]

Thus we see that when Mrs. Shephard's sources are in the oral tradition she can be faithful to them. Yet in narrative technique she is prone to imitate the worst features of oral storytelling instead of the best: meandering waywardness and lack of an integrating emotion or plot, rather than the sparse, dramatic power with which a good raconteur might tell a single joke so well it could not be forgotten.

In some ways, ruining the Round River Drive with that silly fish story is typical of this book. All through its pages Mrs. Shephard has been so loath to give up even one yarn about Bunyan, whatever its source or value, that she has included everything—the dull with the amusing, the long-winded with the terse. The total effect is one of overpowering monotony. For instance, the big kitchen with its enervating enumeration of large griddles, loud dinner horns, long tables, etc., is described no less than three separate times. Paul's hunting prowess is detailed on three other occasions, and we are given three versions of how the Columbia River was dug.[81] In the last case, Mrs. Shephard shoots her best story first, so that it is not even the climax of the two less imaginative yarns. And all three are told by the same narrator, thus lacking the interest we might find were the tales presented as a competition from the liars' bench.

Mrs. Shephard had enough material for a dozen books, and she couldn't bear to let any of it go to waste. My own opinion is that she almost wasted it all by careless or unskilled organization. Her efforts have resulted in a hodgepodge which is surely not a collection of authentic folktales, nor is it good fiction. What is it then? Popularization, distinguished by three factors: the immense number of stories it contains; the author's failure

to differentiate the genres among them; and the essential flatness of her style. Mrs. Shephard has brought a minimum of
imagination to bear upon her material. This was seen as a virtue
by Carl Van Doren, one of several critics who took her at her
word and accepted this book as an actual transcript of lumberjack tales, a folk "document."[82] But when lack of imagination is
accompanied by an absence of reliable criteria for making selections, the result can certainly have limited documentary value.
We can see this failure of imagination and absence of critical
standards in the way Mrs. Shephard adapts motifs from previous popularizers. Mr. Laughead had written about Babe's
depreciation for his audience of literate wholesale lumber dealers. Mrs. Shephard, presumably keeping "as close to the originals as possible," in order to tell the stories "substantially . . .
just as the men in the camps tell them," writes:

Like one of these here efficiency experts would say, the overhead
cost and maintenance for Babe was high, but on account of low
operatin' expense and great efficiency, he was pretty economical
camp equipment.[83]

Some parts of the book, however, are more rewarding than
this. For instance, Miss Turney's story of the fast-growing cornstalk is expanded into a whole chapter; but even here the writing is dull, compared to the effects Thorpe had extracted from
that single motif alone.

Paul's character. Unlike Miss Turney's cowboy yarn, Mrs.
Shephard's stories of Paul in industries other than logging usually show a weakened hero:

 . . . One time Paul'd went in for a little minin' himself. . . .
Paul worked the mine for two months, he doin' all the work and
furnishin' the provisions, and the lawyer sellin' the stock and col-
lectin' the money. Paul said that lawyer wanted to borrow the
Blue Ox, too, so's he could water the stock, but Paul drawed the line
on that.[84]

Mildly amusing; but Paul was outwitted, a sure sign of the
old tradition in decay. His "cleverality" undergoes some other
transformations, too. Some of his best inventions are transferred

to minor characters, while there are several stories including, and similar to, the trip on snowshoes in which Paul is either stupid or makes his discoveries by accident. In one tale, Mrs. Shephard's Paul is challenged by Joe Maufree, and it is Joe who has all the latest equipment. "I'll beat 'em, new-fangled methods and all," vows Paul, but he has to copy his opponent's newfangledness to do it.[85]

As we have seen, the Paul Bunyan of folktale fame was continually improvising new equipment, bringing logging up to date. But it is this very newfangledness which Mrs. Shephard's narrator resents. He grudgingly accepts "the decenter livin' quarters, and the better conveniences, and all that."

It wasn't that so much, but it was the old-time spirit that was gone now. . . .

You couldn't get any of the old-time life and fun back into the men any more, it looked like. Steam heat ain't conducive to it. . . .

Them days the men all knowed each other. . . .

But now it ain't that way no more. Now in the camps the men . . . don't never stay in the same place very long. And there's all kind of 'em. Japs and Hawaiians and Hindoos and Polacks and Bulgarians and I don't know what all, and you never know any of 'em.

. . . And when you do meet one you want to talk to, all they want to talk about is politics or capital and labor or economics or something like that, or else somethin' they read in the Argonaut or Windy Stories or the Literary Digest. Oh, I ain't sayin' it ain't all right. I wouldn't argue with anybody on that. I know they've done a lot of good in bringin' about better workin' conditions and shorter workin' hours and a lot of things like that that we wouldn't of had without them agitators, but a man who's known the old days, when he goes into a camp, misses the fine old spirit we used to have, and can't help but notice the restlessness around him.[86]

This querulous piece of nostalgia is of documentary interest after all. It documents the metamorphosis of Paul at the hands of the popularizers, and the acceptance of the new image by a large public. The attitude expressed in this passage is more likely the voice of an antiquarian writing in dialect than it is that of a lumberjack. It is true that some old woodsmen preferred the *modus vivendi* of their own early days to that of the present. Yet it does violence to the folk concept of Paul Bunyan to resent the inventiveness in him which brought these new ways about. What Mrs. Shephard's narrator really resents is not Paul's inventions, but the breakup of the old camp life, the influx of "foreign" populations, the new mobility of labor—in short, the elimination of the lumberjack folk culture.

From this point of view, the Bunyan stories are romantic echoes of a golden age. The hero, once created as a living image of inventive progress, is now seen as a great lost god. In this book nostalgia for the olden days is only an occasional note. Where it does predominate, however, one can see that the further popularization of Paul Bunyan will transform him into a symbol of the vanished past. This metamorphosis was completed to an obligato of appropriate political overtones, by a writer far more prolific and successful than were all the foregoing authors combined.

6. PAUL IN 1925: JAMES STEVENS' LEADER-HERO

In 1925, two bad books provoked a literary skirmish which lasted for months in the critical journals. Both were titled *Paul Bunyan;* one had been published the previous year by Mrs. Shephard, the other by James Stevens, had just appeared. Since then the Stevens book has sold over 75,000 copies,[87] and it was followed seven years later by a sequel, *The Saginaw Paul Bunyan.*[88] Mr. Stevens has also written over a dozen magazine articles and other communications about Bunyan.[89] As a result of his diligence in working this vein of material, and also of his skill in appealing to a wide public, Mr. Stevens' ideas have become the basis of many subsequent popularizations, especially in juvenile literature. Insofar as one can generalize about the popular concept of our hero, I think it safe to say that the Paul Bunyan most people know more closely resembles the concept of the character in Stevens' books than it does the Bunyan of any other popularizer.

Stevens' theories. Although James Stevens has departed furthest from his oral materials, he has taken the greatest pains of any popularizer to convince his readers of his roots in the old tradition. The introduction to his first book, and the opening chapter of his second, are largely devoted to descriptions of his narrative method and proof that he is in the tradition of the lumbercamp "bards." Despite the assurances to the contrary of Professor Watt, Miss Rourke, Miss Turney, Mrs. Shephard, Professor Dorson, and every other student of the subject, Stevens insists that

each camp enjoyed its chief story-teller; and such a bard could take one of the key stories and elaborate on it for hours, building a complete narrative, picturing awe-inspiring characters, inventing dialogue of astonishing eloquence. . . . It is the method of the old bards that I have attempted to follow in writing this book.[90]

According to Stevens, the most famous Bunyan bard was Len Day, "whose firm of Len Day & Son was one of the largest lumber concerns of Minneapolis in the sixties." Mr. Day is said to have delivered his stories in nightly cantos.[91] Elsewhere Mr. Stevens elaborates his literary program:

The writer who attempts to work the Bunyan material into literary form should . . . write like a literary man and not in feeble imitation of some illiterate woodchopper. . . .
  The epic is my ideal. I set my puny feet in the great trail of Homer. Those myths which he immortalized were first formed, I am sure, by Greek woodsmen, cowboys and sheepherders as they gabbed and dreamed about campfires under the stars. They were uncouthly formed and profanely told. A literary man of those times would have been astonished by the notion that the campfire legends should be literally transposed into writing. I am astonished when I hear similar ideas about Paul Bunyan.[92]

The Stevens method is made still clearer on an early page of *The Saginaw Paul Bunyan:*

I had heard the deeds of the king jack of all loggers recited for nigh on twenty-five years. By the time the down on my chest had grown into a harsh and tawny stubble I myself was fledging into a camp bard. . . . I revised the tales of older bards, giving them whatever form the inspiration of the moment revealed.

For this is the one royal road to truth in the history of Paul Bunyan. It has no documents for the seeker. Truth comes to the Bunyan bard as it comes to the Gospel preacher, in flashes of inspiration. . . . The honest bard never repeats the tale another has told. . . . He takes his text, lets the Bunyan spirit work, and then tries to *cast new light,* as the loggers say, on the . . . grand event of timber-country history.[93]

In short, Mr. Stevens gives himself carte blanche to do whatever "the inspiration of the moment" demands. He insists that epics were reeled off in cantos by lumbercamp "bards," and that in writing a full-length book about Bunyan he is emulating them. Yet he insists that he must "write like a literary man"; this suggests a difference in kind between a literary product and the tales "of some illiterate woodchopper." With the encouragement of H. L. Mencken, who published most of Stevens' chapters in the *American Mercury,* he surrendered himself to "the Bunyan spirit," and did indeed cast new light on old Paul Bunyan.

Paul Bunyan's origin. In addition to confusing his large public about the nature of oral storytelling, Mr. Stevens also propounds and "proves" a fallacious theory of Bunyan's origin. The original Bunyan, whom nobody else has been able to find, was really a warrior in the Papineau Rebellion of 1837. "Sure that the Paul Bunyan stories were of Canadian origin, I questioned many old time French-Canadian loggers before I found genuine proofs." In short, with conclusions already in mind, Mr. Stevens kept asking questions until someone obliged him with the answers he desired. One Z. Berneche confessed to an uncle who had "fought by the side of Paul Bunyon. . . . 'That is truth . . . he fight like hell, he work like hell, he pack like hell.' "[94] Perhaps Mr. Stevens unwittingly played the part of the stranger being "sold" by the native. This is more likely than the only other possibility, that Z. Berneche was the only man of all the French Canadians who could recall a hero who, by his account, should be highly celebrated by that nationalistic people. Neither Marius Barbeau in his collection of *Canadien* folktales, nor Mlle France Royer's survey of the folklore in Québec Province, nor Sœur Marie Ursule in her "Le folklore des Lavalois"[95] even mentions such a Bunyan by name.

But the idea persists that the origin of Paul Bunyan must be in *Canadien* folk tradition. It has been most recently suggested by Max Gartenberg, who adduces ingenious support for this theory in his article, "Paul Bunyan and Little John."[96] Mr. Gartenberg actually checked the Canadian army rosters of the Papineau Rebellion—without success; this should dispose of Paul Bunyan as a *Canadien* George Washington, a role which appealed to Stevens because it made plausible his own story of Paul's forsaking French Canada to become an American citizen. But Mr. Gartenberg goes on to verify an origin for Bunyan in *Canadien* folklore, not by the simple method of comparing parallels (for there are scarcely any), but by comparing opposite characteristics.

Both Mr. Gartenberg and I sought information on this problem from M. Luc Lacourcière, Directeur des Archives de Folklore, at Université Laval, Québec. His reply is of great assistance in settling the issue:

Il se peut que Paul Bunyan ait quelque rapport avec le folklore du Canada, mais je ne crois pas que ce soit par des racines historiques. Pour ma part, je n'ai trouvé sur lui aucune trace ni dans les archives écrites ni dans les imprimés. Son nom est même inconnu ici. . . . Il me semblerait plutôt associé à un personnage des contes populaires canadiens, que l'on appelle quelquefois Bon-Jean. De Bon-Jean à Bunyan (Bun-Yan) le passage est facile. Se serait-il produit à la suite des contes apportés aux Etats-Unis par les "lumberjacks" canadiens dans les chantiers de Détroit ou d'ailleurs? C'est ce que je ne saurais dire n'ayant pas eu le loisir d'étudier cette question.[97]

Of course, the Scandinavian dialects spoken in the woods may have eased the progress from Bon-Jean to Bun-Yan. But the derivation is purely etymological; this Bon (Petit) Jean is no relation whatever to the valiant warrior of Messrs. Stevens and Berneche—nor of the American folk hero whose Yankee prowess we have examined in the last chapter. Mr. Gartenberg, however, goes on to construct what seems to me an unlikely hypothesis. He apparently does not make the distinction between tales from the old oral tradition and those which result from popularizations. And like all proofs derived from parallelism, his concentrates upon the similarities (in this case, the inverted similarities) between motifs abstracted from their cultural settings.

Mr. Gartenberg attributes to the French Canadians a predominant influence upon the lore of an occupational group whose members in considerable numbers derived from other national backgrounds. Paul Bunyan, he believes, is a parody of the French Canadians and their hero, Bon Jean. The latter's cleverness, good fortune, magical powers, and humble origin have their satirized analogues in Paul Bunyan's ingenuity, strength, exaltation of the individual, and democratic spirit. Where Jean outwits talking beast, Paul invents grindstones; the latter's mechanical handiness is an old Yankee trait so typical of American pioneer culture that the assumption of French influence seems gratuitous. The sources of Paul's strength in the defensive self-projection of the occupational group has been examined above; I see little connection between this prowess and the luck which enables Bon Jean to elude the spells of dragons and win the princess' hand. Gartenberg's theory requires the lumberjacks to have been subtle social satirists, expressing their contempt for *sifflets magiques* and *dragons de feu* by endowing their mock Bon Jean with superhuman energy rather than supernatural powers. This is too much to expect from an unlearned folk group which could not compose a literature more complex than the anecdote, and whose narrative lore concerns but a single character. And his proof of Paul's democratic spirit having stemmed from a parody of Petit Jean's ascendancy to a lord's estate rests upon the wrong Bunyan tales—e.g., Paul's behavior "toward the King of Sweden," which was first recorded by Mr. Stevens.

To explain the wide diffusion of the Bunyan lore, Mr. Gartenberg mentions the equally wide diffusion of the French-Canadians among the lumbercamps, and suggests that the satire of their Bon Jean was promulgated among all the other woodsmen. He also remarks that "the American logger would often assume the manner of the French-Canadian raconteur." I find, however, that the humor, characterization, rhetoric, and content of the Bunyan tales is directly descended from the older American lore of Fink, Crockett, and other heroes of our earlier frontier. Certainly the universality of that earlier frontier folklore should suffice to explain its distribution among the last groups to live under similar conditions.

Oddly enough, now that Mr. Stevens' theory has received such an ingenious and scholarly defense as Mr. Gartenberg's, in his most recent account of where his Paul Bunyan material came from, he says nothing about French Canada.[98] In his book Stevens had offered other evidence to support the theory: references in the Bunyan tales to one Joe Murfraw, whose picture Stevens has seen. Murfraw is said to have lived in Québec, and his presence in a Bunyan yarn thus proves that Paul came from there too. But to anyone aware of the way folktale motifs become attached to any other piece of narrative in oral circulation, such a conjunction proves absolutely nothing.

Now, a quarter of a century later, Mr. Stevens tells us that "he wrote without folklore in view, looking instead for the tracks of Hawthorne, Irving, and especially Joel Chandler Harris, who made up stories from one folk fable, 'The Tar Baby.' "[99]

Mr. Stevens' theories in practice. For one who sets his "puny feet" in Homer's tracks (or Hawthorne's, or Irving's, or Harris's), Stevens seems to me to depart in every possible way from the standards of his models and from the concepts of his sources. He intimates that the difference between his book and lumbercamp stories is primarily literary; his inspirations are more literately expressed—he repeats the lumberjacks' tales with grander flourishes than they could imagine. But his deviations are much more serious than these. In his theoretical prolegomena he confuses his readers on every point discussed. In practice, he replaces with his own slick formula the folk concept of Paul Bunyan's character; he substitutes the most puerile form of humor for that which made the best oral tales amusing; and he writes values into the lumbering life which do not appear in the folklore of the woods.

His sources seem to be secondary, and he has used them only in the most incidental way. Unlike the ante-bellum adaptations of folktales, in these the larger fictional design contradicts the concepts of the folktales which are its contributing elements. What Stevens has actually done is simply to appropriate the fabulous landscape of the Bunyan stories as an arena for his own fiction. He retains Babe, and some of Laughead's characters, adds a few dozen more, and includes some key stories from previous sources, but on the whole this book shows small fidelity to either oral tradition or the previous popularizations. Yet it is in many ways the logical culmination of a trend its predecessors began. Stevens adapts Paul Bunyan in such a way that a national public can recognize in him things it wants to see. The occupational hero is lost in the new portrait. Paul Bunyan has become a self-projection of mass-America in the twenties, if not in the entire twentieth century: a grotesque tintype, expert in its mediocrity.

Only the wide circulation of Mr. Stevens' books and stories, and their consequent value as reflections of certain aspects of American popular culture, justify considering them at any length. As literature, they are for the most part painfully puerile, absurdly overwritten, and dramatically vapid.

A lesson in popularization. The natural growth of the original legend had been from the logging industry outward, embracing farming, oil-drilling, cowpunching, etc. But Mr. Stevens must reverse the procedure. His audience consists of people employed at almost every trade *except* logging. Why should an author assume their initial interest in the jokes of "illiterate woodchoppers"? His book makes no such assumption; it opens with Paul as far from being a lumberjack as it is humanly possible to be. The hero is a *student!* Let the bookworm represent all white-collar, sedentary, or intellectual employment, and you have a paradigm of an American reading public. It is a truism that the average reader identifies himself with the hero of his book or comic strip. The public, then, sees itself reading, reading, reading in Paul's Canadian cave. But—

Vague ambitions began to stir in his soul after this and he often deserted his studies to dream about them. . . . Somewhere in the future a great Work was waiting to be done by him.

. . . .

And he dreamed deeply now of great enterprises; his dreams were formless, without any substance of reality; but they had brilliant colors, and they made him very hopeful.[100]

Great student though he is, Paul had never had a single creative idea until now.[101] He didn't think of this one himself, to be sure, but merely developed a hint given him by Bébé, his pet calf:

The thought struck him that his student's life was finally over; there was nothing more for him to learn; there was everything for him to do. The hour for action was at hand.[102]

What American He-Man will not follow our hero now? Without ever having learned to think, Paul now scorns booklearning and dedicates himself to an active life outdoors. Here is a well-blazed trail of escape for clerk, salesman, floorwalker, teller, or soda jerk. Back to Mother Earth with Paul Bunyan!

This first chapter (like the rest of the book) is stylistically half-cooked, but its recipe contains plenty of ingredients for capturing reader interest. One of the few themes as effective as Back-to-the-Woods is 103 per cent Americanism. Thus far Paul has spelt his name Bunyon, and called his calf Bébé. Now he dreams two dreams. In one he sees the words "REAL AMERICA" written in fire; in the other, a forest is being sheared of its trees. It takes him all the winter and half the spring to deduce their subtle implications, but at last he realizes that "Real America was his Land of Opportunity." He sets out to find it, and ceremoniously observes its discovery:

Now Paul Bunyon lifted his hands solemnly and spoke in the rightful language of Real America.
"In becoming a Real American, I become Paul *Bunyan*," he declared. "I am Paul *Bunyon* no more. Even so shall my blue ox calf be called Babe, and Bébé no longer."[103]

But neither chauvinism nor bathos fully accounts for the popularity of Stevens' *Paul Bunyan.*

Paul's inventiveness. Inventiveness is one trait of Paul's which has been consistently propagated in these popularizations. Yet in them we have witnessed the decay of that preternatural cleverness which made Perry Allen's Paul the comic genius of a folk. In this book the decay of folk comedy is complete and the folk concept of genius becomes a parody of the Germanic *Kultur* hero.

For Mr. Stevens, Paul's inventiveness functions in two directions. On the one hand he invents logging and the practical tools and techniques of the industry;[104] on the other, he solves fantastic problems. But Paul must exert Gargantuan labors to produce an idea the size of a stillborn mouse. We have noted the months of concentration necessary to unravel his apocalyptic dreams. Here is an example of his mighty intellect at work upon a practical problem:

And he brought all his inventive powers to the problem of felling the stonewood trees. In eleven days and nights he devised eight hundred and fifty systems, machines, and implements, and from this galaxy he selected a noble tool.
Paul's new invention was the double-bitted ax.[105]

More challenging problems require more fantastic solutions. In one case, Paul devised a plan to log The Mountain That Stood On Its Head; he loaded his shotgun with squares of sheet iron, and shot the blades at the trees.[106] But just as often the problem is too much for Paul, until some other less intelligent creature gives him the answer. Thus the ox persuaded him to give up studies for action. It was stupid Hels who first mistook spread canvas for a lake; from his error Paul got the idea of attracting black ducks to its surface, thus solving the problem of what to feed his crew for dinner.[107]

Paul's practical inventions are simply the commonplace equipment of the old-time hand methods in logging. One might imagine that Paul as Inventor would naturally continue to originate further improvements; not so for Mr. Stevens. Paul is undone by the "Evil Inventions" of one Ford Fordsen, an ordinary mortal logger. Ford Fordsen introduces industrialization, and Paul becomes a wistful giant, nostalgic emblem of an irretrievable golden age. This awkward paradox is the *Deus ex machina* which brings the book to a close.[108] Thus the popularizer kills off the folk hero whose adventures "illiterate woodchoppers" had sustained for seventy years. But Stevens' hero is unrooted in any living situation, and the author's imagination has created neither a consistent character nor a believable fantasy.

Paul's character. Stevens' Paul is unlike his folk prototype in personal relations too. He is anything but shrewd. He is in fact so naïve a trusting fool that his supremacy is continually being threatened by subordinates whose envy or ambition he has unwittingly allowed to flourish. He flattered Hels Helsen and depreciated himself until both Hels and the men put the credit where he said it was due.[109] Likewise, Paul "trusted without doubts his boss farmer," John Shears, with the natural consequence that Shears soon plotted to overthrow him.[110] And in the end Ford Fordsen outwits him. Had Paul any sagacity at all, these problems would never have arisen.

Not only is Paul a dolt at handling his men; he has no moral standards. Stevens spins out a feeble chapter about a lie which Shanty Boy, best storyteller in camp, wonders whether he need tell. Paul wants Shanty Boy to keep the men's minds off the frightening journey they must take to the woods each morning in a sled drawn by Babe, so the "bard" has to tell tall tales. (This is surely a flimsy pretext for yarning in the tall tales' natural climate.) Shanty Boy objects,

". . . if I'm going to make my stories any thicker, I'll jest have to stir a few lies into 'em.

.   .   .   .

"You've learnt all the loggers to hate lyin' jest like you do yourself. . . . Yet, no lyin', no loggin', seems to be the fact o' the matter."
Paul Bunyan pondered doubtfully for some time. Moral issues baffled him always.

He finally decides that business is business, so "Logging must go on. You may lie, if necessary, during the period of emergency."[111]

Paul as Leader-Hero. Originally, the lumberjacks created Paul Bunyan in their own image. James Stevens overthrows their self-projection. In its place, working "like a literary man," he erects a vulgarized caricature of a Hegelian World-Historical-Personality:

We have made history; and that is what matters. After all, industry is bunk; making history is the true work of the leader-hero.[112]

Mr. Stevens makes perfectly plain the proper attitude of the lumberjacks toward their "leader-hero":

. . . the Big Swede . . . now gazed worshipfully on his conqueror.
(page 51)
John Rogers Inkslinger . . . declaimed "There, Mr. Bunyan, is the proof of my worth and zeal. . . . From them I learned to worship you."   (page 68)
He turned away, and Hot Biscuit Slim watched him worshipfully . . .   (page 99)
Little Meery . . . stopped to look worshipfully on his hero, his lord, his king, Paul Bunyan.   (page 121)

This reverence for the leader is accompanied on Mr. Stevens' part by an equal contempt for the led. The men are virtual morons. They become paralyzed with laughter at the antics of a jumping fish, and when the camp is about to move they display "their usual childish excitement."[113] Their chief pleasures are eating and working. Much as they enjoyed gorging themselves at Paul's fabulous table,

His own loggers, however, took the cookhouse glories as a matter of course, and they never realized what inventiveness, thought and effort were needed to give them such Sunday dinners. . . .[114]

Paul has all the worries; the men are not supposed to think. Hels Helsen "could sleep so well because he lacked imagination."[115] Hels represents brute strength and ignorance — and ambition. He is "The Bull of the Woods," true, but he has no brain. Yet he dares to challenge Paul's supreme authority. Upon learning this, Paul bursts into the one fair sample of lumber-

jack invective used in the book. Mr. Stevens explains the roots
of his anger:

So Hels Helsen had rebelled and become an independent logger. If
competition had been necessary to the logging industry the greatest
logger himself would have invented it. But he knew that equality
was an evil thing; a powerful rival was not to be tolerated; for the
sake of the grand new race of loggers, if for nothing else, Hels Helsen
must be put in his proper place.[116]

After a ferocious fight which leaves the spectators shell-
shocked, Paul emerges victorious. "Now that there is peace and
understanding between us we can perform impossible tasks,"
he says.[117] While a good rousing fight was common enough
among lumberjacks, I believe that this episode, when seen in
the light of its context, is something more. Hels is the threat of
labor—stolid, unimaginative, but ambitious and determined—
to the prerogatives of management. The Homeric combat is the
class struggle, crudely burlesqued.

Throughout the book, Paul is not only the leader-hero of Hels
and the rest, but he is their employer also. Bringing his powerful brain to bear upon their common problems, Paul evolves a
set of maxims such as might adorn the office walls of Len Day
in the grand old ruthless days of laissez faire. These are the
maxims of Paul Bunyan:

The strawboss is the backbone of the industry.[118]
"The test of great leadership is originality," mused Paul Bunyan.
. . . "The hero inspires, but the thinker leads. I shall now think."[119]
The hero is even more heroic in disaster than in triumph. Be true
to your pretensions.[120]
Treasure this always: a logging crew works on its stomach.[121]
Paul . . . formed one of his great reflections; Meals make the
man.[122]

Work is the great consoler, for in it men forget the torments and
oppressions of life. And nothing is more tormenting and oppressive
to men of muscle than ideas. My loggers shall forget them. And
strong discipline shall release them from the troublous responsibilities of independence. Again I shall have a camp of men who toil
mightily and make the hours between supper and sleep jolly with
merry songs and humorous tales.[123]

It is hard to believe that this monopolistic timber baron, with his tribe of serfs in jolly peonage, is supposed to be a replica of Perry Allen's Paul Bunyan. Yet this is the form in which the American public has taken Paul Bunyan and made him its own. America's conservatism is as deeply rooted as its forests, and the image of the Leader-Hero was as quickly accepted as it was easily made. Chalk up another strike for Mr. Stevens, who adds Rugged Individualism to Back-to-the-Woods and 103 per cent Flag-Waving as the unfailing ingredients of a popular success.[124]

Mr. Stevens is now handling public relations for the West Coast Lumberman's Association.[125]

Social satire. In the later chapters of *Paul Bunyan,* Mr. Stevens turns from the problems of monopoly capitalism in the land of the Blue Snow to give other subjects his attention. With the logging *décor* as a rather awkward background, he thwacks three targets handy in the twenties: prohibition, professors, and poetry. Recoiling from the fine arts, he leads the lumberjacks into a climate of "Hesomeness." In this happy condition they are betrayed by the triple evils of machinery, the ten-hour day, and the lure of women. These elements complete the Stevens recipe for popularization. They also complete the denigration of a folk hero.

In a chapter called "The Kingdom of Kansas," we learn that the prairie state was once ruled by the monarch Bourbon, and at that time enjoyed all the jovial sporting vices for which Kentucky is now famed. Duke Dryface ended the liquid golden age by putting raw sap in the drinks. The happy jacks and all the king's men got the blind staggers, and that was that.[126]

Professors and poetry are swatted together in "New Iowa." In particular, Mr. Stevens burlesques one Professor Sherm Shermson. In this passage the bad writing is perhaps exceeded by the bad taste, since this is a thinly veiled attack upon the critic Stuart Sherman.[127] For readers who are unaware of this, however, the burlesque remains a disapproval of higher education in general. For a certain segment of the American public, this is almost as popular as flaying the devil.

Mr. Stevens is thoroughly grounded in the Theory of Phi-

listinism. He has Paul attack poetry with the armament traditional among the unenlightened middle class:

He felt that all art was dangerous for his loggers; he felt that poetry
was especially so. This he learned in his attempt to log off New Iowa.
For there the loggers all turned poets and nearly ruined the logging
industry.[128]

(It is interesting that Paul himself enjoyed "noble rimes," but
he considered that his men were unfitted to enjoy the arts.)
Well, in New Iowa the climate is so mild and the vegetation so
luxuriant that the poetic impulse is stirred in the woodsmen:

> I doffed among the daisies snide
> Till their wan petals mortified.
> Egregious as incessant Noah,
> I swamped in carnal Iowa.[129]

Paul roars his riders of the winged horse into silence: "Are you
still loggers, or have you really degenerated into poets?"[130] He
stomps the "pink meadows" and the "lavender river" into a
swamp of mud, and the shamed lumberjacks follow their
Leader-Hero—to the He Man Country.

Only one lumberjack stayed behind—Bab Babbitson, whose
poems had chanted

> Here is the land of opportunity.
>
> .   .   .   .
>
> People will want to buy farms here some day.
> Let's organize a company and sell shares.[131]

Babbitson, you see, "was the one man in all that mighty
host who was not a born logger. And now he had found his
own country."[132] This is very funny. His motto, "Here is the
land of opportunity," is the very one with which the Leader-
Hero himself had begun these adventures. Is this an oversight,
or a coincidence? Whatever the case, it indicates a kinship of
spirit between Mr. Stevens' Bunyan and the boosterism of the
Babbitts he is so clumsily burlesquing. As evidence in support
of this thesis, I suggest a comparison of Chapter XI in Lewis'

book (Geo. F. Babbitt at the camp in Maine) with these few
morsels from "The He Man Country":

Each man chewed at least three cans of Copenhagen and a quarter-
pound of fire cut during his first twelve hours in the woods.
"P-tt-tooey! P-tt-tooey! P-tt-tooey!" sounded everywhere among
shouted oaths and coarse bellowing.

.   .   .   .

As Paul Bunyan said, "Etiquette and dainty speech, sweet scents,
poetry and delicate clothes belong properly in the drawing-room,
the study and the sanctum. They are hothouse growths. Loggers
should take pride in hard labor and rough living. Anything that helps
their hesomeness makes them better men."[133]

A final word on Bunyan vs. poetry. No sooner has Paul ex-
tricated his men from the carnality of poetic New Iowa than
he "remembered his old whimsical query: 'If Springtime comes
can Drives be far behind?' "[134] And Mr. Stevens has no compunction whatever about celebrating the rapture of Hot Biscuit Slim and Cream Puff Fatty (!) in these terms:

It was their high moment. They would not have traded it for all the
glory that was Greece and the grandeur that was Rome. . . . They
had intimations of immortality.[135]

Souls of Poets dead and gone, *in pace requiescat!*

Just as this book began with the double-barreled blast of
Retreat-to-Nature and Superpatriotism, so it ends on another
sure-fire charge from the popularizer's typewriter. At the same
time that Bunyan is being undone by the evil inventions of
Ford Fordsen, the happy-go-lucky tribe of lumberjacks who
followed him in worshipful obedience are betrayed. The agent
of betrayal is that species which is responsible for the failure
of Hesomeness in all human history: women. Paul has never
known them, and says,

If they do exist in other lands it is easy to see why there is no great
industry, no marvelous inventions and no making of history in any
place but my camp. Even as memories or fancies they are nui-
sances.[136]

When real live females invade the camp and pretty up the
bunkhouses with curtains, grass, and flowers,

Then Paul Bunyan did what every true man, whether ditch-digger or king, has often longed painfully to do. He now did that which men are forever attempting in their imaginings. He lifted the woman person in his hand and observed her as a naturalist observes a small kitten or a mouse.[137]

The Leader-Hero, impervious to feminine wiles, alone can enact the creed of "Work! Work! Work!"; lesser men give in to temptation, and sacrifice some of that devotion to wives, homes, babies. These are the responsibilities which shackle the Hesome imagination, and from which a large proportion of the American public—including George F. Babbitt—passionately desires, in its immaturity, to be free. Mortals, bound by balls of mortgages and chains of silk stockings, can only aspire to the abode where Paul Bunyan spits "P-tt-tooey" from afar.

7. A FABLE FOR CRITICS

Since the Shephard and Stevens books appeared during the same season, they were naturally juxtaposed and compared by reviewers. This flurry of critical activity stirred up a slight skirmish on the border between literature and folklore. None of the critics involved seemed to recognize that the proper terrain for the battle of these books was neither folklore nor literature, but the no man's land of popularization. Four prominent critics who took sides in the controversy were Percy MacKaye, Constance Rourke, Carl Van Doren, and Stuart Sherman.

Mr. MacKaye was choice of the *Bookman* to review the two Paul Bunyan volumes. He dismissed Esther Shephard's with one sentence, and proceeded to make the following prophecy:

A comparison of the two books will reveal Mr. Stevens' method as an artist and the excellence of his style, vitally plastic and fecund with imaginative insight and observation. His epic is told in a fluent and vivid prose, simple, powerful, clear and un-selfconscious, which shows him to be an accomplished master of his medium, a native writer likely to rank very high in the future.[138]

Mr. MacKaye's "only regrets" are that Stevens turned away from his folk theme to "journalistic allusions," and that he too rarely used the lumberjacks' native speech.

Miss Rourke, writing in the *Saturday Review of Literature,* found the Shephard version "a source book and a record of a very high order." Of Mr. Stevens' stories she had this to say:

Some of his narratives are undoubtedly private invention. But they are invention kept within the happy bound of a substantial tradition; old and new, they have the windy breadth, the loose and casual structure, the sly pitfalls which everywhere characterize the Paul Bunyan stories.[139]

This is one of the few opinions of Miss Rourke's with which I would disagree. I gain courage in my disagreement from a letter she wrote nine years later, after she had performed the pioneer scholarship in this field which produced her masterpiece, *American Humor.* She seems to have changed her mind about the value of Paul Bunyan tales written down by anyone but the raconteurs themselves:

Almost everyone who becomes fascinated by Paul Bunyan, and many old-timers who are led into story telling, fall into the error of believing that they can match the best of the oral tales. . . . Literary people are especially given to this illusion. . . . There is a certain austerity about the best of the old tales, and the old story-tellers, which few of a later generation can match. Many people see in them only preposterous exaggeration, but most of the central body of the stories contain trickery as well, sometimes of a fairly subtle order, or at least resting on a fairly complex knowledge of life in the lumber camps.[140]

Carl Van Doren had first met Paul Bunyan in the Turney chapbook, and in 1923 had expressed the hope that Paul might meet his Marlowe soon. Comparing Miss Turney's method of telling the tales through one narrator to the way in which the Robin Hood ballads were drawn into one sequence, he concluded that it would be "a shame" if Paul Bunyan were to end merely in a jestbook.[141] Two years later, reviewing Shephard and Stevens in the *Century,* he regarded the differences in their methods as illustrative of the "current great problem of American literature." Mrs. Shephard's book he found to be "a document" in which "there are no signs of any special creative enterprise." However,

> James Stevens . . . has undertaken to go further. . . . To make a burlesque epic out of what was only a collection of folk-tales, he had to choose among his materials with a high hand. . . . Mr. Stevens was in the position that Marlowe was in when he determined to make a play out of the Faustus legends. . . . To have done as well as Marlowe, Mr. Stevens must have been a better artist. This he is not. He has gusto and energy, but he seems never to have quite made up his mind exactly what he wanted to do. . . .
> Nevertheless, Mr. Stevens is on the right road, for he has deliberately deserted document for art. . . . The defects of [his] work are in part due to his own inability to leave his documents far enough behind. . . . [Also] he has allowed himself to be now satiric and now sentimental, to employ now mock-heroic and now burlesque, now to bring his narrative to bear upon actual conditions, and now to send it off into the blue sky of comic fancy.[142]

Stuart Sherman, who reviewed the books for the *New York Herald-Tribune*, had been introduced to Bunyan tales through the recitations of Carl Sandburg. He became so interested by the subject, and by the contrast between Mrs. Shephard's and Mr. Stevens' books which "professed to be doing the same thing and to have similar access to first-hand information," that he took the trouble to track the stories down himself. Following Mrs. Shephard's acknowledgments, Sherman read the Stewart and Watt article, Laughead, and Turney. He concluded that as the Bunyan tales moved westward their hero changed in form from a superlumberjack to a nature myth, clothing himself "in the enterprises of all pioneers." He saw the stories in the Turney booklet not as

> primitive lumberjack stuff . . . but the booming voice of the "bigger, better, busier" Pacific Coast, where modern machinery and efficiency experts have displaced rude muscle and untutored wit.[143]

Mr. Sherman accepted the Turney and Shephard books as authentic transcriptions of folktales, and believed, with Professor Watt and others, that the stories existed as a cycle. He is on firmer ground in his attack on Mr. Stevens:

> . . . he rouses great expectations. One indispensable talent, however, he lacks: he has no gift whatever, so far as this book shows, for

imaginative and persuasive American lying—that is, for poetical and creative lying. There is only one tall story between the covers of his book which completely took me in. . . . "It is the method of the old bards that I have attempted to follow in this book."

That is a "whopper."

.   .   .   .

Briefly speaking, Mr. Stevens has converted Paul Bunyan from folklore to farce, and prepared it for the motion pictures, the burlesque show, or the comic strips—probably with some dim satirical intention.[144]

These, then, are the respective opinions of a sentimental antiquarian, a student of American traditions, and two critics trained in academic and literary disciplines. As one might expect, the greater the critic's background in both folklore and literature, the firmer is the basis of his judgments. Messrs. Van Doren and Sherman showed their literary good taste in preferring Shephard and Turney to Stevens. Both these critics raised interesting questions which I hope the present study may help to answer. Mr. Van Doren still hoped that someone would be a satisfactory Marlowe to Paul Bunyan's Faustus; has anyone used this native myth to enrich our literature? Mr. Sherman, not quite distinguishing between folktale pure and folktale popularized, sees the stories of Miss Turney and Mrs. Shephard as reflections of the mechanized energy and commercial tumult of life in the modern American West. To what extent do these popularizations show the dominant traits of their readers' culture?

These are significant questions with which I shall try to deal in the following pages. The reader may have noticed, however, that the conclusions of these critics all stem from considerations of literary discipline and personal taste alone. None of them seem aware of Paul Bunyan's transformation into a symbol of unfettered free enterprise and managerial paternalism—a point I have stressed perhaps beyond the measure of necessity because of its absence in the writings of others. I mention this now because I believe that to evaluate with thoroughness and justness books about a former folk hero—books which purport

still to be in folk traditions—the critic should include literary
anthropology as well as *bellelettrisme* on his scales of judgment.

8. MR. STEVENS TRIES AGAIN

The popularity of the two *Paul Bunyans* attracted
other popularizers to the theme. Instead of following the chro-
nology of their publications, it might be better to break the
sequence in order to summarize briefly Mr. Stevens' sequel to
his big success. *The Saginaw Paul Bunyan*[145] appeared in 1932,
and I find it a more satisfactory book in many ways than was
its predecessor. Paul is still a Leader-Hero, the men are still
treated with condescension, and the humor is still pretty puerile,
but there are several improvements over the author's previous
volume. For one, Stevens has minimized the descriptive patches
in tones of penny-postal mauve, which had made his style so
offensive to good taste. For another, the second book is much
less of a homiletic tract on What America Owes to Good Old-
Fashioned Capitalism and Why We Should Have It Again.
The third improvement is the reason for the second: the tensions out of which the plots are produced actually have relevance to lumberjack life.

In four chapters Paul struggles mightily against rivers: an
angry river, and a deep river; two rivers too puny to carry logs
he infuses with self-confidence and melted snow. The weather
declares war on him, and for two chapters he is besieged by
high winds and mud rains. The trees themselves are adver-
saries. In one instance, the timber is mobile, trotting around
so fast it can scarcely be chopped; in another, trees are made
of rubber, and bounce. Further tensions arise from the threats
of animals, both real and fabulous. Paul hunts the Goebird in
a chapter as much reminiscent of Kipling as of an axe-swinging
raconteur; one might subtitle it, "Or, How the Animals Lost
Their Tails." In another, the Dismal Saugur and the Hodag
battle each other without help from Bunyan on either side.
Chapter XI, "The Bully Bees," drags out interminably what

Mr. Laughead had amply presented in two paragraphs. Later in the book, Babe has a battle with Pokemouch, the Red Beaver.

Many of these themes resemble those of the oral tales examined in Chapter III. Yet the manner of their telling is almost always very far from the oral style. For one thing, the humor usually derives from the antics of Stevens' characters, and Hels Helsen's distaste for taking baths is certainly not comedy on the same scale as "Breaking the Jam." Mr. Stevens separates the heroic from the comic, and thus his stories lack the intriguing ambivalence which characterized the original oral versions of similar themes. Although his style is less lurid than previously, it is still not often effective. Despite the dozen combats which comprise the plot, *The Saginaw Paul Bunyan* remains for the most part monotonous and dull. After all, for how many pages can an adult reader remain interested in struggles between the hero and no less than four rivers, all of which are personalized in the same naïve fashion? Almost all the stories are dragged out far too long.

Paul also conquers three rival "heroes." One is Shot Gunderson, Iron Man of the Saginaw, who is outmaneuvered into knocking himself through the ice, where he rusts to death and becomes the Mesabi Iron Range. Joe Le Mufraw is a rival logger who employs beavers instead of lumberjacks, and is split in half by Paul. Thus the joke about two Joe Mufraws, one named Pete, is appropriated from the Laughead pamphlet. The third rival is Squatter John, the greedy farmer.

Chapter XIII, "The Colossal Cornstalk,"[146] is the one instance in either of Stevens' books in which he develops a theme from oral tradition without condescension or distortion. In fact, this one story follows the methods of the ante-bellum writers, and does for the tale of the fast-growing corn, first told of Bunyan in Miss Turney's book, what Thorpe, Hooper, and Longstreet did for the oral yarns of their day. He captures with great gusto the whoppers implicit in the yarn itself. Rivers dry up, cracks open in the earth, the dust is so thick the men have to swim through it to reach the shanties! As in the first version, Babe winds a chain around the great cornstalk and it chokes itself to death. It takes three days to fall, and sets off tornadoes, thunderstorms, and earthquakes. Squatter John, however, is a new figure, and he represents the lumberjacks' antagonist—the new race of farmers who moved in as soon as the land was cleared, staked their fences, and tied themselves to their lands and their money. The colossal cornstalk is Squatter John's secret weapon, with which he will ruin the lumber country and drive Paul and his men away. He's a wily curmudgeon, and when Paul catches up with him,

fist and boot were of no avail. He had no compunction whatever about taking kicks and blows. Nothing but mortgages would take the heart out of the great squatter and beat his spirit down. So Paul Bunyan slapped one mortgage after another on his adversary until Squatter John was groaning wretchedly under seventy-nine.

"I give up," he groaned. "I got enough. I'm your'n fer life, Mr. Bunyan. I was licked when you slapped the third mortgage on, but with seventy-nine mortgages on me I'm your'n till doomsday and ferevermore."[147]

The cornstalk itself turned the Round River into the Great Lakes, and its base still exists today, as the Michigan lower peninsula. This story shows what James Stevens might have accomplished with the rest of the Bunyan material. To contrast "The Colossal Cornstalk" with the meretricious chapter in the first book about John Shears' revolt reveals the difference in his hands between the right and the wrong way to treat the same theme. It is too bad that he chose the method of "The Colossal Cornstalk" so rarely.

While the political symbolism of his first book is crowded out of most of the pages of the second by all these conflicts, it turns up again in full force in the final chapter. All through the book Paul Bunyan had looked down upon the human nature of his lumberjacks:[148] the qualities in them which made them argue among themselves and feel dissatisfied with the bully life of incessant working Paul offered them. By the end of the book, the tenure of their contracts with him is over, and they are now free to go and enjoy the Year of the Good Old Times. Paul meanwhile has become interested in using animals to do their work. He had already trained whales to guide logs down-stream[149] and he observed with interest the industrious beavers employed by Joe Le Mufraw. He was struck by their "delight-ful lack of human nature. . . . The beaver jacks chopped trees, trimmed logs, and strictly attended to the business at hand as they worked."[150] Never stopping to argue politics or religion, they would make ideal employees. But he discovers that men, too, have kindness in their hearts, and that makes them his kin. He cannot leave them to exercise Free Will and fall into the clutches of King Pete of Europe, who will make them slaves in his snoose mine. "That's how their Year of Good Old Times would surely end. No more Free Will. I'm protecting my kin."[151] So Paul appeals to their pride; they refuse to let beavers replace them, and follow him out of the Saginaw, burning their bridges behind them.[152]

Thus Mr. Stevens in his two best sellers has contributed forty chapters of Paul Bunyan tales, among which but one story is faithful to the spirit of the old-time folktales. But the popularity of his books, and of his stories rewritten by other hands, shows that they are faithful to another, later spirit wide-spread in America. Paul Bunyan emerges from his hands as a symbol dramatizing the ideals of the *arrière guard* in industrial management and in industrial publicity. In this form Bunyan first met a wide public and became a household name. In what shape did the literary carpenters of the past twenty-five years hammer out the figure of the timbergod?

9. LUMBERJACKS IN THE NURSERY

As far as I know, Mr. Stevens' sequel was the last pop-ularization to present Paul Bunyan to an adult audience. Ex-cept for occasional magazine articles and stories, almost all the subsequent flood of Bunyan literature has been directed at juvenile readers. The dozen books discussed in this section represent the diffusion of the Bunyan stories through all juvenile age-levels, from the high-school student to the baby with picture books. This reduction in the age of Bunyan's readers took place during the same generation which witnessed the rescue of *Moby-Dick, Robinson Crusoe, Gulliver,* and *Alice in Wonderland* from the Children's Corner. If Paul is to stand beside them as worthy of adult contemplation, I fear it cannot be on the basis of any book discussed in this chapter.

Kenneth M. Gould was the first to call Paul Bunyan to the notice of younger readers. In a two-part article he summarized the Shephard and Stevens books for subscribers to *Scholastic,* the national high-school weekly. Slanted for classroom use, Mr. Gould's first article compared the Bunyan tales to classic mythology. In part two he retold several stories, mainly Mrs. Shephard's. The chief Stevens contribution is the tale about the black duck dinner. This article reproduces Mr. Laughead's illustrations (from his pamphlet). Mr. Gould presented his material as an acknowledged condensation of books he urged his readers to consult.[153] This is a simple courtesy few other popularizers have emulated.

Subsequent Bunyan books may be divided roughly into three classes. First and most numerous are those which repeat the tales in Shephard (and thus in Turney and Laughead too). A smaller group reprints or retells stories original with Stevens. A third group contains several books which attempt to combine all of America's legendary heroes into one story; in these Paul usually predominates as the hero of heroes. While the Stevens economic program and political symbolism are not adopted for their own sake, the prevailing status of Bunyan as an industrialist does in many ways resemble his role in that author's books. However, the notion that Paul is beset by rivals in his own camp is usually not taken over. Only in the renditions of Untermeyer and Auden (discussed in Chapter V) do we find incidents similar to the rebellions of Hels or John Shears.

I should hesitate to propose that Paul's position as industrialist, or employer, is due solely to the influence of Mr. Stevens' writings. It was a natural outcome of the popularizing process, in which as we have seen the local customs, cant, and comedy of lumberjacks themselves must be replaced by a broader frame of reference in action, speech, and humor. America has idolized Henry Ford and Thomas Edison, and re-gards as monuments to their virtues the companies which bear their names. As our children must be reared in our own faith, Paul Bunyan in juvenile books is required by the nature of things to be a boss and an industrialist rather than merely a superlumberjack.

Paul Bunyan and His Great Blue Ox, "retold" by Wallace Wadsworth, was issued in 1926, and combines some of Stevens' characters with many of Mrs. Shephard's stories.[154] The new material is chiefly an enumeration of several fantastic animals. The narrative method differs from the Shephard and Turney models in that the story is told in the third person. As this diminishes the feeling of participation so necessary in chil-dren's books, it is difficult to see in what way Mr. Wadsworth has made his retelling more suitable for youngsters. The style is not particularly distinguished for simplicity, or for anything else. Paul remains a doer of miscellaneous big deeds.

Three years later Rachel Field edited an anthology, *Ameri-can Folk and Fairy Tales*.[155] She included two chapters from Stevens' *Paul Bunyan*, which I do not find to belong under either category in her title. It is interesting that she did not feel impelled to simplify his style.

Glen Rounds, author of *Ol' Paul* (1936), is much more enter-prising in his treatment of Paul Bunyan than was Mr. Wads-worth. He too uses characters from Stevens, but the general concept of Paul derives from the Shephard book. In addition to reiterating their stories, Mr. Rounds tells new ones of his own, or retells theirs with new twists. And he has wit, and style. His book is one of the better specimens in this exhibit. The narrator says of Paul and his crew,

These men, I'm proud to say, were friends of mine, and of all the oddments in my warbag, I think the thing I set most store by is the letter of recommendation Ol' Paul gave me when I left, informing whoever it concerns that I was probably the biggest liar he'd ever had in camp.[156]

Mr. Rounds earns this title. He retells the usual stories of fabulous beasts (some of which he borrowed, I think, from Mr. Wadsworth); he describes Paul's hunting dogs, and also the inevitable griddle. He goes beyond these stock achievements. Taking a cue from Mr. Laughead's mosquito-bees, he crosses bedbugs and bobcats, producing bedcats. As in *The Saginaw Paul Bunyan*, Ol' Paul tames a river and outwits trees —this time the river is a whistler, and the trees pop into burrows at the sight of an axe. And further than these switches, Mr. Rounds gives us some new material.

One day Ol' Paul gets a letter from the Government telling him he'll have to log the desert off. It seems that the Tired Eastern Business Women going out there for their vacations, were complaining that they couldn't see the desert because of the trees. . . . Along with the letter is a hand-painted picture showing him what the Government thinks a desert should look like.[157]

As the trees were too thorny to be cut, Ol' Paul tries tunneling under them, blasting, and burning, without success. At last he decides to drive 'em into the ground like tent pegs. That's why the desert has no trees. Paul built the Rockies as a windbreak to protect from drafts the men he had hired—the Swedish King insisted on it. So he fills prairie-dog holes with sourdough; that made the Rockies.[158]

In these later stories Paul's shrewdness is considerably sharpened. He tries crossbreeding plants:

At first he tried to cross an apple tree, a yellow pine, and a sawmill to get a tree that would keep the best features of all three. The idea was that if he could have a tree that would grow lumber already cut, the boards hanging like apples, he could get rid of all his loggers and hire apple or apricot pickers instead. Which of course would be a big saving, as everyone knows that fruit pickers work cheaper than lumberjacks, and feed themselves, which in itself is no small item. Besides that, he could deal direct with the consumer, as the Plankavos, as he hoped to call them, would do away with the sawmills, except for the few needed to provide sawdust for butcher shops and saloons.[159]

Mr. Rounds's satire is at once genial and wry. When Johnny Inkslinger tells Paul that he has invented arithmetic with fig-

ures that can be seen as well as thought, and written down
for future reference,

As you can well imagine, Ol' Paul is pretty excited by this time. Here
is mass production in figures, the same as he has in logging. And
the fellow seems to be a real artist, so probably could be hired for
practically nothing.[160]

Most of the other writers find the end of their Bunyan books
something of an embarrassment. Paul must be made to disap-
pear in body but linger in spirit, and that is a test too difficult
for them to meet with conviction. But Mr. Rounds outwits the
field. His final page shows a little drawing of a lumberjack,
legs crossed, yarning from his shanty bench: "It seems that
Ol' Paul . . ."—which is just how such a book should end!

Next man to enter the Bunyan Sweepstakes was Dell J. Mc-
Cormick, whose *Paul Bunyan Swings His Axe*[161] enlivened the
juvenile market in 1936. This is a simplification of several
Stevens stories. Three years later he followed it with *Tall
Timber Tales*[162] in which the tales for the most part come
from Mrs. Shephard. McCormick is adept at writing in primer
style, and these books could probably be enjoyed by children
too young to find Shephard, Stevens, or Rounds rewarding.

In 1941 Miss Turney reëntered the field, this time with a
three-color picture book, printed in fifteen-point Goudy Bold,
for the benefit of Big Paul's smallest fans. *Paul Bunyan, The
Work Giant* is written in the simplest English possible. The
stories, each a paragraph long, emphasize Paul's constructive
energy and inventiveness. No new material is included.[163]

The infiltration of Paul Bunyan into juvenile literature is
given a seal of finality by two articles in the 1947 edition of
Compton's, the encyclopedia for children. Under "Paul Bunyan"
is printed a reiteration of Mr. Stevens' version of the French
Canadian origin. The *Compton's* people, however, must have
felt that the use of women as an "evil" *deus ex machina* with
which to end the "myth" was somehow not suitable for their
earnest young readers, who are instead instructed that

Paul Bunyan ruled over the woods from the Winter of the Blue Snow
until the Spring That the Rains came up from China and discouraged

his heroic lumberjacks so badly that they became ordinary men again. Then Paul saw that his work was ended, and he disappeared into the forest.[164]

The article on "Story-Telling" also refers to Bunyan, mentioning the books by Laughead, Shephard, and Stevens, and repeating the Stevens theory with some qualifications.[165] This space in a standard juvenile reference work indicates how thoroughly the popularizers have performed their task. Paul Bunyan is now indeed a part of our children's heritage.

Besides the foregoing writers, who drew their material only from the Bunyan books examined earlier in this chapter, there is another set of popularizers who combined stories of Paul with tales of other American heroes. The first author to do this was, as far as I know, Frank Shay, whose book, *Here's Audacity!*, appeared in 1930.[166] Mr. Shay says that "we are an industrial nation, therefore our heroes are audacious industrialists." Paul Bunyan, Pecos Bill, John Henry, Kemp Morgan of the oil fields, Casey Jones, Old Stormalong, and West Virginia lumberjack Tony Beaver represent, to him, simply different regional personifications of the same hero.[167] Now the occupational and geographic boundaries are breaking down.

While men stuck to their trades their heroes thrived and maintained their individuality. It has been the task of the writer to reestablish each hero in his own environment; to keep him within his own province.[168]

In *Here's Audacity!* this is accomplished by devoting a chapter to each hero named above. The subchapters on Paul's boyhood and youth, on Babe, on Paul's gang, and on Round River and Pyramid Forty duplicates the Shephard and Turney material with some variations. Mr. Shay's version of the Round River Drive is among the best I have seen. The distinction of his contribution lies, however, in the sharper delineation he gives to Paul as a clever entrepreneur. In "Paul Bunyan at Puget Sound," Paul has dealings with Billy Puget, George Hood, and their slick lawyer, all of whom attempt to withhold from him the money that is rightfully his. Unlike Mrs. Shephard's story of Paul as a miner, here he gets the best of them, lawyer

and all.[169] "Paul Bunyan and Jim Hill" takes as its point of
departure the old ballad about how Jim made the bums ride
the rods on his railroad. Here he hires Paul to build a fence
along the tracks. In the ensuing battle of wits over the money,
Paul uses both shrewdness and his fabulous powers. Paul
Bunyan is now a businessman who performs physical marvels
for a tidy profit.[170]

The next popularizer to present a panorama of American
heroes was Anne Malcolmson, whose *Yankee Doodle's Cousins*
(1941)[171] is intended for a younger audience than that to
which Mr. Shay addressed himself. Mrs. Malcolmson writes,

The yarns that have grown out of young America belong to children,
as much by right of sympathy as by right of heritage. Paul Bunyan
and Pecos Bill are ten years old at heart. Their humor, their wildly
romantic exaggerations, their quixotic naivete, their lack of self-
consciousness and their hard-headed adaptability to circumstances—
all these are qualities of the average fifth-grader.[172]

Following this belief, she finds it necessary to make few
changes in Mr. Stevens' chapter on the Americanization of
Paul Bunyan. She also uses another Stevens chapter and some
material from a book by C. E. Brown[173] which strongly resembles Miss Turney's stories.

Bethene Miller brought our hero up to date in a picture
primer of 1942, *Paul Bunyan in the Army*.[174] Paul is joined by
Pecos Bill, Joe Muffrau, Kemp Morgan, Big (John) Henry,
Alfred Bulltop Stormalong, and a jeep. All contribute to the
Allied victory with such marvels of military science as seining
the sea for submarines, and bombing Germany with redwood
logs. In this sanguinary nursery tale, Paul and his corps of
demigods represent American production and armed might.

A book which attempts to combine the lumberjack Bunyan
of Mr. Shay with the G. I. Paul of Miss Miller is Walter Blair's
Tall Tale America.[175] The method is similar to that employed
in *Here's Audacity!* in that each hero is given a chapter in
which he appears in his own milieu. Paul rates two chapters,
Chapter 12 as a lumberjack, and Chapter 15 as "Scientific Industrialist in the Oilfields." In the final chapter, No. 17 ("We've

Still Got Heroes"), an absent-minded professor turns up at the Pentagon with a solution to the war manpower problem.

In retelling the tales about Bunyan, Professor Blair has drawn on John Lee Brooks and others for the oil-country stories. For his timber tales Professor Blair consulted Laughead, Wayne Martin, Esther Shephard, Glen Rounds, Stewart and Watt, and Miss Turney—all of whose books have been discussed above—and also *Paul Bunyan Tales* by Charles E. Brown (Madison, Wis.: The Author, 1922). He has studiously avoided the works of Mr. Stevens. I found Professor Blair not quite at home in a juvenile style. His versions, however, do emphasize the ways in which Paul Bunyan has gripped the American imagination in an industrial age.

10. HAROLD FELTON'S POTPOURRI

In forty years the Paul Bunyan tales had undergone printing, revision, redaction, and transmogrification into almost every conceivable form. The hero of the oral tradition, rooted in Yankee and backwoods folkways, had all but disappeared in the constant reworkings of old material and infusions of new, which kept the hero up to date and in the public favor. From the original shrewd and mighty lumberjack whose triumphs over natural terrors rewarded his partisans with comic release from fear, the hero had become successively a nature god, a simple giant, a gigantic simpleton, an emblem of industrial paternalism, and a shrewd entrepreneur. In his latest form he represented American warpower to a generation of babies scarcely old enough to be aware of war. All that now remained was for an anthology to collect this literature, and to provide selections upon which some judgment of its merits might be based.

Just such an anthology appeared in 1947: *Legends of Paul Bunyan,* compiled and edited by Harold Felton.[176] The dimensions of this book are commensurate with those of its subject. It measures 108 anecdotes and a big bibliography between the covers, and the covers are heavy boards of forest green. Mr. Felton has ransacked odd corners of the library to unearth several selections from newspaper columns of the 1920's, and from little-known or defunct periodicals. Much of this material has been virtually inaccessible till now, and all followers of Paul Bunyan owe Felton a debt of gratitude for making it available. Physically the book is sumptuous: immense type, rich paper, many illustrations in color.

This being said, however, any serious student of the Bunyan stories and the American folktale will find much to regret in the choice of selections, the general arrangement, and the editorial method of this anthology. The great bulk of its material comes from various popularizations of the original folktales; from Mr. Felton's choices one could scarcely trace the changing concept of the hero through the mutations suggested above. The editor has limited his selections for the most part to stories of Paul in the lumbering and construction industries; the reader of these *Legends* would never guess the extent to which tales of prowess in farming, ranching, mining, and railroading became attached to Paul Bunyan's name. Contributions from the oil fields are given a scant four pages. And the gradual shift in the nature of "Paul's Cleverality" from inventiveness to the shrewdness of the entrepreneur is not to be traced in this book.

Although the anthology includes an apparent diversity of material, reading through its selections in order is a depressing ordeal. Most of the tales are so poorly written, redundant, and devoid of adult interest as to convince almost anyone that if Paul Bunyan literature has fallen to the estate of the nursery, that is only its just desert. Many of the selections were originally written as juvenile literature, but no distinction is made between them and those intended for maturer readers. It's hard to tell which is which.

The collection is seriously weakened as a reference work by a total failure to distinguish between the several varieties of sources it includes. To Mr. Felton, apparently, anything that has ever been written about Paul Bunyan constitutes a Bunyan "legend." Nowhere is there any indication that a Paul Bunyan story slanted for a national magazine is perceptibly different in kind from a recitation taken down from a lumberjack raconteur. Instead the material is simply arranged under topical headings: "Paul the Baby and the Boy," "Paul the Man," "Food and the Kitchen," "Paul's Great Inventions," etc. Thus the actual folktales transcribed from lumberjacks by Professors E. C. Beck and H. A. Watt, and from oilriggers by Professor J. L. Brooks, are scattered among overblown dilutions, distortions, and misrepresentations of "the bardic tradition" by Stevens and the other popularizers. In verse, too, there is the same jumble of *genres*. A stirring ballad from oral tradition is reprinted (on p. 109) from Beck's fine collection; there is also the pedestrian doggerel of T. G. Alvord, Jr., and Douglas Malloch, and the still less distinguished quatrains of the editor. Completely submerged among these folk-type rimes and anecdotes are "Paul's Wife," by Robert Frost, and Part 47 of *The People, Yes* ("Who made Paul Bunyan?"), by Carl Sandburg —two of the rare attempts by first-rank artists to make something intelligible out of the disordered mess which now comprises the Paul Bunyan "tradition."

Characteristic of the confusion evident in this volume is the thirty-two page bibliography appended to the text. This is a slightly enlarged version of a list which appeared several years ago in the *Journal of American Folklore*.[177] It discriminates between tales, poetry, drama, music, art, and criticism, but within these categories it lists any and all items without prejudice.

Legends of Paul Bunyan is clothed in the appurtenances of scholarship but is completely wanting in critical insight. The intelligence which assembled it was that of a cataloguer rather than a scholar. The literary level of most of its contents is so flatly reiterative that even the general reader may find his initial enthusiasm for Paul Bunyan soon bogs down. Confronted by the disorganized mass of Paul Bunyan lore, the editor of this book had a great opportunity to clear the underbrush from the sound timber and impose a critical order upon the superabundance of his material. Mr. Felton lost his opportunity. His collection, while making available some little-known material, presents its entire contents as "legends," and so perpetuates the common misunderstanding that all the popularizations of Paul Bunyan are valid as folklore.

The possibilities of the Paul Bunyan legends—the real ones —for literature are scarcely to be guessed at from the selections in this book. *Legends of Paul Bunyan* presents a phalanx of poor stuff by writers essentially uncreative. Is it not strange that no one included in this anthology, or the present chapter, has had the creative energy and insight to write a real novel about Paul Bunyan? That with the sole exception of Robert Frost, none had been able to present real characters? That not one of the popularizers had given the tales the dramatic structure of competitive conversation? I fear that the hundreds of articles and dozens of books already written on the Bunyan lore have ruined it beyond reclamation for more intelligent writers. Yet there have been at least four attempts by writers of stature to integrate this traditional or semitraditional lore into their own interpretations of American life. The poems of Frost and Sandburg I have mentioned above; there are also an operetta by W. H. Auden and Louis Untermeyer's novella. Perhaps they will show whether the Bunyan myths offer anything of value to the artist who is looking for symbols to express the imaginative nature of his country's people.

CHAPTER FIVE

Toward a National Literature

1. THE SEARCH FOR AN EPIC

A national literature is inevitably based upon the traditions of its country. It must exemplify the national character, and be expressed in the forms and the diction to which time and usage have imparted both familiarity and honor. Ultimately, it has to draw upon the nation's myths about itself, in whatever manifestations they may appear. In France, Italy, Germany, and England, these patterns are quite clear. They are the result of slow centuries of growth, the gradual emergence from feudal folk cultures of increasingly complex societies which, over the years, have preserved some aspects of their earlier forms and thus developed their individuality. But what of America?

"We Yankees . . . are born in a hurry, educated at full speed, our spirit is at high pressure, and our life resembles a shooting star, till death surprises us like an electric shock."[1] So Sam Slick said of us a hundred years ago. We never had time for our traditions to mature with the grave dignity of Roland or Faust. Folk concepts which in England were slowly nurtured into the saga of Beowulf and the *Gest of Robin Hood* here sprouted into the incongruous Bunyan in the anecdotal lore of our frontier. Popular writers on the one hand reduced this hero to a gross simpleton, and on the other made of him a crude archetype of America's newer deity, the industrial tycoon.

At least four poets, however, have not been content to let Paul Bunyan die of mental malnutrition and esthetic anemia at the hands of authors examined in the last chapter. Robert Frost, Carl Sandburg, W. H. Auden, and Louis Untermeyer do not have very much in common, but each has chosen Paul Bunyan for his subject in one literary effort. What they share in their treatment of Paul Bunyan is their attempt to make the Bunyan legend assume for America the role that national myths have always played in the literatures of other lands. In addition to recasting the Bunyan stories in more highly developed literary forms than had either the folk raconteurs or the popular writers, they each see in Bunyan something more significant than merely an occupational hero. They regard him as a symbolic personage who embodies heroic virtues somehow central to the spirit of our history and the character of our people. Yet their Paul Bunyans are by no means alike; we find four distinct interpretations of the folk hero. Where their ambitious undertakings have succeeded, we may find the strength this part of our heritage offers contemporary American literature. Where they have failed, we can see its limitations as the raw materials for a national epic.

2. ROBERT FROST: INDIVIDUALISM IN EXILE

Frost's fame as a regional poet is so great that to many people south of Boston, to copy New England is to copy him. As Mark Van Doren has said, Frost earns his universality by reaping "all the advantage there is in being true to a particular piece of earth."[2] This is something other than being a regionalist. While Frost's wry farmers may really represent New Hampshire character, it is probably true that they are spokesmen for a view of human existence everywhere, as seen by a poet who happens to stand among stone fences. Despite the patina of his silver birches and the fragrance of his apple orchards, Frost is less concerned with local color than with symbolism—not in the Baudelairian sense, but with a symbolistic style and method of his own. Fidelity to regional fact or regional fantasy is not the point of pride with him that it was to Mark Twain, who boasted of his faithful rendering of no less than seven dialects in *Huckleberry Finn*. In fact, it is surprising that a writer who so often draws upon his neighboring farms and farmers for atmosphere should so rarely use the fantasies which are as deeply rooted in New Hampshire's hills as are the birches or the people themselves. Among the handful of his poems on such traditional themes are "The Witch of Coös," "The Pauper Witch at Grafton," and a poem about Paul Bunyan.

Although he has lived most of his life in or near the original Bunyan country, Mr. Frost has evidently based his poem, "Paul's Wife," on a collection of tales from the other end of America: Miss Turney's *Paul Bunyan Comes West*. This is the passage in Miss Turney's chapbook upon which "Paul's Wife" is built:

A feller by the name of Murphy tells 'bout how Paul found his wife in the heart of a great white pine an' didn't never let no one see her but 'tain't so. Paul's wife wuz regular folks an' she never set in no moonlight spoonin' with Paul. . . . She cooked for 300 men, usin' a donkey boiler with the top tore off to bile beans in when the extra hands wuz needed.[3]

The first sentence of this quotation is unique among the oral or popularized versions of Paul Bunyan then extant. Nowhere else had this lyrical tone been approached, and even here it was introduced only to serve as contrast with the standard exaggerations of frontier comedy. Yet of all the motifs Miss

Turney included in her chapbook, this was the one which most appealed to Robert Frost. And this is how, in his expert hands, Miss Turney's rough hint is polished into lyricism and dignity:

> It was gone.
> And then beyond the open water, dim with midges,
> Where the log drive lay pressed against the boom,
> It slowly rose a person, rose a girl,
> Her wet hair heavy on her like a helmet,
> Who, leaning on a log looked back at Paul.
>
> .   .   .   .
>
> Falling in love across the twilight mill-pond.
> More than a mile across the wilderness
> They sat together half-way up a cliff
> In a small niche let into it, the girl
> Brightly, as if a star played on the place,
> Paul darkly, like her shadow.[4]

"Paul's Wife" is a lyrical narrative of 157 lines. The story is told by someone who learned it from Murphy, the only man who saw Paul find his bride. In the beginning,

> To drive Paul out of any lumber camp
> All that was needed was to say to him,
> "How is the wife, Paul?"—and he'd disappear.
> Some said it was because he had no wife,
> And hated to be twitted on the subject.[5]

Several other reasons are offered, including "one more not so fair to Paul"—that he had married a mere "half-breed squaw," who was "not his equal." But no one wanted to drive Paul away. With his great prowess he was welcome anywhere, stripping the bark from tamarack logs, toting the load with a shrunken harness—"You know Paul could do wonders."

> But I guess
> The one about his jumping so's to land
> With both his feet at once against the ceiling,
> And then land safely right side up again,
> Back on the floor, is fact or pretty near fact.
> Well this is such a yarn.[6]

These motifs are what Frost uses from the oral Bunyan tales. What follows, however, is not "such a yarn" at all, although in telling it he does impart "fact or pretty near fact" with the scrupulous attention to detail that characterizes artistic lying everywhere. However, the restrained cadence and the diction of his blank verse are something else again. The style is Frost's alone. His is the conversational tone which made such verse seem strange and radical in 1920, and beyond the changes of taste or fashion a generation later. Of course, it has its sources in New England's hard-bitten speech. It would seem that Frost has given voice to what his taciturn neighbors might think and feel but seldom say. The idiom, however, is a personal achievement on the highest plane of poetic discipline, and bears very little resemblance to the exuberant lingo of the frontier even when some of the selfsame anecdotes are clothed in it.

To frontiersman or lumberjack, the feats of Paul Bunyan were an end in themselves. Thus the proper idiom for folktales was one which caught the wit and power of their hero. But to Frost these anecdotes are only the appurtenances of a more important theme. Rather than the hero's supernatural strength and cleverness, he sees the human part of Paul as most essential. This is a side the folktales never did develop. Their greatest weakness was in characterization; despite the stupendous exploits and inventive cleverness, Paul himself often seemed a walking shadow. But Robert Frost makes character mean all. If his Paul is to be a hero, the heroism will be based upon a concept of Paul Bunyan as a man, not as a semimythical gigantic marionette.

> Paul was what's called a terrible possessor.
> Owning a wife with him meant owning her.
> She wasn't anybody else's business,
> Either to praise her, or so much as name her,
> And he'd thank people not to think of her.
> Murphy's idea was that a man like Paul
> Wouldn't be spoken to about a wife
> In any way the world knew how to speak.[7]

Paul Bunyan stands apart from other men not because of his prowess (which they admire and welcome) but because of a sensitivity and a lyrical nature they do not share. Conquest of the wilderness lingers vestigially in Paul's "same old feats of logging," but this is only incidental. Instead the emphasis is, unexpectedly, upon his marriage to nature's beauty, as well as on his identification with her power.

The poem refashions a popular legend to restate Frost's most constant theme—the sanctity, dignity, and inviolability of the individual. Thus "any way the world knew how to speak" will be in opposition to these qualities of Paul's spirit—an echo of the earlier poem, "Home Burial." In this vision of Paul Bunyan, individuality takes the sophisticated form of heightened sensibilities. And Paul, the vigorous hero of the woods, flees from his fellow lumberjacks into the same sort of exile as that which makes the sensitive personality homeless in the modern world.

This is the new dimension Mr. Frost has given to Paul Bunyan. Yet however successfully a poet may assimilate a myth, there is always something in it which he cannot capture or subdue. Just because the myth was known before he found it, and will always be known more widely in other forms than his, the poem he writes cannot exist in independence. Rather, it must find its place in the atmosphere the myth itself creates, and, in the minds of those who know that myth, exert its influence upon all other versions. Thus may the tradition and the individual talent be mutually enriched. "Paul's Wife" is not among Frost's major or most successful works; yet it has an interest of its own in showing how a great poet gave a folk tradition a new interpretation, and reworked it into the patterns of his art.

3. SANDBURG AND "THE PEOPLE"

Among the half-dozen poets who began the Little Renaissance in the twentieth century's second decade, no two have less in common than Frost and Carl Sandburg. How strange that they should both have chosen to write about Paul Bunyan! It is not so strange, however, that once they made their common choice, the resulting poems show great differences in language, content, feeling, and ideas.

Sandburg, of course, writes in the populist tradition.[8] He derives his strength from Whitman and William Jennings Bryan, but even more so from the flat prairies, the erupting cities, and the banter and questions of the plain people who live in them. Just as the faith of the populists holds that the political good is inherent in "the people," so their esthetic maintains that the beauty and truth which are the province of art arise out of communal experiences, rather than from those of the hypersensitive individual alienated from his society. Thus the populist poet looks to "the people," rather than to the subjective self or the literary tradition. Sandburg in his earlier poems was often a sentimental lyricist; his attempts to describe cityscapes in terms of neo-Wordsworthian natural beauty are not at all characteristic of his populism. But on the whole his chief concern is to record the multitudinous voices of America. This he attempts to do, with the hope that out of that variegated record a stronger single voice—the national consciousness itself—will emerge.

His most ambitious and successful effort in this direction is the volume *The People, Yes.* In this book the forty-seventh section, or canto, is devoted to Paul Bunyan, and therefore is the locus of our attention here.[9] The volume begins with a re-telling of the story of the Tower of Babel; indeed, the rest of the book is mainly devoted to recording the babble of many tongues. True to the positive faith in the moral grandeur of the people, the faith in their compassionate humanity and good-natured resilience under adversity which the affirmation of his title suggests, Sandburg in this book allows the people to unfold their own drama in their own words. His role is largely that of the sensitive recording ear, attuned to catch the most significant notes out of the endless murmuring and laughter. He records these notes, and uses such fragments from the Tower of Babel to lay the foundations for a new tower, which all the people shall enter and understand because they have each contributed to its building.

Sandburg's esthetic and his method are much more populist than were those of Walt Whitman, his most significant literary ancestor. Although Whitman threw down the gauntlet against pistareen decorum in his art, it was upon a traditional sense of craftsmanship applied to fresh ideas and new forms that he ultimately relied. Sandburg's concept of the poet's role does not embrace the painstaking effort of Whitman to achieve in the very texture of his language organic forms arising from the tensions of the ideas the images suggest. Whitman's most successful idiom was fresh because he had assimilated new influences into the language of poetry. The rhythms of the sea, the solemnity of the King James Bible, the incremental repetitions of biblical verse and nineteenth-century oratory, and the "barbaric yawp" of the backwoods boaster were combined to fashion language into a diction new to poetry. This combination was an act of discipline, an operation of intelligence and will, which in time produced an idiom that was the natural expression of the poet's mind.

Sandburg more literally draws his language from the spoken tongues of the people. He strongly relies upon his raw material to suggest or supply the finished forms of his verse. This may be described on the one hand as high faith in the artistic possibilities of the untutored public imagination; but on the other hand it is also a lack of craftsmanship in the individual poet. *The People, Yes* seems to sprawl like the prairies themselves. Some of its sections read like the published proverb collections of the American Dialect Society. Sandburg's casual stanzas are so difficult to reconcile with the discipline expected in traditional poetry that even his favorable critics approach his most successful book with a mixture of admiration and confusion.[10] There is, however, more form in Sandburg's verse than meets the eye. The most distinguished parts of *The People, Yes* are those in which the poet succeeds, or nearly succeeds, in imposing form upon his almost intractable materials. Sandburg's method, surprisingly, is the development of ideas by indirection—it is the method of the best modern poetry that Sandburg shares, despite the apparent looseness of his language. For these reasons, his poem "Who made Paul Bunyan" must be read in context if one is to understand what significance Carl Sandburg has given this hero in *The People, Yes*. To present this section by itself, as it appears in Felton's *Legends* and Botkin's *Treasury*, is to rob it of most of its meaning. To understand it fully, we must consider its context: Sections 36 through 47. Here we shall find the significance of Paul Bunyan in the entire poem, and we shall discover, too, several of Sandburg's major themes.

In this portion of *The People, Yes*, Sandburg's theme is recovery: recovery from the economic paralysis of the depression, and more immediately, recovery of human dignity from the ravages of want, hopelessness, and fear. The assertion,

> "I am zero, naught, cipher,"
> meditated the symbol preceding the numbers,

introduces six verse paragraphs which argue that money brings status, pride, and selfishness. Then,

> Said the scorpion of hate: "The poor hate the rich. The rich hate the poor. The south hates the north. The west hates the east. The workers hate their bosses. The bosses hate their workers. . . . We are a house divided against itself. We are millions of hands raised against each other. We are united in but one aim—getting the dollar. And when we get the dollar we employ it to get more dollars."

The capitalistic economy makes men inhuman. In the next section they wrangle over "what is mine" and "what is yours" and "who says so?" Yet along with the arguing and hating there is joking and laughter, though the humor may be wry indeed.

Sandburg describes the farmers who had overproduced their crops and cattle until they were themselves near starvation. Theirs is the smoldering hatred that verges on violence:

> "I want to shoot somebody but I don't know who.
> "We'll do something. You wait and see.
> "We don't have to stand for this skin game if we're free Americans."

Speaking through the many voices he has chosen to speak

for him or to echo in his own words, Sandburg is moved to
anger by the greatest of all injustices: the disavowal of human
dignity, the crushing of men and of Man by the economic
machine.

> Have you seen men handed refusals
>   till they began to laugh
>   at the notion of ever landing a job again— . . .
> Have you seen women and kids . . .
>   . . . fighting other women and kids
>   for the leavings of fruit and vegetable markets
>   or searching alleys and garbage dumps for scraps? . . .
> The rights of property are guarded
>   by ten thousand laws and fortresses.
> The right of a man to live by his work—
>   what is this right? . . .
>   and why does it speak
>   and though put down speak again
>   with strengths out of the earth?

What are these strengths out of the earth? In the next section, Number 39, two strengths are suggested. First, "They got
his drift when he laughed," and second,

> The strong workman whose blood goes into his work
>   no more dies than the people die.

These were the flags of hope for "more than one pioneer."

The theme of Section 40 is, "We live only once"; we are all
played for suckers by one another, but fate in the end makes
suckers out of all the players. Meanwhile,

>   plans
>   programs, inventions, promises,
>   games, commands, suggestions,
>   hints, insinuations pour
>   from professional schemers
>   into the ears of the people

But as we learn in Section 41, the people are unpredictable.
You can't regulate them. Section 42 presents twenty-seven
proverbs and jests which illustrate their diversity and their
humor. In 43, people are compared to eggs.

> What sort of an egg are you? . . .
> Under the microscope Agassiz studied one egg:
>   chaos, flux, constellations, rainbows:
>   "It is a universe in miniature."

Similarly, one man is a paradigm of humanity. There follow twenty-six samples of the jokes and quips of the people. These, like the egg, are microcosms which suggest more than they seem to contain. In Section 45 these jests accumulate with growing intensity:

> They have yarns
> Of a skyscraper so tall they had to put hinges
> On the top two stories so to let the moon go by,
> Of one corn crop in Missouri when the roots
> Went so deep and drew off so much water
> The Mississippi riverbed that year was dry. . . .
> Of the man who drove a swarm of bees across the Rocky Mountains
>   and the Desert "and didn't lose a bee,". . .
> Of the boy who climbed a cornstalk growing so fast he would have
>   starved to death if they hadn't shot biscuits up to him, . . .
> Of mosquitoes: one can kill a dog, two of them a man . . .
> Of Paul Bunyan's big blue ox, Babe, measuring between the eyes
>   forty-two ax-handles and a plug of Star tobacco exactly . . .

From Sandburg's long list of yarns I have abstracted those which point toward the climax of this portion a few pages later. The six motifs quoted above had all been previously attached by either lumberjacks or popularizers to the so-called "cycle" of Paul Bunyan. Sandburg has long been familiar with this folklore; in 1924 he contributed the yarns he knew to Esther Shephard, who used them in her popularization, *Paul Bunyan.* In their present context these fragments of the Bunyan yarns are piled helter-skelter one upon another; the list includes other folktale motifs, too, from cowboys, engineers, farmers, sailors, sheepherders, and Negro section gangs. A common bond of humor links them in their diversity. These are the incongruities the people laugh at. Sandburg brings the old yarns up to date, too, with jokes about the high-pressure salesman who sold a cop the idea of jumping off the Brooklyn

Bridge; the oil man in heaven who succumbs to his own suggestion that there are gushers in hell; and four "fantasies heard at filling stations in the midwest." They are simply old tall tales mechanized:

A Dakota cousin of this Ohio man sent six years of tin can accumulations to the same works, asking them to overhaul his car. Two weeks later came a rebuilt car, five old tin cans, and a letter: "We are forwarding you five parts not necessary in our new model."

And the old game of selling the bumpkin is revived by the sharpers who convince an Iowan that for twenty-five dollars they will turn the Masonic Temple on its turntable while he stands in the tower. But these later versions of old American whoppers do not displace their traditional ancestors; Rip Van Winkle, the Headless Horseman, the Flying Dutchman, Mother Carey, and Jim Liverpool all linger in the popular imagination. So too does "Mike Fink along the Ohio and the Mississippi, half wild horse and cock-eyed alligator, the rest of him snags and snapping turtle."

Beneath the proselike surface of *The People, Yes* there is a steady quickening of the pulses of the imagination, charged and recharged with infusions of energy from one after another of these fantastic jokes and wild exaggerations. Then, for an instant, the pace is changed:

Of the woman born deaf, blind and dumb, the vaudeville audience
asked questions: . . .
And the woman enjoyed answering these questions from
people born with sight and hearing:
"I liked it. I liked to feel the warm tide of human
life pulsing round and round me."

This compassion and kinship must not be obscured by the self-assertive rantings of Mike Fink, nor forgotten in the derision of the many which comedy often directs against the single person.

But "They got his drift when he laughed." And they laugh again and again, these nameless, fameless people in *The People, Yes*, till out of their laughter an image of their own aspirations is born. The isolated jokes and yarns are clustered about a single character in whom the people see themselves:

Who made Paul Bunyan, who gave him birth as a myth, who joked him into life as the Master Lumberjack, who fashioned him forth as an apparition easing the hours of men amid axes and trees, saws and lumber? The people, the bookless people, they made Paul and had him alive long before he got into the books for those who read. He grew up in shanties, around the hot stoves of winter, among socks and mittens drying, in the smell of tobacco smoke and the roar of laughter mocking the outside weather. And some of Paul came overseas in wooden bunks below decks in sailing vessels. And some of Paul is old as the hills, young as the alphabet.

In these twelve poems (36-47), the scraps of comic folklore have consistently grown in length and continuity from short proverbs and one-line jests to one-paragraph anecdotes, and now, in Section 47, at last to a full poem on a single subject. The increasing length is accompanied by an acceleration of intensity. "Who made Paul Bunyan" is the climax of this development, and the rhapsodic flow of its first paragraph is among the high points of Mr. Sandburg's book and of the Paul Bunyan tales in any form.

Why should Paul Bunyan emerge as the climactic image of the age in this portion of *The People, Yes?* We remember that eleven poems ago the chain of comic links that led to Paul was fastened to the dull weight of despair. The progression from "I am zero" and

> what punishments handed bottom people
> who have wronged no man's house
> or things or person?

to the ecstatic affirmation of "The people, the bookless people" is a record of the resilience of the human spirit. For Sandburg the Bunyan stories are a major triumph of the collective imagination. They fulfill in this poem the selfsame function that they played in the lives and the art of Perry Allen, Matt Surrell, and the hundreds of anonymous raconteurs who told them in the woods, when logging was a folk life which inherited directly the comic traditions of the old frontier. The conquests

of terror by laughter, of despair by comic ingenuity, and the
victory of the indomitable human spirit over adversity are once
again the geneses of the Bunyan stories.

> The people will live on.
> The learning and blundering people will live on.
> They will be tricked and sold and again sold
> And go back to the nourishing earth for rootholds,
> The people so peculiar in renewal and comeback,
> You can't laugh off their capacity to take it.

So Sandburg writes in his final section. The progression cul-
minated by "Who made Paul Bunyan" is among his most im-
pressive demonstrations of that "renewal and comeback."

But what of the tales themselves? In the first, the Seven
Axmen dance by the light of the sparks from their hobnailed
boots, and "The commotion of the dancing that night brought
on an earthquake and the Big Onion River moved over three
counties to the east." In the second, Paul stops a rainstorm
by climbing a waterspout and turning it off. The third retells
the old yarn of the big mosquitoes whose sting killed oxen;
Paul sent for bumblebees to kill them off, but the insects intermarried and their children had stingers at both ends. Next, a
description of Paul's immense kitchen; finally, Benny, the Little
Blue Ox, who "grew two feet every time Paul looked at him,"
and "ate the red hot stove; and that finished him."

These are all motifs which had been published previously
in the popularizations of the Bunyan stories by W. B. Laughead,
Ida Virginia Turney, Esther Shephard, and James Stevens.
Whether Sandburg learned them from oral sources or read
them watered-down in the books of these writers, his retelling
of these motifs here lacks a distinctive flavor. Only the intro-
ductory paragraph has a truly individual tone. The flatness of
his diction and the choice of anecdotes combines to defeat the
poet's purpose. What was intended as a culmination of his efforts turns out an anticlimax which reveals two endemic weaknesses of Sandburg's art. One is his poetic language, the other
his social thinking. A philosophy which appears so full of hope
that liberal democracy will in the end prevail contains denials

of those very hopes within its own statements of affirmation.

It is Sandburg's personal triumph to have fashioned from the intransigent materials of these dozen poems a form which has the power to invoke our sympathies for the "bottom people," and which invites us to rejoice with them in the imaginative conquests of their hero, Paul Bunyan. But we must also ask whether it was really of moment in 1936 to assume the guise of old Paul Bunyan, so big his footsteps made earthquakes, so strong he turned off waterspouts. The natural elements were not our important enemies then. Neither does it seem especially relevant to thump the expansionist tub with hosannas of a three-mile table and an ox of fantastic size. Is not this a retreat into the vanished past? The Paul Bunyan tales are not even commonly told now among the lumberjacks; how is the poet justified in resurrecting them as a symbol of the contemporary popular imagination?

Sandburg is not using Paul Bunyan narrowly to represent the loggers' hero. Accurately, he saw that these tales of Paul do convey the sense of certain aspects of our national character, and these aspects are not yet extinct simply because bulldozers have displaced ox teams in the lumbercamps. The concepts of character which such folklore preserves from our past and presents to our future are the tenets of individualism which the pioneers needed to practice in order to survive. The virtues of the pioneers, which the Bunyan tales and other legends keep still fresh in the public mind, derive from their heroic struggle to establish human life where for ages thunderstorms had reigned unchallenged. We admire their indomitable energy; the skills and ingenuity with which they fashioned homes in a hostile wilderness; the persistence with which they seized, held, and populated the resisting earth; and their individualism, forged in the heat of unending adversity, danger, and toil. "The people will live on," Sandburg writes; "You can't laugh off their capacity to take it."

But when civilization overtakes the rugged settlement, how useful are these same virtues? The pioneer ethic of individualism was seldom fitted to deal with interpersonal relation-

ships on other levels than self-assertive violence. The tradition
of lawlessness was so cherished on the frontier that such a
man as Judge Roy Bean could be celebrated in oral tradition
as a hero. Bean was that member of the bench who declared,
"I am the law west of the Pecos," held court in a barroom, and
said, "The jury will now deliberate; and if it brings a verdict
short of hangin' it'll be declared in contempt."[11] Paul Bunyan,
too, represents Activity and Will, free from Responsibility, Con-
science, or Coöperation. In many ways this frontier individualism is the very antithesis of life in a democratic civilization.
While these pioneer virtues may still be admired among "the
people," primitive individualism of this sort survives most vigor-
ously in the ethic of old-style business executives, who, in the
assertion of their rights of ownership, leave no ground for intelligent analysis in the solution of economic problems.

The depression was the greatest of such problems. Apparently Sandburg proposes to solve its attendant problems of
poverty, hopelessness, and fear by exhorting "the people" to
remember Paul Bunyan and the virtues of the pioneers. This
is really cold comfort for those bottom people who find themselves at the bottom exactly because there is no longer room
in America for men to emulate Paul Bunyan. Sandburg's of-
fering is more a testament of his faith in the will of the people
to survive than it is even a hint toward any constructive program. He does not suggest the application of rational intelligence in the continual effort to find an equitable balance
between the rights and desires of the individual and the institutions with which he lives. In Sandburg's panoramic representation of American life, as Zabel suggests, "he is pulled by
so many claims on sympathy and forbearance that nothing
survives the prodigious outlay of tolerance and compassion."[12]
Like many another native radical he has faith and good intentions, but has not penetrated to the core of those appearances
which he records so faithfully. It is hard, too, to reconcile his
celebration of rugged individualism with his well-known interest in the Socialist movement.

In resurrecting the dying folklore of a vanished way of life

Sandburg resembles his only important literary forebear. Whitman, writing at the moment when industrialization was changing the landscape of the cities and the tempo of the people's lives, saw not the factory and lathe but the teamster, trapper, and Indian squaw. Both poets attempted to create an imaginary portrait of America. Both portrayed the expansive youth of the nation, but missed the maturer visage in which that youthfulness is interfused with other elements. In the modern struggle for survival, energy and resilience and determination—and even a sense of humor—are no longer enough. While these qualities may have helped avert the explosion of baffled anger into senseless violence in the 1930's, they alone did not restore our economy or regenerate our character. To maintain that they did so, or could do so, is a sentimental fiction, romantic but untrue.

A literature employing national myths may well be romantic, but if the romance is a fiction inadequate to the truth, then neither the myths nor the literature they inspire will be living things. Sandburg has performed a remarkable achievement in delineating our comic heritage, and suggesting its possibilities for poetry. But in his emphasis on the resilience and the energy of the people he overlooks many other strands in American culture which should be represented in the epic panorama he has attempted to write. The omission of these strands seriously weakens the validity of his achievement.

4. AUDEN'S AMERICAN DEMIGOD

A neglected document in the career of W. H. Auden is his libretto for the operetta, *Paul Bunyan*. With music by the English composer, Benjamin Britten, *Paul Bunyan* represents the only large-scale attempt by the poet to write for a popular audience. *Paul Bunyan*, however, was performed only once, for a one-week run by the Columbia University Theatre Associates in May 1941.[13] Mr. Auden was evidently dissatisfied with his script, for he has not attempted to revise it for pub-

lication; three incidental lyrics, included in his *Collected Poetry*
in 1945, are the only parts of the operetta which he has offered
in print.[14]

In response to a query about his operetta, Mr. Auden wrote,
"The choice of subject was dictated by the demands of Boosey
& Hawkes for something suitable for high schools. The sources
were the New York Public Library."[15] It would seem that he
began *Paul Bunyan* under three handicaps: the piece was com-
missioned in a form with which he had had no previous experience; it was directed toward an audience for whom he had
never written before; and his interpretation of the hero was
limited by what he discovered about Paul Bunyan in the library.
What he found there, naturally enough, were the books by Mr.
Stevens and Mrs. Shephard. Most of the touches of folk humor
come from Shephard. But it was Stevens' *Paul Bunyan,* with
its bathetic defense of laissez faire in the lumber industry and
its roughneck attack on education and poetry, which proved
the unlikely starting point for Auden's play.

Mr. Auden has always found the simplicity and integration
of folk life appealing, and has contrasted these qualities to their
opposites which he sensed in the life about him. Here he deals
with the Amercian scene—*Paul Bunyan* is one of his earliest
treatments of America—in terms of our frontier history and our
most popular myth. Aspects of its theme foreshadow *The Age
of Anxiety;* its versification seems a tentative rehearsal for the
virtuosity in *The Sea and The Mirror.* But its major interest
lies in two other directions. In this libretto Mr. Auden gives
fresh strength to a much-manhandled theme from American
folklore. And he deals directly, though sometimes facetiously,
with an important dilemma in the history of the culture he has
lately accepted as his own.

Plot. His operetta has a simple story. Paul Bunyan gathers a
crew to tame the continent. Hel Helson is his foreman, Johnny
Inkslinger his bookkeeper. Tiny, his daughter by an unhappy
marriage, arrives after her mother's death and falls in love with
Slim, the camp cook. The men taunt Helson into rebelling
against Paul; he is beaten in fair fight and is reconciled with

Bunyan again. As the wilderness is cleared, some of the men turn from logging to the occupations of civilized life. John Shears leads the farming contingent, who take to the soil with Paul's blessing. At last Babe, the Blue Ox, tells Paul that his work is done. The gang has a farewell Christmas party. Helson becomes a builder of high-tension power lines; Slim and Tiny go to New York to run a big hotel; Inkslinger is called to Hollywood. And Paul moves on to other deserts where his spirit is still needed to subdue the wilderness.

Thus there is one main plot (conquering the wilderness) and two subplots (Slim and Tiny's courtship, and Helson's revolt). In addition, there is yet another element running through the play. Auden satirizes reactionary politics, the vulgarities of advertising, and the vacuity of the glamorized dream life presented by Hollywood and the slick magazines. These realities of the present, some of which appear as Paul Bunyan's prophetic dreams, are contrasted to the happy state of natural man in which the action takes place.

Characterization. Paul Bunyan is a godlike Father-figure, a Promethean symbol embodying the collective will to mastery over the wilderness which leads all pioneers to clear the ground for civilization. When that work is done, Paul recognizes that he is no longer needed there, and so moves on. Bunyan never appears on stage in this operetta; he is a mythical personage whose deep, meditative voice fills the forests and the theatre. Paul Bunyan is epical, not comical, in this conception.

The chief human character in the play is Johnny Inkslinger. In Stevens' book he was merely a huge, devoted bookkeeper, but for Auden, Johnny represents speculative intelligence. Already civilized, he critically evaluates the crude society in which he is fated to exist. A man of sensitivity and literary ambition, he is frustrated by the demands made upon him merely to survive in a frontier community. Mr. Auden suggests that his talents are later to be deflected from artistic to commercial ends, for Inkslinger leaves the frontier to take a movie job in Hollywood. A pathetic rather than a heroic figure, he nonetheless holds the play together and functions as factotum, master of ceremonies, critic, and asker of leading questions. Esthetic, discontented with society, proud in his isolation, he is also the creative personality thwarted in the crude new world. It is interesting that these last are the qualities that Frost deemed heroic and attributed to Paul himself.

Hel Helson, also appropriated from the Stevens book, is brute strength. He has ambition, too, and a weakness for flattery. Stevens had represented his revolt against Bunyan as a crude parody of the class struggle in which Paul, as Management, emerged triumphant. Auden's Hel, however, has no real quarrel with Bunyan; it is simply that his crew takes advantage of his weakness and momentarily inflames his vanity. After the fight he knows enough to place the cause of his former discontent in their bad counsel. Where Stevens had John Shears plot to destroy Paul, Auden makes no problem of his desire to become a farmer.

Babe is evidently the animal strength and instinctive wisdom which are a part of Paul himself. Like his master, Babe is never seen on stage. In some ways he is Bunyan's mentor; we learn (from the narrator who sings ballads as interludes between the scenes) that Babe advised Paul to get a wife, and later, to leave for another country.

These characters might have been combined to make an integrated story; they might have been the cast of a successful operetta based on our so frequently misused folklore. The poet seems never to have decided, however, exactly what sort of a play he had set out to write. It is by turns an epic, a romance, and a satire; consequently, the total effect is confusing. Yet its parts have a value greater than that of their sum. Since Auden gives free run to his virtuosity, assigning a distinctive style to each of the characters in the play—who in turn each expresses a different mood—we may approach its significance through its versification.

Versification. There are six of these styles: Paul Bunyan's voice, the folk humor, the satire, ballads, other lyrics, and a litany.

1. *Paul's voice* usually speaks in sonorous free verse, ap-

propriate to the dignity and oracular wisdom of the divinity. This is his greeting:

It is a spring morning without benefit of young persons.

It is a sky that has never registered weeping or rebellion.

It is a forest full of innocent beasts. There are none who blush at the memory of an ancient folly, none who hide beneath dyed fabrics a malicious heart.

It is America but not yet.

Wanted. Disturbers of public order, men without foresight or fear.

Wanted. Energetic madmen. Those who have thought themselves a body large enough to devour their dreams.

Wanted. The lost. Those indestructibles whom defeat can never change. Poets of the bottle, clergymen of the ridiculous gospel, actors who should have been engineers and lawyers who should have been sea-captains, saints of circumstance, desperadoes, unsuccessful wanderers, all who can hear the invitation of the earth. America, youngest of her daughters awaits the barbarians of marriage.[16]

At the opening of the second act (there are only two) Paul sees that his task is almost done, and that "the aggressive will is no longer pure":

Virtuosos of the axe, dynamiters and huntsmen, there
has been an excess of military qualities, of the resourcefulness
of thieves, the camaraderie of the irresponsible, and
the accidental beauties of silly songs.

Nevertheless you have done much to render yourselves unnecessary.
Loneliness has worn lines of communication.

Irrational destruction has made possible the establishment of a civilized order.

Drunkenness and lechery have prepared the way for a routine of temperance and marriage.

Already you have provoked a general impulse towards settlement and cultivation.[17]

When civilized order, cultivation, and marriage succeed the wilderness that had been Paul Bunyan's challenge, he speaks again:

Now the task that made us friends
In a common labor, ends;

For an emptiness is named
And a wilderness is tamed
Till its savage nature can
Tolerate the life of man.

.   .   .   .   .   .

Other kinds of deserts call
Other forests whisper Paul. . . .
Here, though, is your life, and here
The pattern is already clear
That machinery imposes
On you as the frontier closes,
Gone the natural disciplines
And the life of choice begins.[18]

These speeches by themselves have the dignity of an epic. Paul is now a personage to whom neither folk humor nor social satire is congenial. Yet Mr. Auden's script is preëminently comic in tone. The comedy proceeds from other voices than that of Paul Bunyan himself.

2. The *folk humor*, which Mr. Auden cannot immediately attach to Paul as Father-figure, is nonetheless concerned with him. To introduce comic motifs from Shephard and yet not intrude upon the serious conception of the hero, Auden employs the device of having a narrator sing ballad couplets entr'act. Unfortunately, in these the author fails to overcome the banality of his sources. The couplets are mere doggerel; their humor depends solely upon the hero's giganticism.[19] Had Mr. Auden been familiar with a few genuine Bunyan folktales, or had he been able to distinguish between the more and less authentic parts of Mrs. Shephard's book, these ballads might have been much more interesting.

3. *Satire.* In the body of the play, however, much of the humor results from Auden's satire of contemporary popular culture. The verse reads (and sounded in performance) like an attempt to modernize Gilbert and Sullivan, although Auden's aim may have been merely to imitate the flippancy of a Broadway musical. He satirizes movie stars ("In our embraces we select / Whatever technique seems correct / To give the visual effect / Of an Eternal Passion"[20]), but the tone is trivial and

the ironic touch slides off the surface of the subject. He pokes fun at advertising, too.[21] Mr. Stevens' Bunyanesque maxims for business executives are satirized in the sycophantic sniveling of Helson's cronies after Hel, fighting Paul at their instigation, had been knocked out:

Cronies 1 & 3: We are all put here on earth for a purpose. We all have a job to do and it is our duty to do it with all our might.

Cronies 2 & 4: We must obey our superiors and live according to our station in life, for whatever the circumstances, the Chief, the Company, and the Customer are always right.[22]

4. *Ballad forms.* The emergence from this occasionally vapid script of several incidental songs indicates that Auden is most successful as a lyric poet. He uses the strength of the old English ballad tradition to give a communal quality to some of his lyrics; these are more complex than the narrative ballads sung in the interludes. One is Paul's dream of defeat, which he holds as a warning to the pioneers about to enter the wilderness. This song, " 'Gold in the North,' came the blizzard to say," is reprinted in Auden's *Collected Poetry.*[23] In "The Mocking of Hel Helson" he employs the question-and-answer structure of "Lord Randall." This is what Helson hears after the men have taunted him to "stand up for his 'rights' ":

1st Question

Heron, heron, winging by
through the silence of the sky,
What have you heard of Helson the brave?

Heron

O I heard of a hero working for wages,
Taking orders just like a slave.

Chorus

No. I'm afraid it's too late.
Helson will never be great . . .[24]

5. *Other lyrics.* Among the other lyrics, the loveliest is a little prothalamium, "Carry her over the water."[25] This has a

ballad feeling about it but differs slightly in form; its refrain ("Sing agreeably, agreeably, agreeably of love") is more charming than the straightforward diction of the narrative ballad.

A tighter compression characterizes "The single creature leads a partial life,"[26] a metaphysical interjection by the dog and cats who are the bunkhouse pets. These lyrics, quite independent of the Bunyan theme, are among the operetta's most successful fragments.

6. The final number of the operetta is a *litany,* employing the antiphonal structure of ecclesiastical music. This, too, is a form expressing communal emotion, and is therefore eminently suitable for the climax of a play which honors a folk hero. It shows in a little space the strengths and weaknesses of Auden's *Paul Bunyan.* This passage immediately follows Paul's farewell, quoted above:

Chorus: The campfire embers are black and cold,
                The banjos are broken, the stories are told,
                The woods are cut down and the young are grown
                   old.

Trio: From a Pressure Group that says I am the Consti-
                   tuition,
                From those who say Patriotism and mean Persecu-
                   tion,
                From a Tolerance that is really inertia and delusion

Chorus: Save animals and men.

Tiny & Slim: Bless us, father.

Paul Bunyan: A father cannot bless.
                May you find the happiness that you possess.

Chorus: The echoing axe shall be heard no more
                Nor the rising scream of the buzzer saw
                Nor the crack as the ice-jam explodes in the thaw.

Trio: From entertainments neither true nor beautiful nor
                   witty,
                From a homespun humor manufactured in the city,
                From the dirty-mindedness of a Watch Committee

Chorus: Save animals and men.

Helson: Don't leave me, Paul. Where am I? What's to become
               of America now?

Paul Bunyan: Everyday America's destroyed and recreated
               America is what you do,
               America is you and I
               America is what you choose to make it.

Chorus: No longer the logger shall hear in the Fall
               The pine and the spruce and the sycamore call.

Paul Bunyan: Good-bye, dear friends.

Chorus: Good-bye, Paul.

.   .   .   .

Johnny: Paul, who are you?

Paul: Where the night becomes the day,
              Where the dream becomes the fact,
               I am the eternal guest
               I am way, I am act.[27]

The strength of this operetta is in Auden's conception of
Paul Bunyan. He is way, he is act; and he is also dream, and
wisdom. The dream is man's eternal desire for mastery over
his environment. The wisdom recognizes the consequences of
the act and the way by which that dream may be fulfilled.
Paul is a Promethean hero who brings men to a civilization
he himself cannot enjoy. Like Moses, another Promethean pioneer with a similar dream, he does not suffer except in being
excluded from the life that is to come. But in Auden's play,
that life is compounded of such hypocrisy, tinsel, and shallow-
ness that Paul Bunyan's exile to a fresher wilderness is only
to be envied.

Auden's satire contradicts his epic. This was just the case
with the original folktales, too; but in them heroism was deflected into comedy in order to ridicule fear by asserting the
resilience of the imagination, a process which Sandburg under-
stood so well. As oral tradition continued into an era when
physical hardships diminished, we have seen how the heroic
elements in the Bunyan stories became subordinated to the
comic. These in turn were diffused in subject and changed in

tone from positive assertions of man's power to the mere burlesque one finds in the Stevens popularizations. But Auden's
inability to sustain the epic tone is due to other causes besides the decayed condition of the pseudo-lore with which he
worked.

Mr. Auden is convinced that America betrayed its possibilities for matching material achievements with moral greatness
when "the life of choice" followed "the natural disciplines."
Instead of the ideal commonwealth Paul's spirit might have
made possible, he finds America oppressed by vulgarity, intol-
erance, pressure groups, prurience, "And the aggressive will is
no longer pure." Auden must interpret his hero in terms of
what America promised to be, and what history and observation have shown it to become. He might have done better,
then, to have written a tragedy; or, like Lowell in *The Biglow
Papers* or Melville in *The Confidence-Man,* he might have
drawn characters and symbols from American folklore and
created a biting satire on the failure of our culture "Where
the dream becomes the fact."

Neither tragedy nor satire of such magnitude, however, was
Auden's intention. The litany shows that his intentions were
perhaps not sufficiently clear to himself, since the tone of this
short excerpt changes almost line by line. Like the rest of the
script, it is serious, satirical, and poignant by turns. In a work
of only forty typewritten pages the effect is so self-contradictory
that no consistent direction gives the libretto dramatic force.
And as a play for high-school audiences this operetta has still
other weaknesses. It could only mystify most teen-agers with
its erudite vocabulary, tricky rimes, and sophisticated references to Marx and Freud, while some of the opinions in the
play are perhaps too unconventional to be broadcast in a
public-school auditorium in these times of unadventurous
conformism.

Yet granting all these faults, the libretto lies in undeserved
neglect. In this half-serious comedy Auden treats some of the
aspects of American culture and character which T. S. Eliot
went to England to avoid. Yet now the temper of Auden's

thought is closer to Eliot's than it has ever been in the past. In *Paul Bunyan* we can see his ambivalence toward America: half celebration, half disenchantment. Finding the abundant promise of folk life unfulfilled in America, the poet can hardly follow Paul Bunyan into still another wilderness. He can, however, attempt to live where "an emptiness is named," and contemplate the age of anxiety with the comfort his faith provides.

5. LOUIS UNTERMEYER: THE GLORIOUS PAST

The most recent Bunyan book of any artistic consequence is *The Wonderful Adventures of Paul Bunyan,* by Louis Untermeyer.[28] This is quite a luxury item, copiously illustrated in color and lavishly printed and bound by The Heritage Press. Boys and girls with rich uncles will find the contents as well as the covers of this book enjoyable. In five hundred ways it repeats what has been written before by Laughead, Turney, Shephard, Stevens, Wadsworth, Rounds, and others; but always with a difference. The distinction is very simple: Mr. Untermeyer has one great advantage over the popularizers, and that is good writing. He has the style to capture the tactile surfaces of experiences, and the imagination to give the myths dramatic organization. In a little space I will quote from his book to prove it. First I wish to take up another source of his superiority over his predecessors in juvenile Bunyan fiction. This is his literary method.

His method is bound up with his style. Both together produce something no other juvenile writer has been able to make of Paul Bunyan: a believable fantasy. In this book Paul is surrounded by a coterie of companions—Johnny Inkslinger, Hot Biscuit Slim, Febold Feboldson, Little Meery, Shanty Boy, and Galloping Kid. Most of these names are familiar. But Untermeyer's characters resemble their namesakes in Stevens only in name and occupation. Here everyone is a hero—not quite so much a one as Paul himself, but a somewhat smaller prodigy cut from the same pattern. Feboldson actually is a latter-day hero of the Midwest, "discovered" by Paul Beath a few years ago.[29] He seems to be a master mechanic patterned after Paul, but I doubt that Febold stories were told in oral tradition *before* Mr. Beath made his discovery public. Galloping Kid is an ex-cowboy. Later in the book we meet a pommel-puller still on the job: Pecos Bill, the hero of the western range. This is fine high-spirited stuff at which we will look in a moment.

In a general way the plan of Mr. Untermeyer's book follows the gradually changing outline of Bunyan's adventures first perceived by Stuart Sherman (See Section 7, Chapter IV). He begins in the East as a superlumberjack, and takes on the attributes of a nature myth in his westward travels. Mr. Untermeyer, however, has kept his hero a lumberjack throughout, and does not attempt to convert him into a symbol of commercial life. Not until the final chapter, when the land has run out of trees, does Paul turn from lumbering (and occasional hunting) to other occupations. He briefly engages in construction work, and in farming, but both he and his men find these activities uncongenial. Paul leaves for Alaska where there is real work to be done. The men, however, have discovered women, and have a hankering for home, family, and less strenuous labors. This conclusion follows the Stevens formula for ending the Bunyan tales, but there is a world of difference in feeling between Mr. Stevens' crude and corny betrayal of "Hesomeness" and the poignant realization of Mr. Untermeyer's Paul that his work in this country is over.

Drawing on the previous books about Bunyan by Stevens, Shephard, and Turney,[30] Mr. Untermeyer has exercised discrimination in choosing what he wanted from an overabundance of materials. He achieves a certain unity, at least by comparison with the popularizations, by sticking close to the logging stories. His immediate sources are secondary, yet he captures the gusto of frontier yarning much more successfully than do the authors who furnished him the tales he retells. He recounts the *Wonderful Adventures* by two narrative methods. One is similar to theirs: rambling, discursive, but much better written, with description crisper and more convincing. The other resembles the craft of the ante-bellum writers: pyramiding of comic tensions, dramatizing the narrative by use of several characters for competitive yarning, and the skillful use of a supple vernacular prose.

The most noteworthy chapter in this respect is the third, "Around the Fire." It begins with a meal. After they have eaten, Paul suggests that they look at a tree they have just chopped down. (They felled the tree as in the MacGillivray story; see Section 2, Chapter I.) "That tree isn't just lumber, it's history," Paul says. On the tree's rings he traces the dates of the Civil War, Washington crossing the Delaware, Columbus discovering America, and finally, the center ring shows the date "when Adam and Eve took their first walk in the Garden of Eden."[31] The men are silent for a bit, till Johnny Inkslinger speaks up. He can match history with the story of a tremendous cornstalk—to which he adds a few new flourishes. But the Galloping Kid won't be outdone by that. Back in Montana, where he comes from, there's a mighty remarkable sheep-counter. He could look at a herd of sheep and tell you in a minute how many sheep were there. How does he do it? "It's easy. I just count their feet and divide by four." Hot Biscuit Slim has a better one than that: "Iowa may be the state for corn, and Montana for sheep, but Texas is the place for temperature." Seems a man from Texas went to Michigan, and the first snowflake he saw stiffened him out so he wouldn't come to. As a favor to his folks they decided to cremate him and ship his ashes home.

Two hours later they opened the door of the oven, and there was the man from Texas sitting bolt upright. He was shivering.

"Hey there!" he yelled, "close that door! Do you want me to catch my death of cold in a draft like this!"[32]

Well, only Febold has yet to speak. After some urging, he finally agrees:

"All right," he said, "I'll talk about mules. Leastways I'll talk about one mule. Coal black. Name of Mabel. Wonderful worker. Couldn't be led and couldn't be licked; but she never knew when she had enough."

One day it seemed Mabel had died, so they skinned her for her hide. Next day they found her standing on all fours, "mostly good as ever. She had just been tired and had gone to sleep, and hadn't waked up during the skinning. You couldn't lick Mabel." Of course, they couldn't leave her like that; so they got a sheepskin, spread it over her, and fastened it with blackberry thorns. "You couldn't hardly tell the difference—it was a black sheep skin just as black as Mabel."

"Come Spring at shearing time Mabel had grown the thickest wool coat you ever saw. They sheared eighty pounds off her back. And, underneath the wool, where the blackberry thorns had gone through the sheep skin, they picked forty-five quarts of blackberries!"

As they take off their boots, Shanty Boy strums his guitar and sings:

We're goin' out to Michigan
To chop that tall jack-pine.

He kept on strumming for another minute or two. Then he, too, turned in. You couldn't hear a thing except the whip-poor-wills still echoing each other, and a deep breath that was maybe the men or maybe the forest yawning. Then the whip-poor-wills got tired and stopped. Even the earth stopped breathing. It was quieter than the Day before Creation.

This is an effective introduction to the characters and the fabulous world in which they move. In the next chapter everyone is heading for Paul's camp, and Paul tries to devise a way to count them. He tries multiplying the fallen trees by three, but that doesn't work. Then he figures he'll divide the number of hotcakes by twenty, since that's how many each man eats for breakfast. Here Mr. Untermeyer allows himself to be detoured in the fashion of Mrs. Shephard, as he describes the griddle, how it was made, how Paul brought it to camp, how hotcakes are a specialty with Slim, what reveille was like at Paul's camp. . . . Finally Johnny reminds him that counting hotcakes won't count men because they eat the cakes so fast Slim can't keep track of them.

Next is the Winter of the Blue Snow, and the monsters are appropriated from Mrs. Shephard.[33] These animals attack the camp. Each of the men conquers one of them, and Paul fights the dread Guyascutus, which he tames as a kitten and keeps for a pet. This chapter should be the last word on how Bunyan conquered fear of animals in the lumbercamps.

As in Stevens, Paul finds Babe in the Great Lakes, and feeds him until he is big enough to work. As in Shephard, he measures 42½ axehandles and a box of tobacco between the eyes. But in other descriptions Mr. Untermeyer demonstrates a style no mere popularizer had achieved:

It was a pretty sight to see. The log raft floating away, Paul singing and Babe pawing the ground. The big blue water and the white logs flashing by in the sunshine. And there was the smell of the pine and balsam sweetening the air. And there were the sounds of the forest far off—the scolding of the squirrel, the call of the thrush, and the axes biting into the clean wood.[34]

This is but one of a great many passages in which the sentient qualities of experience are vividly evoked. These descriptions give immediacy and reality to the whole book, and by their strong sensory appeal they help win acceptance for the fabulous yarns which surround them. This seems a sophisticated level of the practice of the oral raconteurs, who interspersed their fantasies with realistic references to the life around them. This particular style of descriptive prose, however, is not evolved directly from the oral tradition. The style has been seen before. It was perfected in the greatest book which ever drew upon the folklore of the frontier:

The river looked miles and miles across. The moon was so bright I could 'a' counted the drift-logs that went a-slipping along, black and still, hundreds of yards out from shore. Everything was dead quiet, and it looked late, and *smelt* late. You know what I mean—I don't know the words to put it in.

This, of course, is from *Huckleberry Finn*.[35]

Untermeyer injects a new note into the Bunyan stories by incorporating into them another strand of folklore: the Big Rock Candy Mountain. Adapting this song from the hobo jungles[36] for juvenile consumption, Untermeyer changes "the rock-and-rye springs" to "lemonade" but all in all what remains is a lumberjack Land of Cockaigne. Interesting in this connection is an interpretation of "Paul Bunyan and Rip Van Winkle," by Louis LeFevre, in which Paul is seen as "the drive of impotent mankind for power," and Rip as "the age-old rebellion . . . against the compulsion of irksome labor."[37] Here momentarily we have a combination of both, but of course the power drive is dominant, and so Mr. Untermeyer soon has Paul on his way again. He logs the Mountain That Stood on its Head; the lumberjacks ride Sidehill Winders, which have one set of short legs for climbing hills. The chapter, "Paul's Hunting," is another respite from logging as Untermeyer retells the old yarns about using one bullet to bag a fantastic catch of game.

Another pause is the arrival of Pecos Bill, whose biography takes up most of the ninth chapter. When his father's plow horse died, Pecos Bill stepped into harness; this is reminiscent of "Sut Lovingood's Daddy Acting Horse."[38] When Bill's father finds "There are folks livin' in another cabin less than three days' walk from here," he cries, "This state's gettin' too crowded. We're headin' west where a man can have elbowroom!" This calls to mind Dan Boone's famous cry. Little Bill strays into a cave of coyotes, and like the folk heroes of many another wilderness, he is raised by beasts and thinks himself one of them. Rejoining humankind at fifteen, he learns all the tricks of the cowboys, but never forgets his animal wisdom. Thus, like Paul Bunyan, Pecos Bill is a demigod with powers over nature. He rides into Paul's camp:

"Yeeeow! I'm a ring-tailed roarer!" he shouted gleefully digging in his spurs and swinging the live rattlesnake until it whistled about the lion's ears. "I ride cyclones; I give a hurricane a head-start and beat it by a mile! I outstare the sun, and lightning bounces off my back! I can run faster, jump higher, dive deeper, stay down longer, and come out dryer than any man alive! I can straddle an earthquake, and—listen to me spout!"

·   ·   ·   ·   ·   ·   ·   ·   ·   ·   ·   ·   ·   ·

"Stranger," said Paul, "you come mighty sudden. Where are you from and where do you think you're going?"

That's a challenge to Bill, and "the battle raged for hours." Of course they fight to a draw. At last Paul says, "Let's you and me have some breakfast." After a short stay, Bill moves on; Paul "couldn't hold Pecos Bill any more than you can gather moonshine or hold the wind in your fist."[39]

As they log their way across the country, most of the best things that happened to Paul in other books happen to him and his crew in this one. At last they reach the coast and build the Columbia River. Then things start to go wrong somehow. Babe overeats, and before he recovers he swallows the stove. There is little logging to do, and the men seem to lose interest in their work. It is spring, and they have discovered girls. One of the women speaks to Paul, asking him to "let the men go. You will tell me that you need them. But we women need them more."

"But the work?" said Paul.

"The work will get done," she said lightly. "You're the mightiest logger in the world. . . . But what you don't finish will be done by machines. The machines will come in, and the lumberjacks will have to find new places to go—or old places, a ranch or a farm, or just a home."[40]

But Paul must first consult the men. He tells them he's leaving for Alaska. Best place yet: "Salmon as big as whales. Bears weighing over two tons each. Gold, if you want it. . . . Everything you need just for the taking." But one by one his crew declines.

There was a silence which nobody knew how to break until a small sound broke it. It was the sound of a girl laughing.

"It's good-bye then," said Paul. "I've got to go. I don't know what I'll find for Babe and myself, but I'm sure I'll find something. We've all had great times together, and we won't forget them. But—well, I don't know how to say it—and I guess there isn't anything more to say."

He shouldered his axe and was gone.

.   .   .   .

Perhaps he still calls Babe and strides across the mountains; perhaps it is his ghost that roams the earth where the forests used to be. His spirit lives, and the legend grows larger. You won't hear the last of Paul Bunyan until the last tree is down.[41]

There is a dramatic entity in this. An important aspect of the book is the stories Mr. Untermeyer has chosen *not* to put into it: the hundreds of tales in which Paul Bunyan branches out into other industries, and in which he exhibits business acumen. Combining the content of the earlier lumberjack tales with the narrative methods of the ante-bellum regional writers and the crisp, clean prose style of Mark Twain, he sustains a comic intensity and a unity of tone. By not attempting to make Paul Bunyan keep abreast of the times, Untermeyer avoids two courses which would diffuse that intensity and alter the tone. One is to change the hero's character in order to follow the ways in which his attributes were carried into American life after the frontier was closed. This would be to make Paul into a sly and somewhat unscrupulous entrepreneur. The other alternative is to do as Mr. Auden did: keep Paul pure, but show the moral deterioration of "the aggressive will" in the men who surround him.

Instead, Mr. Untermeyer stays in the past, and gives us a story that is at once epical in scope, comic in treatment, and nostalgic in feeling. Bringing into the Bunyan tales such other folk traditions as Pecos Bill and the Big Rock Candy Mountain adds a welcome variety. Untermeyer lets his hero log the land from Portland, Maine, to Portland, Oregon, and puts him through the fabulous paces known in older, simpler times. Then, when his work here is over, and his urge to tame new frontiers no longer stirs men from their bunks at daybreak, Paul Bunyan moves on, free to find another land where he is needed. In that way, America feels poignantly his loss.

6. WHAT DOES THE SYMBOL SYMBOLIZE?

Our four authors have explored a wide range of possibilities in the literary development of the Bunyan stories. Frost worked quite outside the oral and written traditions, drawing upon them only for incidental details and the germ of an idea which he developed in his own way. Like Jonathan

Edwards two centuries earlier, he saw the power and the beauty of Nature; but where the Puritan divine had seen them as the majesty and benevolence of God, the poet called them Paul Bunyan and Paul's wife and joined them in a union of love beyond the profanation of the common world. Sandburg and Auden both followed the concept of Bunyan into modern times, *The People, Yes* with hopeful affirmation, the operetta with disenchanted satire. Untermeyer returned to the original environment of the Bunyan myths with a comic-epic tribute to a bygone era of our history.

Frost and Untermeyer were more successful than Auden or Sandburg in establishing unity of tone and thematic coherence in their semimythical materials. But it is the latter authors who tried to bring Paul Bunyan up to date and give him contemporary significance. What stood in the way of their success?

After his decades of heroic labors, Paul Bunyan in oral tradition and popularization alike has now assumed a guise which is no longer heroic and a burlesque which lacks the deep psychological roots of folk comedy from the frontier. Paul Bunyan lives on in the popular imagination, but he is not the same as he was. In addition to the propagandistic elements in Stevens' books, Paul has been used as a spokesman of varied political views. He appears in an editorial cartoon in the *Country Gentleman* opposing a Missouri Valley Administration.[42] Archie Walker of the Red River Lumber Company received a letter "from Colonel Howe (F.D.R.'s aide) asking him whether the Bunyan motif might be used to popularize the N. R. A. For some reason this never panned out."[43] But in a recent issue of the Ford Motor Company house organ, *Ford Times,* Paul and his Blue Truck, Babe, save the State of California from the wildcat schemes of one Loud-Mouth Johnson, a "progressive."[44] On the other hand, "A commissar of Soviet Russia was interested in the propaganda angle and wanted a copy [of Mr. Laughead's *Marvelous Exploits*] for translation."[45] In addition to such conscious manipulations of the hero, Paul Bunyan continues to be popularized as a symbol of great size and strength. The National Broadcasting Company's western

stations recently carried an elaborate dramatization of Paul
Bunyan,[46] and an educational motion picture on "Paul Bunyan
and Johnny Inkslinger" was released in the spring of 1951.[47]
In neither of these productions did Paul Bunyan resemble his
lumbercamp forebear with much versimilitude.

By now the traditional figure of Bunyan has been quite lost
in these newer manifestations. In popular culture the concept
of Paul Bunyan has become the idealization of giganticism and
success by any means. Hence the smart deals Paul pulls in
Frank Shay's book are, in the public mind, consistent with the
Herculean achievements of Paul Bunyan's earlier days; indeed,
as we have seen, in the books by Laughead, Turney, Shephard,
and Stevens, where the general public first met the hero, his
old-time prowess became increasingly interfused with entre-
preneurial shrewdness.

Yet the material progress of America may in one sense be
viewed as a consequence of the Bunyan idea. While that
achievement has by its very magnitude been epical in scope,
now that we know the human cost of what Mr. Auden called
the impurity of the aggressive will, it is not so easy to take
the comic view of our national destiny. But Paul Bunyan was
a comic demigod for other reasons, reasons which were good
in their time. In the first Paul Bunyan of oral folktale, the
heroism and the comedy developed together out of the same
psychological sources, and so in the telling of the best tales,
heroism and humor were fused in artistic unity. In the second
Paul of the popularizations, these two elements became dis-
jointed: the hero grew larger and larger, more mechanical, less
human, while the fulsome comedy of the frontier shrank to
irrelevant buffoonery. Whoever attempts to create the third
Paul Bunyan in art, as a symbol of American life, is faced with
the difficult task of reconciling these two earlier—and contradictory—portraits of the hero. The first Paul is obviously the
more inviting subject; Mr. Untermeyer accepted the invitation
in his *Wonderful Adventures.* But the second figure is much
closer to contemporary reality. Mr. Sandburg attempted to sub-
stitute Paul I for Paul II, not recognizing the differences be-

tween them. Mr. Auden saw these differences and contrasted Paul I with the popular culture that supplanted him with Paul II; obviously, the earlier Paul is out of place.

But what of the folktales from the original frontier? Did they fare any better in the uses creative authors made of them? No one has ever written a successful epic about Mike Fink or Davy Crockett, although the Crockett stories in the almanacs give many hints of what such an epic might have been like. Yet both the oral tradition in which their adventures were developed, and the almanac and newspaper stories which set them down, contributed significantly to American literature. We have already seen the accomplishments of the ante-bellum humorists in democratizing the language of fiction, portraying local color, and depicting regional fantasy and character. Mark Twain, of course, is the culmination of this tradition, but he is not alone in his uses of the fantasy, characterization, and humor of the folk. Their energy, self-deification, and rhythms of speech contributed to Whitman's thought and style, and thus have influenced American poetry ever since. Howells, in *Their Wedding Journey*, considered the folk hero Sam Patch as an apothegm of American greatness; he reveals his debt to the folk traditions of Yankee character and to earlier regional satirists in his portraits of old Grandfather Latham in *The Lady of the Aroostook*, as well as in the picture of Maine village life in *A Modern Instance* and New England character in *The Rise of Silas Lapham*. And, as Richard Chase has recently made plain, Melville in *Moby-Dick* shows the influence of such phenomena of popular culture as the Barnum sideshow, the folk stereotypes of Yankee, frontier, and Quaker character—indeed the quest for the fabulous beast is itself a motif traditional in American folklore.[48] Ishmael, himself, Chase finds to be "a literary-mythical version of the American folk hero . . . the New England spirit partly Westernized," and traces many parallels between Ishmael and his presumed prototype, Haliburton's Sam Slick.[49] Chase describes Melville's style as that "required by the basic relation between fact and fantasy in American folk art."[50] In *Israel Potter*, Melville turned from the epical view of American folk traditions to their satirical use. The objects of Melville's satire are the failings in the American culture he cherished; these he was to see most clearly in *The Confidence-Man,* the bitterest fable ever written against the background of our native traditions.[51] Melville appropriated the stereotypes of contemporary folklore and popular literature and transformed them into symbolic representations of the American character, of the promise of American democracy, and of the hidden dangers to the American experiment which are inherent in our national temperament and our egalitarian commitment. This is indeed a transfiguration of the homely legends of American folklore. Having subtly blended them with grander myths from classical and Christian traditions, Melville used these native materials with an awareness of potential evil which, by contrast to their optimistic comedy, gives his satire great dramatic power.

Are there further gifts the popular traditions of Paul Bunyan may yet bequeath to American writing? I am afraid we shall not find an epic in Paul Bunyan, or in any other mythical character like him. Perhaps the literary future of Paul Bunyan lies in the direction Melville chose a century ago, an interpretation nobody has yet applied to this hero in our time. Is Paul Bunyan really a Prometheus whose noble visions for mankind are undone by human weakness? This was Mr. Auden's view. Had he traced the development of the original legends into the lineaments of Paul Bunyan's second character, he might have arrived at the thought I am suggesting now. Paul Bunyan may not be the genial demigod he seems. Power without restraint, achievement without moral responsibility, may embody something other than the most admirable features of the American character and the national past. There is a possibility for a stunning satire here, a satire whose hero would wear the mask of Deity and the robes of Epic. When, in due time, these deceptive guises would be cast aside to show the creature that had grown behind them, we might discover why it is Paul Bunyan can no longer assume a human shape, or guide the human spirit toward constructive goals.

Notes to Chapter One

1. See *The Autobiography of David Crockett* with introduction by Hamlin Garland (New York, 1923); Richard M. Dorson, "Sam Patch, Jumping Hero," *New York Folklore Quarterly*, I, 133-51 (August, 1945); Constance Rourke, *American Humor* (New York, 1931), p. 74; and Florence Elberta Barnes, "Strap Buckner of the Texas Frontier," in *Man, Bird & Beast* (Publications of the Texas Folklore Society, VIII [Austin, 1930]), pp. 129-51.

2. Constance Rourke asserted thirty years ago that there was no live prototype for Bunyan. See her article, "Paul Bunyon [*sic*]," *The New Republic*, XXIII, 176 (July 7, 1920). I am certain she was right; for a detailed discussion of the question of Paul Bunyan's origin, see pp. 96-99.

3. This fact has led to the charge that Paul Bunyan did not exist in oral tradition before the tales were first circulated in print. I offer two proofs to the contrary. First is the traditional nature of the stories examined in Chapter III, many of which had been told independently of Bunyan for over a hundred years. Second is the testimony of six ex-lumberjacks from western Pennsylvania and New York State, each of whom was questioned by Professor Herbert Halpert, an experienced folklorist. Dr. Halpert asked his informants how old they were when they first heard about Paul Bunyan; several years later he requestioned the same men, and got consistent answers, which indicate that Paul Bunyan was known in this old lumbering region between 1895 and 1907. (This unpublished material, which Dr. Halpert has generously made available for the present study, is referred to hereafter as "Halpert MS," with key letters indicating the informant, date, and place of interview. See Bibliography, under I A, Tales and Motifs from Oral Tradition.) On the reliability of this data, Dr. Halpert advises: "You'll notice that there's rarely more than a couple of years' difference when a man explains twice when he heard something. I'd place considerable credence in such statements. I think people can associate their *early* memories pretty well, certainly within a 4–5 year span. I've occasionally had the chance to check with other people on the dates someone suggests for an event and there's often considerable

reliability. Not always, of course. On the other hand, it certainly works out better than asking 'How many years ago was that?' . . . When a man refers to the period *after* he was 20, he's likely to be less reliable. Probably early events have less competition and get more firmly fixed." Letter dated July 16, 1951.

4. K. Bernice Stewart and Homer A. Watt, "Legends of Paul Bunyan, Lumberjack," *Transactions of the Wisconsin Academy of Sciences, Arts and Letters,* XVIII, Part ii, 641 (1916).

5. See Edward O'Reilly, "The Saga of Pecos Bill," *Century Magazine,* CVI, 827-33 (October, 1923). Stormalong appears in *Here's Audacity!* by Frank Shay (New York, 1930), pp. 17-31. The best work on Fink is by Walter Blair and Franklin Meine, *Mike Fink, King of Mississippi Keelboatmen* (New York, 1930). See also Guy B. Johnson, *John Henry: Tracking Down a Negro Legend* (Chapel Hill, 1929); and Owen Francis, "The Saga of Joe Magarac, Steelman," *Scribner's,* XC, 505-11 (November, 1931). B. A. Botkin conveniently reprints some of these citations in *A Treasury of American Folklore* (New York, 1944): Pecos Bill, pp. 180-85; Stormalong, 185-92; Fink, 7-9 and 30-50; John Henry, 230-39; Magarac, 246-54.

6. Although the yarns about Mike Fink had circulated widely in ante-bellum newspapers, his fame had been quite forgotten until he was resurrected by Blair and Meine. *Op. cit.,* p. 250.

7. Richard M. Dorson, "America's Comic Demigods," *The American Scholar,* X, 389-401, esp. 391-95 (Autumn, 1941).

8. *Ibid.,* p. 394.

9. *Ibid.,* p. 396.

10. For a recent example see "Paul Bunyan Toss Startles French," *New York Times,* Sunday, January 9, 1949, Sec. 1, p. 44. Paul, attempting to duplicate George Washington's feat of throwing a dollar across the Potomac [*sic*], heaves a wagon wheel across the ocean. Here Bunyan is simply a symbol of size and strength; the story is set in a national frame of reference (the myth about Washington), and has nothing to do with the logging industry or the life of the lumberjacks.

11. James MacGillivray, "The Round River Drive," *Detroit News-Tribune,* July 24, 1910, p. 6, illustrated section. Reprinted in *Legends of Paul Bunyan,* ed. Harold W. Felton (New York, 1947), pp. 335-41.

12. The joke is at least a hundred years old. Dorson, in *Jonathan Draws the Long Bow* (Cambridge, 1946), p. 128, gives a New England version which appeared in the *Exeter News Letter,* October 19, 1841.

13. Douglas Malloch, "The Round River Drive," *The American*

Lumberman, No. 2032, April 25, 1914, p. 33. Reprinted in Felton, *op. cit.,* pp. 341-50, and Botkin, *op. cit.,* pp. 206-12. According to W. W. Charters, "this . . . was the joint production of Mr. Malloch and Mr. MacGillivray." Charters substantiates this statement by quoting his correspondence with MacGillivray; see "Paul Bunyan in 1910," *Journal of American Folklore,* LVII, 189 (July-September, 1944).

14. See note 4.

15. Max Gartenberg, "W. B. Laughead's Great Advertisement," *Journal of American Folklore,* LXIII, 446 (October-December, 1950).

16. Ed Crane, "Paul Bunyan—Hoax or Hero?" *Minneapolis Sunday Tribune,* September 7, 1947, p. 23. Mr. Laughead writes of this interview, "He has colored it up for a Sunday feature, but has his facts straight about the evolution of the Red River version and the circulation of the book." Letter to author dated January 4, 1948.

17. Laughead, *Introducing Mr. Paul Bunyan of Westwood, Cal.* (Minneapolis: The Red River Lumber Company, n.d. [1914]). Westwood was then only one year old. "Westwood (population 2600 and growing) was built during 1913 by The Red River Lumber Company for the benefit of its employees. . . . Most of the population is from Minnesota—old employees of The Red River Lumber Company." The company had recently begun logging operations on its California holdings, but the main offices remained in Minneapolis.

18. Gartenberg, "W. B. Laughead's Great Advertisement," p. 447.

19. Crane, "Paul Bunyan—Hoax or Hero," p. 23.

20. Laughead, *Tales About Paul Bunyan, Vol. II* (Minneapolis: The Red River Lumber Company, n.d.). This title first appeared in 1916; Mr. Laughead writes that the copy he furnished me appeared in 1916 or 1917 (Letter dated July 5, 1951). The pages of neither this nor the first booklet were numbered; the story about Babe appeared on the ninth page of both editions.

21. Laughead, *The Marvelous Exploits of Paul Bunyan* (Minneapolis, 1927), p. 7; *ibid.* (1929), p. 7; *ibid.* (1935), p. 7; *Paul Bunyan and His Big Blue Ox* (1944), p. 7. The editions prior to 1944 had the given title on their title pages, but their covers bore the legend "Paul Bunyan and His Big Blue Ox." As the booklet came to be known by the name on its cover, the title was changed to that name in 1944.

22. Gartenberg, "Laughead's Great Advertisement," p. 448.

23. Robert Frost, "Paul's Wife," *Century Magazine,* CIII, 84-88 (November, 1921). Reprinted in *New Hampshire* (New York, 1923),

pp. 44-48; *Collected Poems* (Garden City, 1936) and (New York, 1949), pp. 235-39; and in *The Pocket Book of Robert Frost's Poems*, ed. Louis Untermeyer (New York, 1936), pp. 40-45.

24. See R. M. Dorson (ed.), *Davy Crockett, American Comic Legend* (New York, 1939), pp. xv-xxvi, 20-23, 47-48. For instance, "Sal Fungus war one of the most poundiferous gals in old Alligator Clearing . . . she could scalp an Injun, skin a bear, grin down hickory nuts, laugh the bark off a pine tree, swim stark up a cataract, gouge out alligator's eyes, dance a rock to pieces, sink a steamboat, blow out the moonlight. . . . But her heart growed too big; and when I left her to go to Texas, it burst like an airthquake, and poor Sal died." (p. 55.)

25. Frost, *Collected Poems*, p. 235.

26. Wayne Martin (as told to B. A. Botkin), "Paul Bunyan on the Water Pipeline," *Folk-Say, A Regional Miscellany* (Norman, Oklahoma, 1929), I, 57-58.

Notes to Chapter Two

1. Earl Clifton Beck, *Songs of the Michigan Lumberjacks* (Ann Arbor, 1942), p. 287.

2. R. M. Dorson, "Folk Traditions of the Upper Peninsula," *Michigan History*, XXXI, 51 (March, 1947).

3. Martha Warren Beckwith, *Folklore in America* (Poughkeepsie, 1930), p. 1. I have drawn upon Chapters I and II of this book for background to the ensuing discussion, and have also used the following sources not indicated by footnotes: Franz Boas, "Literature, Music, and Dance" and "Mythology and Folklore" in *General Anthropology* (Boston, 1938), pp. 589-626; Lord Raglan, "The Scope of Folklore," *Folk-Lore* (London), LVII, 98-105 (September, 1946).

4. Beckwith, *op. cit.*, p. 4.

5. *Ibid.*

6. Stith Thompson, *The Folktale* (New York, 1946), p. 4.

7. Francis B. Gummere, *Old English Ballads* (Boston, 1894), p. xcvii.

8. Ruth Benedict, "Folklore," in *Encyclopedia of the Social Sciences* (New York, 1931), VI, 291.

9. Thompson, *The Folktale*, pp. 4, 428.

10. The most comprehensive demonstration in American scholarship of this approach is Stith Thompson's *Motif-Index of Folk-Literature* (Indiana University Studies, Nos. 96-97, Vol. I [Bloomington, 1932]).

11. Alexander Hagerty Krappe, *The Science of Folk-Lore* (New York, 1930).

12. Thompson, *The Folktale*, p. 434.

13. C. Marius Barbeau, "Contes populaires canadiens," *Journal of American Folklore*, XXIX, 1-136 (January-March, 1916). See also Soeur Marie Ursule, "Le folklore des Lavalois" (Québec, 1947).

14. Barbeau, *Folk-Songs of Old Québec* (National Museum of Canada, n.d.), pp. 9, 11, 24-25, 31-36, 60-64.

15. For a recent survey of some major causes and effects of the unassimilation of French Canada, see Miriam Chapin, "French Canada—Can It Survive?" *Harper's Magazine*, CLXLVII, 80-87 (November, 1948).

16. A. Irving Hallowell, "Myth, Culture and Personality," *American Anthropologist*, XLIX, 547 (October-December, 1947).

17. Benedict, *op. cit.*

18. Henry James, *Hawthorne* (London, 1879); reprinted in *The Shock of Recognition*, ed. Edmund Wilson (Garden City, 1943), p. 428.

19. Dorson, *Jonathan Draws the Long Bow* (Cambridge, 1946), p. 11.

20. Benedict, *op. cit.*

21. Constance Rourke, *Davy Crockett* (New York: Harcourt Brace, 1934), pp. 251-58, contains a complete bibliography of Crockett almanacs.

22. From the title page of *Ben Hardin's Crockett Almanac . . .* (New York & Philadelphia, 1842). Quoted in Rourke, *Davy Crockett*, p. 253.

Notes to Chapter Three

1. C. Lanman, *Adventures in the Wilds of the United States and British Provinces* (Philadelphia, 1856), I, 330, quoted by Richard G. Wood in *A History of Lumbering in Maine, 1820-1861* (Orono, 1935), p. 186.

A philological note on the synonymous terms for "lumberman" is here in order. In their invaluable book of Maine folklore, Fannie Hardy Eckstorm and Mary Winslow Smyth remark, "The use of 'shanty' and 'shanty boy' for 'lumber-camp' and 'lumberman' deserves comment. They are prevailingly Western in use; when found in Maine at present they are comparatively recent introductions from the Provinces or from the West, and in the West they mean respectively what we mean by 'wangan-boat' and 'river-driver.' The

senior editor never heard either word used by any old woodsman.
. . . Yet in all these oldest songs both words are frequently found
instead of the common 'lumbercamp' and 'lumberman.' Clearly the
use was poetical. Probably the words were carried West through
the songs and there found an extension of their meaning." And
again, "This [1916] is the first time the editors ever saw the word
'lumberjack' used by a woodsman. It was not introduced into the
Maine woods until the time of the World War, and is still little
used and less liked by woodsmen. . . . The early word for working
in the woods was 'logger,' which was followed by 'lumberman.' Later
this was reserved for the operators, while the laborers were called
'woodsmen.' Even now, 'woodsmen' is the word always used by the
great companies and the employment offices when advertising for
men to go into the woods." *Minstrelsy of Maine* (Boston, 1927),
pp. 29-30 and 174.

As the present study is not restricted to the folklore of Maine
lumbercamps, I have felt free to use these various terms inter-
changeably.

2. Henry David Thoreau, "Ktaadn," *The Maine Woods* (Boston
& New York, 1906), pp. 5-6.

3. *Ibid.*, pp. 46-48. For an excellent detailed account of early
logging methods see Wood, *History of Lumbering in Maine,* pp.
83-127.

4. Wood, *op. cit.,* p. 229; see also pp. 226-33.

5. Daniel Stanchfield, *History of Pioneer Lumbermen in the
Upper Mississippi* (Collections of the Minnesota Historical Society,
9:346), quoted in Wood, p. 233.

6. Richard M. Dorson, "Folk Traditions of the Upper Peninsula,"
Michigan History, XXXI, 50 (March, 1947). Ninety-four years
earlier, Thoreau too had found the lumberjacks a rough crew: "The
most interesting question entertained at the lumberers' camp was,
which man could 'handle' any other on the carry; and, for the most
part, they possessed no qualities which you could not lay your hands
on." Thoreau chose to sleep in an Indian wigwam rather than the
lumbermen's cabin, because the former was cleaner. *The Maine
Woods,* p. 148.

7. Allan Nevins, *The Emergence of Modern America, 1865-1878*
(New York, 1927), p. 129.

8. Frank Shay, "The Tall Tale in America," in *Folk-Say, A Regional Miscellany,* ed. B. A. Botkin (Norman, Oklahoma, 1930),
p. 129.

9. Here is a fight "Down in Wisconsin fifty years ago" recollected
by ex-lumberjack Swan Olson of Negaunee, Mich.: ". . . So I took

him by the hair—all lumberjacks had long hair—and pumped him up and down in the water. Then finally I pulled him up on the ice. He was pretty well tame. His clothes froze stiff as bark—they were rattling. I hoisted him up into the sprinkler, inside the tank. I pulled the plugs out, and let out the three barrels of water. (If I'd put him on top the tank he'd a fallen off, or froze to death.) I put him into a barrel, and had the horse hoist him up the slide and dump him into the tank. I put the slide on hooks and drove like a son of a gun to the camp, about a mile and a half.

"They took him into town and he never come back no more." Richard M. Dorson, "Personal Histories," *Western Folklore*, VII, 31-32 (January, 1948).

10. For examples, see Phillips Barry, *The Maine Woods Songster* (Cambridge, 1939), pp. 30-31; Earl Clifton Beck, *Songs of the Michigan Lumberjacks* (Ann Arbor, 1942), pp. 92-95; Eckstorm and Smyth, *Minstrelsy of Maine*, pp. 64-70; Franz Rickaby, *Ballads and Songs of the Shanty-Boy* (Cambridge, 1926), pp. 168-72, reprinted in *A Treasury of American Folklore*, ed. B. A. Botkin (New York, 1944), pp. 848-51; and Elmore Vincent, *Lumber Jack Songs with Yodel Arrangements* (Chicago, 1932), pp. 12-13.

11. Rickaby, *op. cit.*

12. Guy B. Johnson, *John Henry, Tracking Down a Negro Legend* (Chapel Hill, 1929), pp. 45-54.

13. From the singing of lumberjack Emery DeNoyer of Rhinebeck, Wisconsin, on American Archive of Folksong Recording No. 5, issued by The Library of Congress, Washington 25, D. C.

The "scaler" is "One who measures logs and estimates the board feet contained in them by use of the logging scale . . . a mathematical table of mensuration . . ." Wilbur A. Davis, "Logger and Splinter-Picker Talk," *Western Folklore*, IX, 122 (April, 1950).

14. For various versions, see Barry, *op. cit.*, pp. 52-53; Beck, *op. cit.*, pp. 133-36; William Main Doerflinger, *Shantymen and Shanty-boys* (New York, 1951), pp. 236-40; Eckstorm and Smyth, *op. cit.*, pp. 82-90; Emelyn Elizabeth Gardiner and Geraldine Jencks Chickering, *Ballads and Songs of Southern Michigan* (Ann Arbor, 1939), pp. 270-72; Roland Palmer Gray, *Songs and Ballads of the Maine Lumberjacks* (Cambridge, 1925), pp. 3-9; Rickaby, *op. cit.*, pp. 11-14, reprinted in Botkin, *op. cit.*, pp. 847-49; and Vincent, *op. cit.*, pp. 2-3.

15. K. Bernice Stewart and Homer A. Watt, "Legends of Paul Bunyan, Lumberjack," *Transactions Wisc. Acad. Sciences, Arts, and Letters*, XVIII, Part ii, 644 (1916); reprinted in *Legends of Paul Bunyan*, ed. Harold W. Felton (New York, 1947), p. 101.

16. See Wood, *History of Lumbering in Maine*, p. 100.

17. Rickaby, *op. cit.;* Botkin, *op. cit.*

18. Beck, *op. cit.*, Nos. 52, 53, 55, 56; Eckstorm and Smyth, *op. cit.*, "The Drowning of John Roberts," pp. 45-48.

19. See note 15.

20. *The Writings of Benjamin Franklin*, ed. Albert Henry Smyth (New York, 1905), I, 292.

21. Beck, *op. cit.*, p. 75.

22. Constance Rourke, *American Humor* (New York: Harcourt Brace, 1931), p. 43.

23. *Ibid.*, p. 76.

24. Franz Boas, "Literature, Music and Dance," *General Anthropology* (Boston, 1938), p. 594.

25. Rourke, *American Humor*, Chapters I and II; Walter Blair, *Native American Humor* (New York, 1937), pp. 3-101.

26. Blair, *op. cit.*, p. 23.

27. See Dorson, *Jonathan Draws the Long Bow* (Cambridge, 1946), Chapters I, III, and IV; and Botkin, *A Treasury of New England Folklore* (New York, 1947), Parts I-III.

28. Seba Smith, *The Life and Writings of Major Jack Downing of Downingville, Away Down East in the State of Maine* (Boston, 1833); *'Way Down East or Portraitures of Yankee Life* (Philadelphia, 1866).

29. Rourke, *American Humor*, p. 76.

30. Beck, *Songs of the Michigan Lumberjacks*, pp. 285-86. Herbert Halpert reported some of these comic motifs current in 1945 in Alberta, Canada, and among American servicemen from the South. For clinching the mosquito bills, see "Tales from Calgary, Alberta," *California Folklore Quarterly*, IV, 45 (January, 1945), and "Tales Told by Soldiers," No. 16, *ibid.*, p. 372 (October, 1945). In the latter article, Nos. 14A and 14B give variants of the still bigger mosquitoes. These yarns recorded by Professor Halpert were told separately, each as a story unto itself, with no mention of Paul Bunyan.

31. The unexpected twist at the end of the story is a device which Mark Twain recognized as characteristic of the oral anecdote; he used it in Jim Baker's story of the bluejay who filled a cabin with nuts. See *A Tramp Abroad* (Hartford, 1879), pp. 27-32.

32. Dorson reprints an account published in 1675 by John Josselyn "of a Sea-Serpent . . . that lay quoiled up like a Cable upon a Rock at Cape-Ann." A generation earlier, in 1641, Obediah Turner reported that "at Cape Ann ye people have seene a monster like unto this, wch did there come out of ye sea. . . . And my praier to God

is yt be not ye olde serpent spoken of in holie scripture yt tempted our greate mother Eve and whose poison hath run downe even unto us, so greatlie to our discomforte and ruin." *Jonathan Draws the Long Bow*, pp. 26-27; 133, 134-137.

33. For a contemporary Italian-American survival, see D. G. Hoffman, "Stregas, Ghosts and Werewolves," *New York Folklore Quarterly*, III, 325-28 (Winter, 1947).

34. For descriptions of other such creatures, see *The American Imagination at Work*, ed. Ben C. Clough (New York, 1947), pp. 200-222.

35. Marjorie Edgar, "Imaginary Animals of Northern Minnesota," *Minnesota History*, XXI, 353-56 (1940).

36. Stewart and Watt, "Legends of Paul Bunyan, Lumberjack," p. 647.

37. Even Audubon enjoyed playing tricks of this kind. For an account of how he hoaxed the naturalist Rafinesque, see Rourke, *American Humor*, pp. 50-53.

38. *Sketches & Eccentricities of Colonel David Crockett of West Tennessee* (New York, 1833), p. 164; reprinted in Botkin, *A Treasury of American Folklore*, p. 56.

39. Rourke, *American Humor*, Chapter II.

40. Transcribed from the recitation of lumberjack Perry Allen, St. Louis, Michigan, 1938; recorded by Alan Lomax for the Folklore Section, Music Division, Library of Congress. Recording No. 2264-B2.

Another possible source of this tale in actual experience is suggested by Thoreau in his essay on "Ktaadn": "Now and then we passed what McCauslin called a pokelogan, an Indian term for what the drivers might have reason to call a poke-logs-in, an inlet that leads nowhere. If you get in, you have got to get out again the same way. These, and the frequent 'runrounds' which come into the river again, would embarrass an inexperienced voyager not a little." *The Maine Woods*, p. 56.

41. For an instance of how discursive, redundant, and uninteresting an oral tale may sound from the lips of an inept raconteur, compare the recorded version of "The Round River Drive" by Bill McBride, Library of Congress Recordings 2259-B2 and 2260-A1, with Perry Allen's. See also James MacGillivray, "The Round River Drive," in Felton, *Legends of Paul Bunyan*, pp. 339-41.

42. An IWW publicist, Walker C. Smith, tells the shocking story of company town vigilantes firing broadsides into a boatload of workers who had sailed from Seattle to Everett, Washington, on Sunday, November 5, 1916, to hold a free speech rally. At least six workers were killed, but no inquest was held into their deaths. Two

vigilantes died, possibly from the drunken marksmanship of their fellow deputies. After the massacre, 74 of the workers were imprisoned for weeks, deprived of their right of counsel, beaten, fed on gruel, and indicted for murder. Finally, after protracted litigation, the Wobblies were cleared. *The Everett Massacre: A History of the Class Struggle in the Lumber Industry* (Chicago, n.d.).

43. For two versions of "the truth" about Joe Hill, see Wallace Stegner, "I Dreamed I Saw Joe Hill Last Night," *Pacific Spectator,* I, 184-87 (Spring, 1947); and Ralph Chaplin, *Wobbly* (Chicago, 1948), pp. 184-93. For songs by Joe Hill, see *Rebel Song Book,* ed. Samuel H. Friedman (New York, 1935), pp. 54, 56-57.

44. Perry Allen, Library of Congress Recording No. 2265-B2.

45. Edward O. Tabor and Stith Thompson, who worked together as lumberjacks at Palmer, Oregon, four years before Mr. Laughead's first booklet appeared, reported this and some of the following motifs in notes they kept at that time. See their note, "Paul Bunyan in 1910," *Journal of American Folklore,* LIX, 135 (April-June, 1946). Laughead gives this motif too, in *Introducing Mr. Paul Bunyan . . .* (1914), p. 4; *Tales About Paul Bunyan . . .* (1916), p. 2; *The Marvelous Exploits of Paul Bunyan* (1922 and all subsequent editions), p. 7. He also tells us that Paul dug the Great Lakes as Babe's water hole (pp. 4, 2, and 33, respectively, in the above editions; p. 20 in the 1944 printing).

46. Robert P. Tristram Coffin, "Paul's Lake," in *Primer for Americans* (New York, 1943), p. 68. This is a rimed version of a tale which Coffin claims to have heard from his father's hired man.

47. Tabor and Thompson, "Paul Bunyan in 1910," p. 134.

48. In MacGillivray's "Round River Drive" the snow is black.

49. MacGillivray, *op. cit.,* p. 338 in Felton's *Legends of Paul Bunyan.*

50. Rourke, *American Humor,* pp. 37–38. See Thoreau's *Walden* (Modern Library edition, p. 294) for an earlier version.

51. *Davy Crockett, American Comic Legend,* ed. Richard M. Dorson (New York, 1939), p. 14.

52. Rourke, *Davy Crockett* (New York, 1934), pp. 241-43; also in Blair, *Native American Humor,* pp. 285-86.

53. Dorson, *Davy Crockett . . .,* p. 10.

54. Tabor and Thompson, "Paul Bunyan in 1910," p. 135; Stewart and Watt, "Legends of Paul Bunyan, Lumberjack," pp. 643-44; Mac-Gillivray in Felton, *Legends of Paul Bunyan,* pp. 337-38.

55. Rourke, *American Humor,* pp. 46-48.

56. MacGillivray in Felton, *op. cit.,* pp. 336-37.

57. Laughead, *Marvelous Exploits* (1922 *et seq.*), p. 16; *Paul Bunyan and His Big Blue Ox* (1944), p. 30.

58. Bill McBride's recitation on Library of Congress Recording No. 2260-A1.

59. Halpert MS "C." (See Bibliography, I, A.)

60. Notation on Halpert MS "C."

61. Stewart and Watt, *op. cit.*, pp. 647-48.

62. Dorson, *Jonathan Draws the Long Bow*, pp. 81-82.

63. Blair, *Native American Humor*, pp. 28-29.

64. Dorson, *op. cit.*, pp. 82, 83-85.

65. "The Pedlar's Fright," from *Mince Pie for the Million* (Philadelphia & New York, 1846); reprinted in Dorson, *Davy Crockett . . .*, pp. 130-31, and also in Botkin, *A Treasury of American Folklore*, p. 389.

66. Albert D. Richardson, *Beyond the Mississippi . . .* (Hartford, 1867), pp. 137-38, 140-41; reprinted in Botkin, *op. cit.*, p. 395.

67. John Lee Brooks, "Paul Bunyan: American Folk Hero" (Unpublished Master's thesis, Southern Methodist University, 1927), p. 40.

68. *Ibid.*, pp. 40-41.

69. *Ibid.*, p. 35.

70. *Ibid.*, pp. 31-32. Note the similarity to the John Henry story suggested here.

71. *Ibid.*

72. Tabor and Thompson, "Paul Bunyan in 1910," p. 134. Stewart and Watt found some tales about Paul Bunyan's childhood on his father's farm, which "seem to be . . . like the animal fables [about fantastic creatures], mere appendages." *Op. cit.*, p. 648. Later, W. B. Laughead was to expand these hints, naming several members of the Bunyan family. See Chapter IV.

73. Halpert MS "D."

74. Halpert MS "E–1."

75. Laughead in 1914 had "colored boys with hams tied to their feet skate around on the griddles to grease them. No one but the colored brethren could stand the heat." (*Introducing Mr. Paul Bunyan . . .*, p. 15.) By 1944, however, he had eliminated these offensive remarks. Now the motif reads, "The griddle was greased by boys who skated . . ." (*Paul Bunyan and His Big Blue Ox*, p. 13). The earlier version, however, was probably closer to the oral tradition; thus we find "Negroes" in MacGillivray (Felton, *op. cit.*, p. 336), and "two niggers" in "Shock" Wormuth's version, 1946, although when he told the same story five years earlier he had mentioned "four, five men" instead (Halpert MS "E-2" and "E-1").

Still another variation was given me by Mr. Theodore White of Philadelphia, who was at Boulder Dam in 1932 and learned, from a photographer named Ben Galaha, that the hams were strapped to the ox's feet!

76. Tabor and Thompson, *op. cit.;* Stewart and Watt, *op. cit.,* p. 643; MacGillivray, *op. cit.,* p. 337; Harold W. Thompson, *Body, Boots & Britches* (Philadelphia, 1940), p. 131.

77. Laughead, *Introducing Mr. Paul Bunyan . . .,* p. 17; Stewart and Watt, *op. cit.,* pp. 642-43; Laughead, *Paul Bunyan* (1944), p. 13.

78. Laughead (1914), p. 14.

79. For some "cute Yankee tricks," see Dorson, *Jonathan Draws the Long Bow,* pp. 78-94; also Botkin, *A Treasury of American Folklore,* pp. 18-82.

80. Wayne Martin (as told to B. A. Botkin), "Paul Bunyan on the Water Pipeline," in *Folk-Say, A Regional Miscellany,* ed. Botkin (Norman, Oklahoma, 1929), I, 57-58; reprinted in *A Treasury of American Folklore,* p. 628. Wayne Martin's stories are derived from such unBunyanesque sources as a poem by James Whitcomb Riley and short stories from *The Saturday Evening Post* (*ibid.,* p. 626, note), and demonstrate the second round of the oral tradition—referred to as Dorson's fourth stage in the development of the American folk hero. See Chapter I.

In the Halpert MS, text "C," Paul builds a buttermilk pipeline to Buffalo, where he also erects a ferris wheel and sells Dutchmen rides and drinks at once. The Dutchmen were so greedy that they drank till they "busted,"—"and Paul would throw 'em over on the Canadian side." Evidently this fragmentary text is all that remains of a yarn satirizing the Germans, but what the story ever had to do with Paul Bunyan as a lumberjack is not at all apparent.

81. See *The (Old) Farmer's Almanack . . . for the Year of Our Lord 1947* (Dublin, N. H., 1946), pp. 47-48, for the tale of the "sharp trader" who outwitted himself when he sold his own whiskers.

82. Rourke, "Paul Bunyon," *The New Republic,* XXIII, 179 (July 7, 1920).

83. James Stevens reconstructs such a conversation in "An Old Logger's Foreword" to Felton's *Legends of Paul Bunyan,* p. ix. This is quite unlike the method Mr. Stevens himself uses in his own stories about Paul Bunyan.

84. Mark Twain, *Life on the Mississippi* (New York, 1917), pp. 22-23.

85. Emerson Bennet, *Mike Fink: A Legend of the Ohio* (Cincinnati, 1848), pp. 24, 83, quoted in Botkin, *op. cit.,* p. 57.

86. Laughead, *The Marvelous Exploits* . . . (1935), p. 2; *Paul Bunyan and His Big Blue Ox* (1944), p. 2.

87. See Stith Thompson, *Motif-Index of Folk-Literature* (Bloomington, Indiana, 1932), Sections J and K, "The Wise and Foolish" and "Deception."

88. Mody C. Boatright, *Folk Laughter on the American Frontier* (New York, 1949), p. 61.

89. Perry Allen, Library of Congress Recording No. 2264-B2.

90. The motifs which comprise this masterful little yarn are scattered throughout Laughead's *Marvelous Exploits* (1922 and subsequent editions), but their combination in this story, and the dramatic style, are apparently Perry Allen's own work. Thus, on p. 11, Laughead writes, ". . . an idea of the size of the tables is gained from the fact that they distributed the pepper with four-horse teams"; on p. 13, "It used to be a big job to haul prune pits and coffee grounds away from Paul's camps." Note how Perry Allen put himself into the story, and tightened up the language of these passages. His talents as a raconteur will be examined in Section 10 of this chapter.

91. Rourke, "Paul Bunyon," *The New Republic*, XXIII, 177 (July 7, 1920).

92. Brooks, "Paul Bunyan: American Folk Hero," pp. 21-22. For a similar description of how tales—in this case, not about Paul Bunyan— were told "when some greenhorn or tenderfoot—an eastern visitor, was present," see Herbert Halpert, "Tall Tales from Calgary, Alberta," *California Folklore Quarterly*, IV, 32 (1945).

93. Dorson, *Davy Crockett, American Comic Legend*, p. xviii. This tradition is still going strong in Al Capp's comic strip, "Li'l Abner."

94. MacGillivray, in Felton's *Legends of Paul Bunyan*, p. 339.

95. Dorson, *op. cit.*, p. 123.

96. Brooks, *op. cit.*, p. 41.

97. The substitution of mechanical process for a character's personal identity occurs in more sophisticated arts than this folktale fragment. Compare, for instance, Charlie Chaplin's metamorphosis into a walking cogwheel in *Modern Times*. And John Dos Passos has his journalist-hero Jimmy Herf (in *Manhattan Transfer*) sum up ten years of his life as a one-paragraph news story (Penguin edition), p. 324.

98. Perry Allen, Library of Congress Recording No. 2265-B2. For several motifs from oral tradition of sounds freezing in the air and not being heard until spring, see Halpert, "Tall Tales from Calgary,

Alberta," Nos. 28-30, and additional references in appended notes, *California Folklore Quarterly*, IV, 43 (1945).

99. Beck, *Songs of the Michigan Lumberjacks*, p. 5.

100. See note 90.

101. Perry Allen, Library of Congress Recordings 2265–B2 and 2266–B2.

102. Laughead, *The Marvelous Exploits of Paul Bunyan* (1927), pp. 7 and 36. I am indebted to Mr. Max Gartenberg for having suggested these parallels. If Perry Allen actually had a copy of Mr. Laughead's booklet, it was probably an edition which contains the introduction used in 1927 and 1929 (and perhaps in other editions which I have not seen), since Allen also knew the story of Paul Bunyan's birth which Mr. Laughead quoted in those editions from an article by Esther Shephard (see Section 5, Chapter IV). By the 1935 edition, Laughead had dropped his earlier introduction.

103. "Some of us . . . had no idea when we were writing that the job would ever be read by serious critics or historians. If we had we might have kept some record of when, where, how, and from whom we got the stories." Letter from W. B. Laughead, dated June 25, 1951.

104. Laughead, *The Marvelous Exploits . . .* (1927), p. 26.

105. According to Herbert Halpert, who also recorded tales from Perry Allen, Perry is the exceptional lumberjack who makes a conscious effort to connect his motifs.

106. Dorson, *Davy Crockett . . .* , pp. 25-26.

Notes to Chapter Four

1. The development of the arts in a heterogeneous democratic society is best described by de Tocqueville in *Democracy in America* (New York, 1945), Part II, Chapters 9, 11, 13-14. The triple cleavage is discussed in some detail by Dwight Macdonald, "A Theory of Popular Culture," *Politics*, I, 20-23 (February, 1944); for an application to music, see D. G. Hoffman, "The Folk Art of Jazz," *Antioch Review*, V, 110-20 (Spring, 1945).

2. Walter Blair, *Native American Humor* (New York, 1937), pp. 63-64.

3. *Ibid.*, pp. 75-79.

4. The phrase is the title of a book by John S. Robb (Philadelphia: Carey and Hart, 1846).

5. Quoted in Blair, *op. cit.*, p. 66.

6. Thomas Bangs Thorpe, "The Big Bear of Arkansas," first published in *The Spirit of the Times*, 1841; reprinted by Thorpe in *The Hive of "The Bee Hunter"* (New York, 1854) and by Blair, *op. cit.*, pp. 337-48.

7. Blair, *op. cit.*, pp. 337-38.

8. *Ibid.*, p. 338.

9. *Ibid.*, pp. 338-40.

10. *Ibid.*, p. 340.

11. *Ibid.*, pp. 341-42.

12. *Ibid.*, p. 342.

13. *Ibid.*, pp. 342-43.

14. *Ibid.*, p. 345.

15. *Ibid.*, p. 347.

16. *Ibid.*, p. 348.

17. Judge (Thomas Chandler) Haliburton, *Sam Slick: The Clockmaker* (Philadelphia, n.d. [1836?]), pp. 15, 16; also in Blair, *op. cit.*, p. 229.

18. Haliburton, *op. cit.*, p. 18; Blair, *op. cit.*, pp. 231-32.

19. Haliburton, *The Attaché; or Sam Slick in England* (New York, 1856), p. 87; also in Blair, *op. cit.*, p. 236.

20. Augustus B. Longstreet, *Georgia Scenes* . . . (Atlanta, 1835). "The Horse Swap" is reprinted by William Rose Benét and Norman H. Pearson in *The Oxford Anthology of American Literature* (New York, 1938), I, 308-12.

21. Joseph G. Baldwin, *Flush Times in Alabama and Mississippi* (New York, 1853). The chapter, "Ovid Bolus, Esquire," is reprinted in Blair, *op. cit.*, pp. 356-67; selections quoted from pp. 357, 358-59. Baldwin's mock-heroic treatment of frontier material is evident in the name of his character.

22. George W. Harris, *Sut Lovingood* (New York, 1867), p. 40.

23. *Ibid.*, p. 44.

24. Johnson J. Hooper, *Adventures of Captain Simon Suggs* . . . (Philadelphia, 1843), p. 24.

25. Harris, "Parson John Bullen's Lizards," *op. cit.*, pp. 48-49.

26. Hooper, "Captain Simon Suggs Attends a Camp Meeting," *op. cit.*, pp. 118-33; reprinted in Blair, *op. cit.*, pp. 316-25.

27. Hooper, "A Night at the Ugly Man's," *The Widow Rugby's Husband* (Philadelphia, 1851), pp. 41-51. Passage quoted from p. 45.

28. W. B. Laughead, letter dated July 6, 1951.

29. *Ibid.*

30. *Ibid.*

31. Tabor and Thompson, "Paul Bunyan in 1910," *Journal of American Folklore,* LIX, 134 (April-June, 1936).

32. Max Gartenberg, "W. B. Laughead's Great Advertisement," quotes a letter from Laughead to this effect, with corroboration from Esther Shephard. *Journal of American Folklore,* LXIII, 447 (October-December, 1950).

33. As I could not obtain a copy of the 1922 edition of *The Marvelous Exploits of Paul Bunyan,* I give the pagination of the 1927 printing, which I assume to be identical with it.

34. *Paul Bunyan* . . . (1944), p. 26.

35. *Ibid.*

36. *Ibid.*

37. *Ibid.,* p. 27.

38. *Ibid.,* p. 30.

39. *Ibid.,* p. 31.

40. *Ibid.,* p. 38.

41. *Ibid.,* pp. 18-19.

42. *Ibid.,* p. 29.

43. *Ibid.,* p. 17.

44. *Ibid.,* p. 41.

45. *Ibid.*

46. The story of the stretching harness is here (*ibid.,* p. 8), as is the yarn about the pea-soup pond (p. 9). Bunyan's kitchen is described too (p. 13).

47. *Ibid.,* p. 34. For one source of Big Ole, see Laughead's account of how he named his characters, quoted on p. 80. Laughead adds, "For Ole there was also a recollection of a strong man who carried a heavy load, sinking knee-deep in solid rock. He could have had an origin in connection with Paul Bunyan. Some say it was Paul who sank into solid rock." Quoted by Gartenberg, "Laughead's Great Advertisement," p. 447.

48. *Paul Bunyan* . . . (1944), p. 25.

49. *Ibid.,* p. 20.

50. *Ibid.,* p. 14. This motif was recently culled from oral tradition. Ex-woodsman "Shock" Wormuth of Shinhopple, New York, told Herbert Halpert that Paul "kept two or three men with wheelbarrows wheelin' prune pits out o' the camp. The chipmunks fed on them there and got as large as tigers—and they called 'em 'tigermunks.'" Halpert MS "E-2."

51. *Paul Bunyan and His Great Blue Ox,* p. 16. Laughead writes, "I had heard of double end mosquitoes in connection with Paul. Bringing bees overland on foot has been told of other frontier characters, but whether this preceded the Paul Bunyan myth or not I

do not know." Quoted by Gartenberg, "Laughead's Great Advertisement," p. 447.

52. *Paul Bunyan* . . . , p. 17. "The Ant story p. 23 of '27, '29, and '35 editions was a faked story and was dropped from later editions." Letter dated July 6, 1951. Apparently Mr. Laughead misremembered, for the story is still in the 1944 edition, p. 17, with "roadhouses" replacing the earlier "bootleggers" and "cars" replacing "automobiles."

53. Laughead writes, "About 'Benny' for the little blue ox, I am not so sure, but probably invented it. He is made up from scraps and it is possible I had heard him named." Quoted in Gartenberg, *op. cit.*, p. 447.

54. *Paul Bunyan and His Big Blue Ox*, p. 29.

55. See pp. 55-56.

56. *Paul Bunyan* . . . , pp. 40-41.

57. Gartenberg, *op. cit.*

58. *Paul Bunyan* . . . , p. 43. The hair-combing motif is reminiscent of a stanza from "Old Dan Tucker."

59. Letter from W. B. Laughead dated July 6, 1951.

60. *Ibid.; Paul Bunyan's Playground* (Minneapolis, n.d.).

61. Ida Virginia Turney, *Paul Bunyan Comes West* (Boston, 1928), p. viii. This is a reissue by Houghton Mifflin of the 1916 chapbook, which is now out of print and very difficult to obtain. Mr. Dale Warren of Houghton Mifflin Co. informs me that the 1928 book "was slightly enlarged from the material contained in the pamphlet." Letter dated January 31, 1949.

62. *Ibid.*, pp. 4-5.

63. *Ibid.*, pp. 7, 33.

64. *Ibid.*, pp. 25-27.

65. *Ibid.*, p. 23.

66. *Ibid.*, p. 38.

67. *Ibid.*, pp. 41-42.

68. *Ibid.*, p. 37.

69. *Ibid.*, p. 28.

70. *Ibid.*, pp. 6-7.

71. *Ibid.*, p. 23.

72. Charles Oluf Olsen, "Analytical Notes on Paul Bunyan" (Typewritten ms, Portland, Oregon, 1938), p. 041.

73. Homer A. Watt, "Notes" to "Paul Bunyan Provides for His Crew," in *The Rise of Realism*, ed. Louis Wann (New York, 1933), p. 779.

74. Esther Shephard, *Paul Bunyan* (New York: Harcourt Brace, 1924), p. v.

75. *Ibid.*, pp. xi-xii.

76. Shephard, "The Tall Tale in American Literature," *The Pacific Review*, II, 412 (December, 1921). Reprinted by Laughead in *The Marvelous Exploits of Paul Bunyan* (1927 and 1929 editions), p. 4.

77. Perry Allen, recitation on Library of Congress Recording No. 2266–B2.

78. Shephard, *Paul Bunyan*, pp. 3-4.

79. *Ibid.*, pp. 51-54.

80. *Ibid.*, pp. 54-55.

81. *Ibid.*, pp. 19-23, 129, 132-33, 164-67; pp. 6-9, 101-2, 115-19; and pp. 188-89.

82. Carl Van Doren, "Document and Work of Art," *Century*, CX, 243 (1925).

83. Shephard, *Paul Bunyan*, p. 104.

84. *Ibid.*, pp. 198-99.

85. *Ibid.*, pp. 60, 97-100, 170; 153.

86. *Ibid.*, pp. 175-76.

87. James Floyd Stevens, in *Twentieth Century Authors*, ed. Stanley J. Kunitz and Howard Haycroft (New York, 1942), pp. 1343-44. The sales must be much higher now, for *Paul Bunyan* was reissued in 1948.

88. James Stevens, *The Saginaw Paul Bunyan* (New York, 1932).

89. See bibliography in *Legends of Paul Bunyan*, ed. H. W. Felton (New York, 1947), pp. 389-90.

90. Stevens, *Paul Bunyan* (1925), p. 6. Yet on the preceding page he writes, "The Paul Bunyan stories . . . are not a narrative; they exist, rather, as a group of anecdotes which are told among a group of camp men. . . ." See also the repartee Stevens reconstructed to demonstrate the casual method in which oral tales were told; this quite contradicts his theory of "bards." "An Old Logger's Foreword" to Felton's *Legends of Paul Bunyan*, p. ix.

91. Stevens, *Paul Bunyan*, p. 4.

92. Stevens, letter dated March 16, 1934, to Mellor Hartshorn, included in Hartshorn's unpublished Master's thesis, "Paul Bunyan: A Study in Folk-Literature" (Occidental College, Los Angeles, 1934), pp. 168-69, 174.

93. Stevens, *The Saginaw Paul Bunyan*, p. 14.

94. Stevens, *Paul Bunyan*, p. 2.

95. C.-Marius Barbeau, "Contes populaires canadiens," *Journal of American Folklore*, XXIX, 1-136 (January-March, 1916); France Marie Royer, "Contes populaires et légendes de la Province de

Québec" (Montréal, 1943); Sœur Marie Ursule, C.S.J., "Le folklore des Lavalois" (Québec, 1947).

96. Max Gartenberg, "Paul Bunyan and Little John," *Journal of American Folklore*, LXII, 416-22 (October-December, 1949).

97. Letter from M. Lacourcière, enclosing a copy of his letter dated October 6, 1947, to Mr. Gartenberg.

98. Stevens, "Folklore and the Artist," *The American Mercury*, LXX, 343-49 (March, 1950).

99. *Ibid.*, pp. 347-48. Mr. Stevens shows considerable unawareness of how much Joel Chandler Harris owed to folklore—a debt which is suggested by Stella Brewer Brookes in *Joel Chandler Harris—Folklorist* (Athens, Georgia), 1950. See also my review in *Midwest Folklore*, I, 133-38 (Summer, 1951).

100. Stevens, *Paul Bunyan*, pp. 16, 18.

101. *Ibid.*, p. 20.

102. *Ibid.*, p. 24.

103. *Ibid.*, p. 27.

104. *Ibid.*, pp. 29, 32, 52, 56.

105. *Ibid.*, p. 150.

106. *Ibid.*, pp. 43-46.

107. *Ibid.*, pp. 104-5.

108. *Ibid.*, pp. 238-40.

109. *Ibid.*, pp. 40-47.

110. *Ibid.*, pp. 116-31.

111. *Ibid.*, pp. 142-43.

112. *Ibid.*, p. 52.

113. *Ibid.*, pp. 158, 194.

114. *Ibid.*, p. 95.

115. *Ibid.*, p. 57.

116. *Ibid.*, p. 47.

117. *Ibid.*, p. 52.

118. *Ibid.*, p. 31.

119. *Ibid.*, p. 43.

120. *Ibid.*, p. 65.

121. *Ibid.*, p. 71.

122. *Ibid.*, p. 85.

123. *Ibid.*, p. 193.

124. A further taste of how rugged is Mr. Stevens' individualism: " 'Audacity!' exclaimed Paul Bunyan . . . 'The ten-hour day! Thunderation! What an unheard of thing! Is the sun shining? Do I wear whiskers? Do men chew with their teeth? Is Babe a blue ox? And —do loggers work twelve hours a day? What devils do trail me!

Ideas; poetry; floods; women; the ten-hour day—what next?' " *Ibid.*, p. 234.

125. In lamenting the decline of the oral tradition, Mr. Stevens states the basic tenets of his reactionary philosophy in the plainest language possible: "This art is perishing simply because Universal Education, and other blights, curses and evil inventions of democracy are destroying all the old simplicity, imaginativeness, and self-amusement of plain American life." *Ibid.*, p. 7.

126. *Ibid.*, pp. 140-68.

127. *Ibid.*, pp. 188-89. See also Stuart Sherman, "Paul Bunyan and the Blue Ox," *The Main Stream* (New York, 1927), pp. 71-79, discussed on pp. 111-12 of the present study.

128. Stevens, *op. cit.*, p. 190.

129. *Ibid.*, p. 202.

130. *Ibid.*, p. 205.

131. *Ibid.*, p. 203.

132. *Ibid.*, p. 206.

133. *Ibid.*, pp. 210, 213-14.

134. *Ibid.*, p. 215.

135. *Ibid.*, p. 112.

136. *Ibid.*, p. 234.

137. *Ibid.*, p. 241.

138. Percy MacKaye, "A Homer of the Logging Camps," *Bookman*, LXI, 473 (June, 1925).

139. Constance M. Rourke, "The Making of an Epic," *Saturday Review of Literature*, II, 81 (August 29, 1925).

140. Rourke, letter to Mellor Hartshorn, dated March 23, 1934, reproduced by Hartshorn in "Paul Bunyan: A Study in Folk-Literature" (Los Angeles, 1934), pp. 173-74.

141. Carl Van Doren, *The Roving Critic* (New York, 1923), pp. 105-7.

142. Van Doren, "Document and Work of Art," *The Century*, CX, 243-45 (1925).

143. Stuart Sherman, *The Main Stream* (New York, 1927), p. 76.

144. *Ibid.*, pp. 77-79.

145. James Stevens, *The Saginaw Paul Bunyan* (New York, 1932).

146. *Ibid.*, pp. 178-92.

147. *Ibid.*, p. 191.

148. *Ibid.*, pp. 19-99; 112; 131; 151-52.

149. *Ibid.*, pp. 102-13.

150. *Ibid.*, p. 248.

151. *Ibid.*, p. 258.

152. *Ibid.*, p. 260.

153. Kenneth M. Gould, "An American Hercules," *Scholastic,* VII, 10-12 (October 31, 1925) and 10, 29 (November 14, 1925).

154. Wallace Wadsworth, *Paul Bunyan and His Great Blue Ox* (New York, 1926).

155. Rachel Field (ed.), *American Folk and Fairy Tales* (New York, 1929).

156. Glen Rounds, *Ol' Paul* (New York, 1936), p. 16.

157. *Ibid.,* pp. 89-90.

158. *Ibid.,* pp. 111-15.

159. *Ibid.,* pp. 87-88.

160. *Ibid.,* p. 132.

161. Dell J. McCormick, *Paul Bunyan Swings His Axe* (Caldwell, Idaho, 1936).

162. McCormick, *Tall Timber Tales* (Caldwell, Idaho, 1939).

163. Turney, *Paul Bunyan, The Work Giant* (Portland, Oregon, 1941).

164. *Compton's Pictured Encyclopedia and Fact Index* (Chicago, 1947), II, 276.

165. *Ibid.,* XIII, 303k-303l.

166. Frank Shay, *Here's Audacity! American Legendary Heroes* (New York, 1930).

167. *Ibid.,* pp. 7-8.

168. *Ibid.,* p. 11.

169. *Ibid.,* pp. 212-19.

170. *Ibid.,* pp. 220-25.

171. Anne Malcolmson, *Yankee Doodle's Cousins* (Boston, 1941), pp. 229-60.

172. *Ibid.,* p. viii.

173. *Paul Bunyan and Tony Beaver Tales* (Madison, Wisconsin, 1930).

174. Bethene Miller, *Paul Bunyan in the Army* (Portland, Oregon, 1942).

175. Blair, *Tall Tale America* (New York, 1944).

176. Harold W. Felton, *Legends of Paul Bunyan* (New York, 1947).

177. *Ibid.,* pp. 379-411. The bibliography originally appeared as "Paul Bunyan Twenty-Five Years After," compiled by Gladys J. Haney, *Journal of American Folklore,* LV, 155-68 (1942), and enlarged by Herbert Halpert, "A Note on Haney's Bibliography of Paul Bunyan, *J.A.F.L.,* LVI, 57-59 (1943). Halpert recognized the bibliography's shortcomings, and suggested "that treatments of folk heroes based more immediately on field data or from direct handling

of printed sources are preferable to, and should be distinguished from, literary popularizations based on these treatments." *Ibid.*, p. 57.

Notes to Chapter Five

1. This quotation is attributed to Sam Slick by Constance Rourke in *American Humor*, p. 73. I have not found it in Haliburton.

2. Mark Van Doren, "The Permanence of Robert Frost," *The American Scholar*, V, 190-98 (Spring, 1936).

3. Ida Virginia Turney, *Paul Bunyan Comes West* (Boston, 1928), p. 8. See note 61, Chapter IV.

4. Robert Frost, "Paul's Wife," in *Collected Poems*, pp. 235-39, lines 105-10, 131-36. See note 23, Chapter I, for other appearances of this poem.

5. *Ibid.*, lines 1-5.

6. *Ibid.*, lines 49-54.

7. *Ibid.*, lines 150-57.

8. I use the term "populist tradition" in a general sense, to denote that political and esthetic philosophy influential in the Middle West, which was for a time represented by the Populist party and after the demise of that organization continued to influence liberal democratic thought in the region. Its chief tenets are an optimistic view of progress, derived in turn from a faith in the innocence, moral vigor, political righteousness, and eventual triumph of "the people." Although Sandburg was active in the Socialist rather than the Populist party, his devotion to this position leads me to consider him as a literary spokesman for the movement just defined.

9. Sandburg, *The People, Yes* (New York: Harcourt Brace, 1936), pp. 97-99.

10. Willard Thorp, in the *Literary History of the United States*, writes: "*The People, Yes* is one of the great American books. But, as has often happened in the history of our literature, its new matter required a new form, and the form is hard to name. Some of the one hundred and seven sections of the book are poems in the usual Sandburg manner, on such themes as the death of those who die for the people, or the common man as builder, wrecker, and builder again. Some sections merely assemble the collective wisdom of the people, on property, war, justice, and the law. . . ." (pp. 1183-84.)

At the time *The People, Yes* appeared, Morton Dauwen Zabel, in a very perceptive review in *Poetry* ("Sandburg's Testament," XLIX, 33-45 [1936]), wrote that "hardly a fifth of the volume is classified

by any definition as poetry, although any definition of poetry must
include the purpose and imagination that runs through its pages.
. . . *The People, Yes* . . . proceeds through 107 sections that alter-
nate, on no apparent principle of contrast or structure, between
personal episodes and mass movements, local anecdotes and epic
generalities, lists of scenes, trades, occupations, and causes, passages
of vague symbolic imagery, long catalogues of popular phrases,
catchwords, clichés, and proverbs, and intervals of gnomic lyricism."
And Horace Gregory and Marya Zaturenska, in their appreciation
of Sandburg in *A History of American Poetry,* dismiss his best book
as a jumble in which "the kind of knowledge that can be gained
by reference to the files of *The World Almanac* [was] thrown and
heaped together half humorously." (p. 248.)

11. Ruel McDaniel, "Necktie Justice," quoted in Botkin, *A Treasury of American Folklore,* pp. 135-36. On p. 141 Botkin reprints
another story about Judge Bean which includes the following item
from the *El Paso Daily Times,* June 2, 1884: "Somebody killed a
Chinaman and was brought up standing before the irrepressible
Roy, who looked through two or three dilapidated law books from
stem to stern, and finally turned the culprit loose remarking that
he'd be d——d if he could find any law against killing a Chinaman."
Nonetheless, according to Mody Boatright, "a charlatan like Roy
Bean . . . was tolerated by the dominant social group, the ranchers,
and the Rangers, because he was of use to them in the suppression
of lawlessness." *Folk Laughter on the American Frontier,* p. 120.

12. Zabel, "Sandburg's Testament," *Poetry,* XLIX, 33-45 (1936).

13. One copy of the mimeographed acting script of W. H. Auden's
Paul Bunyan is in the possession of the Columbia University Music
Library, where it is filed under the name of the composer, Benjamin
Britten. This library also has a manuscript score for voices and
piano accompaniment. The words to two songs are included in the
score but not in the script, while the score lacks the three interlude
ballads sung by the narrator.

14. Auden, *Collected Poetry* (New York, 1945). These lyrics appear in Part III, Nos. iii, vii, and xxxii.

15. Letter from W. H. Auden dated January 17, 1949.

16. Auden, *Paul Bunyan,* p. 1–1–6. (In the pagination of the
script, the first figure refers to the act, the second to the scene, and
the third to the page.)

17. *Ibid.,* p. 2–1–1.

18. *Ibid.,* pp. 2–2–12 and 13.

19. *Ibid.,* p. 2–in–9 ("in": Interlude); also pp. in–1–4 and 5; and
1–in–13, 14.

20. *Ibid.*, p. 1–2–25.

21. *Ibid.*, p. 1–1–9.

22. *Ibid.*, p. 2–1–7.

23. *Ibid.*, pp. 1–1–11 and 12; *Collected Poetry*, pp. 202-3.

24. *Paul Bunyan*, pp. 2–1–3 and 4.

25. *Ibid.*, p. 2–2–11; *Collected Poetry*, pp. 199-200. There are several differences between the text in the script and the published version: Line 3, "culver's" for "culvers"; the third stanza:

> The preacher shall dance at your marriage
> The steeple bend down to look
> The pulpit and chairs shed suitable tears
> While the horses drawing your carriage
> Sing agreeably agreeably agreeably of love.

26. *Paul Bunyan*, pp. 1–1–10 and 11; *Collected Poetry*, p. 230. Variants: Line 1, "lives" for "leads"; line 2, "eye" for "mind"; line 4, "Through him I scent" for "I scent in him"; line 5, "draws" for "calls"; lines 9-10 and 11-12 are inverted.

27. *Paul Bunyan*, pp. 2–2–13 and 14.

28. Louis Untermeyer, *The Wonderful Adventures of Paul Bunyan* (New York, 1945).

29. Paul R. Beath, 'Febold Feboldson," in Botkin, *op. cit.*, pp. 227-30. Beath's material first appeared in a Nebraska Federal Writers pamphlet for 1937.

30. In response to a query on his sources, Mr. Untermeyer informed me, "As you surmise, my own 'recreation' is an amalgam. . . . I had read much of the Bunyan literature and I found particularly rewarding the books by Stevens, Shephard, and Turney (more or less in that order) but I hope to make a more 'cohered' book by attempting some kind of chronological growth (which was only sketchily accomplished in my book) plus an imaginative and perhaps poetic style. Some of this I got from talks with a few lumberjacks in Minnesota, but most of it I'm afraid is merely my own attempts at a semi-colloquial, semi-poetic vocabulary." Letter dated July 8, 1951.

31. Untermeyer, *Wonderful Adventures*, pp. 11-12.

32. *Ibid.*, pp. 14-15. This is the old joke Robert W. Service made famous in "The Cremation of Sam McGee."

33. Esther Shephard, *Paul Bunyan*, pp. 29-34.

34. Untermeyer, *Wonderful Adventures*, p. 39.

35. Mark Twain, *The Adventures of Huckleberry Finn* (New York, 1918), p. 48.

36. Botkin, *op. cit.*, pp. 884-86.

37. Louis Le Fevre, "Paul Bunyan and Rip Van Winkle," *The Yale Review*, XXXVI, 66 and 73 (Autumn, 1946).

38. George W. Harris, *Sut Lovingood* (New York, 1867), Chapter I.

39. Untermeyer, *Wonderful Adventures*, pp. 71, 74, 75, 77, 78.

40. *Ibid.*, p. 128.

41. *Ibid.*, pp. 130-31.

42. Jerry Doyle, "A Job for Cooperation" (Cartoon), *Country Gentleman*, February, 1949, p. 180.

43. Max Gartenberg, who learned this information from W. B. Laughead, furnished it to me in a letter of July 18, 1951.

44. William Hazlett Upson, "Paul Bunyan versus Loud-Mouth Johnson," *Ford Times*, XL, 27-31 (September, 1948).

45. Gartenberg, "W. B. Laughead's Great Advertisement," *Journal of American Folklore*, LXIII, 448 (October-December, 1950).

46. "Paul Bunyan Prances" was presented by the Standard Oil Company of California on April 7, 1949. The script seems to be based on Louis Untermeyer's *Wonderful Adventures of Paul Bunyan*, with certain additions, omissions, and changes. Shanty Boy arrives at Paul's camp, asks employment as a singing odd-job hand, and sings a stanza of the old ballad "The Jolly Lumbermen" (also known as "Colley's Run-I-O") to qualify for the position. He offers to do Paul's figuring, but Paul already has Johnny Inkslinger who invented figuring and counts sheep by dividing their legs by four. We meet Galloping Kid, whose role in this script is merely to introduce an orchestral excerpt from Aaron Copland's *Billy the Kid* suite. Next, Paul dreams of a land of milk and honey, sets out with Babe to find it, and moves his camp to the Big Rock Candy Mountain. He sings the song, then complains that the men got so fat they didn't want to work; instead they became careless and fancy free. (Orchestra: Excerpt from Leonard Bernstein's *Fancy Free*.) Then Shanty Boy sings "A Shantyman's Life" and Paul sings the rest of "Colley's Run-I-O." Paul found Babe in the Winter of the Blue Snow, and asks Shanty Boy to ride a bicycle up and down the table to pass out griddle cakes. We learn that Paul dug Puget Sound, piled rocks for the Grand Coulee Dam, straightened crooked roads, and dug the Grand Canyon. Now it is spring; the men don't have their hearts in their work. Paul suddenly sees why: A WOMAN! As in Stevens' *Paul Bunyan*, the hero picks up one of these female creatures, scrutinizes her, but finally lets her go. Paul offers to take the men where "trees are so tall it takes three men steady lookin' for ten days to see the top," but they've had enough logging. Their refusal to go on with Paul must be drawn from Stevens instead of

Untermeyer, as it lacks the poignance of the latter's chapter. Paul
sets out to invent a machine to replace the axe and to search for
more and greener pastures for himself; "women folks is too distract-
ing" for him. His tag line is Untermeyer's last sentence: "You won't
hear the last of Paul Bunyan until the last tree is down."

Paul's voice is loud and uncouth, a glorification of strength without dignity, in this broadcast. (These notes are made from a transcription of the program.) There is no drama, no suspense, no characterization, no development, and no plot in this pastiche, which
fails completely to take advantage of the strong points in the Untermeyer book that furnished most of its motifs. In addition to the
compositions by Bernstein and Copland, some of the music was
taken from a Paul Bunyan suite by William Bergsma. According to
Felton's bibliography (*Legends of Paul Bunyan*, pp. 394-95), this
is "a Ballet for Puppets and Solo Dancers," composed in 1939.
"James Stevens' *Paul Bunyan* was used as a source."

47. The film is distributed by Impco, Bergenfield, N. J.

48. Richard Chase, *Herman Melville* (New York, 1949), chapter
II, especially pp. 75-102. For detailed references to frontier char-
acter and the use of frontier vocabulary in *Moby-Dick*, see also
"Melville's Backwoods Seamen," by C. Merton Babcock in *Western
Folklore*, X, 126-33 (April, 1951). The following remarks about
Melville are paraphrased from my review-article of Chase's book
and Melville's *Confidence-Man*, "Melville in the American Grain,"
Southern Folklore Quarterly, XIV, 185-91 (September, 1950).

49. Chase, *Herman Melville*, pp. 67, 68. In chapter IV, we have
seen another parallel to *Moby-Dick* in the popular literature and
folklore of the time: Thorpe's "The Big Bear of Arkansas." But
Thorpe's story is comic throughout, and by a miracle greater than
any the hunter could contrive the Big B'ar falls dead at his feet:
"That bar was an *unhuntable bar, and died when his time come.*"
This is the American dream of Man's easy triumph over Nature,
which Melville so acutely criticizes in *Moby-Dick, Israel Potter,* and
The Confidence-Man.

50. Chase, *op. cit.,* p. 73.

51. In tracing this native background Mr. Chase again relies
chiefly on Sam Slick as the dominant folklore element in the title
character. I think there are more extensive parallels in native myth,
and while I cannot prove that Melville knew or used them all,
there is some value in mentioning them because of the light his
satiric use of similar elements casts upon the myths themselves.
There is as much of Simon Suggs as of Sam Slick in the confidence
man. He, like Suggs, finds it "good to be shifty in a new country,"

and like Suggs at the camp meeting, he works the spiritual side of the street. At the same time he presents himself as a Johnny Appleseed, the Americanized Prometheus or Orpheus who, in peddling Easy Chairs, Pain Dissuaders, and Confidence, lightens the burdens of man's life in that same new country. He also has affinities to the corruptness, inhumanity, and cruelty of Mike Fink, while he parodies the Promethean and Jovian prowess of Davy Crockett in "Sunrise in His Pocket." In preaching his gospel of confidence he lures all victims to throw their judgment and money into his hands, to jump blindly wherever he leads them. Their confident submission is surely akin to the brainless braggadocio of Sam Patch, who leapt the Niagara just to prove that "Some things can be done as well as others."

Bibliography

Part I. Original Sources

A. Tales and Motifs from Oral Tradition

Allen, Perry. "Paul Bunyan Tales," recorded by Alan Lomax on Library of Congress Recordings Nos. 2264–B2, 2265–B2, and 2266–B2.

Beck, Earl Clifton. *Songs of the Michigan Lumberjacks*. Ann Arbor: University of Michigan Press, 1942.

Brooks, John Lee. "Paul Bunyan: American Folk Hero." Unpublished Master's thesis, Southern Methodist University, Dallas, 1927.

Halpert MS. Paul Bunyan tales from oral tradition, collected by Herbert Halpert from the following informants:

    A.   Fred Ginther, age 63, St. Mary's, Elk County, Pennsylvania, August 23, 1949.

    B-1.   Frank Odell, Peakville, New York, August 22, 1941.

    B-2.   Frank Odell, July 10, 1946.

    C.   Albert Peterson, age 62, Fish's Eddy, New York, August 19, 1941.

    D.   Gabriel Simon, age 71, Ridgway, Elk County, Pennsylvania, August 23-24, 1949.

    E-1.   "Shock" Wormuth, Shinhopple, New York, August 18, 1941.

    E-2.   "Shock" Wormuth, July 10, 1946.

    F.   Irvan Wormuth, July 10, 1946.

McBride, Bill. Recitation on Library of Congress Recordings Nos. 2259–B2 and 2260–A1.

MacGillivray, James. "The Round River Drive," *Detroit News-Tribune,* July 24, 1910, p. 6, illustrated section. Reprinted in *Legends of Paul Bunyan,* ed. Harold W. Felton, pp. 335-41. New York: A. A. Knopf, 1947.

Martin, Wayne (as told to B. A. Botkin). "Paul Bunyan on the Water Pipeline," in *Folk-Say, a Regional Miscellany,* ed. B. A. Botkin. Norman: University of Oklahoma Press, 1929.

Rourke, Constance Mayfield. "Paul Bunyon [*sic*]," *The New Republic,* XXIII, 176-79 (July 7, 1920).

Shephard, Esther. "The Tall Tale in American Literature," *Pacific Review,* II, 412 (December, 1921).

Stewart, K. Bernice, and Homer A. Watt. "Legends of Paul Bunyan, Lumberjack," *Transactions of the Wisconsin Academy of Sciences, Arts, and Letters,* XVIII, Part ii, 639-51 (1916).

Tabor, Edward O, and Stith Thompson. "Paul Bunyan in 1910," *Journal of American Folklore,* LIX, 134-35 (April-June, 1946).

Thompson, Harold W. *Body, Boots & Britches,* pp. 129-31. Philadelphia: J. B. Lippincott, 1940.

B. POPULARIZATIONS OF PAUL BUNYAN

Blair, Walter. *Tall Tale America.* New York: Coward-McCann, 1944.

Coffin, Robert P. Tristram. "Paul's Lake," in *Primer for America,* p. 68. New York: Macmillan, 1943.

Compton's Pictured Encyclopedia and Fact Index. Chicago: F. S. Compton, 1947. See articles on "Paul Bunyan" and "Story-Telling."

Felton, Harold W. (ed.). *Legends of Paul Bunyan.* New York: A. A. Knopf, 1947.

Field, Rachel (ed.). *American Folk and Fairy Tales.* New York: Scribner's, 1929.

Gould, Kenneth. "An American Hercules," *Scholastic,* VII, 10-12 (October 31, 1925) and 10, 29 (November 14, 1925).

[Laughead, W. B.]. *Introducing Mr. Paul Bunyan of Westwood, Cal.* Minneapolis: The Red River Lumber Company, n.d. [1914].

——. *Tales About Paul Bunyan, Vol. II.* Minneapolis: The Red River Lumber Co., n.d. [1916 and 1917].

——. *The Marvelous Exploits of Paul Bunyan . . . Collected from Various Sources and Embellished for Publication.* Minneapolis: The Red River Lumber Co., n.d. [1927], 1929, and 1935.

——. *Paul Bunyan and His Big Blue Ox.* Westwood, California: The Red River Lumber Co., 1944 (30th Anniversary Edition).

——. *Paul Bunyan's Playground.* Minneapolis: The Red River Lumber Co., n.d. [1935 or 1936].

McCormick, Dell J. *Paul Bunyan Swings His Axe.* Caldwell, Idaho: Caxton Printers, Ltd., 1936.

——. *Tall Timber Tales, More Paul Bunyan Stories.* Caldwell, Idaho: Caxton Printers, Ltd., 1939.

Malcolmson, Anne. *Yankee Doodle's Cousins.* Boston: Houghton Mifflin, 1941.

Miller, Bethene. *Paul Bunyan in the Army*. Portland, Oregon: Binsford and Morts, 1942.

"Paul Bunyan Prances," Standard Education Hour, National Broadcasting Company, April 7, 1949 (transcription).

"Paul Bunyan Toss Startles French," *New York Times,* Sunday, January 9, 1949, Sec. I, p. 44.

Rounds, Glen. *Ol' Paul*. New York: Holiday House, 1936.

Shay, Frank. *Here's Audacity! American Legendary Heroes*. New York: Macaulay, 1930.

Shephard, Esther. *Paul Bunyan*. New York: Harcourt Brace, 1924.

Stevens, James. *Paul Bunyan*. New York: A. A. Knopf, 1925.

——. *The Saginaw Paul Bunyan*. New York: A. A. Knopf, 1932.

Turney, Ida Virginia. *Paul Bunyan Comes West*. Boston: Houghton Mifflin, 1928.

——. *Paul Bunyan the Work Giant*. Portland, Oregon: Binsford and Morts, 1941.

Upson, William Hazlett. "Paul Bunyan versus Loud-Mouth Johnson," *Ford Times*, XL, 27-31 (September, 1948).

Wadsworth, Wallace. *Paul Bunyan and his Great Blue Ox*. New York: Doubleday, 1926.

C. LITERARY TREATMENTS OF PAUL BUNYAN

Auden, W. H. (with Benjamin Britten). *Paul Bunyan* (operetta libretto). Mimeographed acting script, n.d. [1941].

Frost, Robert. "Paul's Wife," in *Collected Poems*, pp. 235-39. New York: Henry Holt, 1949.

Sandburg, Carl. *The People, Yes*. New York: Harcourt Brace, 1936.

Untermeyer, Louis. *The Wonderful Adventures of Paul Bunyan*. New York: The Heritage Press, 1946.

Part II. Secondary Sources

Auden, W. H. *The Collected Poetry of W. H. Auden*. New York: Random House, 1945.

Babcock, C. Merton. "Melville's Backwoods Seamen," *Western Folklore*, X, 126-33 (April, 1951).

Barbeau, C.-Marius. "Contes populaires canadiens," *Journal of American Folklore*, XXIX, 1-136 (January-March, 1916).

——. *Folk-Songs of Old Québec*. National Museum of Canada, n.d.

Barnes, Florence Elberta. "Strap Buckner of the Texas Frontier," in *Man, Bird & Beast*. (Publications of the Texas Folklore Society, VIII, 129-51.) Austin, 1930.

Barry, Phillips. *The Maine Woods Songster*. Cambridge, Mass.: Powell Printing Co., 1939.

Beck, Earl Clifton. *Songs of the Michigan Lumberjacks.* Ann Arbor: University of Michigan Press, 1942.

Beckwith, Martha Warren. *Folklore in America.* Poughkeepsie, New York: The Folklore Foundation, Vassar College, 1931.

Benedict, Ruth. "Folklore," *Encyclopedia of the Social Sciences,* VI, 288-93. New York: Macmillan, 1931.

Blair, Walter. *Native American Humor.* New York: American Book Co., 1937.

——, and Franklin J. Meine. *Mike Fink, King of Mississippi Keelboatmen.* New York: Henry Holt, 1930.

Boas, Franz. *General Anthropology.* Boston: D. C. Heath, 1938.

Boatright, Mody C. *Folk Laughter on the American Frontier.* New York: Macmillan, 1949.

Botkin, B. A. (ed.). *A Treasury of American Folklore.* New York: Crown Publishers, 1944.

—— (ed.). *A Treasury of New England Folklore.* New York: Crown Publishers, 1947.

—— (ed.). *Folk-Say, a Regional Miscellany.* Norman: University of Oklahoma Press, 1929 and 1930.

Brookes, Stella Brewer. *Joel Chandler Harris—Folklorist.* Athens, Ga.: University of Georgia Press, 1950.

Chapin, Miriam. "French Canada—Can It Survive?" *Harper's Magazine,* CLXLVII, 80-87 (November, 1948).

Chaplin, Ralph. *Wobbly.* Chicago: University of Chicago Press, 1948.

Charters, W. W. "Paul Bunyan in 1910," *Journal of American Folklore,* LVII, 188-89 (July-September, 1944).

Chase, Richard. *Herman Melville: A Critical Study.* New York: Macmillan, 1949.

Clough, Ben C. (ed.). *The American Imagination at Work.* New York: A. A. Knopf, 1947.

Crane, Ed. "Paul Bunyan—Hoax or Hero?" *Minneapolis Sunday Tribune,* September 7, 1947, illustrated section, p. 23.

[Crockett]. *The Autobiography of David Crockett,* with an introduction by Hamlin Garland. New York: Scribner's, 1923.

Davis, Wilbur A. "Logger and Splinter-Picker Talk," *Western Folklore,* IX, 111-23 (April, 1950).

De Noyer, Emery. "The Little Brown Bulls." American Archive of Folksong Recording No. 5. Washington: The Library of Congress.

Doerflinger, William Main. *Shantymen and Shantyboys: Songs of the Sailor and Lumberman.* New York: Macmillan, 1951.

Dorson, Richard M. "America's Comic Demigods," *American Scholar*, X, 389-401 (Autumn, 1941).

—— (ed.). *Davy Crockett, American Comic Legend*. New York: Rockland Editions, 1939.

——. "Folk Traditions of the Upper Peninsula," *Michigan History*, XXXI, 48-65 (March, 1947).

——. *Jonathan Draws the Long Bow*. Cambridge: Harvard University Press, 1946.

——. "Personal Histories," *Western Folklore*, VII, 27-42 (January, 1948).

——. "Sam Patch, Jumping Hero," *New York Folklore Quarterly*, I, 133-51 (August, 1945).

Doyle, Jerry. "A Job for Cooperation" (Cartoon), *Country Gentleman*, CXIX, 180 (February, 1949).

Eckstorm, Fanny Hardy, and Mary Winslow Smyth. *Minstrelsy of Maine*. Boston: Houghton Mifflin, 1927.

Edgar, Marjorie. "Imaginary Animals of Northern Minnesota," *Minnesota History*, XXI, 353-56 (1940).

Francis, Owen. "The Saga of Joe Magarac, Steelman," *Scribner's Magazine*, XC, 505-11 (November, 1931).

Franklin, Benjamin. *The Writings of Benjamin Franklin*, ed. Albert Henry Smyth, Vol. I. New York: Macmillan, 1905.

Friedman, Samuel (ed.). *Rebel Song Book*. New York: Rand School Press, 1935.

Gardner, Emelyn Elizabeth, and Geraldine Jencks Chickering. *Ballads and Songs of Southern Michigan*. Ann Arbor: University of Michigan Press, 1939.

Gartenberg, Max. "Paul Bunyan and Little John," *Journal of American Folklore*, LXII, 416-22 (October-December, 1949).

——. "W. B. Laughead's Great Advertisement," *Journal of American Folklore*, LXIII, 444-49 (October-December, 1950).

Gray, Roland Palmer. *Songs and Ballads of the Maine Lumberjacks*. Cambridge: Harvard University Press, 1925.

Gregory, Horace, and Marya Zaturenska. *A History of American Poetry, 1900-1940*. New York: Harcourt Brace, 1946.

Gummere, Francis B. *Old English Ballads*. Boston: Ginn & Co., 1894.

[Haliburton, Thomas Chandler]. *The Attaché; or Sam Slick in England*, "By the Author of 'Sam Slick the Clockmaker,' . . . Etc." New Revised Edition. New York: Stronger and Townsend, 1856.

——. *Sam Slick; the Clockmaker*. Philadelphia: T. B. Peterson, n.d. [1836?].

Hallowell, A. Irving. "Myth, Culture and Personality," *American Anthropologist*, XLIL, 544-55 (October-December, 1947).

Halpert, Herbert. "A Note on Haney's Bibliography of Paul Bunyan," *Journal of American Folklore*, LVI, 57-59 (January-March, 1943).

——. "Tales Told by Soldiers," *California Folklore Quarterly*, IV, 364-76 (October, 1945).

——. "Tall Tales and Other Yarns from Calgary, Alberta," *California Folklore Quarterly*, IV, 29-49 (January, 1945).

Haney, Gladys J. "Paul Bunyan Twenty-Five Years After," *Journal of American Folklore*, LV, 155-68 (July-September, 1942).

Harris, George W. *Sut Lovingood, Yarns Spun by a Nat'ral Durn'd Fool*. New York: Dick and Fitzgerald, 1867.

Hartshorn, Mellor. "Paul Bunyan: A Study in Folk-Literature." Unpublished Master's thesis, Occidental College, Los Angeles, May, 1934.

Hoffman, Daniel G. "The Folk Art of Jazz," *Antioch Review*, V, 110-20 (Spring, 1945).

——. "Stregas, Ghosts and Werewolves," *New York Folklore Quarterly*, III, 325-28 (Winter, 1947).

——. "Melville in the American Grain," *Southern Folklore Quarterly*, XIV, 185-91 (September, 1950).

——. Review of *Joel Chandler Harris—Folklorist* by Stella Brewer Brookes, *Midwest Folklore*, I, 133-38 (Spring, 1951).

Hooper, Johnson J. *Adventures of Captain Simon Suggs, Late of the Tallapoosa Volunteers; together with "Taking the Census," and Other Alabama Sketches*. Philadelphia: T. B. Peterson and Bros., 1843.

——. *The Widow Rugby's Husband, A Night at the Ugly Man's, and Other Tales of Alabama*. Philadelphia: T. B. Peterson and Bros., 1851.

James, Henry. *Hawthorne*. London, 1879. Reprinted in *The Shock of Recognition*, ed. Edmund Wilson. Garden City: Doubleday Doran, 1943.

Johnson, Guy B. *John Henry: Tracking Down a Negro Legend*. Chapel Hill: University of North Carolina Press, 1929.

Krappe, Alexander Haggerty. *The Science of Folklore*. New York: Dial Press, 1930.

Le Fevre, Louis. "Paul Bunyan and Rip Van Winkle," *Yale Review*, XXXVI, 66-76 (Autumn, 1946).

[Longstreet, Augustus Baldwin]. *Georgia Scenes, Characters, Incidents, &c., in the First Half Century of the Republic*, "By a Native Georgian." New York: Harper and Brothers, 1840.

Loomis, C. Grant. "Davy Crockett Visits Boston," *New England Quarterly*, XX, 396-400 (September, 1947).

Macdonald, Dwight. "A Theory of 'Popular Culture,'" *Politics*, I, 20-23 (February, 1944).

MacKaye, Percy. "A Homer in the Logging Camps," *Bookman*, LXI, 473 (June, 1925).

Nevins, Allan. *The Emergence of Modern America, 1865-1878.* New York: Macmillan, 1927.

(Old) Farmer's Almanack, Calculated on a New and Improved Plan for the Year of Our Lord 1947. Dublin, N. H.: Yankee, Inc., 1946.

Olsen, Charles Oluf. "Analytical Notes on Paul Bunyan." Typewritten ms, prepared for the WPA Oregon Federal Writers Project, 1938, in the possession of the Oregon State Library, Salem.

O'Reilly, Edward. "The Saga of Pecos Bill," *Century Magazine*, CVI, 827-33 (October, 1923).

Raglan, Lord (Fitzroy Richard Somerset). "The Scope of Folklore," *Folk-Lore* (London), LVII, 98-105 (September, 1946).

Rickaby, Franz. *Ballads and Songs of the Shanty-Boy.* Cambridge: Harvard University Press, 1926.

Rourke, Constance. *American Humor, A Study of the National Character.* New York: Harcourt Brace, 1931.

———. *Davy Crockett.* New York: Harcourt Brace, 1934.

———. "The Making of an Epic," *Saturday Review of Literature*, II, 81 (August 29, 1925).

———. "Paul Bunyon [*sic*]," *The New Republic*, XXIII, 176-79 (July 7, 1920).

———. *The Roots of American Culture.* New York: Harcourt Brace, 1942.

Royer, France Marie. "Contes populaires et légendes de la province de Québec." Unpublished Master's thesis, McGill University, Montréal, 1943.

Shay, Frank. "The Tall Tale in America," in *Folk-Say, A Regional Miscellany*, ed. B. A. Botkin, II, 382-85. Norman: University of Oklahoma Press, 1930.

Sherman, Stuart. *The Main Stream.* New York: Scribner's, 1927.

Smith, Seba. *'Way Down East, or, Portraitures of Yankee Life.* Philadelphia: John E. Potter, 1854.

Smith, Walker C. *The Everett Massacre: A History of the Class Struggle in the Lumber Industry.* Chicago: IWW Publishing Bureau, n.d.

Stegner, Wallace. "I Dreamed I Saw Joe Hill Last Night," *Pacific Spectator*, I, 184-87 (Spring, 1947).

Stevens, James Floyd. Autobiographical sketch in *Twentieth Century Authors,* ed. Stanley J. Kunitz and Howard Haycroft, pp. 1343-44. New York: H. W. Wilson, 1942.

——. "Folklore and the Artist," *American Mercury,* LXX, 343-49 (March, 1950).

Stewart, K. Bernice, and Homer A. Watt. See under Part I, Original Sources.

Thompson, Stith. *The Folktale.* New York: Dryden Press, 1946.

——. *Motif-Index of Folk Literature.* (Indiana University Studies, Nos. 96-97, Vol. I). Bloomington, 1932.

Thoreau, Henry David. *The Maine Woods.* Vol. III in *The Writings of Henry David Thoreau.* Boston & New York: Houghton Mifflin, 1906.

Thorp, Willard. "The 'New Poetry,' " in *The Literary History of the United States,* ed. Robert E. Spiller, pp. 1181-84. New York: Macmillan, 1948.

Thorpe, Thomas Bangs. *The Hive of "The Bee Hunter."* New York: D. Appleton, 1854.

Tocqueville, Alexis de. *Democracy in America.* New York: A. A. Knopf, 1945.

Twain, Mark. *The Adventures of Huckleberry Finn.* New York: Harper and Bros., 1918.

——. *A Tramp Abroad.* Hartford: American Publishing Co., 1879.

Untermeyer, Louis (ed.). *The Pocket Book of Robert Frost's Poems.* New York: Pocket Books, 1943.

Ursule, Sœur Marie, C.S.J. "Le folklore des Lavalois." Unpublished thèse de Docteur en Lettres, L'Université Laval, Québec, 1947.

Van Doren, Carl. "Document and Work of Art," *Century Magazine,* CX, 242-47 (1925).

——. *The Roving Critic.* New York: A. A. Knopf, 1923.

Van Doren, Mark. "The Permanence of Robert Frost," *American Scholar,* V, 190-98 (Spring, 1936).

Vincent, Elmore. *Lumber Jack Songs with Yodel Arrangements.* Chicago: M. M. Cole Publishing Co., 1932.

Watt, Homer A. "Paul Bunyan Provides for His Crew," in *The Rise of Realism,* ed. Louis Wann, pp. 270-73, 779. New York: Macmillan, 1933.

——, and K. B. Stewart. See under Stewart, Part I, Original Sources.

Wood, Richard G. *A History of Lumbering in Maine, 1820-1861.* (University of Maine Studies, Second Series, No. 33.) Orono, 1935.

Zabel, Morton Dauwen. "Sandburg's Testament," *Poetry: A Magazine of Verse,* XLIX, 33-45 (October, 1936).

Manuscript Letters

Auden, W. H. January 17, 1949.
Gartenberg, Max. July 18, 1951.
Halpert, Herbert. July 16, 1951.
Lacourcière, Luc. May 3, 1948.
Laughead, W. B. January 4, 1948; June 25, 1951; July 6, 1951.
Untermeyer, Louis. July 8, 1951.
Warren, Dale. January 31, 1949.

Motif-Index to the Paul Bunyan Stories

The following index lists motifs and characters in the Bunyan tales discussed in this book. It is not intended as a comprehensive survey of all Bunyan motifs, but rather as a convenient aid in tracing the development of the narratives through the three stages of oral tradition, popularization, and literary application. Because of the intermingling of these three strata, however, it is inadvisable to draw conclusions about the transmission of motifs from the entries in this index without consulting the pages in the text to which they refer.

Motifs are generally listed by key word. All the yarns in which Paul creates a geographical phenomenon, such as the Grand Canyon or the Great Lakes, are referred to under the heading "Landscape"; the one exception to this includes Puget Sound and the Columbia River, listed instead under "Construction gang," as Paul is said to have dug them while working in that industry. The tales involving Babe are all listed under "Blue Ox, Babe the Big," while under "Kitchen" appear references to all the yarns about Paul Bunyan's cook-shack. When names of characters are alliterative they are listed under the first name. The abbreviation "pop." of course stands for popularization; the listings give the pages of this book on which the motif appears in any of the popularizations discussed.

Since the entries indicate only those motifs discussed in the present study, it should be remembered that many motifs in the works examined are not mentioned in this text, and so do not appear in this index. It should be possible, however, to trace the characteristic development of the Bunyan traditions on the basis of the motifs and characters included here.

Name and Subject Index

Also by Daniel Hoffman:

Poetry

An Armada of Thirty Whales
A Little Geste
The City of Satisfactions
Striking the Stones
Broken Laws
The Center of Attention
Brotherly Love
Hang-Gliding from Helicon: New & Selected Poems 1948–1988
Middens of the Tribe

Criticism

Paul Bunyan, Last of the Frontier Demigods
The Poetry of Stephen Crane
Form and Fable in American Fiction
Barbarous Knowledge: Myth in the Poetry of Yeats, Graves, and Muir
Poe Poe Poe Poe Poe Poe Poe
Faulkner's Country Matters
Words to Create a World: Essays, Interviews, & Reviews of Contemporary
   Poetry

As Editor

The Red Badge of Courage and Other Tales
American Poetry and Poetics
Harvard Guide to Contemporary American Writing
Ezra Pound & William Carlos Williams

About the Author

Writing *Paul Bunyan* as his M.A. thesis at Columbia fifty years ago, Daniel Hoffman first devised his unique analysis of the creative interrelationship between American folklore and literature of first intensity. This approach informs such later studies of his as *Form and Fable in American Fiction* and *Faulkner's Country Matters.* Perhaps best known among his critical writings is his National Book Award finalist, *Poe Poe Poe Poe Poe Poe Poe.*

The insights in these books are enriched by Hoffman's own experience as a poet. He is the author of ten books of poetry, including *Brotherly Love,* another National Book Award finalist. Dr. Hoffman is the Felix Schelling Professor of English Emeritus at the University of Pennsylvania, and the Poet in Residence at the Cathedral of St. John the Divine, where he administers the American Poets' Corner.